Praise for Stefne Miller's debut novel,

salvaged

"*Salvaged* made me laugh, cry, smile, pout, and even make the little 'aww' noise out loud! I loved every single part of this book, and I may just have to read it again someday (and I rarely, if *ever*, reread a book)."

—Briana, B.A.M. Book Reviews

"*Salvaged* is one of the most beautiful stories I have ever read. It was touching and heartbreaking and full of feelings that I could really relate to. I think every teenage girl will feel some connection to Attie, and this book needs to be added to everyone's to-read lists (or piles)."

—Katie, Katie's Book Blog

"Beautiful. Magical. Amazing. A true, unyielding gift. *Salvaged* is a powerful story of love, pain, and hope, all wrapped up in a beautiful story... I opened this book and found, instead of a story, a life, a gift."

—Jenn, Book-Crazy.com

"Romance has been redefined! *Salvaged* was amazing. I fell in love with the whole story. Edward Cullen, Stefan Salvatore, you've been replaced. *Salvaged* had me captivated from when I started reading to even now because I am desperately waiting for a sequel."

—Maddie, Confessions of a Book Addict

"*Salvaged* is one of the cutest books I've read in a long time and one that I highly, highly urge you to pick up because I'm sure you'll love it just as much as I did."

—Lauren, Lauren's Crammed Bookshelf

"Simply put, *Salvaged* is magical and one that will stick with me for a very long time."

—Julie, Bloggers [[heart]] Books

"*Salvaged* is simply one of the best love stories I have ever read."

—Erica, The Books CellarX

"*Salvaged* is a story that spoke to my heart, spoke to my soul. It was truly an amazing, heartbreakingly beautiful story."

—Loni, A Casual Reader

"This novel blew me out of the water, ripped my socks clean off, and sent them hurtling into orbit. *Salvaged* was so well written and emotionally engaging that I couldn't stop reading it. The quality of the author's writing and her mastery of dialogue makes this novel stand shoulders above many 'shallow' teen novels on the shelves these days. I can't say enough good things about this book! It's making my best Christian fiction of 2010 list."

—Michelle Sutton, Author of *Never Without Hope*

"Author Stefne Miller's book *Salvaged* is a truly beautiful reading experience. You get to hear the story from both Attie's and Riley's points of view, tying the story together wonderfully."

—Ursula Gorman, Author of *Old Acquaintances*

"This book is a must read for parents, grandparents, and teenagers."

—Elaine Littau, Author of *Nan's Journey*

Rise

STEFNE MILLER

a love story

TATE PUBLISHING & Enterprises

Published by Tate Publishing & Enterprises, LLC
127 E. Trade Center Terrace | Mustang, Oklahoma 73064 USA
1.888.361.9473 | www.tatepublishing.com

Tate Publishing is committed to excellence in the publishing industry. The company reflects the philosophy established by the founders, based on Psalm 68:11,
"The Lord gave the word and great was the company of those who published it."

Book design copyright © 2011 by Tate Publishing, LLC. All rights reserved.
Cover design by Rebekah Garibay
Interior design by Lynly D. Grider

Published in the United States of America
ISBN: 978-1-61777-358-7
1. Fiction, Christian, Romance
2. Fiction, Coming of Age
11.03.14

Rise

chapter 1

The earth orbits the sun as the bright star keeps close enough to give just the right amount of light and heat to allow for life but far enough away that it doesn't do damage. The sun keeps a safe distance while at the same time its sole purpose is to exist for the benefit of the beautiful sphere that hangs so majestically in the universe. God designed them to perfectly exist with each other, and I'd come to a place of realizing that even if only for a time, Attie's existence was heavily dependent upon my ability to protect her and shine light in her direction. At the same time, I had to give her enough room to live her own life. I also knew the connection was fragile and that as I navigated the space just outside her world, if her life were to start to spin out of control, I wouldn't be able to come closer and intervene without causing more damage. I understood that I was created to be a part of her life, but only at a safe distance.

Looking back at how far Attie had come in such a short time, I was awed. I wondered if her new journey with the Lord had run its course and her life would return to normal—or at least what would be normal to most people. He'd asked her to join him on a journey, and although they'd already experienced a difficult adventure together, we quickly realized that the journey wasn't coming to an end; it was just beginning.

Our universe, the one that seemed to only include us, was about to be hurled into an entirely new solar system. It started as she stood trembling with a look of panic on her face. She was terrified; it was a fear of what might come and a possible doubt that this particular new adventure wasn't going to be all that I'd made it out to be. She wasn't sure that she'd made the right choice. She wasn't sure that joining me on *our* adventure had been such a great idea.

"Okay, now all you're gonna do is stick your arm in there and wiggle it around." Kent acted out his directions as he spoke. "When the fish latches on, you grab a hold of his insides and pull with all your might. I'll be right here, and I'll grab him when you pull him out."

Attie looked over at me, eyebrows arched high and eyes huge, then looked back at Kent. "Explain what you mean by the fish latching on. What are you describing, exactly?"

"Well, he's in there protecting his eggs, and he's gonna think you're trying to steal them, so he's gonna bite you."

Attie's arms flew out of the water and into the air as if she were a thief throwing her hands up in surrender. "Riley!"

"Yeah?"

"You didn't tell me that this little adventure was going to require me to literally risk life, limb, and digits."

"Come on, Charlie, you can do it. It'll be fun."

She looked back over at me and stuck out her tongue while Tammy sat next to me laughing.

"Ten bucks says she doesn't do it," Tammy said.

"Naw, she'll do it."

"No way, Riley. Look at her, she's scared to death. I can tell ya right now, I wouldn't be doing it."

"Me either," Anne added. "That girl's crazy."

My attention focused back on Kent and Attie. "You're on. I'm in for ten. I say she does it."

"So he's literally going to bite me?" Attie asked.

"That's right," Kent said with a quick nod.

"And what insides am I supposed to be grabbing on to, exactly?"

"You'll grab his gills from the inside."

"His gills?" Her hands opened and closed nervously as she flapped them in the air.

"Yep."

"Come on, Attie," Curt urged. "I've got your back."

"That's so encouraging, Curt … Riley!"

"Yeah?"

"If this is so darned safe, why isn't your butt in the water with me?"

"I gotta videotape it. Mom and Dad'll get a kick out of it."

"Can't you have one of the girls tape it?"

"They're taking pictures. Now just shush and get on with it, for cryin' out loud."

"You shut your mouth. No urging me to get on with it from people safely sitting on the shoreline, got it?"

"Got it." I glanced at Tammy, rolled my eyes, and then looked back at my petrified girlfriend.

Kent grabbed one of her arms and led her closer to the catfish den. "Enough wasting time, Attie. Heck, we'll be lucky if we haven't scared him off by now."

"I can't believe I'm doing this. What in the name of all that's holy am I doing? I can't believe I agreed to this." Of course she was rambling. She always rambled when she was nervous. It was one of the things she was known most for. Well, that and her dramatics. "Normally I'm a pretty smart girl, but this, this is not smart."

"Come on, Charlie, don't start psyching yourself out."

"You can't be a sissy, Attie. It's gonna be fun—promise. Now I'll be right back." Kent went under water for several seconds before popping back up. "All right, he's right there. He's ready for you."

"Oh, wonderful."

"Remember what I said. Reach on in, wiggle your fingers, and then when he grabs a hold—"

"Drag him on out."

"That's right. Drag him out here, and Curt and I'll be waiting for you."

"Gotcha." Attie's eyes closed, and her head bobbed frantically. "I can do this. I can do this. I can do this."

I rose to my feet. "Come on, babe, make me proud!"

"One … two …" She took a deep breath. "Three." Next thing I knew, she'd disappeared into the murky water.

Kent's head snapped in my direction in apparent shock. "She's doing it! I didn't think she'd actually do it!"

I tried to keep the video camera steady and focused as I excitedly watched and waited for her to pop back out of the water.

"Where is she?" Anne asked.

I quickly glanced over at the girls who stood with cameras ready to snap as soon as she exited the water.

"Give her some time," Kent insisted. "It can take a second to find the hole."

We all fell silent as we watched the water … and watched … and watched.

The more time passed, the more worried I got. "Kent?"

"Give her some time."

"Kent!" Tammy screamed. "Where is she? You go in there and bring her back out this instant!"

Attie's head exploded through the surface just as I started to sprint into the water after her.

"Ow, ow, ow, ow! Get him off! Get him off! Dear Lord! Curt, get him off!"

Curt and Kent rushed to her as the fish violently jerked around on her arm. It flung her arm around so much that I was afraid the fish was going to pop her shoulder completely out of socket. That *really* would've made her mad.

"Hold on to him," Kent yelled. "Hold on to the sucker."

"Get him off!" she shrieked.

"Kent, you get him off of her right now!" Tammy screamed.

"Give me a second; I'm working on it. Stop moving your arm, Attie."

"I'm not moving my arm—he is! He's big as fire!"

Curt slid a net up over the catfish as Kent worked at unleashing its grip on Attie's arm.

Tammy looked over her shoulder at me. "Ooh, Riley, she's gonna be so mad at you."

"Naw, she's loving it."

"She's got a fish swallowing half her arm, and she's screaming her head off. She's gonna be ticked."

I ignored the crazy redhead and kept my eyes on the spectacle in front of me. "That's my girl! You're doing great."

"Nobody told me that catfish have teeth! Get him off!"

"He doesn't have teeth," Kent said as he worked on prying the fish off her hand. Every time he'd get a grip, it managed to slip out of his hands again. "Heck, Attie, he's as stubborn as you."

Finally, the fish let go of the bait, and Attie was freed. Yanking her arm away, she fell back into the water and onto her back. A large smile spread across her face. "Man, that was fun."

I looked over at Tammy. "Told ya so. You owe me ten bucks."

Attie's nose crinkled in a smirk as she made her way back toward the shore. "You've got to give it a try, Anne. Heck, everybody's got to give it a try. It's scary but fun."

"How bad did it hurt?" Anne asked.

Attie held out her arm and exposed several small red marks that formed a circle around her wrist. "Oh, it hurt all right, but it'll be okay. That's by far one of the craziest things I've ever done."

"And the most redneck thing you've ever done," Tammy added.

"Redneck, huh? Is that why I'm suddenly in the mood for barbecue?"

I kissed her on the nose and got an adorable giggle in return. "Barbecue's not redneck; it's southern. There's a difference." Attie was shivering, so I grabbed a towel, wrapped it around the catfish warrior, and gave her a hug. "You made me proud."

"Did you see how big it was, Riley? That thing was massive. He was so heavy I didn't think I'd be able to lift him, but I did it. I really can't believe I did it. Another first," she said proudly.

"That's right, another first." I squeezed her tightly to me as Tammy raced toward the water with her camera held up to her eye. "Bring it up here, Kent. I've gotta get a picture of the monster catfish."

He and Curt waded through the water. "It's a big one. I'd say about eight pounds or so. Not bad for your first time noodling."

"You mean my last time noodling."

Kent frowned. "Aw, you aren't gonna do it again? You're a natural."

"No way. I'm moron enough to try just about anything once, but I'm not a total idiot. If that would've been a bigger fish, it could've really done some damage. I'll leave the noodling up to you boys. But really, Tammy, you've got to give it a go."

"No way, sister. I'll live vicariously through you and your antics."

Attie's bottom lip protruded as she made sad eyes toward her best friend. "I guess that'll do."

"So can we do something girlie for a change?" Anne asked. "Let's go soak up some rays while the boys play."

I grabbed Attie as she turned to go. "Forget something?"

"What?"

I held up her *Salvaged* bracelet. "Don't you want this back?"

"Of course. I'm glad we took it off. That fish would've yanked it right off my arm."

I secured it in place around her wrist.

"It just so happens that the bracelet hits just the right spot," she said.

"The right spot?"

"That's right where you used to kiss me, before you were allowed to really kiss me."

"It is?" I lifted her arm, moved the bracelet a little out of the way, and kissed her wrist. "Is that where it was?"

"It was a little lower."

I kissed her again. "There?"

"A little higher."

"Here?" My lips were millimeters from her skin.

"Right there."

My lips grazed her skin one last time.

"You two are completely grossing me out," Tammy groaned. "Save it for when you're alone."

Being alone was something I had a whole new appreciation for. Now that Attie and I were actually an item, all of our alone time had to be spent outside the house. The new rules laid out by my parents and Joshua meant that not only were we never alone in the house, we also weren't allowed to touch if we were inside. Therefore, we were spending a lot of time outside. Practically sun up to sun down during the end of summer was spent exploring riverbanks, walking to the playground, working in the yard—anything we could come up with. I'd never enjoyed mowing the lawn more in my life, and even Attie's scars were starting to get a little bit of color due to the sunlight. All the time outside was definitely a good thing.

Tammy yanked Attie out of my grasp and dragged her toward a small hill at the side of the riverbank. I watched as they laid their towels on the ground and made themselves comfortable before joining the guys in a game of football.

• •

(Attie)

"Now who is this playing on the iPod?" Tammy asked as we lay out on our towels.

"Chris Tomlin," I said, reaching over and turning up the volume.

"I like his voice. This isn't so bad for Christian music."

"He's one of my favorites."

"Mine too," Anne added. "I saw him in concert a little while back. He was great."

I glanced over at Riley and the boys playing ball by the water. "I would love to see him in concert. You might even want to see him in concert, Tammy. He's just your type."

"And what type is that?"

"Good looking," Anne offered.

The bright light reflected off the water and stung my eyes, so I turned my attention back to Tammy. "And he plays guitar—you like that."

"He's hot and he plays guitar?" she asked.

"Yes."

"And he's a Christian?

"Yes."

"And he sings Christian songs while standing on stage looking good and playing guitar?"

"Yes."

"I can't go then."

"Why?" we asked.

"It kinda defeats the purpose of going to a Christian concert if you're lusting after the guy on stage, don'cha think?"

Anne sat up, laughing. "Tammy, that's ludicrous. Only you would think of something like that. Who does that?"

"I did," I confessed. "Just before the car accident, I went to see a musical in New York. It was called *The Rock and the Rabbi*—"

"*The Rockin' Rabbi*?" Tammy asked. "Was it some guy dressed like a rabbi dancing around the stage?"

I laughed at her misunderstanding. "No. *The Rock and the Rabbi*, not the Rockin' Rabbi."

"Oh."

"Anyway, it's the story of Jesus and his disciple Peter. It was great and the music was incredible, but the problem was the guy playing Peter. He was extremely good looking. I felt guilty the entire time because I was sitting there thinking a disciple was attractive. One of Jesus's disciples, for crying out loud. I was completely disgusted with myself."

"Well, he wasn't a real disciple," Anne said. "I don't think you should feel bad about that."

"Anne, he was standing on stage singing 'You Are the Christ,' and all I could think about was how completely drool-worthy he was."

She laughed and shook her head. "Well, yeah, that's pretty bad."

"So back to this guy playing right now," Tammy interrupted. "Chris Tomlin?"

"Yeah, him. I'm Googling him tonight when I get home. I've gotta see what he looks like."

"You'll be an instant fan," I promised.

"Time to turn." Anne flipped over onto her stomach and made herself comfortable again. "I bet Tess would swoon over him."

"Tess swoons over just about anything male. She'd probably hyperventilate," Tammy said as she flipped over as well.

"That's for sure," Anne agreed. "Now thanks to you two, I probably can't ever see him in concert again. You've ruined it for me."

"Oh, don't you worry; it won't be the last thing we ruin for you. We're a terrible influence on you."

"Trust me, Tammy, I already know that."

"You should probably limit the time you spend with us."

"Are you kidding? And miss out on all the fun? No way."

"Well then, you'd better get yourself all prayed up so you can resist our evil ways. Or at least mine away."

Anne laughed. "Oh, Tammy. Your bark is bigger than your bite. It's not like you're a big heathen or anything."

"Well, don't tell anyone else that. I've got a reputation to uphold, you know."

"Whatever."

I listened to the girls banter back and forth until I began to drift off to sleep. For the first time in a year, I was finally sleeping in peace, and it was safe to nap without fear of having a nightmare.

Just as I lost consciousness, I heard a whipping noise, followed by icy cold water drops spreading across my body. I opened my eyes to find a mop of wet, brown hair shaking over me.

"Good grief, Riley Bennett!"

chapter 2

By the time we got home from our fish wrangling expedition, my skin was on fire. Ignoring pleas from Riley, I'd refused to put on sunscreen and was now paying the price. Knowing that he would never let me hear the end of it, I secretly slathered my body in aloe and then joined him in the hallway by plopping down into my beanbag chair. As soon as my skin made contact with the pleather, the back of my legs felt like thousands of tiny needles pricked into them. I hid my anguish behind a pretend sigh.

"Worried about tomorrow?" he asked as I placed the heel of my foot onto his knee.

"Pretty much."

In reality I felt like a prisoner making her way to the guillotine. Everyone knew that Tiffany was already busy trying to stir up trouble and that I was left to walk into a wasps' nest. My only hope was that she didn't have as much influence over the students as Tammy and Anne seemed to think.

Holding a small brush in his hands, he carefully painted crimson polish onto my toenails. "You'll cause a stir for the first few days…" He softly blew on my big toe. "But you'll become old news pretty fast."

"I sure hope so."

"Plus, you'll be so busy you won't even have time to think about it, what with school, cheering, and classes at UCO." He jammed the brush back into the bottle and looked up at me with a scowl. "How are you gonna fit everything in?"

"I only have classes a couple of nights a week. Really, it's not a big deal."

"It just doesn't seem like you'll have much time for yourself."

"Or for you?"

"I guess."

"Don't worry, Riley; I'll make time."

"You better." He started painting again. "How else are you gonna find time to get your toenails painted?"

I held my foot up in the air and inspected his paint job. "Gosh, you're pretty good at that."

"What do you expect? I'm an artist."

"Lucky for me, I have a professional doing the job. I don't even think you got any on my skin. When I do it I have to go back with a Q-tip and clean up around the nail."

"Since I don't need to protect you at night anymore, I've got to find something to make myself useful."

"There are other things you can do to make yourself useful."

His eyebrows arched over blazing green eyes. "Not inside this house, there aren't. We've gotta be outside these walls for that— assuming you're talking about my incredible kissing skills."

"Yes, those would be the skills I was referring to."

I heard Pops's footsteps, signaling he was making his way up the stairs. Due to his size, he couldn't have snuck up on us if he'd wanted to.

"Attiline, you ready for school tomorrow?"

"I think so."

He leaned against the doorframe going into Riley's room, and I thought back to our conversation about how he came up with the nickname Attiline. It still surprised me that we'd been such a large part of each other's lives for so long. It also reminded me that I needed to download *Sweet Caroline* from iTunes and give it a listen. "Nervous?" he asked.

"Yes. What if the mean kids pick on me?"

"If the mean kids pick on you, I'll turn my head the other way while Riley kicks the crap out of them. Nobody's gonna pick on our girl, are they, Riley?"

"Not if I can help it."

Pops looked at the nail polish in Riley's hand. "You thinking of going to cosmetology school, son?"

"Maybe. What of it?"

"I just never know what I'm gonna get with you, do I?"

"I don't wanna make this parenting gig too easy on you."

Pops laughed. "Easy on me? I'm having to police two lovebirds that are living in my upstairs. That's enough to make my hair go gray."

Riley ran his fingers through his own head of thick hair. "Well, I hate to tell you this, but your hair was already going gray."

Pops looked over at me and smirked. "I guess the beautician would know."

"Don't look at me. This is a no-win situation. I'm keeping my mouth shut."

Riley tossed me the nail polish. "You're supposed to take my side, Charlie. We're a team, remember?"

"And risk getting kicked out of the house? No thank you."

"No, Attiline, I already told Riley he'd be the one to go if one of you had to move out. We like you much more than we do him."

"Who can blame you? In that case..." I threw the polish back to Riley. "Get busy, cosmetology boy. You still have the other foot to do."

The evening hours rushed by, and I was sure that it was only because I was dreading the next day so much. If I'd actually been looking forward to the next twenty-four hours, time would've practically stood still. At least that's the way it worked for me, anyway.

I tossed and turned in bed for most of the night before I finally gave up on falling asleep and tiptoed to Riley's bedroom door.

"Riley? Psst, Riley."

He didn't budge, so I ran back to my closet, grabbed a flip-flop, ran back, and threw it toward his bed. I ended up hitting him in the face by accident.

"What the …?" He sat up and looked around the room in a panic before setting his eyes on me. "What was that?"

"A flip-flop."

"You threw a shoe at me?"

"I called your name several times. You wouldn't wake up."

He looked over at his clock as he scratched his head. "Charlie, it's three o'clock in the morning."

"I realize that. I couldn't sleep."

"And if you can't sleep, I'm not supposed to sleep either?"

"Isn't that how we work?"

He scratched his head again before swinging his legs over the side of the bed. "That's how you work, anyway."

I dropped my head and slowly turned to go to my room. "You don't have to come out here if you don't want to. I was just wanting to spend some more time with you, that's all."

It was an act, of course.

"I'm coming. Just give me a sec to wake up, for cryin' out loud. I was in the middle of a REM cycle."

I turned back to him. "Well, you don't have to get testy with me."

Riley looked at me with a crooked grin. He wouldn't ever turn down spending time with me, no matter what time it was.

"I'll wait out here."

Slumping into the beanbag chair, I waited for my knight in shining armor to keep me company. Within a matter of moments, he drifted out of his room, pulled his beanbag chair next to mine, and plunged in.

He moaned. "Happy now?"

"Yes. I feel much better."

"So was it a bad dream or nerves?"

"Nerves."

"That's an improvement."

"I'm really bothered by the fact that your dad didn't put us in any classes together. What was he thinking?"

"He was thinking, *How on earth am I gonna keep these two away from each other for the majority of the day?*"

"Now that you say that, I can totally hear him thinking that."

"That very question has probly been haunting his mind for weeks."

"I'm sure it has."

"But you're gonna be fine. You've got the girls in some of your classes—at least he gave you that. And we do have the same lunch hour."

"Yes, there is that."

He turned on his side and laid his head on the back of the bag. "Did you know that we might actually be able to exist without seeing each other sixteen hours a day?"

I turned to face him. "You don't say?"

"That's what I hear, anyway. I've heard that spending time apart makes the heart grow fonder."

"I don't think my heart can get any fonder."

He looked surprised. "Well, that was adorable."

"It was also true."

He shook his shaggy head as if he were trying to escape a daze. "I totally lost my train of thought. What were we talking about?"

"School."

"Oh yeah. Maybe we can catch a peek at each other as we mosey down the hallway. Maybe I'll wink at you."

"That would be nice. I might actually wink back…and maybe throw in a flirty wave."

"Now that would make my day for sure, the flirty wave and all."

"Do you think we should act normal or be coy?"

"I say we leave everybody guessing. They've all heard rumors; what's wrong with confusing them a bit? Play a few mind games maybe?"

"I'm in."

"So we act like we know each other—obviously."

"Obviously."

"But we don't act like we actually love each other. No holding hands or anything. It's strictly business," he said.

"Cool."

"It'll drive everybody crazy."

"Good. It *is* my goal in life to make sure everyone's as wacked out as I am."

"This could very well do it."

"I love it when you act all devious. It's really sexy."

He laughed loudly before burying his head in the beanbag chair so his parents wouldn't hear and then looked back over at me. "I think my heart just exploded when you said that. You're on a roll, and it's only three o'clock in the morning."

"I'm most creative in the wee hours."

He leaned toward me, and his fiery eyes caused my heart rate to increase. "Maybe you should start waking me up more often."

"Do I note wishful thinking in your voice?"

"Yep. I kinda miss the ol' days of sleeping next to you on the floor."

I placed my hand on his head and pushed him back into the chair. "Oh, Riley, you really are cute."

We sat and talked about school until sleepiness finally took hold and my yawning increased as my eyelids grew heavy.

"I'm tired now. I'm going to sleep." I stood to make my way to my welcoming bed as he reached out and clutched on to my arm.

"Wait just a minute! I'm wide awake."

"I'm going to bed."

"That's just wrong, Atticus Elizabeth Reed." His arms folded across his chest, and a scowl perched on his face. "Completely and utterly wrong."

"Fine." I plopped back into the beanbag chair.

"Thank you."

"Uh-huh."

Another large yawn escaped my throat, and seeing my sleepiness caused him to feel a little bit sorry for me.

"Okay, if you can answer one question right, I'll let you go to sleep."

"Do I have to? I'm tired."

"You gotta."

"What is it?"

"Name the schools of the Big Twelve Conference."

"Riley!"

He wagged his finger at me. "You have to name them if you wanna go to sleep."

"Fine."

"I'll count."

"Oklahoma, Oklahoma State, Iowa State, Texas Tech, Texas A&M, Baylor, Nebraska, Colorado, Kansas, Kansas State…"

Riley kept count on his fingers as I listed them.

"Missouri…"

"Can she do it? One more… can she do it?"

"Oh, and what's that other orange team I hate? Oh yeah, Texas." I stood and started making my way toward my bed.

"See, this is why I love you. You really are a dream girl."

"Goodnight."

"She even knows the schools of the Big Twelve…" I listened to him talk to himself as he walked back into his room. "She's my dream girl, darned right. I sure can pick 'em."

I turned and stuck my head out my door. "Them? You can pick them?"

He peeked around the doorframe. "You, I meant. I sure can pick—you."

"Nice try."

"You're the only one for me, Charlie."

"Go to sleep, Riley."

chapter 3

I lay in bed dreading the day a little too long, and by the time I dragged myself out of the comfy covers and toward the shower, everyone else was gone. Boomer and Baby were the only ones left, and they both sat on the landing staring at the front door in hopes that someone would come back home.

"Baby, do you realize I'm the one that cared for you and helped restore your health?"

She glanced back at me for a moment but went right back to watching the door. Riley had quickly become the center of her world, and nobody else would do. Who could really blame her?

"Fine, see if I give you a snack when I get home, you ungrateful dog."

Walking into the bathroom, I spotted a new drawing. Riley must have drawn it and then taped it to the mirror after I went back to bed. It was a replica of a photo Tammy had taken of him and me together. I was proudly holding my catfish, and he was pointing at it and smiling.

My collection of Riley artwork was growing larger and larger by the day, and I constantly wondered what he was going to draw next. It was one of the highlights of each and every day, and I'd started storing them in a shoebox. It was the shoebox from the first pair of shoes that Marme bought me after I arrived.

I went through my normal routine of getting ready for the day and didn't bother to put on any more makeup than I normally would.

I didn't really like to wear makeup, and Riley wouldn't have liked it even if I did. He liked me "au naturel," or so he said.

Finally picking up some steam, I rushed through a bowl of cereal, tossed some dry food into the dog dishes, and ran out the door. When I jumped into the car, there was a sticky note attached to the steering wheel.

> I filled your gas tank, so you should be set for the week.
> Have a great first day of school. Don't worry; you'll do great!
> Love you! Pops

The note from Pops was a big clue of where Riley got his love of giving notes and pictures. I guessed he'd been getting them from his dad for years and wondered if Riley kept them for safekeeping.

As it was, I had nothing with my mother's handwriting on it. There might have been some items back at the house in Ithaca, but my dad hadn't sent me any of her things. I hoped that in the boxes he'd probably packed away, there was a note of some kind from my mother to me, and I wondered if our handwriting looked similar.

Removing the note, I opened up the visor and stuck it on the mirror for safekeeping before finally putting the car in drive and making the ten-minute drive to my new prison.

• •

"She's arrived!" Tammy danced in circles as I approached what would be my new school building. "Look at her in all her new girl glory."

I walked toward the entrance and my ridiculous best friend. "How on God's green earth are you of all people so peppy this early in the morning? And on the first day of school, no less?"

"Aw, I knew you'd be tortured all day today. I thought it might be fun to witness."

"I appreciate your loyalty and support."

As soon as we made it through the doors, the noise was deafening. I stopped and peered into the office just to my right. I hoped to see Pops, but there were so many parents and students standing at the desk that if he were inside, my view of him was obscured.

The library sat right in front of us, and the cafeteria was snuggled between it and the office I'd just passed. Turning left, Tammy and I walked down the small hallway lined with a single row of blue lockers. I held my breath as I watched students pack the hall, laughing, talking, and slamming locker doors. It felt odd to see everyone dressed in casual clothes. I was accustomed to a strict dress code that composed of a school uniform and no additional items. Everyone standing in front of me looked so casual and so ... foreign.

The more steps we took, the farther away Pops was and the more I felt like I was making my way down a gauntlet.

Once we'd finally made our way down the first hallway, Tammy wrapped her arm around mine, and I watched the locker numbers as she led me through the crowd.

"Where are the girls?"

"Are you kidding me? Tess and Anne wouldn't be late for class if their lives depended on it, and Jen's chasing after some guy on the golf team. That'll keep her occupied for a while."

"Golf team, huh? Does she even like golf?"

"Does anyone?"

"I doubt it."

"She likes the guy, so she'll pretend to like the sport. That's how we do things around here."

"You live a lie?"

"Yep."

"Hmm."

"Don't judge, Attie. We've all got our issues. Some of us more than others."

"I'm not judging; I'm just worried she's going to want us to fake it too. I don't think I could make it through an entire golf match."

"I think it's actually a tournament."

"Whatever. Hey, here's my locker."

My backpack fell to the floor as I dialed the combination. Of course it didn't work. With my luck the way it is, why on earth would I have thought it would work on the first try? Having good luck would have been completely uncharacteristic of me.

I kicked the metal contraption twice before giving the combination another try. "Twenty-seven, nine, seventeen. Abra cadabra." This time the locker door opened easily.

"Nice magic."

"I've got skills."

"Speaking of skills, where's Riley?"

"Watch it. I don't employ any 'skills' when it comes to Riley Bennett, thank you very much."

"I'm not accusing you of anything inappropriate; I'm just saying you've got him under your spell, that's all."

"Uh-huh."

"Anyhoo, I thought the two of you would come together."

I threw the backpack into the locker and shoved it in with my foot. "We're not together."

She grabbed me by the arm. "You broke up?"

"Shh!" I looked around to make sure nobody was listening. "We were never together."

"Huh?"

"It's a little game we're playing, messing with people's minds."

She maniacally rubbed her hands together and gave an evil laugh before speaking in her best Wicked Witch of the West voice. "Oh, how I enjoy messing with people's minds."

"That was creepy."

She shrugged. "I try."

"Anyway, you're going to love it. Riley and I are going to ignore each other."

"That should be interesting to watch. You haven't been able to keep away from each other for months."

"Shh!"

"Quit telling me to shush; nobody's paying us any mind." She looked around the crowded hallway before dramatically rolling her eyes. "Well, actually, everyone's staring at you."

I pretended to dig in my locker. "Please tell me you're joking."

"Wish I could, but people are all up in your business right now."

I kicked my backpack again.

"Turn around," she whispered.

"No."

"It's your man candy."

"My what?"

"Turn around, turn around, turn around, turn around … hey, Riley."

I spun around and practically ran right into him. He smelled amazing, and his tan skin looked like syrup against his butter-yellow golf shirt.

"Hey, Attie." He was going all out, even calling me Attie. He'd probably been practicing all morning, seeing as how he hadn't directly called me "Attie" since we were in the second grade.

I gave a small nod and felt my face and neck begin to flush. "Riley."

The throng of students immediately surrounding us became noticeably quieter. I imagined their ears perking up, much like Baby's did when we called her for dinner. Our fellow students wanted the scoop, and they wanted it now.

"How's your morning?" he asked.

Refusing to make eye contact, I nibbled on my thumbnail. "It's all right. Tammy's showing me around. How about yours?" I finally peeked up at him. He was wearing an adorable smirk.

"Okay. I'm a little tired though. I didn't get much sleep last night. Something kept me up."

My stomach flipped. He was secretly flirting with me right there in front of everyone, and I stood stunned while he smiled proudly at me as he waited for a response.

Quickly, the shyness and nerves fled my body, and I felt my shoulders rise and my chest puff a bit. Two could play his game, and there was no way I was going to let him win.

I returned his smugness with a sly smile of my own. "I'm so sorry to hear that. I hope it wasn't anything serious that kept you up."

"Oh …" He nodded. "It was *very* serious."

"Really?"

"Uh-huh. It's affected me...four months or so? Yeah, about four months."

"Has it always been so serious?"

"Pretty much from day one."

"Day one?"

"It's sorta like it showed up on my doorstep and never left. I've had trouble getting a good night's sleep ever since."

"Really, it's that serious?"

"Yep."

"Maybe you should have yourself checked out, let someone have a really good look at you. You know, someone who really knows your inner workings."

"And outer," Tammy added.

"Yes, Tammy." I threw her a nod. "Definitely his outer workings."

His eyes widened and then narrowed. I was sure his mind was racing.

"Riley?"

He shook his head, which caused a clump of dark hair to fall across his right eye. "What?"

"Maybe you should have yourself checked out."

He gave a knowing nod. "I plan on it."

I desperately wanted to laugh but somehow managed to maintain my cool. "Is that why your eyes are so red? A lack of sleep?"

"No, that would be allergies."

"Allergies?" I asked.

"Yeah, I've been spending a lotta time outside." He bit his top lip, but a small laugh still escaped.

"Really, a lot of time outside?"

"More than usual."

"Doing what, exactly?"

"A little of this. A little of that." He shrugged.

"Nothing too strenuous?"

"Never." My toes went numb as his searing eyes burned right through. "I really try to place limits on myself."

"Limited but enjoyable just the same?"

"Extremely enjoyable." He crossed his arms in front of his chest and grinned his movie-star grin, leaving me completely weak in the knees but still determined to win our war of flirty words.

I glanced at Tammy. Her mouth hung open as she watched our interaction. "Did you hear that, Tammy? Riley's been spending a lot of extra time outside."

She looked over at me. "I hear it's good to spend time outside with all that fresh air and physical activity and stuff. It does the body good."

"And the psyche," Riley added, barely able to hide his amusement.

"Definitely the psyche," I confirmed.

Tammy looked at Riley. "Plan on spending any time outside this afternoon?"

"Quite a bit, actually. Maybe even into the evening."

She gave him a pat on the arm. "Good for you. Have a good time."

"I plan on it." His eyes locked on mine. "So …"

"So," I repeated.

He dropped his gaze, rummaged through his backpack, and pulled out a bagged lunch. "Mom was afraid you'd forget your lunch, so she had me bring it."

I grabbed for it, but he reached across me and put it on the shelf in my locker. The reach brought his face and the scent of his fresh-smelling cologne inches from me.

"You're killin' me," he groaned.

"You started it." I pulled out my schedule and placed it on my binder. "Will you look at this with me?" I spoke loud enough for everyone crowding around us to hear.

Pretending to look at the paper, he leaned into me until his chest rested against my shoulder. "I may have started it, but you kicked it up a notch," he whispered, pointing to the schedule. "You're smoldering right now, do you realize that?"

I lowered my head and pretended to examine the paper more closely. "Evidently you didn't know whom you were dealing with."

A small moan escaped his throat. "Seriously, you need to stop right now, or everyone in this hallway's gonna get a show."

My stomach fluttered at the idea that I could make him nervous so easily. It was cute. I looked up at him out of the corner of my eye. "And what type of show would you be referring to?"

"Let's put it this way: there won't be any doubt how I feel about you."

"And how is that?"

He smiled. "So that's how you wanna play?"

"Uh-huh."

"You're so not fair."

"How much more can you take, Riley?"

"Uh..." He looked back down at the schedule. "Not much more, I can tell you that."

"Do you want to admit defeat now?"

He smiled down at me again. "How about we call it even and continue this later on tonight?"

"Only if you say it."

"Say what?"

"Attie holds all the power," I whispered.

His eyes practically sparkled. "Attie Reed most definitely holds all the power—I gladly gave it over."

I grabbed the schedule and jammed it into my notebook as I raised my voice again. "That's exactly what I needed to know. Thanks so much, Riley."

"You're welcome, Char—Attie."

"I'll be sure to tell your dad how nice you were to help me out. You know, going out of your way to find me and point me in the right direction. I know you have a lot of better things to do. Probably a girl or two waiting around for you somewhere."

"Anytime. Well... try to have a good day."

"I'll do that."

"Maybe we'll see each other at lunch or something?" he said. "Yeah, it'd be best if I found you at lunch. That way I can see if you need anything or have any questions or anything."

"You're so darned sweet, Riley. I'm sure you'll make a girl very happy one day."

A full-blown chuckle escaped before he could stop himself, so he turned it into a fake cough. "Gotta go."

"Toodles."

I turned toward my locker as he bolted down the hallway.

"Jaws are dropped all around." Much like a ventriloquist, Tammy talked through nonmoving lips. "You both deserve an Oscar, and I think I need a cold shower. That was hot. "

"It was fun."

"How on earth did you control yourself? If I were dating him, I'd be kissing him ten times a day and sixty times on Sunday."

"Shame on you. Don't you know Sundays are a day of rest?" I exploded into a fit of giggles and dragged her through the hall. "Come on, get me to my first class."

"Attie!" Jennifer raced up and threw her arms around me.

"Hey, girl. Where's your golfer boy?"

"He had so many girls stalking him it was crazy. He couldn't get anywhere near me."

"*He* couldn't get anywhere near *you?*" Tammy asked.

"Be nice. Not all of us have a Riley Bennett to pine away after us. Where is he, by the way?"

Tammy's head quickly occupied the space between Jen and me. "They aren't together," she announced.

"What?" Jennifer gasped. "You broke up?"

"Shh!"

"You broke up?" she repeated in a whisper.

Tammy exaggeratingly winked several times. "They were never together."

"You weren't? I thought—"

"Good gravy, Jen. Did you not see the winks I threw your direction?"

"I thought you were having an eye spasm."

"An eye spasm? What the … ?"

"So shoot me."

"I'd like to."

"Okay, you two, knock it off." I pushed them away from each other and walked to within inches of my bubbly blonde friend. "For the sake of high school entertainment, Riley and I are acting like we aren't together."

Her eyes grew wide. "Oh."

"Yeah," Tammy interrupted again. "The plan was to torture all the busybodies, but the only person being tortured at the moment is Riley. You just missed Attie literally driving him out of his mind. If he wasn't crazy about her before, he sure is now. I practically had to wipe the boy's chin."

"Always leave them wanting more," I instructed.

"You definitely did that. He probably can't even see straight right now. For an angelic little thing, you sure do have a bit of a devious side."

"It's harmless fun, Tammy."

"Uh-huh." She threw her arm around Jennifer's shoulders. "So anyhoo, we gotta play along with the act."

"I get it. I'm not gonna ruin it. If anyone's gonna ruin it, it'll be Tess and Anne. They couldn't lie to save their souls."

Tammy grabbed our elbows and started leading us toward class. "Well, we're just gonna have to give the girls some acting lessons then, aren't we?"

My first few classes of the day went smoothly. Tess was in my first class, Tammy and Anne were in my second, and Jennifer and Curt were in my third and fourth. One of the girls made sure to escort me to my next class so that I wouldn't get lost and to protect me from unknown predators—or so Tammy said.

Riley passed me in the hallway four times, and each and every time, he was surrounded by a group of people. I was quickly learning that Jennifer was right; he was one of the most popular people in school. I, on the other hand, evidently had the plague. Other than my summer friends and some of the girls from the squad, nobody came near me. I heard my name whispered here and there, and I got a lot of not-so-friendly stares, but I tried to pretend I didn't notice.

Every time Tiffany walked by, she refused to make eye contact and blew right past me like a northern breeze. The whiff of her overly perfumed body left me reeling in a cloud of stinkiness, and I grew to dislike the girl more and more with every second. What on earth Riley ever saw in her was beyond me; how he could go from her to me left me completely puzzled. We had absolutely nothing in common, unless, of course, you counted the fact that we'd both kissed him. And if I ever stopped and took the time to think about that common feature, I'd probably end up vomiting repeatedly.

"Ms. Reed?"

I looked up from my science book. "Yes, sir?"

"You're wanted in the principal's office."

Curt leaned over from his seat next to me. "How'd you manage to get in trouble in less than four classes?"

"I have no idea." Actually, I had a very good idea. Riley's dad must have heard about our little production in the hallway. I felt nauseated at the thought of discussing it with him.

"We were just having fun," I murmured to myself.

"You're excused," the teacher announced. "Take your books in case you're in there for a while."

"Yes, sir." I slowly slid out of the chair, and although I didn't look around to confirm my fears, I assumed that all eyes were on me as I inched my way through the tables and out of the classroom.

Just after closing the door behind me, a wad of paper struck me in the face. I looked in the direction it came from and spotted Riley hiding behind a row of lockers. Making my way toward him, I looked around and noticed the hall was empty.

He grabbed a hold of my shirt, pulled me to him, and kissed me. He hadn't kissed me with such intensity since our first official date. It was nice. Better than nice.

Eventually our lips separated, and he was left wearing a large smile of contentment.

"Riley, you're going to get us in a lot of trouble."

His face flushed as the smile turned into a crooked grin. "It'll be worth it."

"Wow, maybe I should flirt like that a little more often."

He pulled me to him again, but this time our faces froze a few inches away from each other. "As much as I'd love that, it probly isn't such a good idea."

"Too much?" I asked.

"Unfortunately."

"I'll dial it down a bit."

"Good." He quickly kissed me again.

"How'd you get out here?"

"I have connections. I told Dad we should check on you."

"I doubt us mugging in the hallway is what he had in mind."

"Probly not, but it's what I had in mind. Especially after that award-winning performance this morning."

"You didn't do so bad yourself."

"I was just trying to keep up. You kept the zingers coming. I didn't even know your mind could work like that."

"There's still a lot you don't know about me, Riley Bennett."

"As I said, you'll always be a mystery to me."

"I could have kept it up all day."

He laughed as he wrapped his arms around me. "I couldn't have taken it all day."

"How long are we going to keep this act up, anyway? I'm getting lonely without you."

"Just a few days. I don't think I'll be able to stand it much longer than that."

"Me either."

"I talked Matt into trading lockers with me. Now we're right across from each other."

"Look at you, so creative."

He beamed. "Anything to be closer to my girl."

"Your girl?"

"Aren't you?"

"Yes, and evidently you're my man candy."

He laughed. "Your what?"

"It's a Tammy-ism."

"Sounds like a Tammy-ism."

"Hey, thanks for the drawing this morning. I loved it."

"You're welcome. I worked on it last night after you deserted me and went back to bed."

"Sorry. I won't wake you up like that again."

"Did I say I minded?" He kissed me on the forehead before turning me around and giving a small push. "You better get to the office or Dad's gonna come looking for you."

"Which direction do I go?"

He pointed to his left. "Head that way and follow the sounds of hell; they'll lead you right to it."

chapter 4

(Riley)

Even just a few minutes after class let out, the cafeteria was packed. I'd made the mistake of heading to my locker before going to lunch, and now I could hardly make my way through the room.

My sense of smell was immediately assaulted by the scent of school green beans. I hated the smell and had developed such an aversion to it that Mom never made green beans at home. Luckily for me, my mother was the Martha Stewart of central Oklahoma, and she packed my lunch each and every morning. Otherwise, I'd be left to suffer through fake meat and congealed macaroni and cheese like everyone else.

Kent walked against the rush of students and in my direction. "We're in the back. Wanna head that way?"

"I guess."

"You guess?" He slapped me on the forehead. "Don't even try to act cool. I know you've been waiting to see her all day. Only a day and a half of school and you're already going through withdrawal."

"Keep it down or someone's gonna hear you."

"It's louder than a NASCAR race in here. Nobody's gonna hear nothing unless they're standing right next to you."

We squeezed our way through the tables, bodies, backpacks, and books that had been thrown all over the floor.

"You ready for the game on Friday night, Riley?"

I scanned the faces around me until I found a pimple-faced boy smiling up at me. He looked like a freshman.

"Uh, yeah, of course. We should win. Are you going?"

"I'll be there," the boy said.

"Great."

"Maybe we can hang out after? Know of any parties?" he asked.

"I'll get back to you on that."

"Cool." He pushed himself through the crowd and out of sight.

"Who was that?" Chase asked from behind me.

"I have no idea. I've never seen him before in my life." I walked on the tips of my toes trying to catch a glimpse of Attie as I shoved my way toward the back.

A girl jumped in front of me. "Hey, Riley!"

"Hey, Claudia."

"Can you believe it's already the second day of school?"

"Naw, time flies." My eyes scanned the room again.

"Did you have a good summer?"

There was still no sign of Attie. "Incredible. You?"

"It was amazing. My family took a trip to Mexico and—"

I completely blocked out her noise but kept nodding so she would think I was listening. As I pushed through the students, she followed behind. Attie finally came into my line of vision. "That sounds incredible, Claudia. I'll talk to you later."

"Oh." She sounded upset, but I didn't look to find out if she actually was. I figured she'd get over it soon enough.

Attie looked completely out of her element and overwhelmed as I shoved my way through the remainder of the crowd and rushed to the table.

"What's the matter? You look upset."

"Devil girl got a hold of her," Jennifer said.

"Devil girl?"

They both raised their eyebrows at me, causing me to realize what a stupid question it was. "Oh yeah. What did Tiffany want?"

"To be a jerk," Tammy said. "What else is new?"

"It wasn't a big deal," Attie mumbled.

"So what happened?"

"She came walking toward me down the hallway with all her friends surrounding her. I didn't want to be rude, so I said hi to her, and she literally looked the other way and then practically knocked me down when she walked past. They all laughed at me, and musty ol' Wes called me a freak. It was like something out of a bad movie on the Lifetime Channel."

"All Lifetime Channel movies are bad," Tammy said.

Kent tossed his lunch onto the table. "What a bunch of whack jobs. I don't get why people have to act like that all the time. What would it have hurt for her to say hi?"

"It's their MO, Kent," I said. "They've gotta make everyone else look bad to try to make themselves feel more important. One day, they're gonna get what's coming to them, and I hope I'm there to see it."

"Can we just drop the entire subject?" Attie asked. "Really, I'd rather not let those jerks ruin my lunch."

I reached for her hand but remembered our hoax and put my hands back in my lap. She noticed the gesture and smiled up at me.

"If you two are gonna keep trying to fool everyone, you better stop giving each other those googley eyes," Kent warned. "There isn't a soul in this room that's gonna fall for it."

Attie snickered while she looked down and poked at her pasta salad. I picked up a pen and started drawing on my notebook.

"Everyone's talking about her," Tess said. "'Is she the one living with Riley?' 'Is she the one from the accident?' 'Are they really together?' 'I thought he was dating Tiffany.'"

Attie shoved her food out of the way and laid her head onto the table. "Seriously, is it that bad?"

"It's worse." Anne walked up to the table, stood behind me, and stole a Cheeto out of my chip bag. "Tiffany isn't wasting any time trying to take you down."

Attie groaned.

Kent slammed his fist on the table, causing plates to crash, drinks to topple, silverware to scatter, and Attie to pick her head up. "I'd like to knock a few rungs off her ladder, if you know what I mean."

"Actually, Kent," Anne said, "I have no idea what you mean."

"I'll be fine. Everyone will settle down in a few days. I'm sure this doesn't just happen to me, and it happens to new people all the time."

The words that came out of her mouth didn't match her body language. She was bothered by what people were saying about her, and I think I was bothered by it even more. There was no way I was going to let her go through it all by herself. I stood and moved my way around the table. "All I know is that I'm not gonna sit back and let you go through it all by yourself."

"What are you doing, Riley?"

"I'm coming to sit with my girlfriend, that's what I'm doing."

Attie looked puzzled. "But I thought we were trying to keep it secret for a few more days."

"Not anymore. I'm tired of trying to hide it." I straddled the bench and sat down.

She turned, threw her legs onto the bench, and sat cross-legged so we could face each other. "It's only been a day and a half day; you're tired of it already?"

"I was tired of it yesterday when you asked if I enjoyed all my time outside."

"That was a good one, huh?"

I leaned over and kissed her on the forehead. "It got my attention, I'll say that."

"Uh, Riley..." Tammy muttered.

I ignored her and kissed Attie on the nose before reaching for my lunch and pulling it toward me. "So the rest of your day's been okay?"

"Yes. Pretty uneventful. Thanks for leaving the note on my mirror this morning."

"You're welcome. I just thought you should know I was thinking about you. I hate leaving before you wake up."

Tammy slapped me on the shoulder. "Riley!"

I looked over at her. "What, Tammy? What?"

"I think this entire room just went up in flames. I swear I saw heads exploding all over the place."

Looking around, I saw hundreds of eyes looking our direction.

Kent stood and turned to face the crowd. "Y'all just mind your own dang business and eat your lunch. They're just dating; it's not like it's the apocalypse or anything."

Attie laid the top of her head against my chest and looked across the table. "I wish it were still summer. Either that or we could just fast forward a week or two."

"It'll get better, Attie," Anne said as she sat in the spot I'd left empty. "You'll be old news before you know it. Well, after the crap hits the fan, anyway."

"What crap?" we asked simultaneously.

"I talked to several of the girls on the squad today. We vote for captain on Friday after school, and if my count is right, it isn't going to be Tiffany."

"Who's it gonna be?" Kent asked.

"Who do you think, brainiac?" Tammy asked. "Attie, of course."

Kent's eyes grew wide. "Well, that's gonna knock ol' Tiff for a loop. She's been so busy trying to cause you problems that she's lost the support of the only people she had on her side. Heck, it's like going out and mowing your lawn while your house is on fire."

"What does that even mean?" Anne asked.

"Don't ask," Tammy begged. "He makes sense to himself, honest he does."

Tammy leaned toward Anne with an excited grin. "Anyway, back to the cheer squad. So what did you hear?"

"Just that everyone is sick of the way Tiffany's acting. Plus, Attie's the better leader, and her skills are far better."

"She does have great skills," I added.

Tammy gave me a scowl. "We don't need to know that."

Attie lifted her head and punched me in the stomach. "Don't act like you're talking about something you're not really talking about."

"I was acknowledging what a great cheerleader you are."

"You've never even seen me cheer, moron. You don't have a clue what you're talking about."

"I could assume. You're good at everything else."

She lightly punched me in the stomach again. "Quit while you're ahead."

"What?"

"This is serious. It could get bad."

"Nobody's gonna mess with my girl Attie," Kent said. "And let me just say, had they seen you out there noodling, they would have realized you're one tough cookie. Personally, I wouldn't mess with you."

"I don't mess with her," I said. "I just give her what she wants."

"Like I ever have to get tough with you, Riley Bennett."

I grabbed her cheeks in my hand and squeezed until she looked like a fish. "That's my point. You've got me whipped."

She covered my mouth with her hand. "Enough out of you. You aren't helping."

I kissed her on the inside of her hand several times before giving it a lick. She yanked her hand away and wiped it on my shirt. "I knew this cheerleading thing was a bad idea." She was still talking through fish lips. "It's going to be my downfall, I just know it." She finally swiped my hand away from her face and gave me a small thunk on the forehead with her finger.

"I hate to break up the party," Chase whispered, "but said cheerleader is walking our direction."

"You've got to be kidding." Tammy moaned as Tiffany slunk up to the table.

"Hey, Riley."

"Tiffany."

"Uniforms are in, Attie. You might want to check yours out. I noticed it looked a little small. It may be too tiny for your slightly larger frame."

Tammy stood. "Slightly larger frame my—"

Kent covered her mouth.

"She's the size of a tic-tac," I added.

"Thanks, Tiffany. I'll go check it out. Where are they?"

"Coach Tyler's office, of course."

"I need mine too, Attie," Anne said. "We'll go together. Thanks for going out of your way and letting us know, Tiffany."

"It's what a leader does, Anne. We look out for our team."

"Bull crap."

Tammy hid the comment behind a cough, which caused Kent to slap her on the back several times. "There, there, now. You choking on something? Need some water?"

"I need some boots is what I need. It's getting mighty deep in here."

Kent jammed a cookie in her mouth. "Here. Chew on that."

Tiffany ignored them and kept her hostile eyes on me. "Oh, and Attie…"

Attie reached up over her head and pointed to herself. "I'm over here."

"In case you forgot, practice is at three fifteen," Tiffany said.

"Isn't it actually three?" Anne asked.

"Yes, Anne," Attie said. "It is three. I'm glad you said something, or Tiffany would have been late."

"It's the leader in me looking out for the squad." Anne's voice was laced with a bit of sarcasm and tainted with just a smidge of vile, which caused Tammy to give her an approving nod. She loved it when Anne showed her nonholy side. It was usually the highlight of her day.

Tiffany crept away without saying good-bye, and her two drones, otherwise known as Wes and Rick, waddled along behind her.

"Hey, Tiffany," Kent shouted toward her, "you ever need help getting that corncob outta your butt, just let me know. I'll get my pliers. Wes and Rick can take care of their own."

chapter 5

Attie propped up the hanger that held the very small uniform. "I don't know, Riley; it looks a little skimpy. A heck of a lot smaller than the uniforms we wore up north. Is skimpy a southern thing?"

"I thought skimpy was a universal thing," I admitted.

"Not this skimpy. Are you sure it isn't missing some fabric? I don't even know if it'll cover the parts it's supposed to cover, let alone the parts I was hoping it would."

"Maybe it's just an optical illusion. Go in the bathroom and try it on."

She disappeared for a few minutes, and I listened through the door as she talked to herself about the lack of fabric and how there was no way she would go in public looking like a Hooters girl. Her dramatic distress was cracking me up.

"Well?"

"Good grief, I look like a stripper... or an NFL cheerleader, which is just about as bad."

"Get out here and let me be the judge of that." The thought of my girlfriend momentarily looking like a stripper sounded extremely promising, and I couldn't wait to see for myself.

"I'm not leaving this bathroom."

"Oh, come on. Is it really that bad?"

"Yes!"

"Get out here and let me see."

"I don't know, Riley."

"Get out here already!"

After several seconds, the door slowly opened; and when I saw her delicate body in the tiny uniform, I'm pretty sure my jaw slammed to the floor. "You're right. You can't walk out of this house wearing that."

"I knew it." Attie grabbed a hold of the bottom of the skirt and started tugging it toward her knees as she danced nervously around the hallway. It wasn't helping. The skirt didn't budge.

I dropped into the beanbag chair, and Baby immediately made herself at home on my lap as Boomer lay in a clump next to my feet. "Now, wearing it in the house is another thing altogether. You can wear it around here all you want. I won't complain a bit."

She kicked me in the shin. "Dial down the perv factor, will ya?"

"I'll try, but you walk around in something like that and what am I supposed to say?"

"It really is that bad, isn't it?"

"Well, babe, that depends on your definition of *bad*."

"Bad as in if I bend over, everyone's going to see my lady parts."

"Turn around and give it a try."

"Gross!" She crossed her legs at the knee and threw her arms across her bare stomach. "Riley Bennett, cut it out."

"I'm just having some fun."

"What the heck am I going to do?"

"I can't be the judge of this. In all seriousness, it covers more than a bathing suit, so it's not like you're naked or anything. I just think it's a little short for a uniform."

"I feel naked."

"You don't look naked. You just look…uncomfortable. And totally amazing. I'm in heaven right now."

"Riley!"

"Maybe we need another opinion."

"Well, go down and get your mother and bring her up here. Let's see what she thinks."

Without getting out of the beanbag chair, I leaned back and yelled over the stair railing for my mother to get upstairs.

"I could have done that. I meant go down and get her."

"Why? She heard me."

Mom's voice traveled up from the kitchen. "I'm busy making dinner. What do you want?"

"I knew she'd hear me."

Attie tapped her foot on the floor in annoyance. "The entire neighborhood heard you."

"Get up here and tell us if Attie looks like a Hooters girl and is showing off too many of her lady parts." I started laughing and looked back at the stripper. "That'll get her attention."

The heels of Mom's shoes clopped across the hardwood floors as she hurried to join us.

"Told you so."

Mom was completely out of breath by the time she made it to the landing and spotted Attie. "Oh dear," she gasped. "Riley, cover your eyes."

Attie grabbed a towel and wrapped it around her waist. "I knew it! What in the world am I going to do?"

Mom slapped me on the head. "Cover your eyes."

"Good Lord, I've seen her in a bikini. This isn't any big deal. And it was a bikini you picked out, by the way."

"I don't care. Cover your eyes right now or you're grounded."

I slapped my hands over my eyes. "You act like I'm twelve."

"No, I'm acting like you're seventeen and your girlfriend's standing in front of you a quarter of the way dressed—if that."

"I thought she looked good."

"I bet you did."

A smack accompanied an explosion of pain on my temple as Mom's hand again made contact with my head.

"Ow."

"Tom, get up here!"

Although I couldn't see anything, I could hear Mom walk closer to the half-naked cheerleader. "It's okay, Attie. We'll get Pops's opinion. He's the principal, and he'll know if it's too small."

I heard Dad make his way up the stairs and step into the hall-way. "Why are the boy's eyes covered?"

"Well, Tom, it seems we have a little problem with Attie's cheer-leading uniform."

"Little being the word of the day," I added while rubbing my throbbing scalp with the hand that wasn't covering my eyes.

"You'll see," Mom said. "Keep your eyes covered, Riley. Take the towel off, Attie."

"Do I have to?" Attie and I asked simultaneously. I wanted to uncover my eyes, and she wanted to stay covered.

"Yes."

I slightly spread my fingers so I could peek through and watched as she opened the towel. I still thought she looked amazing.

"Uh, no," Dad said quickly. "You aren't wearing that in public."

Attie threw the towel closed before bursting into tears. "Well, what am I going to do?"

I closed my fingers so I wouldn't get caught and listened as Dad walked toward her. It was obvious by the sound of his voice that he was trying not to laugh but finding it hard not to. "Maybe we can get all the girls together and see if you can swap with someone. If not, we'll just have to order you a new one."

"There's no way it will be ready in time for the game on Friday," Attie cried.

"Let me just say," I said with my hand still covering my eyes, "as a player, I would find myself extremely motivated to do well if I had Attie dressed like that and cheering for me on the sideline. Either that or I'd wanna be benched so I could watch her cheer all night."

My mother slapped me on the head again.

"You're digging a grave for yourself, son," Dad warned.

"I just thought you'd want input from one of the people she cheers for."

"You thought wrong."

"Get your mind out of the gutter," Mom insisted.

"Surely we can work something out. I'll go call Coach Tyler right now and find out what we should do. In the meantime, Atti-line, take that loincloth off and get some clothes on."

"Yes, sir."

I heard footsteps disperse in various directions.

"Can I uncover my eyes now?"

Nobody answered.

"Hello?" I peeked through my fingers and realized that the dogs and I had been left alone on the landing.

Unfortunately, the peep show was over, and next time I saw Attie she'd be fully clothed.

• •

(Attie)

Pops paced the family room while Riley and I sat perched on the couch waiting for my uniform nightmare to be solved. "It seems we have a confusing situation on our hands. Coach Tyler said that there must have been a miscommunication when your measurements were taken because the order that was shipped perfectly matched the order that was placed. So either someone took the measurements wrong, or it was written incorrectly on the order form."

"Was anyone else's uniform wrong?" Riley asked.

"No, just Attiline's. Who took the measurements?"

I thought back to the day that the team had their measurements taken. "Coach Tyler."

"And did she write the measurements down as she took them?" he asked.

As if a light bulb went off in my head, I knew exactly what had happened. "No, Tiffany wrote down the measurements as Coach called them out."

Riley jumped off the couch. "That girl has no limits. She did this on purpose."

"What are you talking about?" Pops asked.

"She's been jealous of Attie since the day she got here. Remember that night I came inside after the camping trip and you asked who I'd been talking to?"

"Yeah. You said it was Tiffany."

"She came to confront me about Attie. She came on to me, and when I turned her down, she started calling Attie all kinds of names and stuff. She treats Attie like crap at school and practice."

Pops looked over at me. "Is that true, Attiline? Is Tiffany causing you problems?"

"She's trying to, but I've ignored most of it. When I noticed that she was taking the measurements, I got a weird feeling about it. I should have double checked the list."

"If there's one thing I hate about being the principal of a high school, it's the way the girls treat each other. They can be downright vicious."

Riley sat back down on the couch. "Tiffany is one of the worst, no doubt about it. I just never dreamt she'd do something like this."

"Tomorrow I'll call her into my office and see what she has to say about this. I'm sure she'll deny the entire thing, and honestly, I have no way to prove that she did it on purpose."

"So what do I do about my uniform? I can't cheer on Friday night."

"Coach said that you guys could wear the regular tops with your lightweight sweatpants."

"It's going to be one hundred degrees outside!"

"I guess it'll teach someone a lesson then. I'll go call Coach Tyler." Pops made his way toward his bedroom and left Riley and I to stew on the couch.

Riley stood up and walked to the other side of the coffee table. "Girls amaze me. I just don't get it. Why can't they just have a disagreement and get over it? Punch each other if they have to. This kinda stuff is just nuts." It was as if he'd taken Pops's job of pacing the floor. As he spoke, he followed the same path his father had, only Riley also agitatedly ran his hands through his hair.

"Like Pops said, girls are vicious. Especially ones like Tiffany. I'm afraid to even guess what she's gonna do next."

He finally stopped pacing and turned to face me. "Are you all right?"

"I could be better."

"What can I do to help? Do you want me to hit her?"

"Yes."

He laughed and his anger dissipated.

"I want you to hit her extra hard. Hit her into next Sunday."

"I'm all over it." He threw a fist into the palm of his other hand and pounded it several times.

"Actually, I should sic Tammy on her. It would make her day to get to knock the soup out of that girl."

"Naw, Tammy would enjoy it too much. At least I'd show some remorse . . . maybe."

"Wouldn't that be a sight?"

"I'd buy a ticket to that show," he said.

I sank back into the couch. "Oh boy."

"What?"

"How much do you wanna bet I'll be getting a serious lecture from Jesus tonight? All about forgiving my enemies and praying for my enemies. Yada yada yada."

Riley sat on the coffee table in front of me. "I don't know if you should say 'yada yada yada' when you're referring to words from the Lord. That kind of sarcasm could get you in a lot of trouble. And technically, isn't he always right?"

"Unfortunately."

Riley's shoulders slumped. "I'm afraid I feel a life lesson coming on."

"I hate it when that happens."

My heart sank as our sad eyes locked on each other, and we sat in silence. But slowly, a smile crept onto Riley's face. "Do you wanna go for a walk?"

My mood instantly brightened. "A walk outside?"

"Yeah, a walk outside."

I jumped off the couch and started running for the door, but he caught me and pulled me out of the way so that he could make it out the door first.

As soon as he crossed the threshold, I jumped onto his back, wrapped my legs around his waist, and perched my chin on my arm, which was thrown over his shoulder.

"Where to?" he asked.

"Um…" I pointed to our right. "That way."

He bounded down the stairs and toward the end of the driveway, and within minutes my entire body was trembling as Riley broke out in laughter.

"What's so funny?"

He shook his head.

"What?" I thunked him on the head with my finger. "What?"

"I just pictured you standing outside the bathroom in your cheerleading uniform."

"You think I looked silly? You should have seen yourself sitting in that beanbag chair with your hand over your eyes. And don't think I didn't notice you peeked a few times."

"I couldn't help it. You looked amazing. Slutty, but amazing."

I unwrapped my legs from his waist and jumped down.

"Whoa, where are you going? Come back. We've barely started our walk."

"Do you ever wish I was different?"

The skin between his eyes crinkled in perplexity. "Different how?"

"You know, different-different."

"Different, different?" He stopped walking and lightly grabbed my elbow. "What do you mean by *different?*"

"Easier. More wild. You know, sexy and adventurous."

"You're adventurous. You're the catfish wrangler, remember?"

"I'm serious, Riley. You liked it when I was a little more sultry yesterday morning. Do you wish I were like that all the time? Easier?"

"There's a difference between being easy and being sexy. You don't have to be one to be the other." He scratched his head. "Come to think of it, I don't think you can be both."

"What do you mean?"

"What makes you sexy is your self-confidence. The way you carry yourself. A girl who's easy usually doesn't have self-confidence; that's why she acts the way she does. She thinks that if she acts that way, guys will like her, and that will give her self-confidence. A girl that has self-confidence doesn't have to act or dress like a slut to get a guy's attention."

"But yesterday morning—"

He reached out and tucked a piece of hair behind my ear. "Yesterday morning you weren't easy; you were impossible, and that's hot."

"Oh." We started walking side by side. "But girls like Tiffany don't seem to have any problem getting boyfriends."

"Tiffany has a lot of dates, but she hasn't really had many boyfriends. Not that I know of, anyway. Trust me; guys want girls like her for one reason and one reason only. Once they get to know her, there isn't much there to be attracted to. Look at the way she's treating you. No guy who knows about it is gonna find that attractive."

"You did."

"I caught on pretty fast. Even if you hadn't shown up, I wouldn't have gone out with her again. And really, I was just going out with her because all our friends thought I should … and I was bored."

"That's mighty shallow of you."

"I'm a guy. Shallow's what we do. Or what I did before you. Now I'm deep."

"More like digging yourself a grave. You should stop while you're ahead."

"Trust me, what I was thinking wasn't that bad. It sounded worse as it came out of my mouth."

"Uh-huh. Anyway, so you don't you think she's self-confident?"

"No, she's arrogant. I'd bet that under all the skimpy clothes, big hair, and makeup, she doesn't like herself very much. There's no way she can and still act the way she does."

"But you seemed to like it today when I was dressed in skimpy clothes."

"I'm not gonna lie and say I didn't. You looked good—really good."

I felt my face flush and my ears get hot.

"I'm in love with you, so there's no way I'm gonna see you in that getup and not get a little turned on. But I wouldn't want you walking around like that all the time. Then it would be a turnoff."

"Why?"

"Because if you did, you'd be doing it to get attention. You've already got my attention; who else's do you need?"

"Nobody's." I started chewing on my thumbnail again.

"Trust me, you could wear a trash bag and I'd still find you very sexy."

"Really?"

"Maybe not the chewing on your thumbnail part, although it is cute." He removed my hand from my mouth and kissed my wrists. "Look, I love you just the way you are. You don't need to change a thing."

"I'm glad to hear that."

"Besides, given our circumstances, the more clothed you are, the better."

"I guess that's true. It's a good thing. I really don't feel comfortable in stuff that shows too much skin. Especially having skin as ugly as mine."

"Your skin's not ugly."

"Riley, you're the only person on this planet who doesn't think my scars make me look like Frankenstein."

He grabbed my arm and stopped me from walking. "What's the matter? Why are you bringing your scars up all of a sudden?" I shrugged and started walking again, but he stopped me. "Out with it."

"People at school already look at me funny. What are they going to do on Friday when I'm wearing my uniform? Most of my scars are going to show. I don't know that I'm ready."

"Charlie, you can't hide them forever. And remember, you aren't walking in there alone. You've got me there with you."

He slid his hand in mine, and we started walking again.

"You know, sometimes I see a really a famous model and she has this really ugly boyfriend, and I always wonder how on God's green earth he ever landed someone who was so beautiful. I imagine that's what people say about us. When we walk down the hallway, I picture people saying to themselves, 'How on earth did she get someone as good looking as him?'"

"Spare me."

"I do. I think it all the time."

"Remember what I said back there about you having self-confidence and it making you sexy?"

"Yes."

He laughed. "Never mind. Evidently it's something else that makes you sexy. Your self-confidence needs some work."

"I'm self-confident in some ways, just not when it comes to my looks."

"That's what it is then."

"What?"

"You're flat-out gorgeous and don't even know it. You're humble, and that, my little blonde-headed ball of energy, is sexy."

"Thank you."

"You're welcome. Now…" He grabbed me in his arms and pulled me to him. "Enough walking. Neither one of us needs the exercise, so we might as well get on with what we really came out here for."

I stood on my tippy toes and smiled. "And what's that?"

"Oh…" he said with a shrug before kissing my ear. "A little o' this and a little o' that."

chapter 6

After we finished our walk, I marched to my room and took a deep breath before opening the door. Part of me dreaded going in. I didn't want to know what the Lord was going to have to say, and I had a nagging feeling I was in big trouble.

I exhaled loudly and then opened the door and walked into the room.

"Yada, yada, yada, huh?"

"I knew you would hear that. I didn't really mean it. It was a joke."

The look on Jesus's face showed doubt.

"All right, maybe I meant it—a little. What's my punishment?"

"No punishment, just an assignment."

"An assignment? This is new. You've never given me an assignment before."

"You never know what you're going to get with me." He smiled warmly at me before taking a seat on the corner of my bed. "Get out a piece of paper, a pencil, and your Bible."

I obeyed and sat down at my desk.

"Turn to Colossians chapter three, verse twelve, and let me know when you're there."

When I flipped through the pages of the Bible, I listened to the paper crinkled under my fingers.

"Whoever designed the Bible was so intelligent. The thin paper and the sound it makes when you turn the pages makes you feel smart for some reason. At least it does me, anyway. If it were regular paper, it just wouldn't be the same experience. Don't you think?" I turned to face him and realized he was unimpressed with my observation.

"Can you just get to chapter three please?"

"Yes, sir." I turned back around, quickened the search, and finally found it. "I'm there."

"Are you at verse twelve?"

"Yes."

"Start writing."

"Writing what?"

"Verses twelve through fourteen. Read out loud as you write."

"Just so you know, the words yada, yada, yada will never again escape my lips, I can assure you of that." I placed the pencil on the paper and started reading and writing. "Therefore, as God's chosen people, holy and dearly loved, clothe yourself in ... " I swallowed hard and rolled my eyes.

"I can't hear you."

"... compassion, kindness, humility, gentleness, and patience. Bear with each other and ... " I turned to him. "Do I have to?"

"Keep going."

"Good grief."

"I don't think it says that—and I would know."

I turned back around and focused my eyes on the scripture. "Bear with each other and forgive whatever grievances you may have against one another." I turned to him again. "Are you giving Tiffany this same assignment? Because I think she needs to do it more than I do right now. And Riley, he probably needs to do this too. Tammy for sure does."

"If you don't get it done, you're going to have to write the entire book."

Begrudgingly, I continued. "Forgive as the Lord forgave you, and over all these virtues put on love, which binds them all together in perfect unity." I slapped the pencil down onto the pad and turned to him again.

"You're not finished."

"What? You said to verse fourteen."

"I know I did. But now I want you to get out your dictionary."

"My dictionary?"

"Did I stutter?"

"No." I stomped toward the bookshelf and yanked the dictionary off the shelf. "You sure are getting sassy."

"Now, what were the things you were supposed to clothe yourself in?"

I checked my notes. "Compassion, kindness, humility, gentleness, and patience."

"Good. Write down the definitions to each of those words and say them out loud as you write them."

I groaned again. "Wait till Riley hears about this. I told him I was going to get grief from you as soon as I came upstairs."

"Do you want more words?"

"No."

"Then get busy."

"Fine." I continued the assignment, but if I said I had a good attitude about it, I'd be lying, and that would end up landing me in even more trouble.

"Compassion: a feeling of deep sympathy and sorrow for another who is stricken by misfortune, accompanied by a strong desire to alleviate their suffering."

It didn't make sense. Why should I have to share the suffering of Tiffany? She wasn't suffering; I was! And what misfortune did she have? She had no time for misfortune; she was too busy handing it out to everyone else. I pictured her standing at a perfume counter in the mall handing out little vials of smelly misfortune as people walked by. Come to think of it, that's exactly what her stinky perfume smelled like—misfortune.

"What are the synonyms?" he asked.

"Mercy, tenderness, heart."

"What's the antonym?"

"Tiffany."

"Not funny."

"It's mercilessness and indifference."

"Okay, next word."

"Kindness…Can I ask why you're having me do this?"

"Because you tend to breeze through the scriptures without really thinking about what they mean. I want you to not only read them but understand them. Keep going."

"…the state or quality of being kind."

"And the synonyms?

"Humanity, generosity, charity, sympathy, compassion, tenderness, and good turn."

"What was that last one?"

"Good turn."

"What did you say?"

"Good turn!" I practically screamed the word at him.

"It doesn't say 'turnabout's fair play?'"

"No."

"Hmm. Well, what's the antonym to kindness? And don't say Tiffany."

"Cruelty."

"Next word."

"Humility: the quality or condition of being humble; modest opinion or estimate of one's own importance, rank, etc." I continued before he could even ask. "The synonyms are: lowliness, meekness, and submissiveness. Submissiveness! I am not going to be submissive to her."

He ignored me. "What's the antonym?"

"Oh heck no, I'm not going to be submissive…"

"Attie—"

"I'm not doing that. A person's got to draw the line somewhere, and being submissive to a—"

"Don't even say it."

"Well, you get my point."

"And you're going to get mine. What's the antonym?"

"Pride!"

"Thank you. Next word."

I tried to calm myself a bit and read more gently. It seemed appropriate, seeing as how that was the word we were on.

"Gentleness: not severe, rough, or violent; mild. The synonyms are peaceful, soothing, calm, tender, lenient—this is painful, it really is—docile, and tame. The antonyms are harsh, cruel, violent, sudden, wild, and unruly."

"Next word."

"I'm going to hate this one."

"That's why you're doing it."

"P-p-patience." The word would barely escape my lips.

"There are several good definitions, so make sure you get them all."

"My hand's cramping."

"I don't care."

I gave my hand a dramatic shake and then continued writing. "The quality of being patient, as the bearing of provocation, annoyance, misfortune, or pain, without complaint..."

"What was that?"

"Without complaint!"

"Continue."

"...loss of temper..."

"And that? What was that?"

"Loss of temper!"

"You obviously need to work on those. Keep going."

"...irritation, or the like. An ability or willingness...oh puke...to suppress restlessness or annoyance when confronted with delay. A quiet, steady perseverance; even-tempered care; diligence. The synonyms are: composure, stability—well, I'm obviously neither of those—submissive—there's that dang word again—submissiveness, sufferance—I'm doing plenty of that..."

"What are the antonyms?"

"It doesn't say."

"How about temper tantrums?"

"No."

"Continually asking when something will be over? Saying life isn't fair? Expecting life to be easy?"

I moaned in disgust, leaned forward, and let my forehead bang into the desk. "I get the point. Am I finished yet?"

"One more."

"But that's all the words."

"One more—forgiveness."

I practically broke out in hives but sat back up and allowed my fingers to flip through the dictionary anyway. "Forgiveness: the act of forgiving; to pardon."

"Wait, doesn't it mention forgetting? Making up? Being friends?"

"No." I turned to face him. "Just the act of forgiving."

"Hmm."

"I'm assuming you're being sarcastic."

"You think?"

"Yes."

"Look, Attie, I'm not saying you have to be Tiffany's friend. But I am saying that you need to bear with her and offer her forgiveness."

"To her face?" I screamed.

"No, unless you feel like you need to."

"Heck no, I don't." Without even thinking about it, my arms crossed my stomach in a huff. "And how many times do I have to forgive her? She does a lot of stuff."

"How many times have I had to forgive you?"

"Well, that's harsh. You know, you didn't have to go there."

"Yes, I did. I'm not asking you to do anything I don't do."

"You are the Messiah. I think it's probably a little easier for you."

"Really?"

"Uh-huh."

"Being tortured and hung on a cross?"

"Never mind. I should've known better than to argue with you. You are always right."

"True."

"I get the point."

"And what point is that?" he asked.

"I have to be nice to the girl."

"And?"

"For-f-f…"

"Spit it out."

"Forgive her." I threw myself back against the chair in a fit. "I thought I'd learned this lesson already—with the whole nightmares thing."

"Forgiveness is one of the hardest crosses to bear. You have to pick it up every day and walk it out because as soon as you think you've mastered it, something else happens and you're right back where you started off."

"I'll say."

"I've saved the best for last."

"There's more? I don't think I can contain my excitement," I mumbled.

"Do you even have a filter between your brain and mouth, or do you just say everything that comes to mind?"

"I say everything. Talk to the Father—he didn't give me a filter."

"Oh, he gave you one all right; you just don't choose to use it. But we'll save that conversation for another night."

"Thank God…or you. Whatever. Go on."

"You need to pray for her."

"For whom?"

"Whom do you think?"

"It's not enough that I've got to forgive her? Now I've got to pray for her too?" The blood surging through my veins was practically at its boiling point.

"Yes."

I plopped my elbows on the desk and buried my head in my hands. "This just gets more and more painful by the minute."

"I'm sorry."

I looked up at him and smiled. "Really?"

"No."

I frowned and then buried my face again. "Fine, I'll pray for her."

"Real prayers, Attie, not fake ones. Real prayers, just like the ones you do for your dad."

"All right."

"And I want you to hang that piece of paper on your bathroom mirror, and every morning while you're getting ready, I want you to read it out loud."

"For how long?"

"Until you've mastered it."

"Forever then." I sprung out of the chair and across the room. "You're basically saying it'll be there forever."

"Yes, that's what I'm saying."

I flung open the door and stomped toward the bathroom to wash my face.

Riley peeked his head out of his room. "What was all that yelling about?"

"I just got my butt handed to me by the Lord."

"I figured you would. I told you not to say yada, yada, yada."

"Shut it, Riley!"

I heard him laugh as I slammed the door behind me.

chapter 7

Marme stood in front of the stove stirring up one of her wonderful dinner concoctions. The house smelled like roasted garlic, and my stomach was already growling in order to make sure I knew it was past our usual dinnertime. Marme was a planner, and even my stomach had learned her schedule, but school being back in session meant we were on a new routine. Riley had football and I had cheer practice every day, and then I also had class at the university on Tuesdays and Thursdays starting next week, so dinner was officially pushed back to seven thirty on all weekdays but Wednesday due to church. With four people and four active lives, life was going to get confusing, and my stomach and I would have to get used to the new routine.

I stepped toward the sink to grab a tomato and practically trampled Baby. She too was unsettled with the changes and hadn't left my side since I'd been home. She'd settled with me seeing as how Riley hadn't made it through the front door yet. Baby didn't seem to enjoy ten hours a day with no humans at home to answer her every demand. Boomer, of course, sat like a bump on a log in his chair, and I was sure that he offered her no company whatsoever. He was too old and out of shape for a puppy with so much energy, and entertaining a lonely Baby was the last thing on his aging mind.

"No youth group tonight?" Marme asked.

I shook my head. "Nope. Not sure why. Something about schedules, I think."

"How was school today? No drama, I hope."

"No, ma'am. It was a relatively calm day. Tiffany was a little witchy at practice, but that's nothing new."

"I wish she'd just move on already."

"Do you know if Pops got anything out of her about the uniform situation?"

"I haven't heard. But if she didn't act up at practice, maybe he scared her enough to keep her under control."

"I sure hope so."

"And what about Bob? How are you two doing at school?"

"Fine. We only see each other between classes every once in a while." Marme and I had grown so accustomed to calling Riley "Bob" that it was now second nature and we were now calling him "Bob" in every conversation, not just to avoid the awkwardness of talking about me dating her son.

"So you do realize you need a plan, right?"

"A plan?" I stared down at the tomato in front of me. I'd never been very good at getting them sliced without all the insides squeezing out. "I think I'm doing this wrong."

"Who cares what they look like? Just get them in the salad."

"I thought you cared."

"You've lived here for almost four months and you've prepared over fifty salads. I'm kinda used to them not looking perfect."

"Oh."

"And," she continued, "I think your messy salads taste much better than my pretty ones ever did."

"You're just saying that."

"No, I'm not. Now seriously, we need a plan." Marme could change a topic faster than Riley could change the channel on the remote, and both would leave me in slight confusion until my brain caught up.

I carefully held the tomato so that I wouldn't cut my finger as the knife blade made its way through. "A plan for what?"

"A plan for you and Bob. You know, some guidelines."

"Good grief, Marme, I've already got boundaries coming out the ying-yang. How many more do I need?"

"I'm not talking about boundaries. I'm talking about guidelines. There's a difference."

"They sound the same to me."

"Boys like a challenge, and with you and Bob living under the same roof, it's going to be difficult to be a challenge."

I tossed the tomatoes into the bowl and grabbed a cucumber. "What kind of challenge are we talking about? I think Riley—I mean Bob—sees me as a challenge already."

"There's a difference between being a challenge in the way you're talking about and the way I'm talking about. You don't have a choice but to be a challenge in the way you're talking about—we've laid out rules about it. I'm talking about something totally different."

My cloud of confusion hadn't lifted yet. "Then what are you talking about?"

"I think girls today don't respect themselves enough. They don't realize how special they are and that they deserve to be pursued—they shouldn't be the pursuer."

"Hasn't Bob already done the pursuing? I mean, we're together."

"I know, but you can't ever let them take it for granted. Boys tend to get lazy, and no matter how great I think Bob is, I betcha he'll get lazy if you let him."

"Lazy?"

"If they know you're going to make all the effort, they don't."

"They don't?"

"Nope. Trust me. I've been a schoolteacher for years, and I see it happen all the time. The guy gets lazy and stops calling or texting or whatever it is you kids do these days, so the girl is the one calling all the time. Guess what happens?"

I stopped peeling the cucumber and looked at the strips of green peel that had piled up in curls. "I haven't the foggiest idea."

"The once lazy boy turns into a bored boy. The chase is over, and they're ready to move on."

"Really?"

"Yep."

"You're sure about this?"

"As a matter of fact, what I hear most boys say is the girl became 'needy.'"

"Needy? Well, I'm certainly not that."

"I know you're not. And not only are you not needy, what you are is special, and Bob or any other boy needs to treat you like you are. If they don't, kick 'em to the curb."

As weird as it all sounded, she was actually making complete sense. I started peeling again.

"When I was in high school, I wasn't allowed to call boys. My mother always told me that if a boy wanted to talk to me, he'd call. Now at the time, I thought it was the stupidest thing I'd ever heard, but now I look back and think she was a genius."

"So you never called a boy?"

"Never. Not even if the boy was my boyfriend."

"You're kidding."

"Nope. It gets better. One of my dad's rules was that I wasn't allowed to go out with a boy unless he asked me at least the Thursday before the weekend."

The cucumber slipped out of my hand and onto the floor. Quickly glancing over my shoulder, I made sure she didn't notice, picked it up off the floor, wiped it on my jeans, and started cutting it into chunks.

She was none the wiser and kept right on talking. "It sounds crazy. But his point was that if a boy wanted to go out with me enough, he'd plan in advance to do it; and if he waited until the last minute, then I probably wasn't his first choice. He was a guy, so I figured he'd know."

"So what did you do if a guy asked you out on Friday morning?"

"I told him no or told him that if he wanted to spend time with me, he could come hang out at my house with me and my parents."

"And what did they do?"

"If they really liked me, right then and there they would ask me to go out the next weekend. A few, including Pops, even came over and hung out with my family."

"Really?"

"Yep. Some of them thought it was stupid and never asked me out again, which was fine by me because I figured if they weren't willing to do that for me, they weren't worth my time. But the good ones caught on and followed the rule. If they wanted to go out with me, they asked me early in the week."

All I could do was nod at her brilliance.

"Look, Bob loves you. And I'm not telling you to mess with his head or play games or anything. All I'm suggesting is that you put systems in place that require him to make you the priority you should rightfully be. I also believe that you tell them what your expectations are."

"I'm in." I threw the cucumbers into the salad and reached for the box of croutons. "So what do I do—or not do?"

"Don't call him or text him first—ever."

"Ever?"

"Ever. He needs to have the chance to miss you, and if you're in constant contact with him, he'll never get to that point. So no matter how much you want to talk to him, wait and let him contact you."

"That sounds painful."

"Trust me. If a boy really likes a girl and he knows that she isn't gonna be calling him, he's gonna be picking up that phone and making contact."

"Okay, I won't call or text Bob first. What next?"

"Tell him that if he wants to go out with you on the weekend, he needs to make sure to ask you before Thursday. Otherwise, you'll be making other plans."

"What else?"

"At least one weekend a month, make plans to be apart. Neither one of you should be so into each other that you can't hang out with your friends every once in a while when the other one isn't around."

"Fair enough."

"In order for a relationship to be healthy, it needs to be respected. You and Bob are very special people, and you should treat each other that way. You probably need to ask him if he has any requests he'd like to make too. He might have one or two. I know Pops did."

"What were his?"

"He just had one. He'd always hated it when he was dating a girl and she would hang all over him in front of his friends. It embarrassed him. So I never did. As a matter of fact, I never even made contact with him if his friends were around. I figured if he wanted to talk to me, he would. And guess what?"

"He did."

"He always did."

"I wonder what Bob's going to say about this."

"If he has an issue with it, tell him to take it up with us. That's what I did. I always said that they were rules that my parents made and I had to follow. So they could either follow or get lost. Bob will follow the rules; you don't have to worry about that. And just wait, you'll feel more special than you ever have before."

"Why is that?"

"Because every time that phone rings and you see it's him, you'll know he's calling because he wanted to talk to you. And every time he holds your hand in front of his friends, it'll be because he's proud to have you there. You'll know that you're important to him—important enough for him to make an effort."

"That does sound nice."

"There's nothing wrong with making a boy work for it a little bit." She peeked over my shoulder at the salad. "Whether Bob and I were related or not or whether you were like family or not, I'd want both of you to be treated well by the people you choose to spend time with. Like Dr. Phil always says, 'Ya teach people how to treat ya,' and you're ensuring that Bob's gonna treat you the way you deserve—not that he wouldn't have already, but this ensures it."

She grabbed the breadbasket off the counter and made her way toward the table. "Oh, and one more thing."

"Yes, ma'am?"

"Don't think I didn't see you drop that cucumber."

"You saw that?"

"I'm a mom. I see everything."

Riley burst through the back door. "That's no lie. She does see everything. You can't get away with anything around here."

He slid past me toward the sink, and as he did, he allowed his hand to slightly graze my back before reaching into the salad bowl for a piece of cucumber. I slapped his hand just before he grabbed one.

"Wash your hands first. You're dirty from practice, and I don't want my salad all gross with germs."

Marme looked up at me and smiled but kept my cucumber-dropping incident between the two of us.

He placed his mouth right next to my ear. "Since when are you concerned about getting my germs?"

"Step away from the young lady," Marme announced. "You know the rule; leave enough room between you for Jesus to walk through."

"That's the most ignorant rule I've ever heard. Where did you come up with it?"

"Your grandfather gave the same one to me, so I'm passing it on to you."

He flipped on the faucet. "What does it even mean?"

"It means to stay away from her, that's what it means."

"Gotcha."

I picked up the salad bowl and took it to the table. "And speaking of which, Riley, is there anything I do that annoys you?"

He stopped lathering his hands and looked over at me. "Is this a trick question?"

"What do you mean? Is there a lot that I do to annoy you?"

"Uh…"

"Would you like me to rephrase the question?"

"That might be a good idea."

"I know I do a lot that drives you crazy, but I mean more like, in front of your friends. Do I do anything in front of them that you wish I wouldn't? Or is there anything other girls do around guys that you want to make sure I don't do? You know, stuff that'll embarrass you."

He started lathering again. "I don't think so. You don't do most of the annoying stuff other girls do, so I haven't really thought about it."

"Well, what do other girls do that annoys you or your friends?" Marme asked.

She and I both sat down at the table and made ourselves comfortable as Riley contemplated whether or not he wanted to incriminate himself.

He turned off the water, flapped his hands in the air to dry them, and then jumped onto the counter and wiped them on his jeans. "What's all this about?"

"We're conducting research," Marme said.

"What kind of research?"

"What do girls do that annoys boys kind of research. We really want to know. Just boy and girl interaction type stuff, not generalities or anything."

"I can't speak for all guys."

"Then just speak for guys like you. The good guys. The kind a girl like Attie would actually want to get attention from."

"I don't want her getting attention from other guys."

"Stop being difficult," she snapped. "You know what we mean."

I could almost see his brain turning in his head as he stared into space. "Well... calling all the time, texting every other second..."

Marme and I looked at each other and shared a grin.

"...acting too needy for attention. Most guys don't like that. And then, as a general rule, stalking would be a definite no."

Marme leaned forward. "And by stalking you mean what?"

"Following them around school, driving by their house, asking people for information about them all the time. You know, stalking-type stuff. I mean, let's be honest, how many girls who acted like that actually landed the guy they were stalking?"

"Probably not many. Go on," she said.

"Talking real loud and shrieking to try to get a guy's attention—that really drives me crazy. Basically, I think girls just need to act normal. I don't know of any of my friends who are attracted to a girl that tries too hard."

"So you want them to play hard to get?"

"Not necessarily hard to get, but there's nothing attractive about easy to get. If I like a girl, which of course I do …" He looked at me and winked. "I'm gonna let her know."

"That's true. You did tell me."

"See."

"And what about once they get the guy? How should they act then?" Marme asked.

"The same as they did before. Why should it change?"

"I don't know. That's why I'm asking you."

"Nothing should change. Attie didn't change how she acts." He looked over at me again. "Did you?"

"I don't think so."

"I mean, if I liked you enough to ask you to be my girlfriend, why would I want you to change once I got you? It wouldn't make any sense. Are we done now?"

"Why? You don't like all the questions?" Marme asked.

"I just don't see the point. Attie's got me. Why does she need to know how to get me?"

"I don't need to know how to get you. I need to know how to keep you."

His forehead creased. "Why are you worried about that?"

I shrugged.

"Charlie, I'm not gonna go anywhere. If you haven't scared me off up to this point, why on earth would you think you would now?"

"I don't know."

He jumped off the counter and sat in the chair next to me. "Mom, give us a sec."

Without saying a word, Marme left us alone in the kitchen, and I got the sinking suspicion that our impending conversation wasn't going to be a good one.

"Okay, I thought of something you do that annoys me."

"What?" I regretted asking him in the first place and most certainly didn't want to hear what he was about to say.

"You doubt us all the time, or at least me and my feelings for you, anyway. That I don't like, and if you do it enough, it could cause problems. Insecurity is not attractive, especially coming from someone who has nothing to be insecure about."

I felt my face start to crumble.

He softly rubbed his thumb on my forehead as if he were trying to erase the lines caused by my emotions. "I'm sorry if I hurt your feelings."

"You've never come right out and told me something you didn't like about me before."

"First off, you asked. And second, it's not something I don't like; it's something that irks me sometimes."

"I asked if there was anything I do around your friends to annoy you, not for just anything in general. That was an in-general statement, and I wasn't prepared for it."

"I'm sorry. I didn't mean it to upset you."

I was in full-blown pout mode, and his apology wasn't helping. I think he knew he was in trouble.

"Why don't you tell me something that I do that irks you and that way we'll be even?"

"You don't do anything that irks me."

"Sure I do. Nobody's perfect."

"You practically are."

"Come on. There's gotta be something."

I searched the crevasses of my mind, and within seconds, one popped up. "I got it."

"For not thinking I had any, that sure did come to you fast. What is it?"

"Straws."

His eyebrows arched high. "Straws?"

"Yes. You walk around chewing on straws all the time, and it totally grosses me out."

"Straws?"

"You chew them until there's hardly anything left, and then you leave them lying around the house or in your car. I can't even stand to look at them."

"Well—"

"And sometimes you coil them up and stick the whole thing in your mouth at once, and then when you finally spit it out and put it somewhere, it slowly starts unraveling. Seriously, it makes me want to vomit."

"I get the point."

"They have your teeth marks all over them and saliva and stuff. Really, it's—"

"I get it!"

"Oh."

"No more straws. Got it."

"Or toothpicks."

"Forget I asked." He jumped out of his seat, stomped to the refrigerator, and threw open the door.

"I'm just saying that you do it with toothpicks too. Maybe it's a nervous tick or something. Chewing gum might help, and it's not nearly as gross."

"I get the point, for cryin' out loud. Enough already."

"You're not mad, are you?"

"Not mad. I'm annoyed!"

Marme sheepishly walked back into the kitchen and looked over at me with wide eyes. "Evidently you two annoy each other a little more than you thought."

Riley slammed the refrigerator door and looked fiercely at his mother. "This is your fault. You started it."

"My fault? I was trying to help."

"Don't you get on to her, Riley Bennett. I hate it when you talk to Marme like that."

"Oh really?" His face turned crimson. "Since you're getting it all out in the open, why don't you just keep on going? What else don't you like about me?"

"Nothing!"

"It sure doesn't sound like it."

"I just don't like it when you disrespect your mother like that. You should be nicer to her. You're lucky you have a mother at all."

His jaw tightened, and his eyes practically burned holes right through my body. I wanted to shrink away into nothingness and avoid his glare altogether, but all I could manage to do was squirm in my seat.

After what felt like forever, he finally released his hostile glare and stomped out of the room. "I'm leaving so I don't say or do something I'll regret."

Marme followed behind him. "You get back here. Dinner's ready."

"Leave me alone. I'm not hungry."

I listened to his feet clomp all the way up the stairs, across the hallway, and finally into the room where he slammed his door shut.

Pops promptly followed behind, made him walk back down the stairs, apologize to his mother and me, then quietly walk up the stairs and close his door properly.

After that, I didn't see him the rest of the night.

chapter 8

(Riley)

The first four classes of the day were horrible. I hadn't laid eyes on Attie all day, which meant she was avoiding me. The fact that I hadn't run into her once in the hallways made it obvious that she was somehow making it to each class without taking her normal routes or stopping by her locker. Not that I cared what other people thought, but let's just say I wasn't the only person to notice. At least a dozen people asked if we were all right or if we'd broken up. News, or non-news in our particular case, moved very fast in our school, and the last thing I needed was for Attie to get a whiff of the rumor and have it throw her into a panic.

Chalk the entire episode up to another big screw-up and over-reaction on my part. I'd just told her that insecurity was something that could cause problems between us, and then I turned around and gave her even more to be insecure about. What was meant to be a conversation to make her feel better ended up making her feel worse. Not smart.

When I made it to our lunch table, she was nowhere to be seen. I went ahead and sat down with the group, but when she hadn't shown up in ten minutes, I went searching for her and finally found her in the very last place I looked—my mother's classroom. They were eating lunch together at one of the food prep stations.

As soon as Mom saw me, she got out of her chair, left the room, and shut the door behind her. Of course, she didn't leave without giving me the all-too-familiar "I'm not happy with you" stare-down that mothers give their kids when they can't full-out yell or hit them due to the fact that other people are around. Between seeing Attie slumped over her lunch and Mom look at me like I was pond scum, I felt like a complete heel.

"I'm a jerk," I announced.

Attie didn't look up and didn't say anything.

"I went and took something small and turned it into something bigger than it needed to be. I'm sorry. But babe, there's no need to avoid me."

She didn't look up at me but at least spoke. "I'm not a big fan of confrontation." I was happy to hear her voice, even if it was squeaky from stress.

"What makes you think there woulda been a confrontation?"

She shrugged and kept her gaze on the counter.

"Charlie, just 'cause we're crazy about each other doesn't mean we aren't gonna argue. Everyone argues every once in a while."

I took the seat my mother left empty and looked over at her. She wouldn't look back.

"Plus, given your dramatics and my overreactions, we're bound to have it out every once in a while." The silence was deafening, and I wanted to know what was going on in her crazy blonde head. "Talk to me. Will you look at me please?"

When she didn't lift her head, I climbed onto the counter, sat cross-legged, and waited for her to join me. She didn't move.

"Charlie, please—"

She sighed but gave in, climbed onto the counter, sat with her knees touching mine, and let me take her hands in mine. She still wasn't looking at me, although I wasn't surprised. She hated to look at me when we used the "knee-to-knee technique."

"What if I can't stop being insecure?"

Her sudden talking shocked me. I lowered my face to hers. "What?"

"What if I can't stop being insecure? I'm actually so insecure that I'm insecure about being insecure, and you said that my being insecure could cause us problems, so now I'm insecure about that too."

"I need to clarify already 'cause I didn't catch all that. All I heard was the word *insecure* about ten times."

"Never mind."

"No, no, no, don't say never mind. Just say it again, a little bit slower this time so I know what it is you're so upset about."

She finally looked me in the eyes. "If I can't stop being insecure, what then?"

"I shouldn't have brought it up. All it did was make matters worse."

"No, you were absolutely right. I'm totally insecure, and I don't know what to do about it. Trust me, I don't want to be that way. Insecure people make me nuts … more nuts than usual. I'm not normally a needy person, and being insecure makes it seem like I am."

"No, it doesn't. You don't ever come off as needy. Trust me, I would know."

"Are you sure?"

"Positive. The reason the insecurity irks me is because I feel like no matter what I do, I can't convince you that we're good together and that this can work. It's like you can't believe we're good for each other."

"I know you're good for me."

"But you won't let yourself know that you're good for me too. Charlie, you're great for me. You make me happy. The last thing I want is to have you walking around thinking you don't or that for some weird reason you don't deserve me. In reality, none of us deserve anything good, but some of us get lucky and get it anyway."

"And you consider yourself lucky to have me?"

"A thousand percent."

Her nose scrunched a little as she smirked. "Thank you, Riley."

"Are we all good now?" I rubbed the top of her hands with my thumbs.

"I guess."

"That didn't sound convincing. There's something else. What is it?"

She shrugged.

"Out with it."

"It'll sound like I'm insecure, which we've already established I am."

"Then technically you wouldn't be *sounding* insecure; you'd actually be *being* insecure."

"Yes. And you hate it when I'm insecure, so why would I do it more?"

"I don't hate it; it irks me. But for the sake of making you feel better, you might as well just say it. We aren't leaving here till you do."

Still holding her hands in mine and figuring I might be waiting for a while for her to get the guts to spit it out, I lowered my elbows to my knees.

She squirmed around on the counter for several seconds before finally talking again. "Last night was the first time since you gave me my ring that I realized you thought we might not last." The words poured out as if they'd been sitting in her mouth waiting to be freed.

"That's not at all what I was saying."

"It is—"

"It isn't. I said it could cause problems, but my mind never went to the place of believing that it's something worth breaking up over. It just gets frustrating, that's all."

"So you've never thought of breaking it off?"

"No. As I've said five thousand times, you aren't getting rid of me that easy."

"You didn't even think about it last night when you were avoiding me?"

"I wasn't avoiding you; I was avoiding my mother. And you're one to talk—you've avoided me all day."

"Last night you didn't even come out and say goodnight to me, and then you were gone this morning and you didn't leave me a note or a drawing. You even left my lunch on the counter."

"Okay...?" I didn't understand her point.

"So I avoided you because I was afraid you were going to break up with me."

"*What?*"

"I thought that if you didn't actually see me, you wouldn't be able to do it; and maybe by the time you did see me, you would have calmed down and changed your mind."

"No way. There's no way that would've happened."

I leaned forward and laid my forehead against hers. "Charlie, being frustrated doesn't equal wanting to break up. When you love someone, you don't leave just 'cause they drive you crazy. Ask my dad. My mom's a lot crazier than you are, and he hasn't gone anywhere in almost twenty years."

"Well, that's true."

"If being frustrated made someone wanna break it off, you woulda already broken up with me over all of the disgusting straws I leave lying around."

"That's true too."

"I didn't say goodnight because I fell asleep before you came upstairs. And I didn't leave you a note or a drawing and I forgot your lunch because I woke up late and was running behind. I didn't want to be late to the gym. I wasn't thinking clearly, and honestly I didn't realize that me doing those things meant so much to you."

"Of course they do."

"I didn't realize you'd noticed."

"Riley, I keep every note and picture you leave me."

"You do?"

"I love them."

"I'm glad to hear it."

I kissed the tip of her nose and could feel it scrunch under my lips, so either she was smiling or crying. I pulled away enough to take a look and was relieved to see she was smiling.

"So we're okay?" I asked.

"If you're okay."

"I'm perfect. I'm right where I wanna be."

"Me too. I love you," she whispered.

It was one of the few times she'd said it first, and hearing her say it gave me the same rush it gave me when I heard it at the playground the first time.

"I love you too."

I leaned over to kiss her.

"Make room for Jesus to walk through," my mother announced out of nowhere.

I looked over at her in disgust. "Your timing stinks."

"My timing's perfect," she corrected.

"How'd you know when to come back in?" I asked.

She looked at me and smiled. "I'm a mom, and moms know everything."

chapter 9

(Attie)

I trudged into Joshua's living room, dragging my backpack on the floor behind me. As much as I dreaded counseling, I knew that I desperately needed it. School had brought out the worst in me, or at least the worst of my paranoia when it came to Riley. We'd left our cocoon and had started venturing out into the world, and I wasn't liking it one bit.

Joshua laughed as soon as he laid eyes on me. "So, Miss Attie Reed, you called this emergency counseling session. What's up? Did you hear from your dad?"

"Are you kiddin' me? Heck no, I haven't heard from him." I had no intention of thinking about my dad, much less talking about him. I quickly changed the subject. "Why was youth off last night?"

"We never have youth the first week of school. Too much going on."

"I, for one, can attest to that. Our house is in complete chaos right now. Marme's running around like a chicken with her head cut off."

"What's going on? Why did you need to see me?" he asked.

I fell into the large recliner next to the fireplace. "Well, I was called a freak and many other not-so-nice names, but the start of the week rallied when I got to dress like a stripper and get my boyfriend all worked up without even so much as thinking about it. Then the week started to stink again when Riley and I got in an argument and I thought he was going dump me."

"Did he?"

"No, thank God. But I'd say it was an altogether interesting first four days of school."

"Sounds like a winner," he teased. "There's so much to talk about that I'm not even sure where to begin, and I'm definitely afraid to ask why on earth you were dressed like a stripper."

"The always wonderful Tiffany did some dirty work, messed with my cheerleading uniform measurements, and I ended up wearing a loincloth—or that's what Pops called it, anyway."

"Do you know for sure it was Tiffany?"

"Not 100 percent, more like 99.875 percent. She's pretty much going to try to make my life miserable. What's worse is that rumor has it that tomorrow I may be voted captain of the cheerleading squad."

"Attie, that's great."

"Not so much. If it happens, it'll only make Tiffany hate me that much more. She thinks she's a shoe-in, and if I get that spot, I basically become public enemy number one for her and all her followers."

"You can't let someone like Tiffany take away the joy from the good things in your life. You've needed some good things, and now you've got them."

"I know. I don't plan on letting her. I'm just saying she's going to be trying really hard to ruin my life."

"You know what you have to do, don't you?"

I held up my hand in an effort to shush him. "Jesus already told me."

Joshua started laughing and leaned forward in his chair. "Oh yeah. I can't wait to hear this. What did he say?"

"That I had to pray for her and forgive her for all her crap. Well, he didn't specifically say 'crap,' but he said something like that."

"Uh-huh."

"Okay, it wasn't even close, but you get my point."

"But you don't want to forgive her?"

"Of course not, but I will. Lord knows I've already lived through what unforgiveness can do. I just started getting a good night's sleep every night; I don't want to go backward."

"Then it sounds like you're dealing with this the best you know how. I'm proud of you."

"Thanks."

He sat back in his seat again. "So what about Riley? What happened there?"

"He basically came out and told me that he thinks I'm too insecure and it's starting to grate on his nerves."

"Is he right? Are you too insecure?"

"Of course."

"Why do you think that is?"

"Because I'm crazy as a loon and I look like Frankenstein, that's why."

He laughed and shook his head before hiding his smile behind the small notebook he held in his hand. He cleared his throat and then turned serious again. "That may be part of it. But I would have to say there's probably more to it than that."

"Like what?"

His eyebrows arched high, which meant he wanted me to answer the question myself.

I followed his lead. "Well, I'm not for sure, but I'll take a stab in the dark and say it's probably daddy issues."

"Bingo."

"I was afraid that was it."

"I know you were. I think you avoid the topic of your dad like the plague."

There wasn't a bone in my body that wanted to dive into the topic of my dad, so I ignored his prompt. "So you think this is all about some newfound abandonment issues?"

"That probably has the most to do with it, yes. And I think you're going to have to dig deeper and deal with your dad's rejection. We can't just keep skimming over it and hope that it'll go away."

"That may be so, but I've got so much other stuff on my mind right now that I can't even think about going there."

His brow creased as he frowned. "Eventually? Soon, I hope?"

"Soon...er or later." I looked down at my feet and readjusted myself in the chair. "Can we move on?"

"If that's what you want."

"It is."

"Okay, but just know that at some point I'm going to make you talk about it."

I felt my eyes roll. "Okay."

"So anyway, back to your insecurity issues. Personally, I don't think you give a rat's rear what anyone else thinks about your scars anymore, and I think we've already determined that you aren't any crazier than the rest of us. So daddy slash abandonment issues seem to be the logical choice."

"Well, let's face it. If my own dad can walk away, who's to say a seventeen-year-old boy won't?"

"Nobody."

"My point exactly."

"What you've got to figure out is that your value as a person doesn't come from Riley or even your dad. No matter what they think of you, it's what God thinks of you that matters."

"What about what I think?"

"Your opinion of yourself needs to line up with what God thinks, not with what humans think."

"Well, I don't think it does."

"Then you need to work on that."

"And how do I go about doing that?"

"Glad you asked." He got up, walked over to his desk, and rummaged around until he pulled out two spiral notebooks. "Here," he said, handing me one. "I want you to carry this with you everywhere you go, and every time you have a negative thought about yourself, I want you to write it in this notebook. Consider it an assignment."

"Good grief, what's with the assignments all of a sudden? Whatever happened to just talking things out? I've got assignments coming out my wazoo."

"I don't want to know about your wazoo; I just want you to do what I'm asking."

"But if you want me to write down every negative thought I have about myself, I'll be writing all day … and night."

"That's the point. I want you to realize how much negativity about yourself invades your mind and spirit on a regular basis. That can't be good for you, and it can't be good for a relationship, not matter who it's with."

"Fine then, I'll write it all down." I wasn't at all happy about it, and I suddenly felt like he and Jesus were in cahoots with the whole writing assignment thing.

"I'm not finished yet," he announced.

"I was afraid you were going to say that." I looked at the other spiral notebook in his hand. "Is that one for me too?"

"Yep."

"Good grief."

Seeing as how I didn't reach for it, he tossed it onto my lap. "Every night before you go to bed, I want you to get out the list of negatives you wrote that day and get out a Bible …"

I felt my eyes roll in my head.

"… and for every negative thought you recorded, I want you to find something in the Bible that contradicts it. In other words, I want you to find the truth and write that down."

"Is that it?"

"Nope."

"Why am I not surprised?"

"Let's say you wrote: 'Why am I doing this? I'll never get it right.' Then in the Bible you find the scripture that says: 'I can do all things through Christ who strengthens me.'"

"Uh-huh."

"I want you to read through them like this: 'I *am* doing this, and I *will* get it right because I can do all things through Christ who strengthens me.' The goal is to change how your mind works and how you see yourself. God's word doesn't return void, Attie. Eventually his truth will penetrate your mind, and you'll notice the negative thoughts begin to fade away." He sat back in his seat and crossed his left leg over his right. "If you'll do this like I'm asking you to, you'll see it heal that area of insecurity in your life, and all of your relationships will be the better for it. I promise."

"Okay, I'll do it."

"I want you to bring both notebooks with you to our meetings so we can track your progress."

"Whatever you say." I slunk further into my chair. "Have you ever worked with someone as screwed up as me?"

"Get out the notebook. That was your first negative thought."

"Good grief, already?"

"It took less than two minutes."

"See what I'm saying? I'm a nutcase!"

"There was another one. Man, you really will be writing all day."

"I told you so."

I grabbed a pen off the end table and wrote the thought in the notebook. *I'm screwed up.*

He leaned over and handed me his Bible.

I searched through it until a scripture jumped out at me. When I found one, I opened the second notebook and wrote down the scripture.

"Now read it out loud as I told you. The truth."

"I'm not screwed up; I'm fearfully and wonderfully made."

"What does that mean, Attie?"

"It means that God made me this way."

"That's right. What else?"

"He thinks I'm wonderful?"

"Bingo."

I felt myself grin. "I might actually like this assignment."

"I'm glad to hear that, especially seeing how much time you're going to be spending doing it."

"Just add it to my already chaotic and jam-packed life."

"Too much on your plate?"

"Not necessarily too much, but a lot."

"Maybe you should reconsider some of the things you're spending your time on."

"Like what?"

"You tell me."

"Honestly?"

"Of course."

"I think taking classes at the university seemed like a good idea when Cooper talked about them, but now that everything's going on, it seems like a lot. How on earth I let a guy I only knew for a few months talk me into taking on a full load of not one but two schools was beyond me. I guess I was lulled into a trance by his glowing white teeth."

Joshua laughed. "I don't know, but I would agree. Is the additional stress worth cutting a few classes off your total time spent in college?"

"Well—"

"And not only that, do you have any time to enjoy being alive?"

"I hadn't thought about that."

"Attie, you missed out on a year of your life. Do you want to keep missing out on having fun just so you can grow up even faster?"

"Well, when you put it that way, what on earth was I thinking?"

"You were trying to be efficient. But rather than seeing you be efficient, I'd prefer to see you enjoying the life you've been given."

"What do you think Pops would say?"

"I think he'll support whatever you want to do."

I sat up in my chair and smiled over at Joshua.

"Not to change the subject, but you know I have to ask," he said. "It's partly why you're here, and it's what we all agreed to."

"Go ahead."

"Are you and Riley following the rules?"

"To a tee."

"So no problems there?"

"What are you asking me, Josh? Come on out with it."

He placed his elbows on his knees. "Are you struggling at all with limiting the physical aspect of your relationship?"

I copied his body language. "Um, not really, no. I mean, we have our moments, but all in all, we've done really well. I feel sorry for him sometimes—"

"Why?"

"Let's face it: as much as he agrees with the stance we're taking, he'd probably throw it out the window if I let him."

"You think so?"

"Sometimes. And it's not that I don't want to do more; it's just not a good idea. I feel like if we start crossing lines, then it'll become a habit, and we'll just keep crossing every one we draw."

"That sounds about right."

"I mean, don't get me wrong, Riley's never complained or hinted at anything or acted inappropriately—except for that one time at the lake. He's great about all of it; really, he is."

"But you worry that he's going to feel like he's missing out on something. Giving up too much?"

"Yes. And I don't know if he'd tell me if he got to that point. After last night, I can't see an instance where he'd be willing to upset me again, so I think he'd keep it to himself."

"Would it upset you if he told you that he was struggling?"

"No. I realize he's human."

"Maybe you should tell him that. Sometimes the fear of coming clean about something causes it to manifest itself into something bigger. It would probably be a great relief for him if you told him that you understood his situation."

"We talked about it at the very beginning our relationship, but I guess it couldn't hurt to bring it up again."

"I think he'd appreciate it. Maybe just set the record straight again?"

"Why not?"

"You two have your heads on straight, you have goals, and you know what you believe. A lot of kids your age don't have that. So, when you put the two of you together, you get two levelheaded kids who are trying to do the right thing, even when it isn't always the easy thing. I respect that—a lot."

"It's because we've got this great counselor-slash-youth-pastor-slash-friend. He gives a lot of great advice."

"I could give all the advice in the world; it's only when people take it and put it to work that it actually has an effect. You two do that, so it makes my job that much easier."

"Good."

He laughed. "Well, that, and like you said, you have a great counselor." He stood and walked over to me. "We're good here, so let's pray and then let you get home. Anything in particular you want to pray for?"

"Why don't we pray for Pops not to freak when I tell him I'm quitting UCO and Tiffany not to freak if I end up getting the captain's spot?"

He raised his eyebrows at me.

I sighed. "In other words, let's pray for a miracle or two."

· · · · · · · · · · · · · · · · · · · ·

Our family sat at the kitchen table eating Marme's homemade chicken enchiladas and Mexican rice. Of course, the parents wanted a complete rundown of how our week was going, and seeing as how Riley's only response was "fine," I was left filling them in on all the down and dirty details. Riley only nodded, shrugged, and grunted every once in a while in response to a direct question.

"Pops?"

"Yep? Hey, pass the salsa, will you?"

I picked up the jar of sauce and handed it to him. "I think I've made a pretty important decision, and I want to run it past you."

Evidently Riley finally got interested in our conversation because he sat forward in his chair as he took a swig of sweet tea.

"What's that?" Pops asked.

"I'm quitting school."

The shock of my declaration caused Riley to spew most of the tea he'd just put in his mouth all over me, and what didn't fly out of his mouth shot out of his nose when he started laughing at seeing me covered in his beverage.

I was so disgusted I couldn't even respond. All I could do was wipe my face on my sleeve and give my attention back to Pops, who was trying to remain stoic and fatherly rather than laugh at the repulsive shower I'd just taken.

"What do you mean, you're 'quitting school'?" he finally asked.

"Only if it's okay with you."

"Attiline, I realize it's been a tough four days, but you just can't up and quit school like that."

I felt my shoulders slump and my face droop.

"I mean, I know I'm a pushover sometimes, but why on earth would you think I'd be okay with that?"

"It's not even like it's necessary. I mean, you're acting like it's a big deal. I can always go back."

"It is a big deal!" It was the first time he'd raised his voice to me, and I didn't like it. It even caused Riley to slide down in his chair a bit. "If you aren't going to go to school, then what exactly is your plan?"

"To enjoy life."

"Trust me, we'd all like to enjoy life, but sometimes we've got to do things we don't like. You're just gonna have to buck up and live a crappy life like the rest of us."

I shrugged. "Never mind, I'm sorry I even brought it up. It's just—"

"It's just what?"

"Joshua and I thought it sounded like a good idea."

"Joshua agrees with you?" Pops was literally screaming.

"It was sort of his idea."

"*What?*" He was now on his feet and about to start pacing. I could tell because he looked just the way Riley did before he started pacing when he was upset about something.

"Well, with counseling a couple of times a week and church on Wednesday and Sunday nights and football games on Friday nights and Sooner games on Saturdays and cheerleading practice—"

"You can't be on the cheerleading squad if you aren't in school," he said.

"Why not?"

"Attiline, it's a school sport. You can't be a cheerleader on a school team if you aren't going to the school."

"Wait, what?"

"You can't—"

"I'm talking about quitting classes at UCO, not high school."

Pops fell back into his seat. "Oh, thank God."

"What, do you think I'm crazy or something?"

Riley laughed again but this time covered his mouth.

"Shut it, Riley."

"I'm not saying a word," he mumbled from behind his hand.

Pops laid his head on the back of the chair. He looked like he'd been KOed and left hanging in the corner of a boxing ring. "Well, I didn't know what was going through that head of yours, and I didn't know what I was gonna do with you."

"I'm not a complete moron." I was actually a bit offended that they thought I'd be as ridiculous as to think I could quit high school or even think it would be a good idea.

"You don't wanna take classes at the university?" Riley asked.

"They haven't even started yet, so I can get most of my dad's money back."

"Do you think you need to call and ask your dad about it first?" Marme asked.

"No," I snapped. "I don't know, it just feels like I've got too much going on. I don't have any time to—"

"Enjoy life?" Marme asked.

"Yes. That's exactly it."

"I think it's the best idea I've ever heard," Riley said. "Our lives are crazy enough as it is."

"I'm with Riley," Marme said. "I'd like to have you home just hanging around more often. A girl your age doesn't need to be goin' and blowin' all the time. Adulthood will come soon enough; no sense in rushing it."

I looked over at Pops and waited for him to respond. He still hadn't picked his head up off the chair.

"Pops?"

"What?"

"What's the matter?"

"I'm still trying to recuperate from my near heart attack."

"Oh. Well, take your time."

Riley, Marme, and I continued dinner over small talk until Pops finally regained his composure.

"I'm with you three," he announced. "Less is more, at least in this particular situation. If you feel like you've got a handle on everything this winter, you can always go then. Or better yet, you can just wait till next fall like all your other friends. There's nothing wrong with being a normal kid."

"You're assuming she was ever normal," Riley teased.

"I was normal."

"When?" he asked.

I stopped to think about it, and it took awhile because I had to go back quite a ways. "Preschool. I think I was pretty normal in preschool."

"If you can call eating crayons normal."

"It only happened once, Riley. They were the smelly kind, and I thought they were food."

"So it wasn't your sanity that was in question back then, it was your IQ?"

I threw a flour tortilla at him. "Enough out of you, or we won't be taking any walks this evening."

"You win."

"Well, that didn't take much," Pops quipped.

Riley shrugged with a grin. "What can I say? The girl's got skills."

Pops scowled. "I don't wanna know that."

I rolled my eyes at him and took another bite of enchilada.

"Okay, then I'll just say she holds all the power," Riley said.

"They all do, son, and the sooner you figure that out, the better off you're gonna be."

"Thanks for the warning." He picked up the flour tortilla and threw it back at me. "Oh yeah, did Attie tell you what tomorrow is?"

"No," Marme said. "What's tomorrow?"

I rolled my eyes again.

"What?" she asked.

"The team votes for captain."

Marme practically jumped out of her chair in excitement. "Are you gonna win, Attie? I bet you are; I bet you're gonna win!"

"Oh, I don't think so."

"Yeah, she is," Riley announced. "The girls are already talking about it. Just think, Attie's gonna go from zero to hero in less than a week."

"Hero?"

"You're gonna be the captain of the cheerleading squad. In our school, that's a big deal."

Suddenly sick to my stomach, I dropped my fork onto my plate.

"I take it you aren't excited?" Pops asked.

"What part of you thinks Tiffany Franks isn't going to make my life a living hell if I win?"

"No part," Pops said as he gave my leg a pat. "Prepare yourselves. I see a bumpy road ahead."

chapter 10

My stomach felt like a light bulb lighting up the night sky as thousands of beetles flittered around the brightness. The nauseated feeling in the pit of my abdomen was understandable yet upsetting at the same time. Had it been any other circumstance, I would've been happy and excited to hear the announcement that was about to take place; but knowing the possible repercussions should things go my way, I was actually left hoping that I didn't hear my name.

"And this year's captain, with eleven out of eighteen votes, is ..." As Coach Tyler opened the envelope, I almost became physically ill. "Attie."

I immediately shut my eyes and listened to the team scream and begin clapping. I didn't want to see Tiffany's face—hers or her fellow juicers.

"Juicers" was a term invented by Kent. It was used to identify anyone who followed Tiffany, Rick, or Wes. In other words, they were drinking the Tiffany Kool-Aid. When we discussed Tiffany or any of her groupies, we referred to them as "juicers." Although it wasn't the most loving term of endearment, it seemed to fit them perfectly.

I pulled out my notebook and wrote: *I don't deserve this.*

"Congratulations, Attie," Coach Tyler said, interrupting my writing. "Is there anything that you'd like to say?"

I squirmed a bit in my seat as I chewed on the end of my pen. "Just thank you. That's all really." I kept writing. *I can't do this. I'm not good enough.*

"Well, come on up here. Your first order of business is to choose a co-captain."

I closed the notebook and stuck it under my bottom so that I was sitting on it. "I'd rather not choose. Why don't we just give it to the person who got the next highest number of votes?" I assumed the votes were for Tiffany and hoped that being cocaptain would curb some of the resentment that was probably flowing like a tidal wave in my direction.

"All right then. Anne, you came in second place with five votes, so I guess that makes you co-captain."

"What?" Anne shrieked.

Jennifer leaned over and stuck her chin on my shoulder. "I don't even want to look Tiffany's direction."

I nodded.

"How is that possible?" Tiffany's voice erupted from a group of girls in front of me. "I'd like a recount."

Coach Tyler looked down at Tiffany and handed her the ballots. "Feel free to count them. They're all right there."

She snatched them out of Coach's hand and flipped through them. "I'd like a public vote."

"That isn't necessary, Tiffany. You see the ballots; no need to redo the vote." Coach grabbed the forms back out of Tiffany's hand. "You received the remaining two votes. You came in third."

"That doesn't make sense. I specifically had commitments from over half of the squad that they were voting in my favor. Something went wrong."

"Or people didn't want to tell you the truth to your face," Jennifer added. "It is what it is, Tiffany. Attie and Anne are captains. Get over it."

And so it was. My first day as captain was a complete and utter nightmare.

As Anne and I tried to corral everyone for a quick practice before the game, Tiffany individually terrorized each and every girl, demanding they admit whom they voted for. While Mandi, Jina, Casi, Christy, Trish, and Blair refused to answer, Brandee and Mary ran the other direction. Nobody wanted the wrath of Tiffany on them—not even me.

Midway through practice, she ended up "spraining her ankle" and sat out the rest of the time. Once she was no longer in the picture, practice improved, and harmony ended up winning out.

Coach called the girls together so that I could talk to them about a few business matters.

In a desperate attempt to keep my nervous energy contained, I curled my toes inside my shoes and hoped it would stay there rather than have it run up my legs, through my body, and make my voice shake. I didn't know how they'd feel about having to wear sweats at their first game for no other reason than my uniform issues.

"I'm sure you've heard already, but my uniform came back a wee bit small—completely unwearable, actually. So, for the game tonight, our uniform will be our rain resistant pants and the regular uniform top."

"Why should the rest of us have to suffer because your skirt's too small?" Tiffany asked, walking toward the squad with no sign of a limp.

Coach Tyler and I quickly exchanged knowing glances.

"Because we're a team, Tiffany," Anne said. "And that's what a team does."

I ignored both of them. "Ironically, I hear it is supposed to rain tonight, so go ahead and bring all your rain gear just in case. We'll meet up at the field in a few hours for warm-up. Any questions?"

I dreaded a response from Tiffany, but she somehow managed to keep her mouth shut.

"Great. Thanks everyone. See you at six-fifteen."

Tiffany walked to within inches of me and perched her hands on her hips. "So how'd you do it?"

Jennifer was right behind her. "Jealous much?"

"I wasn't talking to you, Jen. I was talking to Attie."

"I didn't do anything, Tiffany. I didn't ask anyone to vote for me; it just happened, and I'm not apologizing for it."

"Well, it should be an interesting season. Let's see how good you are at keeping your squad together."

"Are you trying to turn this into a war?"

She shrugged.

"Why, Tiffany? What's the point?"

"A little fun never hurt anyone."

I felt my back stiffen. "You don't scare me."

"Not yet, anyway." Tiffany's shoulder rammed into mine as she walked past me.

"Oh boo-hoo," Anne hissed in Tiffany's direction. "I can't believe that she's making such an issue of this."

"Get ready, Anne. I have a feeling it's going to get worse. Much, much worse."

And of course, it did.

Things were out of control before the game even started. Tiffany and the two juicers on the team refused to warm up with the rest of the squad and even walked ahead of us and onto the other team's home field.

In an effort to create unity and reduce drama, Anne and I announced that anyone could start a cheer if they knew of one that was appropriate for a given game situation. The team really stepped up and took ownership, and the squad had the fans in a constant state of enthusiasm. It didn't take long, however, before I realized that three squad members participated in every chant unless it was one started by Anne or myself. If we started the cheer, they literally stood still with their arms folded across their stomachs. It was their silent protest of my and Anne's "authority"—an authority that we never actually wielded.

Finally, during halftime I noticed Pops make his way to the fence, call for Tiffany to join him, and watched as he gave her a lecture.

How did I know she was getting a lecture? Body language. I couldn't hear a word that was said, but I did see a lot of finger pointing on his side and crossed arms, eye rolls, and foot tapping on hers.

During the second half, she and the juicers participated in all the cheers, but they sure didn't try very hard to look like they were enjoying themselves. I tried my hardest to ignore them, enjoy the game, and watch Riley put on a show. By the end of the game, he'd scored three touchdowns, and we won, forty-two to seventeen.

Finally in the sanctuary of my car, I plugged in my iPod and sat in the driver's seat writing all the negative thoughts I'd made mental notes of throughout the night. With all the drama going on, there was a lot to write, and I knew I was going to be up late going through the Bible.

The parking lot emptied, and the noise finally died down to a manageable level, but there were still some young kids and parents waiting outside the locker room door. I found it funny that so many children wanted their programs autographed by the players. I guess they hoped that one day one of the players would make it to the NFL and the signatures would really be something special. As they were right now, they were nothing more than the acknowledgment that they wanted to play football for Guthrie High one day too.

Riley finally appeared. He'd showered and changed into a pair of blue jeans and an OU T-shirt. He was handsome as ever, and his shaggy brown hair hung wet, partially covering one eye. As the crowd pushed into him, he strained to see above their heads until his eyes locked on mine and he smiled and gave me a nod.

I could feel myself beam at his acknowledgment. All those people huddled around him, wanting his attention, and all he wanted to do was find me. I felt special. He made me feel special.

Riley signed a few autographs, shook several hands, and took pictures with fellow players before jogging toward me.

"Look at you, you're a celebrity."

"Naw." He kissed me on the forehead before hugging me. He smelled amazing, a wonderful combination of soap and cologne.

"Great game. You made me proud."

"I just wish I could stop and watch you every once in a while."

"You aren't missing much. But there's always basketball season—if I last that long."

"Did Tiff cause problems?"

"You don't want to know." I slid my arms around his body and laid my head on his chest. "Besides, your dad took care of her."

"You sure you don't wanna talk about it?"

"I'm sure. I don't want to waste any of our time talking about her."

"Fair enough. Everyone's going to Braum's. Wanna go?"

"If you do."

"Might as well. More time for us to spend together before going home. Curt said he'd drive. We can leave your car and come back and get it before heading back to town."

"You think it'll be okay here?"

"Yeah. It's a public place. What could possibly happen to it?"

• •

(Riley)

I kicked the tire.

"It's flat. Completely flat. So is the other one. We've only got one spare, so you're gonna have to come get us."

I could hear Dad's heavy sigh through my cell phone. "It'll be about thirty minutes or so before I can get over there. Lock yourselves in the car and I'll be there as soon as I can."

"Okay."

"And Riley?"

"Yeah?"

"Be good."

"Dad, seriously..."

"You're right, sorry. I'm on my way."

I turned and threw the phone into the car. "I swear that man lives in a constant state of paranoia. If he only knew how little actually happened, he'd be shocked."

"Are you talking to me?" Luckily, Attie hadn't heard me.

"No. I'm talking to myself."

"You've been hanging around me too much then. I think I'm a bad influence and you're slightly losing your mind."

"Like I always say, you'll probly lead to my undoing."

Attie sauntered toward the other side of the car and looked over her shoulder at me. "I can't say that I'm upset that we'll have to spend more time alone together."

Her teasing invigorated me. I ran up behind her, grabbed her around the waist, and picked her up off the ground. "You don't have to slash your own tires to spend time alone with me, you know?" I lightly bit the skin on the back of her neck.

"No, but it was a darned good idea. I should thank whoever did it. I couldn't have planned it any better if I tried." I set her down, and she turned to face me. "I wonder if they're watching from afar."

"Hoping to see us get all upset?" My hands rested on her hips, ensuring that she wouldn't wander outside arm's distance.

"Little do they know…" She looked up at me through the corner of her eyes and gave a grin.

"Maybe we should give them a show. You know, really give them something to talk about."

Her arms wrapped around my neck. "Like this?"

"That's a start." My hands slowly slid up the sides of her body.

"So, Riley Bennett, tell me—"

I kissed her neck, mumbled "Mm-hmm," and then kissed her ear.

"What's it like to kiss the most hated girl in school?"

My lips grazed the skin below her right eye. "Give me a second. I'm about to find out."

A giggle escaped her lips before I silenced her.

After several seconds, she jokingly and dramatically wrapped one of her legs around my waist. Even though I knew she was teasing, I admittedly lost what little common sense and any sensibilities I had left. Keeping my mouth attached to hers, I wrapped my arm around her knee and lifted her up until she was forced to wrap her other leg around my waist as well. The thought of our surroundings and situation completely escaped my mind.

She pulled her head away. "That'll really get to them."

"To whom?"

"The juicers."

"That wasn't for the juicers."

"No, who was it for?"

"Me." I was completely energized.

"Oh, well in that case..."

"Hold that thought." I propped her up against the car. "Don't move."

"I'm not going anywhere."

As I set my watch alarm for twenty minutes, her legs tightened around my waist, and I felt her feet cross at the ankles. My mind was spinning.

"What are you doing?" she asked.

"Giving us fair warning. We've got twenty minutes."

"Oh."

"Now, where were we?"

. . . .

Attie looked over at me with a grin. "Well?"

"Well, what?" I put the key in the ignition and turned it enough to start the radio.

"How was it, kissing the most hated girl in school?"

"Amazing."

"Do you feel like a rebel?"

"The luckiest rebel alive."

She threw her feet onto the dashboard in front of her as we waited for my dad to show up. "I can't believe you could hold up me that long."

"I wasn't really thinking about how much you weighed."

"What were you thinking about?"

"You probly don't wanna know."

Her eyes grew large as a blush took over her face and her nose scrunched.

"Anyway, you weigh twelve pounds. I could've held you like that all night."

"And it was a great way for you to keep your hands stationary. Don't think I didn't notice."

I looked down at my hands as they tightly gripped the steering wheel. "I'm running out of ways to creatively keep my hands to myself."

"Well, I wouldn't say you kept them to yourself."

"Hey, at least I didn't cross over into inappropriate territory."

"You were a good boy." She reached across and gave my cheek a gentle pat. "Always are."

I groaned at the thought. "Don't remind me, Charlie. As much as I appreciate your appreciation of my good behavior, please don't remind me."

"Okay. I'll let you keep thinking you've got some bad boy left in you."

"Thanks."

I leaned over to kiss her, and when I did, my hand slid between the seat and the console and rested on a spiral notebook. I pulled it out and read the title out loud. "Lies I Tell Myself."

She grabbed for it, but I held it out of her reach.

"What is this?"

"A notebook."

"I know it's a notebook. What's it mean? What's it for?"

"It's nothing. It's just an assignment from Josh to help me get over my insecurity issues. I'm supposed to write down every negative thought I have about myself."

"Can I look?"

She shrugged.

"I won't if you don't want me to."

"You can; I don't mind."

Making sure not to actually read anything, I opened the cover and flipped through the first several pages. They were all full.

"How long have you been doing this?"

"Since yesterday."

"There's like four or five pages filled already."

"I know. I'm totally messed up." She winced. "Well, crap, there's another one."

"I had no idea you saw yourself like this. We kid about it all the time, but I always thought we were just joking. I didn't know you took it all so seriously."

"We are joking, and I don't take what you and I say seriously."

"Then what is it?"

"Joshua thinks it's mostly dad issues."

I flipped through it again, and although I didn't read the sentences, words like *ugly*, *stupid*, *crazy*, *undeserving*, and *moron* jumped off the page over and over again. I was shocked. Shocked and sad.

"Charlie, none of this is true. You're none of these things."

"Well, that's the second part of the assignment. I have another notebook at home that I write the positive stuff in."

"Then you should've already filled an entire notebook by now. And if you ever need help coming up with the good things, just ask me. I'll be glad to tell you all of them."

"Riley, that won't work."

"Why?"

"Because you're biased."

"No, I'm not. I'm right."

The light from headlights swept across the car, and I regretted that I wouldn't have more time to discuss the notebook. "He's here. Let's go. We can talk more about this later."

"What's there to talk about?"

"Charlie, you've written five pages of negative stuff about yourself in a matter of twenty-four hours. You don't think that's gonna make me worry about you?"

"You don't need to worry about me. Joshua's got it under control. We're working on it."

"You sure?"

"Yes." She leaned over and kissed my cheek. "What's that?"

I followed her gaze and saw a piece of paper tucked under the windshield wiper. "Don't know."

We jumped out of the car as Dad walked up. "How'd you manage to get two flat tires, Attiline?"

"I don't think I did manage it."

She joined us on the driver's side as I grabbed the piece of paper off the windshield and read it out loud.

"We drove by, saw your car, and couldn't resist. We slashed your tires 'cause you're a dumb—"

"Don't even say it," she interrupted. "I bet I can guess how it ends."

Dad snatched it out of my hand. "You've got to be kidding me."

"Evidently not." Attie chewed on her thumbnail and stared absentmindedly at the tire.

"I'm gonna call Stew and report this. You two get in the car. I'll be there in a minute."

When I reached for Attie, she snapped out of her haze. "Let's get in the car, Charlie. Dad's gonna call the cops."

Entwining her fingers in mine, she followed behind as I led her to the passenger side.

"Stew? It's Tom Bennett. Sorry to call you so late..."

I opened the back door and watched as Attie slowly climbed in and lay down in the backseat.

"I'm here in Deer Creek. Attie's front two tires were slashed. Someone left a note about it on her windshield."

When I opened the other car door and climbed in, Attie sat up slightly but quickly laid her head in my lap.

"They really do hate me." There was sadness in her voice, and she said it as if she'd realized it for the first time. "They don't just dislike me; they vehemently hate me. The words in the note prove that."

"They don't hate you, Charlie. They hate what you've accomplished since you got here. They're jealous. They don't know you enough yet to hate you."

She started laughing.

"Okay, that came out totally wrong. Not that people would hate you if they got to know you."

"Nice try." She sat up, stole a glance out the front of the car, and then kissed me before slinking back to her corner of the backseat and grinning over at me.

"I love you." The words spilled out of my mouth like the most natural words I'd ever spoken. They were three of the most honest words I'd ever said.

"You too."

We stared at each other for a few seconds before my dad threw open the car door and climbed in the driver's seat.

"So, Attiline, are you doing okay back there? You aren't too upset, are you?"

Her attention left me and focused on Dad. "No, sir. I'm fine."

During most of the drive home, I sat completely speechless as I watched Attie interact with my dad. Every once in a while she would glance my direction by peeking over her shoulder, but as soon as she realized I was still watching her, she would turn her head back around.

I couldn't keep my eyes off of her. I couldn't help myself. I was done for.

chapter 11

(Attie)

It was late and I was tired. I wasn't tired in a sleepy kind of way; I was tired from the drama. Tired from the temper tantrums Tiffany and her juicers had thrown most of the night and tired from knowing that they hated me enough to slash my tires and leave a disgusting note to make sure I knew just how they felt. I was tired and completely fed up.

Leaving Riley and Pops to fill out the police report downstairs with Stew, I moped up the stairs and into my room.

"Okay, you better be ready to bring it 'cause I'm losing it."

"Bring what?" Jesus asked from my desk chair.

"What am I supposed to do now? Look where praying for my enemies and forgiveness got me. They slashed my freakin' tires."

"Watch your language."

"Sorry." I threw myself onto the bed. "Doing the right thing isn't getting me anywhere. They're acting even worse."

"Didn't I tell you to expect that?"

"Uh, no," I sassed. "A heads-up would've been nice."

"Sometimes when you do the right things and you start living out my will rather than your own, life gets more difficult. You're a child of God, Attie. You're called to be meek and kind no matter how they act."

"But kids at school don't care if I'm a child of God. They don't care if I'm meek or kind or any of that stuff. People don't think I'm nice; they think I've lost my everlasting mind. Which I have, but they don't need to know that. Nobody would put up with this."

"My ways are not their ways. What they think about you doesn't matter."

"That's easy for you to say. They aren't slashing your tires and calling you bad names."

"They are. When they attack you, they attack me. When you hurt, I hurt. You aren't walking through this alone."

"When do you put a stop to this?"

"Who says I do?"

I could feel the anger start to rise in my chest. I wanted to hear him say he'd fight for me, but that wasn't at all what was happening.

"You're going to let it continue?"

"You have to trust me on this, Attie. You may not see it right now, but good will come of this."

"Yeah, I've heard that from you before. More than once. So because I follow you, I have to suffer?"

"No. You aren't necessarily suffering because you follow me, but you're called to follow and trust in spite of the suffering. The true question is whether or not you'll follow even if I don't rescue you. Are you going to follow me no matter how bad you think it is?"

"You're really trying to make this difficult on me, aren't you?"

"Through hardship you learn how to handle more hardship."

"There's going to be more? You're actually preparing me for more? Worse? That's not really what I was hoping to hear."

"Attie, you aren't going to walk through life without suffering through hardship. Nobody does."

"Don't remind me."

"What you need to do is see this as an opportunity to build your character and your spiritual fortitude so that when other things happen, they roll right off you and you move on ahead and do what I've called you to do."

I couldn't speak. The thought of suffering even more than I already had gave me stomach pains.

"I'm not a fortune teller. I'm not cryptically telling you your future. I'm simply saying that bad things happen to everyone, whether they're my followers or they aren't. The sooner you learn to handle those times, the better off you're going to be."

"So in order to learn that lesson, I'm supposed to sit back and do nothing?"

"Yes. Read the list we made together and try your hardest to live it out. Pray that we'll give you the ability to live it out. That's what I want from you."

"What about my friends? They're practically more upset than I am."

"You need to lead by example."

"What if I can't?"

"Rise above it, Attie. You can do this. Don't sink to Tiffany's level; rise."

chapter 12

(Riley)

Attie and I sat in the hallway outside our bedrooms. We were surrounded by our friends, and to no one's surprise, Tammy had quite a bit to say about the tire slashing incident.

"Tiffany sure knows what she's doing. She's an evil genius who has all her devilish minions doing her dirty little deeds. You know she didn't personally slash your tires. One of the juicers did."

"Wretched hillbillies," Kent added. "They've been drinking the Kool-Aid."

"Bring on the pitchforks; it's time for a witch hunt."

"Watch it, Tammy," Anne warned. "We don't want to stoop to their level. We need to rise above all their shenanigans. We've got to show that we're better than that."

Tammy scoffed. "I don't wanna be better than that. I wanna join right in."

"You'd be ashamed of yourself if you did."

"I'll hang my head in shame later, Anne. Right now I wanna kick their butts."

Jennifer raised her hand like she was in class waiting for permission to talk.

"Yeah?" Tammy asked.

"I wanna see them all get publicly flogged. Completely humiliated and laughed at in a very torturous manner. Seriously, how sick am I?"

"About as sick as me," Tammy said.

Jennifer's shoulders slumped. "Oh. A completely unhealthy amount then."

"Okay, you two," Attie interrupted. "I appreciate your willingness to rush to my defense. And I'm grateful that you'd all show up here on a Saturday morning to discuss the possibilities of revenge—"

"I had to gather the troops," Tammy said.

"Well, unfortunately, you're not going to like what I have to say."

Tammy groaned. "Don't even tell me that you're about to say we have to behave."

"That's exactly what I'm going to tell you."

"But Attie, I've spent hour upon hour thinking of ingenious ways to get even with those Kool-Aid snortin' jerks. I have some really good ideas too."

"I'm sure you do. You have a gift."

I'd heard enough. The natives were getting restless, and it was time for someone to talk some sense into them before they planned an all-out attack.

"Look, if we don't react, then they'll get bored and move on to someone else. The important thing is that we don't let them get a reaction outta us. We don't let them have an effect on our lives."

"Riley, they're complete imbeciles. They aren't even smart enough to figure out that we aren't responding," Tammy said.

"They'll catch on eventually. Plus, Dad's on to them now. He'll step in if he needs to."

"Did he tell you that?" Tess asked.

"Yes."

Out of nowhere, Mom yelled up from the kitchen and announced that lunch was waiting on us.

"We'll be right down, Mom!"

"How does she whip stuff together that fast?" Chase asked. "We just got here."

"She's a home ec teacher. She lives for this stuff," Curt said.

"Plus, she's probably hoping we'll keep talking while we're down there and she'll be able to hear what's going on. That woman can be a nosey body," I added.

Attie stood up and walked to the middle of the group. "Back to the business at hand. I get the impression that this is a make or break moment. The juicers keep turning up the heat in hopes that we'll eventually break—act as badly as they are. As soon as we lash out, they win. They prove that we're no better than they are."

"You think they're actually smart enough to give it that much thought?" Tammy asked.

"They probably didn't think that far ahead," Attie said. "Look, I realize this isn't world peace or anything, but in our school we have the chance to set an example for others to follow..."

"Me?" Tammy shrieked. "I shouldn't be setting an example for anyone. Me and example setting are treacherous areas."

"You're a great example," Anne soothed.

Tammy shook her head in disgust. "I should've known better than to hang around a bunch of do-gooders. Now you people expect me to act just as good."

"We aren't asking you to 'act' anything," Attie said. "You are a better person than that, Tammy, and you're one of the most loyal people I've ever met. I'm not asking for everyone to act perfect— I know that's impossible—and I also know that I'm about as far from perfection as a person can get. All I'm asking is that we try to do right, not what feels good. Trust me, I'd like to do a little butt kicking myself; but no matter how good it felt for the moment, it wouldn't be the right thing to do."

"Fine! I'll behave."

"Thank you, Tammy. So we have a deal?" Attie asked. "Nobody responds. We act like nothing happened." She looked at Tammy, who gloomily gave her a nod. Then she looked at Jennifer. "What about you?"

"You know me, I hate confrontation. I talk a big game, but when it comes right down to it, if someone said 'boo,' I'd run the other direction."

"Nice amount of honesty there, Jen," Tammy teased.

"Anne," Attie said, "you'll have to be the one to set the example for the rest of us sinners."

"I'll do what I can. But with Kent and Tammy, I've got my hands full."

Tammy stood and pulled Anne to her feet. "You have no idea how right you are. When it comes to retaliation, I'm like a moth to a flame."

Anne hugged her. "I'm secretly in awe of your love for all things sinister."

"Then stand back, girlfriend. You ain't seen nothin' yet."

"I heard that," Attie said.

"I'm just sayin'. 'Good girl' ain't how I roll, so this is gonna be new to me. Everyone just sit back and watch the show. This could get mighty interesting."

chapter 13

I sprung out of bed in a panic. The once quiet house was suddenly erupting in noise, and the confusion of being half asleep and the unexpectedness of the sounds made it nearly impossible to figure out what I was hearing. My mind ran through the months of the year. It was August, not May, so the chances of it being a tornado were small; but then again, in Oklahoma you never knew what you might get—just like with Attie.

The volume continued to increase as I rubbed my eyes and swung my legs out of bed.

What in the world?

I recognized a rhythm. It wasn't just noise; it was music. But what kind of music, and who would be blaring music at eight o'clock on a Saturday morning?

Drums pounded, horns joined in, and then it hit me.

"Oh, dear Lord."

Disgusted, I lay back in bed. I knew exactly what it was and who was doing it. Who else could it have been?

"Riley!" Attie screamed for me from the living room.

I'm not sure why I didn't expect something like this. It was August 30. To most people in the world, this day was nothing special, but to Attie it was the most important day of the year. Today was the first Oklahoma Sooner football game of the season, and Attie decided the entire house needed to start the day off by hearing the school fight song at an ear-splitting volume.

"Riley!"

"I'm comin', for cryin' out loud!" Not that she could even hear me yell back. "Hold your horses."

I rushed around getting dressed as the floor vibrated under my feet until the song ended and it was finally silent.

"Thank God."

The peace and quiet didn't last long. Within seconds, "Oklahoma" blared from the speakers.

I peered over the stair railing and spotted Attie and my mother marching around the living room. They looked like complete idiots, while Dad stood watching them in slight amusement with his fingers plugging his ears.

Attie spotted me on the stairs and ran to me. She was dressed in jean shorts and a crimson T-shirt with a large OU printed in white on the front. She also wore the OU football helmet that normally sat on my bookshelf. It was several sizes too big for her tiny skull and rolled around on her head as she moved.

"It's today! It's today!" I noticed a large, red foam finger had swallowed her right hand.

"Uh-huh."

"Aren't you excited, Riley? It's the most exciting day of the year."

I was looking forward to it, but I couldn't say my excitement level was anywhere near hers. "I can't wait," was all I could manage to scream over the music.

"Come on, babe, please get excited."

"Well, let me wake up first."

Through the face mask I could see that her face wore a pout. "And then you'll get excited?"

"Yeah."

Standing one stair below me, she smiled up at me. "Thanks."

Seeing her excitement, I couldn't stop myself from smiling back, even if I was completely annoyed.

"See," she said. "You're smiling. It's going to be a great day."

I gave the face mask a small tug, causing the helmet to cover her eyes. "Yeah, it's gonna be great."

Her neck bent back so that she could see me, and I leaned over and peeked into the helmet. Her smile had grown.

"Good Lord, you're cute," I admitted. "And it's a good thing, 'cause otherwise all of this would be very annoying."

A flash of light caught the corner of my eye. Turning toward it, I noticed Mom had just taken our picture.

"That's gonna be the most adorable picture I've ever seen. Riley, you're gonna have to draw that one."

Attie started to run off, but Mom stopped her. "I can't believe I'm about to say this, but Riley, lift up the helmet a little and give Attie a kiss so I can take another picture."

"Seriously?"

"Yes. It'll be so cute, I can't pass it up."

Dad threw his hands over his eyes.

I was happy to oblige, so I grabbed the face mask with my hand, lifted it up to her forehead, and leaned down to give Attie a kiss.

The camera flashed again.

I didn't bother to stop kissing her. I figured I'd keep going until someone told me to stop. Attie's body starting shaking as giggles consumed her. The camera kept flashing, and my lips stayed attached to hers. I was going to take full advantage of the opportunity to actually get to kiss her in the house.

Attie threw her arms around my neck, and through closed eyes I could still see flashes of light strobe in our direction.

"Enough already," Dad interrupted. "How many pictures do you need?"

I kept kissing her.

"Enough," he repeated.

Attie pulled away from me, turned around, and ran back down the stairs toward the stereo.

"Gramps and I have got it all figured out. The game starts at six, so we need to be there by five so that we can watch the players warm up. That means we need to be at Campus Corner by about four thirty, which means we need to leave here no later than two so we have time to swing by and pick up Gramps."

I plopped onto the sofa. "Why do we need to get there so early?"

"I just told you. To watch the players warm up."

"Why do we have to watch the players warm up?"

"Riley, we've got to get the entire experience. Plus, I want to show my support by being there when they warm up."

"You don't watch me when I warm up before a game."

"That's because I'm warming up. If I weren't cheering, I'd show up an hour early and watch you warm up too."

"You would?"

"Sure." It sounded a little strange, but I appreciated her loyalty and enthusiasm.

"Okay." She stood up, grabbed the remote control, and turned to face us. "Are we ready?"

"Ready for what?" Dad asked.

"Behold." She turned and pointed the remote at the TV. "And God said, 'Let there be ESPN.'" She pushed the power button, and the television came to life. "I just got chills."

Dad looked over at me with a grin. "Where did this girl come from?"

"I have no idea. I just sit back and watch the spectacle." I looked back at Attie, who had made herself comfortable on the floor in front of the TV. A reflection of the television bounced off the helmet as it still sat on her head. "You never know what she's gonna do next, that's for sure."

• • • • • • • • • • • • • • • • • • •

Attie walked so fast that the rest of us could hardly keep up. The grown-ups finally handed us our tickets so they could take their time instead of running all the way to the stadium.

"But you'll still be there to watch them warm up, right?" she asked, disappointed.

"We'll be there," Gramps said. "You two go on. We won't be far behind."

Attie wore the helmet all day until we finally left the house and she changed into an OU ball cap. I watched as she bounced along the sidewalk. Her ponytail, which she'd pulled through the opening in the back of the cap, swung in the air.

She gasped, stopped midstep, and latched onto my arm.

"What?"

Her eyes grew large, but she stayed silent.

"Charlie, what?"

She lifted the foam finger and pointed in front of her. It reminded me of the scene in *E.T.* when the small alien extends his ugly finger and points to the moon before saying "Home."

My eyes followed the direction of the finger. She'd just spotted the stadium and was obviously in awe.

"Haven't you ever seen the stadium before?" I asked, looking back at her.

She shook her head slowly. "Not since they added all the new stuff to it."

I grabbed the cell phone out of my pocket and took her picture. She still didn't move.

"That's the coolest thing I've ever seen," she said slowly.

She was fun to watch, and I couldn't take my eyes off of her. I would imagine that the look on her face was similar to a kid walking into Disney World for the first time and laying their sights on Mickey Mouse.

As I stood in awe of her excitement, she grabbed a hold of my arm with her nonfoam hand and started dragging me along behind her. Her feet carried us as fast as they could go.

Now I've heard it said that males and females have an average amount of words that they use on a daily basis. Females, of course, use more words than males. I'd always thought that, like my mother, Attie probably exceeded her number of words every day by borrowing some of mine. Today, just from the time in the car and the walk toward the stadium, I knew for a fact she'd used her total allotment of words for the week—not to mention mine. She wouldn't shut up, and I could barely keep up with the flow of words as they flew out of her mouth. I recognized some of the players' names as she spouted them out, but other than that, it was just a lot of words.

We handed over our tickets to be scanned and finally made our way through the entrance. By this point, Attie was literally skipping. "We've got to get a hot dog and some waters and a chair back and a program. I pretty much memorized the roster, but we should still get a program because I want to see their faces."

As she talked, I added up the amount of money she would be spending within the first five minutes of entering the stadium and realized that if we were going to do this every home game, I was going to need to get a job.

"Maybe a pretzel too? What do you think, Riley? A pretzel?"

"Whatever you want. I'm just along for the ride."

"Well, you have to think it through. We can't get up once we're in our seats."

"We can't get up?"

"No. We might miss something."

I felt my eyes roll but followed behind and held on to all the items as she bought them and shoved them into my arms.

Finally, we made our way from under the stadium and up the ramp to section nine. As soon as we walked out of the tunnel, the field appeared in front of us.

The players, dressed in their crimson jerseys, were warming up on the perfectly maintained field. Even I got a small rush from the sight.

Attie gasped. "I think I might cry."

I turned to her in horror. "Don't you dare cry."

"I can't help it."

"There's no crying in football."

She gave me a puzzled look. "I thought there was no crying in baseball. Isn't that the line? 'There's no crying in baseball'?"

"That was a line from a movie. This is real. There *is* no crying in football."

"But it's beautiful," she said, looking back at the field.

"Football's not beautiful, Charlie. Football's cool or exciting; it's anything but beautiful."

"But look at how gorgeous the crimson helmets and jerseys look against the pretty green grass. It's even prettier than on TV."

I felt my eyes roll again.

A boy scout dressed in full uniform walked up to me. "Can I help you find your seat?"

"Yeah." I showed him my ticket.

"You're going to turn and head up these stairs, go up to row sixty-four, and the seats will be on the left side of the aisle."

"Thanks. Come on, Charlie."

She didn't respond. She stood, jaw hanging wide open, watching the players.

"Come on, Charlie."

I started up the stairs and after making it a quarter of the way looked and noticed that Attie wasn't far behind. The binoculars hanging around her neck beat against her chest every time she bounded up the step in front of her.

"You okay back there?"

"I'm good, but did you see all those girls that are all dressed up for the game? I mean, who wears skirts to a football game, for crying out loud? And why would you? What guy would want to bring a girl to a football game wearing a skirt? Would you want me wearing a skirt, Riley?"

"If it was short enough."

"Oh, shut up…" She continued jabbering away, and I tried to ignore her.

I'd like to think that I'm in pretty good shape, but even for me, the climb was tiring. I spotted our row and then our seats and sat down to wait for Attie. About every ten rows or so, she would stop, turn around, and take a picture with her phone.

"When I die," she said as she finally sat down next to me, "I hope heaven is just like this."

I laughed. "You hope heaven is a football field?"

"No. I hope heaven is *this* football field."

. . . .

Without being obvious, I watched Attie out of the corner of my eye as the band played on the field during the pregame show. I wasn't at all surprised when she burst into tears during the state song. Personally, I would have enjoyed the song more if it hadn't been the fiftieth time I'd heard it that day. Attie had made us listen to it and "Boomer Sooner" over and over again during our drive into Norman.

The band continued, and I watched Attie as she sang the OU chant with her foam finger held high in the air, booed when they played the fight song of the other team, clapped along to "You're A Grand Old Flag," and held her hand over her heart during the national anthem.

She really got a kick out of it when, at the end of the national anthem, instead of singing "and the home of the brave," seventy-five thousand people substituted "brave" by shouting "Sooners." It caused her to jump up and down and scream at the top of her lungs.

Dad tapped me on the shoulder. "How's she doing over there?"

"So far, so good, but 'Boomer Sooner' is about to start. She might just have a heart attack."

As I expected, as soon as the drum line started playing the "Boomer Sooner" riff, Attie lost her mind but quickly settled into watching and clapping along as they marched off the field.

Attie turned to me and went on a description overload about what she thought of the pregame show. Her lips moved a mile a minute until she heard a loud church bell give one ring.

Her eyes grew large, and her mouth slammed shut.

Another bell chime.

Her mouth flew open, and she screamed in my face before turning around to look at the jumbo-tron.

The bell rang again, and she got silent, eyes plastered to the screen as head coach Bob Stoops suddenly appeared on the screen along with past and present players. She named each and every player as they appeared.

The purpose of the video was to get the crowd pumped up, and she was certainly that.

When the team exploded out of the tunnel, Attie screamed and hopped up and down to the point that I was afraid she was going to bump into the person to her right and cause a complete domino effect. I turned and noticed that the rest of our group was so busy laughing at her reaction they weren't even bothering to watch the field.

She was definitely entertaining, and she'd done so much screaming and jumping around before the game even started that I couldn't in my right mind figure out how she was going to last four more hours. Honestly, I was relieved that some of her energy had been burned and she might be calmer during the game itself.

I should have known better than to hope for something so ridiculous.

The Sooners scored four times in the first quarter alone and three more in the second. Attie showed the same amount of excitement for each and every touchdown—not to mention every tackle, every run, every pass, and every field goal. She may not have been worn out, but I sure was, and it was just from watching her and listening to her never-ending play by play.

By halftime, when it started raining, the Sooners were ahead fifty to zero. Luckily, as the rain fell, we were safely sitting underneath the deck above us and didn't get wet. A few minutes in, the announcer asked everyone out in the open to seek shelter due to lightning and thunderstorms nearby. At Attie's insistence, we stayed put.

"After all," she said, "we've got cover."

"Attiline, it's fifty to zero, and it's pouring down rain. Can't we just go ahead and head home?" Dad asked.

Attie looked disgusted. "Do the players get to go home?"

"Well…no."

"Then we shouldn't go either. I don't think true fans should leave until the players have finished playing."

"You wanna stay the entire time?" he shrieked.

"Don't you?"

"I guess?" He was asking himself a question more than agreeing with her.

And so we stayed. We stayed through the one-and-a-half-hour game delay. We stayed through the third quarter in which the Sooners only scored one more time. And we stayed through the entire fourth quarter, even when nobody scored and practically everyone in the stadium but other morons like ourselves had left.

We didn't leave the stadium until almost 10:30 p.m., and by the time we made it to the car, we were tired, sopping wet, and our ears were practically bleeding from her constant talking.

To top it all off, as we climbed in the car and made ourselves comfortable, Attie said something mind blowing.

"Good grief, did you guys hear that obnoxious woman behind us? She would not shut up."

Dad's head turned my direction so fast that I thought he was going to fall over. "The woman was loud?" he whispered. "Is she kidding?"

All I could do was shrug.

Not surprisingly, Attie kept talking. "She complained about this and she complained about that. My Lord, we won by fifty-six points; what does the woman want? Riley, next time, remind me to wear headphones so I can listen to the play by play and I don't have to listen to all that noise."

I hung my head in my hands. "I'll do that."

Next time? Did I even want there to be a next time?

"I say we all get headphones," Dad announced. "You know, to drown out all that noise."

"Oh," Attie said, "so you heard her too?"

chapter 14

Joshua and I stood in the pasture out behind my house throwing the football to each other as we had our debriefing and the females all made dinner in the kitchen. Even though we were several yards away, I could hear them cackling through the open kitchen window. Of course, my mom's voice was the loudest, but Attie's wasn't far behind, and she was giving my mom a run for her money in terms of who talked the most. In that moment, part of me realized that God had a very big sense of humor, and the reality was that I was dating a younger version of my mother. The other part of my mind refused to believe it.

"I heard about the tire incident. What's happened since then?" Joshua asked.

"Not much. As a group, we decided not to respond. We didn't even acknowledge that it happened."

"That was a smart idea."

"Attie gets the credit for it. She's under the impression that if we don't get involved, eventually we won't be any fun and they'll move on and bug someone else."

"And have they? Moved on?"

I caught the ball, lined up the threads in my fingers, and threw it back. "It's only been a couple of weeks, but they haven't really done anything else big like that. Tiffany gives Attie fits at practice and games every once in a while, but the coach has really got that under control. I think she hears things that are said about her, but she ignores it. I've been proud of her."

"I have too. She seems to have risen above all the mess. It'll only make her that much stronger and a better role model for other kids going through the same thing."

"Yeah. I know people are watching to see how she handles it."

"How about you?" He rested the ball between his arm and hip. "How are you handling things?"

"I'm fine. Nobody really gives me problems."

"What about with Attie? How's your relationship?"

"Incredible. Wonderful. I'm crazy about her."

"Living with her isn't causing problems?" He finally grabbed the ball and threw it again.

"No. I think the rules you guys laid out have helped. They kinda keep us from going into boyfriend/girlfriend mode at home. It's more hanging out than anything."

"And when you aren't inside the house?"

"We spend a lot of time outside, I'll be honest. But really, even then we just go for walks or hang out on the front porch. Nothing more than PG stuff, I can assure you. Well, maybe a little PG-13. I mean, there've been a couple of instances where it's been more difficult."

"What's more difficult?"

"Following the guidelines we agreed to. You know, one minute I'll be kissing her and all's fine, and then the next it's all I can do to not cross the line. It's a constant battle."

"I can understand that."

"Like, the first day of school. We were playing a joke on the students and acting like we weren't dating. Well, she started flirting with me in the hallway, and it really messed with my mind. It was all I could think about all day. And the more I thought about it, the more I turned completely innocent remarks into suggestive ones— to the point that by the time I saw her that afternoon, I wanted to break every rule known to man. If she would have shown one weak moment, it would've been all over."

"So she's the one that's keeping this ship afloat—in terms of not going overboard?"

"Mostly. Don't get me wrong; I agree with everything. I wanna wait, but sometimes I don't think clearly."

"That's when you really have to work on taking your thoughts captive."

"Yeah."

"Do you watch the Olympics?"

"That was a random question, but yeah."

"Have you ever watched a gymnast or a diver as they visualize the stunt they're about to do?"

"I've seen them do it."

"They visualize themselves doing it perfectly because the mind and body don't know the difference between reality and imagination. The visualizations—the thoughts—are so real that the body thinks they've actually just performed the act perfectly. They can literally train the muscles of their body and mind by imagining perfect moves."

"I had no idea."

"What I want you to see is that when you let your mind wander into areas that are questionable, when you focus on thoughts that are different from reality, your mind doesn't necessarily realize it isn't real. So it can become much more difficult to resist something that your mind and body thinks it already did."

"It doesn't help that I have done more with other people and before Attie came along. Not everything, but more."

"And don't think Attie doesn't realize that too."

"I know."

"She'll wonder if you always want more."

"The problem is, no matter what I wanna believe, the truth is yes, I always want more."

"You're a seventeen-year-old guy. That's normal. Controlling yourself is going to continue to get more difficult."

"We do better if we just don't get close to the line."

"The line?"

"Yeah. It's this imaginary place that I can feel if we get too close to. It's that point where my mind starts to shut down and my body wants to take over. As long as we stay away from that place, I do pretty good."

"But when you get right up to that line?"

"It's darned near impossible to stop."

"So what do you do at that moment?"

"Stop, or back off and cool down and stay away from each other. But I swear, Josh, sometimes all she has to do is look at me, and I'm right there with my toes hanging over that line just a little bit. We don't even have to be doing anything; it's just that look. And what's worse is that she doesn't even know she's doing it."

He laughed. "Really?"

"Yeah. It's like she's a freakin' Jedi who hasn't figured out that she has the Force, so she walks around with all this power and doesn't even have a clue. It's her eyes and the way she looks at me. Dear Lord, I wanna cross the line right now just thinking about it, and she's not even out here!"

"Well, stay away from me. You keep on that side of the field."

"Lucky for you, you look nothing like her."

"Thank God for small blessings. Although, she is cute."

"She is, isn't she?"

"Yes. You have excellent taste."

I juggled the ball back and forth in my hands as my mind raced. "Can I do this, Josh? I mean, for years? Is it even humanly possible?"

"Oh, it's possible. It's very difficult, and it'll feel impossible at times, but it is possible. All things are possible if you trust that God will help you through it. On your own, using what little willpower you've got, it isn't possible at all."

I felt my eyes roll.

"Look, Riley, you need to stop focusing on what you can't do with Attie and focus on what you can—and I mean that in a completely nonphysical way. You two have a lot of fun together. You carry on some of the strangest conversations I've ever had the pleasure of overhearing, and you seem to be very honest with each other. I mean, is there a topic you won't discuss?"

"Not really." I threw him the ball again.

"Do you realize how rare that is? It's true intimacy. A true connection and an honest and safe environment is where true intimacy is created. That's what you two are forming right now. And in the future, if you guys end up together, then you'll be that much better off because you focused on developing the emotional and communicative aspects of your relationship long before the physical part."

"In my mind, I know that. In my lower region, not so much."

"Well, you're gonna have to learn to ignore the lower region and focus on your mind. And that, my boy, is the struggle of males everywhere. No matter what age, race, or culture."

"Is that supposed to make me feel better?"

"No. It's intended to let you know you aren't alone."

"Can I come out yet?" Attie screamed.

Joshua laughed. "Yes, Attie. You can come out now. It's all clear."

She burst out the door and through the pasture before throwing herself into Joshua's arms. We were both surprised by her affection.

"Congratulations!" I realized by the sound of her voice that she was crying.

"What's going on?" I looked back at the house and saw Nicole and Mom standing in the doorway. Mom had a tissue pressed to one of her eyes. "What's with the crying?"

Joshua smiled over at me with Attie still attached to him. "Nicole's pregnant. Four years of trying and we're finally having a baby." A tear ran down his face as he wrapped his arms around the spunky blonde.

Sprinting to them, I dropped the football and joined Attie in her congratulatory hug until Nicole made her way out and the four of us stood crying and celebrating in a huddle.

It was one of those rare moments when you believe that everything's going well and all's right with the world.

chapter 15

We were learning the hard way that football weekends were exhausting. Friday night games got us home past eleven, and Sooner home games easily turned into eight- or nine-hour days. Night games were most difficult. We usually didn't make it home until close to one o'clock in the morning, and our promise of making it to church every single Sunday was getting difficult. Today was no different.

Attie trudged into the kitchen and plopped into her seat at the table. She looked like she'd been hit by a truck.

"Good morning, sunshine," I teased.

"Hello." She sounded bleak. "My name is Attie Reed, and I'm a Sooner Football-aholic. It's been less than three minutes since my last fix."

Dad placed a mug in front of her and filled it with coffee. "And in what form did this indiscretion present itself?"

"I perused Soonersports dot com."

"How many times today already?" I asked.

"About four, and I'm seriously jonesing to read the sports section of the newspaper."

"We hid it from you already, Attiline. We thought you might be having a problem."

"How'd you guess?"

"Maybe it was all the weird comments you've been making for the last few games." Dad noticed that Attie hadn't fixed her coffee yet, so he grabbed it and added cream and sugar. "What were some of the best ones, Riley?"

"'In Bob we trust' was a good one," I said.

"One nation under Bob," Mom added. "She also threw out the 'Bob bless America' a time or two."

Dad laughed from behind his coffee cup. "Yeah, well, my personal favorite was 'Our Bob who aren't in heaven.'"

Mom walked over with a plate of bacon. "Now when she's talking about Bob, I don't know if she's talking about Bob Stoops or Riley. I think she's equally in love with both of them."

Attie's forehead crumbled as she looked over at me. "Sorry, Riley. I'm sick. I don't think there's any hope for me."

I smiled over at her. "At least you're dedicated. Who knew being a head football coach could get you so much praise and adoration? I wonder if Bob Stoops has ever heard his name used in so many interesting ways."

"He'd be horrified, and they'd probably consider me a stalker and take away my season tickets."

"Probly." I threw her a piece of cinnamon toast. "You're like a super-fan extraordinaire. You've taken it to a whole 'nother level."

As she took a bite of toast, cinnamon and crumbs fell down the front of her shirt. "Good grief, I can't even eat, I've got withdrawal shakes so bad. We aren't even halfway through the season. What in the world am I going to do?"

"We'll put you on a football diet," Dad suggested. "Limit the intake."

"To what?"

"How often do you normally watch it?"

She peeked at him through her fingers as she covered her eyes in shame. "Saturdays, Sundays, Mondays, Thursdays, and Friday nights when we have a school game."

"Maybe cut out Thursdays for a start. We haven't had a movie night since football season started. Maybe we can start doing a movie night every Thursday."

Her face collapsed, but she nodded in agreement before looking down at her shirt and wiping off the crumbs. She stopped midbrush and her face cringed.

"What?" I asked.

She rubbed her chest lightly. "Nothing."

"It doesn't look like nothing. What's the matter?"

She rubbed her chest again and then looked over at my mother with a confused look on her face.

I jumped out of my chair. "Charlie, what? You're freaking me out."

"It's nothing, Riley. It's probably some scar tissue or something; I've just never noticed it before." Her eyes darted in my mom's direction again.

"Where is it?" Mom asked.

"Right here." She rubbed a small area just above her left breast. "I just don't remember it ever being there, and it feels different from the other scars and stuff."

Mom scurried over to Attie and placed her hand on her chest. "Attie, that's not a scar. That's a lump."

Suddenly nauseated, I fell back into my chair.

Mom continued rubbing the spot. "It's definitely round, and it's about the size of a large gumball. How could you have not noticed that before?"

Attie shook her head in confusion. "I...I..."

Mom looked over at me. "Riley?"

"My hands don't enter that territory. How would I know?"

"You don't check yourself regularly, Attie?" Mom asked.

"I didn't know I was supposed to. Do you think it's bad?"

"It could be a lot of things, but it certainly isn't normal. I'll call and get you into the doctor tomorrow."

"Attiline, do you know if cancer runs in your family?"

"Cancer?" The word spilled out of my mouth.

"MeMaw died of cancer," she whispered.

"What kind?" I asked.

Attie looked at me but didn't answer. Her eyes were wide.

Mom grabbed Attie's cheeks, turned her face to her, and gave her a kiss on the nose. "Let's not get all freaked out. I'm sure it's nothing serious. We just need to get it checked out as soon as we can."

"Call the doctor right now," I begged.

"It's Sunday morning, Riley. They aren't open."

The room started spinning, and I felt cold and clammy.

"Babe," Attie said, "you're looking a little woozy. Put your head between your knees."

I leaned over and tried to relax, but the words *Attie* and *cancer* continually ran through my mind.

After a few minutes, Attie appeared under the table. She'd crawled underneath and was peeking up at me with a large grin on her face. "Don't freak out, Riley. I'm fine. I'm sure it's nothing."

"You're crazy."

"About you." She whispered quietly enough that my parents wouldn't hear.

"No, you're just plumb crazy." I slid my chair away from the table as she crawled out and knelt in front of me. "What time do you think we can go see the doctor tomorrow?" I asked.

"We?" Mom asked.

"Yeah, 'we.' I'm not staying here while you go. I'll be losing my mind."

"It'll be during school."

"So? Can't we call the principal and let him know?" I looked over at my dad and waited for him to respond.

"I'd excuse that absence."

"See?"

"And Molly, we'll need to get you a substitute."

Attie struggled to get out from under the table. "None of you need to go. I can go by myself."

"No," we answered.

"Good grief. It isn't that big of a deal. They'll do an X-ray or something and that'll be about it." She ran her fingers through my hair. "Buck up, camper; it'll all be okay. I have a good feeling about this. It's all going to be okay."

chapter 16

Attie slammed her locker door, and the sound reverberated through the empty hall.

"They are not sticking a needle in me. Riley, go tell your mom that they aren't sticking a needle in me."

"Charlie—"

"Don't 'Charlie' me. How would you like a four-inch-long needle stuck in your chest while you're wide awake? Did you see that thing? It's a freakin' thick needle. It isn't happening."

"They need to find out what it is. They've got to do a biopsy on it."

"Then they can do it another way."

"If you do it the other way, you're in the hospital longer. It's actually surgery. We have to worry about them knocking you out, and it'll leave a scar."

"What's one more? It's not like I'll be posing for *Playboy* one day or anything or that anybody else is going to see it." I opened my mouth to say something. "Don't you say a word."

"I wasn't gonna."

"Yes, you were. You were going to make a snide remark about how you definitely wouldn't be seeing it."

A small laugh escaped from my throat. "How did you *know* that?"

"I know you, that's how."

I turned serious again. "So you wanna tell them you're doing it the other way?"

"Yes."

"Surgery?"

"Yes."

"You're sure?"

"Yes."

"Are you gonna call your dad?"

"No way."

"Why?"

"Because he doesn't need to get in involved in something so minor. What makes you think he'd care anyway?"

"'Cause even if he's a jerk, he's still your dad."

"If he wanted to know about stuff like this, he wouldn't have given your parents legal rights to seek medical treatment for me if I needed it."

"I think that was more for emergency type stuff. Not—"

"Riley, enough."

"Am I annoying you?"

"Yes."

"Charlie, I just think—"

"Don't."

"Don't what?"

"Think."

I noticed Tiffany and another student walk up to a locker a few feet away, but I didn't bother acknowledging them.

"Fine. I don't agree with the surgery option, but I'll obviously support whatever decision you make. It's your body."

"Thank you. Are you going to go with me?"

"Do you want me to?"

"Of course. It's a fast procedure. I don't stay the night or anything, but I'll have to sit out the game on Friday night."

"It'll be worth it. We'll be able to have some peace of mind…I hope."

"Yes." The school bell rang, and students immediately poured into the hall. "Riley, let's not tell anyone, okay? I don't want people freaking out over nothing."

"Okay," I said before giving her a kiss on the nose. "It'll be just between us. Our little secret."

"Well, ours and Tammy's."

"Tammy?"

"She is my best friend."

"Yeah."

"And she's Tammy. She'd kick my butt if I didn't tell her."

"You're scared of your best friend?"

"This is Tammy we're talking about. Wouldn't you be?"

"Uh, yeah."

The rest of the day and all the way through Wednesday were three of the longest days of my life. My concentration was even completely off during practice. So much so that Coach finally sent me home early on Wednesday. Although they tried to hide it from Attie, my parents did a horrible job of hiding their concern from me. They acted completely opposite than they normally did. Dad talked a mile a minute about nothing in particular, and Mom was practically silent.

To try to keep Attie's mind off things, Nicole invited her to go along for her doctor's visit on Tuesday afternoon, and Attie excitedly agreed in hopes that she would hear the baby's heartbeat. She was handling all the stress much better than the rest of us. Or, if she was as worried as much as we were, I sure couldn't tell.

For dinner on Wednesday, Mom made Attie's favorite meal: chicken fried steak with mashed potatoes and gravy. She threw in fried okra, buttered corn, and dinner rolls. Complete overkill if you ask me, but Attie seemed to appreciate it, especially seeing as how she wasn't allowed to eat or drink anything after ten o'clock. She practically gorged herself, and then at 9:59, we all took one final bite of carrot cake before calling it a night.

Attie and I slept in our beanbag chairs in the hallway. Well, she slept, and I mostly watched over her. I was worried that the added stress might bring on a nightmare. Luckily, it didn't.

At five thirty in the morning, my dad gave her a hug and loaded her into the car with my mom, Tammy, and me. By six thirty she went back to prep for surgery, and as much as I hate to admit it, Tammy and I both cried as soon as she and Mom were out of sight.

"Don't assume the worst," Tammy urged.

"I'm not."

"We've gotta think positive."

"I am."

"Then why are you white as a ghost?"

"Am I that obvious?"

"Yes."

I fell into one of the waiting room chairs. "Do you think Charlie noticed?"

A large smile formed on her face.

"What? Why are you smiling?"

She pulled her legs onto the chair and folded them underneath her. I'd never seen anyone sit in a chair that way before. "You just called her Charlie," she said.

"I always call her Charlie."

"Not when you talk about her third person."

"Huh?"

"When you talk *to* her you call her Charlie, but when you talk *about* her, you call her Attie."

"Really? I never noticed."

"You just let me into your little world." Tammy glowed at the idea. "You actually like me, Riley."

"No, I don't."

"Yes, you do." Her red head bobbed up and down. "You love me. We're friends and not just 'cause of Attie."

"Fine, I admit it."

"I knew it."

"I love you partly 'cause you love Attie and partly cause you're so darned obnoxious I can't help myself."

She smiled a big, sappy smile. "And I love you. One, because you love Attie, and two, because you're one of the sweetest boys I've ever known."

Something was off. Tammy wasn't being herself. I leaned forward and gave her the look my dad gave me whenever he was about to start an interrogation. "Okay, what's going on?"

She looked confused. "What?"

"You're being really nice. Do you know something I don't?"

She slapped herself on the forehead. "Aw, Attie told me not to be too nice. She said it would worry you."

"It did."

"Honestly, I don't know anything. I was just being nice. It's a rare occurrence. Maybe you should just soak it in. It may not happen again for centuries."

"So you don't know something bad and she just told you not to tell me?"

"No, I promise. If it scares you that bad, I'll never be nice again. I'll go back to being my hateful, opinionated self."

"That might be best."

"You've got it."

"I appreciate it."

"Here," she said, tossing me a magazine. "We might as well make ourselves comfortable. We're gonna be here awhile." I picked it up and opened to the first page just as Joshua and Nicole walked into the room. For some reason, seeing them made me cry.

Without saying a word, Joshua sat next to me, placed his arm around my shoulder, and prayed quietly into my ear.

An hour and a half later, after Nicole and Tammy had fallen asleep in their chairs, Mom walked out into the waiting room. She looked exhausted and worried.

We woke up the girls before Mom gave the details.

"They took her back about fifteen minutes ago. After her IV was in, the doctor talked to her about what was gonna happen."

"What *is* gonna happen?" Tammy asked.

"The incision should be very small, and he's gonna try to go in…" She looked at me and rolled her eyes. "Anyway, someplace not so obvious, if you know what I mean."

"No," Tammy said, shaking her head. "Not really, but go ahead."

"Tammy, Bob and Joshua are sitting right here. I'm trying not to be graphic."

"Oh, that's okay. Attie'll give me all the gory details later. I may even get to see the scar. Are you jealous, Riley?"

"No, and need I remind you my mother and my youth pastor are sitting right here?"

"So?"

"Was she upset?" I asked in an attempt to change the subject.

"A little nervous, but they gave her something to calm her down. She got a little loopy. It was funny."

"What did she say?" I asked.

"She started talking about 'Bob,' and 'Wasn't Bob cute?' and 'Bob's the sweetest boy ever.'"

"Oh good gravy. I hope that's all she said. Was there anything incriminating?"

"I hope so," Tammy said, rubbing her hands together.

"Nope. Nothing incriminating."

A pout formed on Tammy's face. "Bummer."

"They said it shouldn't take long to get the growth removed. They're gonna take it straight to the pathology person; I think that's what they said. We should know if it's anything serious within just a few minutes."

"How long will she be back there?" Nicole asked.

"They said that they will need to monitor her for about an hour after she wakes up. They have to make sure she doesn't have a reaction of any kind. Then we can take her home."

Joshua stood and walked toward the exit. "I'll go call Tom and let him know what's going on. He's already texted me four times."

"And Gramps," I added. "Would you call him too? I know he's really worried."

"I'll make sure to update him."

"What about her dad?" Tammy asked. "Should we call him?"

I shook my head. "No. Attie didn't want us to call him unless there was news of some kind."

Tammy looked surprised. "Really?"

"I don't think she wants him involved in the day-to-day stuff."

"This isn't really day-to-day stuff, is it? I mean, surgery's kinda major."

"It's what she wanted. I'm not gonna push the issue with her anymore. No sense in opening a can of worms unless we need to, which I hope to God we don't." I rubbed my eyes and sat back in my seat. "She's been through so much crap with him that she refuses to even talk about him. If you try to reason with her, it doesn't get through. So—"

"Mrs. Bennett?" We all turned to the nurse. "You can go back in now. She's about to be put in her room."

"That was fast." She hopped up and gave me a pat on the cheek. "Hang in there, Riley. We'll have an answer soon."

"I don't get to be there when they tell her?"

Mom looked sympathetic to my situation. "Hold on for a second." She disappeared behind some doors and within a few minutes came right back out. "They said you could go back. I'll wait out here."

I sprung to my feet. "Really?"

"Go on."

I made it to Attie's curtained-off "room" just as they were wheeling her back in. She was partially awake but groggy.

"I want Riley," she mumbled.

"I'm right here."

"Riley?" Her head turned in my direction, but she could barely hold her eyes open.

"I'm right here."

"What did the doctor say?" she asked.

"Nothing yet."

"Hmm." She struggled to keep her eyes open but eventually lost the battle and fell back to sleep.

I was shocked to see that she wasn't wearing a gown of any kind. Her chest was only wrapped in several layers of gauze, so I pulled the sheet up to cover her. I figured it was the gentlemanly thing to do, and I didn't want her to be embarrassed once she finally came to.

I glanced around the room at all the equipment. Even for a small procedure, there were several machines monitoring her. I had to fight the encroaching memory of when she was lying in the hospital a little over a year before.

Not wanting to think about it, I laid my head on the bed and let myself fall asleep.

"Was Tammy nice to you out there?" she mumbled, waking me up. I wasn't sure how much time had gone by.

"Yeah. She didn't sass me once. It's like she's sick or something. Maybe she should be the one back here."

Attie started laughing and then winced. "Riley, don't make me laugh."

"Sorry, I didn't mean to."

"I told Tammy to act normal or it would freak you out."

"She was anything but normal. I think she's worried."

"Probably."

I wanted to hold her hand, but the one closest to me had an IV in it, so I stroked her hair instead. "How do you feel?"

"A little sore and very groggy."

"Attie?" The doctor opened the curtain. "Is she awake?"

"I'm awake," she answered.

"We've got your test results back."

It was as if time stood still. My heart stopped beating, my hand stopped stroking her hair, and I stopped breathing.

"It's good news."

My body instantly relaxed as relief swept over me.

"It was a calcium growth. Very common and harmless. We'll have it sent off to be looked at further, but I don't anticipate hearing anything different. All you've got to do now is heal and maybe lay off the sodas a bit. Too much caffeine can be a cause of those types of growths."

"You hear that, Charlie? Not so many Route 44s."

"Say it ain't so," she teased.

"The nurse will be in within the next few minutes to take out the IV, and then we'll get you ready to go home. Is there anything else I can do for you? Do you have any questions?"

"No," she mumbled.

"Do you think you could go give my mom the news? She's waiting out in the lobby."

"I'll do that right now. I'll also give her Attie's prescriptions and follow-up information."

"Thank you."

"My pleasure. This is the kind of news I don't mind giving. You two have a good day, and Attie, I'll see you in about a week."

"Okay, thank you."

As soon as the doctor left the room, I covered Attie's entire face in kisses.

"Riley," she mumbled as she playfully tried to push me away. "Stop, we're going to get in trouble."

"By whom?"

"The nurse is going to be in here any minute."

"I don't care." I gave her several more before sitting back down in my chair. "I can't tell you how relieved I am. I was so scared."

"What would you have done if the results would have come back different?"

"I woulda bawled my eyes out, I'm not gonna lie."

"And then what?"

"Are you being serious right now?"

"Yes."

"Um…" It was an interesting, deep, and loaded question. "Well, after spending days crying, I would've done whatever it was you needed me to do. I wouldn't have gone anywhere. It wouldn't have changed anything, if that's what you're getting at."

"Even if I was bald?" she asked with a small smile.

"Even if you were bald. I woulda just bought you a cute OU hat."

"And that's one of the gazillion reasons I love you."

"I love you too. Just promise me one more thing."

Nine

"What's that?"
"No more hospitals."

chapter 17

(Attie)

After briefly checking in with the squad, I gingerly walked out of the locker room and toward the noisy crowd. I really shouldn't have been out of the house so soon after the surgery, but I didn't want to miss the chance to sit with Pops and Marme to watch Riley play. As long as I didn't lift my arms or move around too fast or suddenly, I would be fine. Or at least that's what I told myself.

The stadium was filled with blue and white, and the sounds from the band whipped the fans into a frenzy. For the first time since football season started at Guthrie High, I was wearing jeans. I also wore Riley's extra jersey. I liked wearing his jersey more than my uniform.

Someone walked up to me, and without even seeing who it was, I felt uncomfortable.

"Not cheering tonight, Attie?" Tiffany's voice held its usual malicious tone.

"Not tonight." Trying to escape, I dashed down the sidewalk toward the bleachers.

She continued to chase me down. "Why?"

"I don't feel up for it."

"Personal issues?"

"Sort of."

"So I've heard." Swooping in like a vulture, she grabbed my arm and stopped me midstep. "You live a double life, don't you?"

I jerked my arm out of her hand. "What do you mean by that?"

"I think you know exactly what I mean. Luckily your secret's safe with me. Unfortunately, I can't say the same for others."

My eyes scanned the stadium in hopes that I would catch a glimpse of someone I knew, but the crowd was too large to make out anyone's face. I was stuck dealing with Tiffany on my own.

"My secret?"

"You forget I dated Riley too. I know what he's like, and I know how difficult he can be to resist." She gave a vicious laugh as she folded her arms in front of her. I'd never wanted to punch anyone more in my life. "But I never got myself in the predicament you did."

"Why don't you come right out and tell me what you're talking about, because I don't have a clue."

"It's all over the school. If you hadn't been gone all week, you would've known that."

"What's all over school?"

"The news about your procedure," she whispered.

"That? Why would that be all over the school? And who the heck cares, anyway?"

"Look, when the cheerleading captain gets knocked up—"

"What?" I felt like I'd been punched in the stomach.

"Everyone knows. Quit acting all innocent. Karen saw you at the OB/GYN on Tuesday, and then you end up having a 'little surgery' yesterday. We all know you had an abortion; no need to act like you didn't."

I started walking again, my feet furiously carrying me to the stands as my eyes searched for Pops and Marme. "Have you lost your mind, Tiffany? That's the craziest thing I've ever heard."

"I guess the truth hurts."

I spun around and grabbed her by the arm. "It isn't the truth. I was at the OB/GYN with my friend Nicole. She's the one that's pregnant, not me. My procedure had nothing to do with the office visit. That's the truth, but I wouldn't expect you to care."

"Little innocent princess get her crown tarnished? Wonder if they'll still want you singing up there on stage at church. And poor

Riley. From what I understand, he didn't agree with your decision. I hope the two of you can survive this."

"Don't you worry about Riley and me."

She pulled her arm away from me, gave a grin, and sauntered off, leaving me with my head spinning and black spots forming in my line of vision.

I let myself slowly fall to the ground.

"Attie?"

Feeling cold and clammy, I lay back to keep from passing out.

"Attie!" Tammy ran up beside me. "Are you okay? Do I need to get the team doctor?"

"No, just a little dizzy."

"Wait here, let me get the doctor."

I clutched onto her arm as she started to dart off. "No. I'm fine."

"Are you sure? You look horrible. What if you've got an infection in your incision or something?"

"Oh, I've got an infection all right. A seeping, disgusting, hate-filled infection called Tiffany."

"Oh, sweet Lord above, what's she done now?"

I grabbed her by the chin and forced her to look at me. "If you heard something horrible about me, would you tell me?"

"Of course. Why? What did she say?"

"You haven't heard anything? You haven't heard any rumors?"

"No new ones. But I wasn't there yesterday or today, so—"

"This has gotten completely out of control."

The referee blew his whistle in the background, and the roar of the crowd heightened.

"Attie Reed, tell me right now. What's going on?"

"It can wait. The game started. Wait until I can tell you and Riley at the same time. I don't think I can repeat it more than once."

"Are you sure? This sounds bad."

"I wish I could say you're wrong." The crowd cheered, and the band started playing the fight song. "Here, help me up. My man candy's taking the field."

She pulled me up by the arm opposite the incision and made sure I was steady. "I'm glad to see that you still have your sense of humor."

"That's about all I've got," I admitted.

"Oh, not true." She entwined her arm in mine and led me toward the bleachers. "You've got me."

"Lucky me, and I mean that sincerely."

"Where do you want to sit?"

"Do you mind if we sit with Riley's parents? This is probably going to be the only game where I can do that."

"Sure, I'd love to hang out with my principal on a Friday night. It's what all the cool kids do."

It may have just been my imagination, but as I searched the crowd for the Bennetts, it felt like students were staring at me or talking with someone and pointing my direction. I might as well have been standing there without any clothes on. I felt bare and completely exposed.

By the grace of God, Pops spotted us and waved us down after only a few moments.

I squeezed through the row of screaming fans and gave Nicole, Joshua, and Gramps a hug before taking a seat next to Marme. She wore two large buttons on her jacket. One with a picture of Riley in his uniform and the other was a picture of me in mine.

"Perfect timing," she said, waving her pom-pom in the air. "Riley's about to go in."

"Let's go Blue Jays!" Nicole cheered.

I glanced down at the squad and caught Tiffany glaring in my direction, but then I spotted Riley and watched him take his place on the field. It was time to enjoy watching him play. My latest soap opera episode could wait until after the game.

chapter 18

(Riley)

"Pause, rewind, repeat," Jennifer urged. "She said what?"

"She said that people think I had an abortion. Somehow they found out about my surgery yesterday, and they concocted the abortion story. I can't believe Tiffany would stoop to this level."

"Charlie, we don't even know that she started the rumor."

"The heck we don't," Tess screamed. "My brain can't even function I'm so ticked off. I'm normally not a violent person, but right now I could absolutely knock her block off."

"Tammy?" Attie asked, looking over her shoulder. "You okay? You haven't said anything."

"I have no words … absolutely no words."

"That's a new one," Jennifer said. "She's really gotta be shocked to be speechless."

Tammy perked up. "No wait, I've found the words."

"Brace yourselves," Kent suggested. "This is gonna get ugly."

"That girl is an absolute crime against humanity, and she must be destroyed. An atrocity like her cannot be permitted to exist any longer."

"And there it was," Kent said.

Attie sat in the passenger seat of her car with her head in her hands while Curt, Tammy, Kent, Anne, Jennifer, Tess, Chase, and I sat crammed in the car in a sullen haze. We were floored, and other than Tammy, we weren't sure what to say.

"Who are these people?" Tammy snapped. "Who acts like this? I mean really, I dislike a lot of people, but I would never, ever try to destroy someone like that. I like to joke around, but I would never actually do something that would hurt someone else."

Attie climbed across the front seat and into my lap as Tammy continued to rant. "I mean, hello, people, take out a loan and buy a freakin' clue—we're in high school, for cryin' out loud. Is anything so stinkin' important that you've gotta act like that? I seriously need a barf bag 'cause I'm about to hurl."

"Stick your head out the window," Kent said.

"Remember to breathe," Anne said. "Inhale and then exhale."

"I know how to freakin' breathe, Anne."

"I'm just trying to help!"

Attie buried her face in my neck.

"Everyone cut it out," Jennifer screamed. "This isn't helping the situation."

The car got silent. I looked into the rearview mirror and watched as everyone sat and stared into space.

"Attie," Chase finally said, "what do you want us to do? Do you want us to go out and start defending you? Do we need to set the record straight?"

Attie sat up and looked toward the back of the car. Exhaustion filled her face. "I don't know. My gut reaction is to run out and try to set the record straight, but in reality I don't know if that'll do any good. It could just end up making things worse."

"Charlie, I don't want people walking around thinking that we're like that. If people wanna say we're having sex, that's one thing. It's not the end of the world. But they're accusing us of killing a baby; I'm not okay with that. People think you talked me into letting you have an abortion. I can't stand the thought of anyone believing that we would do that. That *you* would do that. It's so far away from who you are."

"Or who you are, Riley," Anne added. "We all know that."

Attie stroked my cheek with the back of her fingers. "I'm so sorry. I'm sorry I've caused you all this trouble."

"You aren't causing me trouble; don't even say that."

"That jealous wench is causing it," Tess spat.

"I know, but if I hadn't encroached on her territory—"

"She'd be doing it to someone else," I said.

"Excuse me while I pick myself up off the floor," Tammy said. "You're telling us you think this is your fault?"

"A little, maybe."

Tammy thrust forward in her seat. "I call bull crap on that. Tiffany thought she was the cat's meow until you showed up—that much is true, but the proverbial crap hit the fan because she was so jealous of you that she lost all common sense. The girl's a nut job, plain and simple, and she needs a freakin' lobotomy."

"And she needs to be spayed while they're at it," Tess added. "We don't need any Tiffany offspring cavorting around town in the future. They'll just end up causing our kids the same trouble."

"Preach it, sista," Jennifer howled.

"Watch it, guys," Chase warned. "You're whipping yourselves into a frenzy again."

"We aren't whipping into anything," Tammy said. "Tiffany hurled us into it."

Attie threw her hand into the air, motioning for everyone to be quiet. "Can you guys give me the weekend? I just need some time to think."

"That's fine," Tammy said. "But if you're gonna turn around and tell us that we have to behave some more, then I'm gonna have to find a new hobby."

"I'll buy you a painting kit," Attie teased. "Maybe you can teach yourself to paint."

"Deal."

• • • • • • • • • • • • • • • • • • • •

(Attie)

I woke up in the middle of the night and couldn't sleep. My mind raced with horrible ideas of how I wanted to retaliate, and then guilt would overtake me and I'd cry over thinking such horrible thoughts. I was on an emotional roller coaster and desperately wanted off, but the best I could come up with at the time was to make my way down to the kitchen for a snack.

The stove light was on, and I could see Pops standing at the counter as I entered.

"Hey, baby girl. You couldn't sleep either?"

"Nope."

"Why don't you join me? Want some cereal?"

"Sure." I sat down in my seat and watched as he grabbed a bowl out of the cupboard. "Did Riley tell you what happened at the game?"

"He did. What kind of cereal do you want?"

"Frosted Flakes."

"Good choice," he said, smiling. Tucking the box of cereal under his arm, he grabbed the bowl and milk and made his way to the table. "Are you hanging in there?"

"Do I have a choice?" I asked.

"I guess not."

I closed my eyes and listened to the corn flakes fall into the bowl and the milk slosh over them. "This reminds me of when I was a kid and my dad and I would eat a bowl of cereal before we went to bed."

"Nothing like a small sugar rush before tucking in for the night."

"You got that right."

He sat down at the table and looked over at me. "So do you wanna talk about it? I'll listen if you need to talk."

"About the rumor?"

"Yep."

Tears immediately welled up in my eyes. "This is a big one, you know? It isn't a flat tire or being called a name. This is being accused of killing a baby. I don't even know how to grasp it."

"I don't know that you can. It's impossible to make sense out of something that's completely senseless, and that's what this is."

"And cruel."

"Very cruel." He nodded before taking a bite of cereal.

"Would you have believed it? If you'd have just been the principal and we were two different kids who were students. Given the circumstances, would you have believed it?"

He set his spoon down. "You know, Attiline, I've seen so much, I don't know if it would've even fazed me. Yes, I probably would've believed it. Unfortunately, that's the reality of the world we live in. Sex and the consequences of that choice are lived out every day in high schools around the country."

"We've tried so hard to be responsible and pure—for lack of a better term. It's just ironic that this is what we end up being accused of. If it weren't so sad, it might be funny. And Riley...poor Riley, even though he won't say it, I know he's distraught about it."

"Really?"

"We sat out there alone in the parking lot for an hour, and all he could do was say, 'I can't believe people believe that,' over and over again. I think it kills him to know that people who have known him his entire life believe this rumor about him. Nobody even bothered to ask; they just believed it. They don't know any better when it comes to me, but for them to know Riley like they do and still accept it as truth, I don't get it, and I know he doesn't either."

Pops's shoulders sagged, and he shook his head slowly. "For some reason people like to assume the worst about others. I don't think people who know Riley believe it because they think he's actually capable of doing it, but instead they chose to believe it because it's something *they* might actually do if in those circumstances. It suddenly makes it okay if someone like you two does it. It makes them feel better about the choices they make. Maybe it makes them feel less alone, I don't know.

"It probably sounds sick and twisted, but that's really all I can come up with. Let's face it—if in fact you had been pregnant, it would've been a very big deal. You would've faced a lot of public scrutiny and judgment. That's a lot for a teenager to have to own, and it seems so big that unfortunately a lot of kids make the decision that you're being accused of making. So people believing that you two would make that choice isn't so farfetched. Many, many great kids make poor choices and out of that make an unfortunate mistake."

"That makes sense."

"And just for the record," he said, placing his hand over mine, "if you ever found yourselves in that situation, I want you to know that you could tell Molly and me. We might freak out at first, but it wouldn't change the way we feel about you, and we wouldn't love you any less. I don't ever want you to make a decision that could affect the rest of your lives out of fear. There's nothing we can't handle as a family, and there's nothing that can't be forgiven."

"Thank you. You don't need to worry about us though—"

"I realize that, but I still want you to know. You can come to us with anything—anything."

"I appreciate that. Maybe you could share it with Riley too."

"I will. I'll spend some time with him."

"I love that you're so worried about me all the time, but I worry about Riley, and I'm afraid that people don't show him as much concern as they show me. Everything I deal with, he deals with—even more, maybe."

"You're right. I need to make a better effort at that. He's been through a lot in the last year and a half too. I should probably check in on him more often."

I watched as he took another bite of cereal. "What do you think Riley and I should do about this?"

"Tell me what you're thinking."

"I've been living in the Psalms and Proverbs over the last several weeks. They're all about living through crap and how we should handle difficult situations."

"You've got a good head on your shoulders, Attiline. I have a feeling you'll figure out what to do. You'll know what's best. We could all learn from your example."

"I wouldn't go that far."

"I would. If someone attacks me or my family, I have to admit that the Bible isn't the first place I think to go."

"You'd be surprised how much it helps."

He laughed. "I guess it's pretty pitiful when you're surprised that the Bible has some good instruction in it."

"Hey, we're human."

"Yes, we are." He pointed at my bowl. "And you're a human who hasn't touched her Frosted Flakes."

"Oh." I picked up my spoon and took a bite of cereal.

"So about this football obsession of yours, does the Bible say anything about that?"

"Probably chapters."

"Well, if you're gonna be obsessed, now's the right season to do it. We sure are looking good…"

We talked football until we finished our Frosted Flakes, bid goodnight, and I trudged my way back up the stairs to my room, where Jesus sat waiting for me.

"What can I do for you?" he asked, his face full of concern.

"Tell me what to do. What do I tell my friends? What do I say to Riley?"

"You tell me."

"What?"

"Come on, you know where you need to go to find the answer. Tell me what you're going to do."

Even though I was exhausted, I grabbed the Bible off the nightstand and opened it to the middle of the book.

chapter 19

(Riley)

"Riley." I felt my body shake as I pulled myself out of sleep. "Riley," Dad said as he shook me by the shoulder. "Wake up."

I opened my eyes and gave them a rub. "What's wrong? Attie—"

"Nothing, she's fine. Get dressed and meet me out front."

"Where are we going?"

"You'll see. Come on, get up and get dressed."

He left me alone as I climbed out of bed and threw on some clothes and shoes. I checked on Attie as I walked past her room. She was sound asleep in bed, her ear buds still jammed in her ear canals. She must have fallen asleep listening to worship music. It was her new routine. She felt like the music ensured the nightmares wouldn't come back.

I met my dad on the front porch. "Aren't we going to church? What about Mom?"

"I told your mom what we were doing. She'll meet us in a bit." He threw me the keys and started walking toward his truck. "I just wanted to spend some time alone with you."

"Am I in trouble?"

"No. Do you have to assume that every time I want to talk to you, you're in trouble for something?"

"Yeah. That's usually the case, anyway."

"Not today."

We climbed into the truck. "Where to?" I asked as I stuck the key in the ignition.

"The cemetery."

"The—"

"You heard me."

We made a little small talk while we drove to the cemetery, mostly talking about football. Nothing too serious. I figured we'd have plenty of that once we got there.

"Why are we here?" I asked as we walked up to Melody's headstone.

"Yesterday I realized we haven't been here together since the funeral. Your mom and I come here a lot, but I've never been here with you. I'm sorry about that."

"You don't have to be sorry."

"Well," he said, sitting down, "I am. I'm very sorry."

I sat down next to him. "Okay."

"You know, Attiline said something very profound on Friday night."

"She did?"

"Yep. We were up in the middle of the night eating cereal, talking about the gossip that was going around and trying to figure out what to do about it all."

"Uh-huh."

"And she turned to me and told me that everyone spends so much time worried about her that we don't ever worry about you. We don't ever ask you how you're doing."

"She said that?"

"Yep."

"I guess I hadn't noticed."

"Everything that she goes through, you've gone through. You've had the sleepless nights. You had to deal with the tires being slashed and the rumors."

"None of that was directed at me."

"No, but you still dealt with it all. How are you? I mean, how are you holding up in all this chaos?"

"Well, Attie—"

"No. I don't want you to talk about her. I want you to talk about you. How all this affects you."

I looked over at Melody's headstone. "I hate it."

"Go on."

"I don't understand how people who used to be my friends all of a sudden hate me just because of who I'm dating. I mean, they don't even know her. They never even gave her a chance."

"You're talking about her again. What about you?"

"And I feel weak."

"Weak? Why?"

"Because I can't help. I look at everyone around me, you and Mom and Attie and our friends. And I see all the pain, all the grief, all the crap, and there's nothing I can do to make any of it go away. I feel like I spend all my time putting out these small flames, but in reality there's this huge fire just under the surface, and it feels like it's gonna explode at any second. Like I'm putting Band-aids on a gushing wound."

"Son, nobody expects you to fix anything."

"I know; that's what makes it worse. The irony is that I had almost this exact same talk with Attie. We were sitting right here, and she was telling me how upset she was that she couldn't fill the void that Melody and Mrs. Reed left behind, and I was trying to convince her that it wasn't her job, that she shouldn't feel responsible. But I'm right here, feeling sorta the same way. Then you pile all the other crap up on top … Sometimes it just gets depressing."

He turned to face me. "Riley, it hurts you when people attack Attiline, but it also hurts when people attack you. It hurts that your friends believe the rumor about the abortion. It hurts that your friends would think the worst of you, and you can't be so focused on trying to make Attiline feel better about it that you don't deal with your own feelings. You're allowed to have feelings."

"I'm afraid to."

"Why?"

"Because if I go there, if I let myself feel that pain, I'm afraid it'll bring all the other pain back up too."

"Then that means you haven't dealt with it enough. If your emotions are that close to the surface, then you've still got some healing to do. We all do."

Dad pointed to the headstone. "I look at the date on that headstone, the day that my daughter died, and it feels like it was yesterday. That's how it *feels*. Now, the reality is that it was almost a year and a half ago, and for some reason we think we should have moved on by now. We think we should stop feeling the pain, stop thinking about it all the time, and just get over it and get on with our lives. But you know what? I don't think we ever will, and I think we need to be okay with that. I think you need to be okay with feeling pain. When something upsets you, you need to know that you can tell me or your mom or Attiline, and we're still gonna be okay."

I was on the verge tears and wasn't sure how much longer I could contain them.

"I'm so proud of you," he said.

That was it. The tears flowed.

"I can't even begin to describe how proud I am. I look at everything you've been through and how well you've done, and it practically leaves me speechless. Everything you've done for Attiline, how you've been there for her, even before you were together and when there was no personal gain for you to be doing it. You rose up and helped her heal. That's amazing. And all the stuff going on at school and the way you've handled yourself—Riley, the choices you're making are good ones."

"Attie helps with that."

"I know she does, but she can't make you do something you don't want to do, and she can't keep you from doing something you really want. You're making those decisions based on what you know to be right and what you think is best. What more could any parent ask for?"

"Thank you for saying that."

He reached over and pulled me to him in a bear hug. "I love you, son."

"I love you too."

I heard two car doors shut. We looked toward the road and saw Mom and Attie making their way toward us. Attie was barefoot and in her pajamas.

"I told them to meet us here," Dad said. "I thought we should spend some time here with all four of us together."

Seeing them heading toward us and knowing that this would be the first time the four us were at the cemetery at the same time caused my tears to start falling to the point that I could barely see through them. All the emotion I'd stuffed away, all the denial of what the four of us really had in common—it all erupted.

We stood huddled and crying for a long time, although I'm not sure how long. Long enough that all the crying gave me a headache and I could feel that my eyes were swollen.

Finally, my mom sat on the ground, and the rest of us joined her.

"Riley," Attie said from her spot next to my dad, "do you remember the time Melody and I went walking by the creek at Old Man Travis's house and we found a puppy and came home and told you about it?"

"Yeah. You guys wanted to bring it home, but you were afraid you'd get in trouble."

"Yes."

"Why are you asking?"

"Well, lo and behold, on that very night..."

I shook my head as if to warn her not to tell any more, but she ignored me.

"...a puppy showed up on your back porch, and as soon as your mom saw it, she was in love, and that puppy had a new home."

"Boomer?" Mom asked.

I nodded as Attie continued. "I knew you went back to get Melody that puppy, and I knew you sat out at the creek with it until it got dark and then you snuck up to the back porch and left it there right at dinnertime just so your mom would find it. That's the kind of brother you were ..."

Tears rolled down my cheeks.

"...and that's the brother that Melody always talked about. I would complain about you all the time and talk about how mean you were to me and tell all the hateful things you did to me when I'd visit, but she almost always took your side. It drove me crazy. In her eyes you could do no wrong."

"And your point?" I asked.

"My daddy always told me you can tell how a man's going to treat you by the way he treats his mother and his sisters, if he has them."

"That's true," Mom said with a nod.

"Sitting here looking at Melody's headstone made me remember that story and made me realize why it was so easy for me to fall in love with you. I think I figured that if you treated me anywhere near as well as you did Melody, I'd be very lucky to have you."

"Thanks, babe, but you didn't have to tell me that in front of my parents. That's a little embarrassing, don'cha think?"

"I'm telling you the story so that you'd know that even though Melody never told you, she knew it was you that brought Boomer to the house too. It's another reason she loved you as much as she did. She was crazy about you."

"You two were best friends," Mom said. "We could hardly separate you."

"Yeah, well, I remember the time Riley accidently caught Attiline's hair on fire—"

"That was not an accident, by the way," Attie interrupted.

"Yeah, it was too," I said.

"Was not."

"Was too."

"...and Melody ran over and poured her Kool-Aid in your hair to put the fire out. Your hair was purple for two days."

Mom started laughing. "Or the time Elizabeth found all three of you sitting in the kitchen with marshmallow topping all over yourselves and in your hair."

"It was like the Garden of Eden," I said. "Attie found it in the pantry and told us to try it."

"Sure, go ahead and try to blame it on me, but I didn't make you stick your entire arm in the jar."

"Riley, I had to shave your head completely bald," Mom said. "And Attie, I think your mom cut most of your hair off. We couldn't get that stuff out."

"Why were so many of my mishaps hair related?" Attie asked. "It's a wonder I have any hair left at this point."

We sat at the cemetery straight through church and didn't even notice. We were telling stories about Melody and Mrs. Bennett. It felt good to talk about them in a way that didn't depress us. We were remembering the best and funniest things about them, and just doing that accomplished more healing than a month of counseling ever could have.

chapter 20

It was our first day back since Attie's surgery and finding out what our friends and classmates really thought happened. Walking through the door that morning was as bad as what we could have imagined. A lot of finger pointing, whispering, and laughing, as well as a few gasps. All I could do was hold on to Attie's hand as tightly as possible and lead her through the madness. When I couldn't be with her, one of the other guys made sure to stay close to her side. Curt especially became protective, and for someone who used to take part in the teasing, he was none too thrilled with what people were saying about my girlfriend. While Attie had Tammy who wanted to run out and knock everyone's block off, I had Curt. If given the option, he would've personally seen to it that every person who mentioned the incident would never speak again—about anything.

"Proverbs 19:5. 'A false witness will not go unpunished, and he who pours out lies will not go free.'"

The gang and I sat at the lunch table listening to Attie read from her Bible. It was a strange thing to be doing in the cafeteria, but we'd already all lost our cool label by then, so what did we have to lose if anyone happened to notice?

Attie looked at us for a moment before continuing with another scripture. "This one's a lot like the last one. Proverbs 19:9: 'A false witness will not go unpunished, and he who pours out lies will perish.' Proverbs 20:3: 'It is to a man's honor to avoid strife, but every fool is quick to quarrel.' Proverbs 20:20: 'Do not say, "I'll pay you back for this wrong!" Wait for the Lord, and he will deliver you.' Proverbs 25:15: 'Through patience a ruler can be persuaded, and a gentle tongue can break a bone.' Proverbs 26:20: 'Without wood a fire goes out; without gossip a quarrel dies down.' Proverbs 29:11: 'A fool gives full vent to his anger, but a wise man keeps himself under control.'"

Tammy raised her hand into the air. "Is this your not-so-subtle way of telling me that I'm a fool? 'Cause all of those sound like they're directed at me."

Attie put the Bible back into the backpack as everyone's eyes watched and we waited for a response. "No. I'm talking to all of us, and I don't think any of us are fools. I think we're upset, and we should be. There's such a thing called righteous anger, and I think that's what we have, but I also believe we need to be very careful about how we respond … or if we do."

"So what did you come up with?" I asked. "What are we gonna do?"

"I told you I was going to give this situation a lot of thought and get some counsel—and I did. I also spent hours pouring over the Psalms and Proverbs, and much to my chagrin, there are probably hundreds of scriptures about how to handle an attack from the enemy and only a few of them mention attacking back."

"Well, that stinks," Tammy said. "What did those attacking back scriptures say?"

"To seek guidance first and make sure you're supposed to."

"And I reckon you don't think we're supposed to?" Kent asked.

"Right. No matter what we do, people are going to believe what they want about us. I can't spend any more time worrying about what people think. Those who I care about most in the world know me, and they know I wouldn't do what I'm being accused of." Attie turned and looked straight at me. "And Riley, that goes for you too. Is us going around denying the rumors going to change anyone's mind?"

"So we say nothing?" I asked.

"I didn't say that. I think that if people come right out and ask us, we tell the truth. We don't point fingers, make accusations, or act angry. We just tell the truth. My hope is that those that are truly friends will seek you out and give you a chance to tell the truth before they'd believe what someone else said about you."

"And if they don't?"

"Then how good of a friend were they? If they can't give you the decency to either give you the benefit of the doubt or at least ask, then I don't think they're really a friend."

"So what is the truth?" Anne asked. "I don't even know the whole story."

"Last Sunday morning I found a lump in my chest, so I went to the doctor to have it checked out, and we made the decision to get it removed. That's what I was doing on Thursday morning at the surgery center. Tammy was there; she witnessed the whole thing. I even have the scar I can show you—or at least the girls, anyway."

"You don't have to prove anything to us," Chase said. "Are you okay? What did you find out?"

"It's nothing. It was just a growth, no cancer or anything."

"Well, if we didn't even know, how would anyone else find out?" Jennifer asked.

"Don't look at me. I didn't tell a soul."

"I know you didn't, Tammy. Honestly, I've racked my brain trying to figure it out, and all I can think of is that Riley and I were discussing it in the hallway at school one day and Tiffany was standing not too far away. She must have overheard and taken the conversation completely out of context."

Tammy's head shook wildly. "You're giving her too much credit. She could know the truth and still twist it to suit her needs."

"Well, that's neither here nor there. Again, just as in everything else, we can't prove it was her."

"You look really down. Are you okay?" Tess asked.

"I think I'm just worn out from all the drama. It's the constant bombardment of crap that's been flowing our way. If it isn't a rumor or a slashed tire, it's a cryptic message on my Facebook. There hasn't been a day that's gone by that we haven't heard something else that was said about us or an accusation that we said something or did something to them. Every day I wake up and wonder what in the world they're going to do that day, and for the life of me, I can't figure out why they find any of this necessary. Like they have nothing better to do than sit around and dwell on the fact that Riley's moved on and he's happy. And for some reason, until this, most of the fingers have been pointing in my direction, and I've done nothing but keep my mouth shut and try to go with my life.

"I don't get this whole mentality of 'if you're not one of us, then you're the enemy, and we'll do whatever we have to do to take you down, and that includes lying to anyone that will listen.' It isn't enough to stir up a little trouble; they think it's necessary to absolutely destroy people. When you're dealing with people with that mind-set, no matter what you try to say, they aren't going to believe it."

I finally spoke up. "The more I think about it, Attie's right. If we just keep our mouths shut, eventually they'll dig their own graves and the truth'll come out. I may be forty when it finally happens, but it'll happen. They're too stupid to pull this thing off long term."

"And here's the thing," Anne said. "Even if it doesn't look like they're being punished for what they're doing, they are. Just look at the way they act. Nobody that's truly happy with and likes himself or herself acts like that. They may act like they're happy, but I'm willing to bet that deep down inside, they know they're total screw-ups and that if people knew them for what they really were, they wouldn't have any friends at all."

"I don't agree," Attie said. "Not with all of that anyway. I think they're just like the rest of us. They've got issues, and they try to hide them because they're afraid that if anyone knew they wouldn't be friends with them."

"That's what I just said," Anne huffed.

"I'm not done. But the reality is that everyone would like them a lot better if they'd just be themselves and quit putting on the show.

They put on the show in order to hide their true selves, but their true selves aren't any different than the rest of us."

"My head is spinning," Tammy said. "Look, I'm not gonna sit here and try to figure those whack jobs out. Their minds are very dark, and once you get in there, you may not come back out."

"I'm trying to have some compassion for them," Attie mumbled. "I've got to do something to keep myself from being completely overcome with hate."

"I think compassion is a bit much. Why don't you just think of contempt and then dial it back a bit to feeling slightly less than contempt."

"I don't know, Tammy. I'm just going to have to forgive them. They'll never admit they did anything wrong; all I can do is forgive them and move on."

"Gross."

"I didn't say I had to like them or be their friend. My only responsibility is to forgive them."

"And you can do that?" Tammy asked.

"What choice do I have? If I don't, they win. If I don't forgive them, then I end up dwelling on it all the time; and if I give them an ounce of my time or attention, they win. They don't deserve a thought, let alone any of my energy. So this is it. I'm drawing the line; no matter what they do, I'm not going to give it a second thought. Anyway, how much worse could it get?"

Tammy threw her hands over her ears. "Don't say that out loud. It's like you're tempting the evil powers or something. As soon as you say 'what could be worse,' something worse happens."

"True. I take it back. They could do worse; I just won't give it any attention if they do."

Kent stood up and grabbed our trash off the table. "Let's go, guys; we gotta get to class."

We piled out of our chairs, followed him into the hallway, and ended up passing Rick, Wes, Tiffany, and clan in the hallway.

As soon as I spotted them, my arm instinctively wrapped around Attie's waist.

"Who knows, Tiffany," Wes said with an obnoxious laugh, "maybe you'll get lucky enough to barely survive some tragic accident so that you can have a sob story too. Maybe you can get as many sympathy friends as Attie gets."

I started to lunge for him, but Attie held me back. Before I could react, and in what seemed like the blink of an eye, Tammy had Wes on the floor, punching him in the face repeatedly. Students stood cheering as she waylaid on him, and he screamed in horror and tried to cover his face with his arms.

I enjoyed the fact that he screamed like a girl.

His friends didn't bother stepping in to help him, so I finally raced in and tried to pry her off of him.

Words spewed out of her mouth so quickly that I could hardly identify them, but I did recognize a few that I'd have been grounded for if Dad or Mom heard me repeat.

As soon as I grabbed her, Kent ran in to help me restrain her. We each grabbed an arm and pulled her off Wes, and as we did, her legs flailed at him. Unfortunately for Wes, one of her very powerful kicks landed in the "sweet spot," and he was left curled up in the fetal position with his hands between his legs.

I couldn't be sure, but I think I heard him cry for his mommy.

Tammy was still screaming when Dad and several teachers scrambled in to break up the commotion.

"Tammy!" Dad yelled. "Calm yourself down this instant."

Her spirited legs finally calmed, and I set her down and removed my hands from her waist.

Wes slowly stood up, regained his footing, and wiped blood from under his nose. "Get that wench away from me. She's completely insane."

Within seconds, Tammy was assailing him again, and this time it took several adults to pry her fingers from around his neck. By the time she'd finished with him, Wes had claw marks carved in the skin on his face and neck.

I felt almost jovial watching the spectacle and would have joined in on the cheering if it wouldn't have gotten me in major trouble with my principal slash father.

As two teachers restrained Tammy, Dad straightened his shirt. "Get her to my office." He looked over at the rest of us. "All of you to the office. Right now."

"Dad—"

"Riley," he screamed, "get to my office."

"Yes, sir." I placed my hand on the small of Attie's back and led her down the hallway as Tiffany, Rick, Wes, and Kent followed behind. I didn't remove it until we were sitting safely in Dad's office. I watched as he paced in front of the window.

"What in Sam Hill was that out there?"

"Wes, would you like to share with Mr. Bennett the nice comment that you made just before I kicked your—"

"Watch it, Tammy," Dad interrupted.

"Since you were so proud of yourself when you said it, I'm sure you'll have no problem retelling it now," she added.

Wes stared at his feet and said nothing.

The room was silent as Dad took a moment to eye each of us sitting in front of him. Then he picked up the phone, pushed a button, and waited for the person on the other end to answer. "Mrs. Fields, could you please join me in my office? Thank you."

Silence again as we waited for the assistant principal.

The door opened, and a brown-haired woman poked her head into the room. "Yes, Mr. Bennett?"

"Could you please join us in the conference room?" he asked. "Unfortunately, this incident includes my son and Attie, so I don't wanna be accused of preferential treatment in any way."

"Of course, Mr. Bennett." Mrs. Field snapped her fingers several times before telling all of us to meet them in the conference room.

We stood in a single file line and marched out of his office through the reception area and into the conference room.

"Keep Wes and Tammy separated," Dad quietly suggested to his subordinate. "She may not be finished with him yet."

We sat around the conference table, and before Dad or Mrs. Fields could get a word out, Attie stood.

"I'd like to say something."

"Yes, Attie?" Dad asked. It was the first time I'd ever heard him call her Attie.

"I wasn't involved in this particular incident, but for some reason I seem to be the cause of everything that led up to it."

Glancing over at Tiffany, I noticed a small grin sweep across her face, and I had to fight the urge to reach across the table and knock it right back off.

Attie hadn't noticed and continued talking. "Mr. Bennett, I know you're aware of a lot of the things that have gone on over the last few months: the uniform situation, the refusal by fellow squad members to follow my lead, my tires being slashed, the rumors. Really, I could go on and on."

"Yes, I'm aware." His eyes momentarily rested on Tiffany, and then he looked back at Attie.

"I'd asked my friends to ignore all of it, not to respond or retaliate in any way, and up until today, they hadn't. Tammy's a great friend, and I think that hearing what Wes said was the last straw. She ended up taking it out on him all at one time. She wasn't really thinking clearly."

"I appreciate that, Attie, but Tammy is responsible for her own actions."

"I realize that, but I'm asking you to take into account all that she *hasn't* done. Let's be blunt; she could've done a lot worse a lot more often."

Everyone but Tiffany and her clan laughed at the remark.

"I think Tammy's shown amazing restraint given the circumstances."

Dad nodded and motioned for Attie to sit back down.

"One more thing?" she asked.

Dad nodded again before Attie turned and faced Tiffany. "I surrender," she said, holding up her hands at her side. "I can't let this go on anymore. If my being a part of the squad causes you to go through this much trouble to bring me down, then I surrender. It isn't fair to the squad or the rest of the students to have to go through all the drama."

Although Tiffany stared down at her lap, she sat with the same grin plastered on her face. My blood was boiling.

"My dad sent me here to try out for the squad because he thought it would be a great way for me to make friends, and he thought that cheering would bring me some joy. Unfortunately, that isn't how it's been. Joining the team has done nothing but complicate my life more. It isn't fun for me, and I'd dare say it probably isn't much fun for anyone else. So I quit. You win. You can have it all. Trust me, I don't want it—the price for everyone else is too high."

"Attie," Dad interrupted, "are you sure you don't wanna give this more thought?"

"I've given it plenty of thought. There isn't a doubt in my mind that this is the right thing to do. I'm hoping it will stop the war." She looked back at Dad and waited for his response.

"I guess if your mind is made up—"

"It is."

"There isn't anything I can say to change it?"

"No, sir."

"All right then. You need to let Coach Tyler know about your decision."

"Yes, sir."

"Why don't you go ahead and get home? As you said, you weren't a part of this particular incident."

"Yes, sir." Attie made her way around the table and to the door before stopping and facing Tiffany one more time. "I gave in on the squad issue in hopes that it would end all of this nonsense, but if you think that by continuing your tactics that I'll eventually give up Riley as well, you're pitifully mistaken. That's one fight I won't lose."

Hearing the fire in her voice was mind blowing. I wanted to jump over the table and grab her into my arms.

She continued. "You can rest assured that all your accusations against us have done nothing but bring us closer together and make our bond that much stronger. From what I can tell, any chance of the two of you being together was over the second I pulled into his driveway. You've been trying to fight a battle you lost a long time ago. Riley made his choice, and it wasn't you, so get over it."

And with that, my girlfriend bounded out the door, leaving the rest of us in awe.

I glanced back at Tiffany and noticed that the haughty grin had evaporated.

Dad and the assistant principal gave the traditional "appalled and disappointed" speech, and even though it was mostly aimed at Tiffany and her clan, Tammy got a few glares too. I spent the entire lecture wondering why in the world I had to sit through it. I was the one who stopped the fight; I should have gotten a pat on the back and permission to leave with Attie.

"Anything anyone would like to say for themselves?"

The room stayed silent.

"Wes, what do you think should be done with Tammy?"

"She should be kicked out of school," he barked.

"So you don't wanna accept any responsibility for this?"

"Why should I? I didn't do anything wrong."

"You didn't say what you've been accused of saying?"

"Yeah, I said it, but this is a free country, and I can say what I want to say. I can't help it if people get their feelings hurt. That's their problem, not mine."

Dad shook his head in disgust. "Rick? Tiffany? Anything you wanna add?"

They didn't respond.

I couldn't take their smug attitudes any longer. "I've got something I wanna say."

"Go ahead," Dad said. "But watch it."

"Yes, sir."

I stared straight at Rick, the ringleader of the group. Even though Tiffany did most of the dirty work, I knew he was just as involved in all the behind-the-scenes action as she was, and he was her number one encourager.

"The problem you have with Attie isn't that she got the captain spot or that her popularity is growing or that she's dating me. Your problem with Attie is that she doesn't wanna be one of you. You can't stand it that someone has the nerve not to fawn all over you. And since she won't lower herself to act like you, it makes you feel guilty for acting the way you do. It's okay as long as everyone acts the same way—you think it's excusable. But when someone actually sees it for what it is and opts out, it ticks you off.

"I used to be one of you. Remember? We spent a lotta time together, and unlike most of the other people in this school, I've seen you for what you really are. I've been behind the scenes. I've heard the talk, and I've seen the way you act when you think nobody's watching. Not only am I not impressed, I'm disgusted with myself for ever being a part of it, and I'm thankful I got out when I did.

"While you've been trying to cause us all these problems, we could have played dirty—as dirty as you have—but we didn't. And we didn't 'cause Attie didn't want to. She didn't think that retaliation or defending ourselves was worth it 'cause it would only prolong the war.

"Don't think that our silence was a signal of our defeat. You can't lose a war that you weren't a part of. We walked away from every battle you threw our way not 'cause we couldn't defend ourselves but 'cause we chose not to. You weren't worth the effort.

"Attie is choosing to give up her position on the team not 'cause she's weak but 'cause she's strong enough to make the choice to do what's best for the team as a whole. She realizes that all the drama isn't good for anyone."

I finally looked at Tiffany. "I'll be willing to guess that she'll even cover your butt when she steps down. And that, Tiffany, is the sign of a true leader. You should try taking some notes."

"Enough, Riley," Dad said sternly. "I think they get the point."

"I doubt that," Tammy said.

"Tiffany, Wes, Rick, Kent, and Riley, get on home. None of you are allowed to go to your respective sports practices today. I want you to go straight home too, do you hear me? I'll make sure your coaches know not to expect you. Tammy, you stay put."

I gave the clan time to leave the room before giving Tammy a hug. "Good luck."

"Don't worry about me. Whatever your dad does to me is worth the butt kicking I got to give today."

Dad cleared his throat. "I wouldn't say that in front of me if I were you. Go on, Riley," he snapped. "Get on home."

I ran out of the room and headed home to Attie. When I arrived, she was working on her homework in the side yard. She'd laid a blanket on the ground and was lying on her stomach writing in a notebook.

She looked up as she heard me approach. "How'd it go? What's Tammy's punishment?"

I stood several feet away. "I don't know. I had to leave before he told her."

"Are you all right? You look agitated."

"Come here," I requested.

She lifted herself up until she was on her knees. "Why, what's wrong?"

"Nothing, just come here."

She jumped to her feet and made her way toward me. "You're scaring me. What's the matter?"

As soon as she was within my reach, I placed my hand on the back of her neck and pulled her to me. "I've never felt more incredible than how you made me feel today."

The skin between her eyebrows crinkled. "When?"

"When you told Tiffany that you wouldn't give me up."

She laughed. "That?"

All I could do was nod.

"Well, it probably doesn't come close to how you make me feel every day. It's the least I can do. And besides, it's true. I won't give you up. Not for anybody."

chapter 21

(Attie)

Surrendering my position from the squad seemed to have succeeded. The harassment stopped for the most part, and other than a few nasty glances from Tiffany every once in a while, I was left almost completely alone by the juicers.

The abortion story quickly lost steam. Several of Riley's friends and most of the girls on the squad sought out the truth, and once we had the opportunity to tell what really happened, the truth began to win out over the gossip. Jesus had been right. We'd done what he said and didn't try to defend ourselves. Our choice not to get in God's way left him the ability to bring the truth to light, and our plan worked so well that even Tammy had to admit that no defense was the best defense of all.

What was meant to cause us pain and isolation actually ended up causing people more concern for us. When we told people what the surgery was really for, they were genuinely worried. It felt as if we became more likeable in people's eyes rather than unlikeable.

Homecoming arrived, and I watched from afar as the cheerleading squad decorated the football players' lockers and hung banners in the stadium. I went in to say hello before the game started but missed them. They'd already left the locker room.

Just before I turned off the light, I heard crying from behind the last row of lockers. It wasn't a quiet little cry; it was a heartbreaking sob. Glancing around, I noticed that I was the only person in the room other than the person who was obviously distraught, and I wasn't sure if I should check on her or just leave her alone. Eventually the fear that the person was hurt won out, and I followed the wailing until I spotted her.

Of all people ...

"Tiffany? Are you all right?"

As soon as she turned and saw it was me, her cries got heavier. "Go away."

"Do you need me to get you a doctor or something? Are you hurt?"

"No."

My feet wanted to move away from her, but my spirit wouldn't let me. "Is there anything I can do to help?" I asked the question while at the same time I wanted to slap myself for being so ridiculous.

"Like you'd ever help me." She turned away from me. "Just leave me alone, Attie."

I wanted to do as she said. Oh, how I desperately wanted to leave her alone. I just couldn't.

"I don't think I should—leave you alone."

"Why?"

"Because you sound hurt."

"I already told you I'm not hurt. Not physically anyway. There's nothing you can do to help."

"Look, Tiffany, I realize that I'm pretty much your mortal enemy; but if you need to talk, I'm willing to listen."

She remained silent, and finally, after several seconds of no response, I turned to go.

"He didn't come," she whispered.

I turned back to her. "What?"

"My dad." She sniffled. "He was supposed to escort me for homecoming. He said he'd be here and then called and cancelled a little while ago."

"Oh." I walked over and sat on the bench next to hers. "Does he live here in town?"

"No. He lives in Dallas."

"Your parents are divorced?"

"Yes."

"May I ask why he didn't come?"

"His new girlfriend has some party or something. She's practically my age. Heck, he could be going to *her* homecoming."

"Really?"

"No. I think she's in her early twenties or something."

"What about a stepdad? Do you have a stepdad that could escort you?"

"I have a stepdad, but he's number three."

"Number three?"

"My third stepfather, and we aren't close."

"What about your mom?"

"She can't make it."

"I'm sorry." I lay back and balanced myself on the bench. "Dads sure can suck sometimes, can't they?"

"Yes." She wiped her nose on a towel. "He doesn't really want anything to do with me. He's moved on with his life, and I don't fit in the picture."

"I know that feeling all too well."

"You do?" She seemed shocked at my admission.

"Coming to Oklahoma was supposed to be a new start for my dad and me—since my mom died."

"What happened?"

"He sent me here early. He was going to come at the end of the summer, but one week before he was supposed to show up, he called and said he wasn't coming. He'd actually never planned on coming. Never bought the house like he said he did, nothing. He just wasn't coming."

"Why didn't you go back to New York? Was it because of Riley?"

"No. My dad didn't want me to go back. He flat out didn't want me at all. It was too painful to have me around—or so he said."

"So that's why you live with Riley's family, because your dad doesn't want you?"

"Pretty much. My Gramps lives in the back of the vet clinic, so he doesn't have any room for me, and I have no place else to go. I'm lucky the Bennetts let me live with them, especially after everything that happened with Melody. I don't know what else I would do. I would have nowhere else to go."

"I didn't realize…" She turned silent for a few minutes. "You seem happy at the Bennetts'," she finally said.

"I am. But I'd give it all up if I could have a father that actually loved me enough to want me with him."

"Had you and your dad been close before your mom died?"

"Very close."

"My dad and I were never close. He left when I was five."

"Oh?"

"He left my mom for my babysitter."

"Your babysitter?" I practically tipped off of the bench, I was so stunned. "You've got to be kidding me."

"I wish. My mom caught them together one day when he was supposed to be at work. She came home early, and there they were, kissing on the couch."

"Where were you?"

"My brother and I were watching television or something. I don't really remember much about it."

"That's good, I guess."

"The only thing I remember is that he left that night and didn't come back. Ever. He never came back."

"Not even for a visit?"

"No. He sends birthday cards and Christmas gifts, and he sends me tons of money and stuff, but if I want to see him, I have to go to him."

"When was the last time you saw him?"

"Two years ago. When I went to visit, he never actually spent time with me. Whatever girl he was dating at the time usually got stuck watching me while he was at work or out with his friends. I got tired of going and coming back upset every time. It's easier this way."

"But you went ahead and asked him to escort you for homecoming?"

"To him, importance comes from being pretty and popular and powerful. It's status. He's even on Facebook and has over one thousand friends. Everything's a popularity thing for him, and everything's about image. I think that's why he keeps getting younger and more beautiful girlfriends. I thought maybe if he knew I was on the homecoming court he would think—"

"You were worthy of his time?"

She nodded.

"And of his love." It was a statement for me as much as it was for her. I knew exactly how that felt.

"Yes," she whispered as she lay back onto the bench.

Trying to forget who I was talking to, I closed my eyes. "My mom used to tell me that when I was little, I would stack five or six magazines on top of each other and then stand on top of them, wait for my dad to count to three, and then I would jump off and take a bow. Neither one of us could get enough. I couldn't get enough attention from him, and he couldn't give enough. He'd tell me how amazing I was, how beautiful I looked, how talented I was. There's no telling what all he said, and I believed every word of it. I believed that he truly saw me that way. For years, having my daddy tell me I was beautiful and special was it for me, my pinnacle. Then suddenly I wasn't those things to him anymore. I'm not those things, not to him, anyway."

"But you're those things to Riley, or at least it seems like it. I've never seen him act like this over a girl."

"To some extent, I guess that's true. To Riley, I've practically hung the moon, and I feel the same way about him. But one thing I've learned through all of this dad stuff is that we can't walk around getting our value from some guy. People are human, and they change their minds or they make horrible choices. Our worth can't be left hanging out there depending on what some fickle person thinks about us.

"Just by the very nature of our dads' relation to us, they should think we're the most amazing things ever; but for some reason they don't, and it hurts. It seems to go against nature and all that God had in mind for families, but it's our reality, and our reality, in this particular area, stinks."

"Tell me about it."

"When I found out my dad wasn't coming, that he didn't want me, I nearly lost my mind. Literally almost lost my mind. If Joshua hadn't knocked me out and I would have actually tried to process it right then, I probably would have gone comatose. I still haven't really gone there and thought about it. I'm afraid to. I'm afraid of the damage it will do to me if I really let it sink in."

"So how do you keep from dwelling on it?"

"It would sound weird to you."

"Try me. I want to hear."

"For every negative thought I have about myself, I've written out a scripture from the Bible that tells me the truth. And the truth is always opposite of what I've told myself."

"How can that be enough?"

"What other choice do I have? If those things aren't true, then what's the point? But, if the Bible is true and God is real, then the Creator of the universe and everything on it and in it and everything that has ever been and will ever be sees me as beautiful and worthy . . . and sees *you* as beautiful and worthy. If he thinks that, doesn't that make it so?"

I looked over and saw her shrug.

"I choose to believe we're worthy, you and me. No matter what our dads or some guy may think. We're pretty darned awesome, and they're missing out if they don't see that."

"I need to choose to believe that too," she whispered.

We lay on our respective benches in silence for several minutes as we processed the conversation. Tiffany had stopped crying, but when I glanced at her again, it was obvious she was still upset.

"You know," I said, "it's unfair that kids get stuck having to suffer the consequences for their parents' problems and crappy choices.

Like we don't have enough problems of our own, we've got to worry about theirs too."

"That's for sure."

"I don't know what it is that allows a parent to cut off all feelings for their kids and act like they don't exist."

"It's selfishness," she said.

"I guess you're right. That's probably exactly what it is."

"They want what they want, and they don't care who they have to hurt to get it—even if it's their own kid."

"It's sick," I said.

"And twisted," she added.

"So then we're sick—"

"And twisted."

As we laughed at our predicament, the air in the room seemed to lighten, and the tension drifted away. We were simply two girls, each having our own issues and trying to figure out how to survive in a difficult and selfish world—trying to survive without their dads.

"I overheard your conversation and misunderstood." Her comment came out of nowhere and caught me off guard.

"What conversation?"

"I heard Riley say that he didn't agree with you having surgery but that it was your body and he'd go along with whatever you decided."

"Oh."

"I assumed—"

"You assumed wrong."

"I think part of me was happy to find out you weren't actually perfect, that you made a mistake."

I couldn't help but laugh. "You thought I was perfect before that?"

"Pretty much."

"I'm so far from perfect—you have no idea. Perfect and I are millions of miles apart."

"It doesn't seem that way."

"Nobody's perfect, Tiffany. Surely you know that."

"Well, some people sure do seem more perfect than others."

"They just hide their crap better," I said.

"Riley seems to think you're perfect."

"I think he sees us as perfect for *each other* more than he sees *me* as perfect. Trust me, he knows what a screw-up I am. He probably knows it better than anyone else."

"It must be nice to have someone who loves you for who you really are."

"When Riley and I first saw each other this summer, I was a person who'd been completely stripped of everything I thought I was or believed. All I had was the real me—the hurt, scared, lonely me. There was no show. I didn't pretend to be something I wasn't, and it wasn't so much because I knew better; it was because I couldn't. I was so exhausted from life that I couldn't have put on a show for him if my life depended on it. He literally got a no makeup, hair in a mess, sweatshirt and sweatpants wearing, up at night screaming, neurotic, scarred girl who'd lost most everyone she'd ever loved. I was a complete mess."

"Sounds so appealing," she teased.

"Doesn't it? I was a catch; what can I say?"

"What on earth did that boy see in you?"

"I have no idea. Honestly, I have no idea."

"I do," she whispered. "You're a good girl."

I groaned.

"I don't mean that in a bad way. I mean that you're a good person; that would be attractive to most people—even to people who want to hate you. Maybe that's why they do."

"Because I'm good?"

"Because they aren't—we aren't."

"None of us are. We can try to be good and we can make the right choices, but when it boils down to it, none of us are inherently good."

"Okay, then. You're good-er."

"I'll take 'good-er,' only 'cause it'll shut you up."

"Thank you for that."

"So who are you going to have escort you?" I asked.

"Nobody. I'm on my own."

"Surely we can think of someone to do it."

"Who?"

"Riley would do it if I asked him."

Tiffany almost fell off the bench. "Riley? You'd ask Riley to escort me?" She sat up, swung her legs over the side of the bench, and leaned toward me. "You would do that? For me?"

"Sure. Well, for you and for the amusement of the entire school."

"That's really cool of you."

I sat up and faced her. "You have no idea, Tiffany. I'm a very cool person," I teased.

"I'm starting to see that." Her voice sounded sincere, and for some reason having her act so nice was making me feel uncomfortable.

"We better get out to the game. They're going to realize that we're both missing and think we've killed each other. I'll go track down Riley and tell him what he'll be doing during halftime."

"You go on out. I'm going to freshen up a bit."

"All right." I hopped off the bench and started for the exit.

"Attie?"

I turned to face her.

"I'm about to tell you something that I'll completely deny if you ever repeat."

"Okay." I braced myself for some earth-shattering news.

"I thought it was awesome the way Tammy kicked Wes's butt. It made my year—you have no idea how many times I've wanted to do the very same thing. He can be such a jerk to everyone around him."

"I think it made a lot of people's year." I turned to go again.

"And Attie?"

I turned around again.

"Thanks for listening. I know I didn't deserve to have you be so nice."

"We all deserve to have people be nice to us Tiffany, even you." I laughed.

"Go on," she encouraged. "I'll be out in a minute."

As I walked out of the locker room, part of me was in shock that Tiffany and I had a conversation. The other part of me worried that the entire thing had been an act and she would somehow use all the information she'd gathered against me. I'd have to wait to see which it was.

I knocked on the football locker room door and waited for someone to answer. Soon, one of the trainers stuck his head out.

"Yeah?"

"I need to see Riley Bennett please. It's a minor emergency."

• •

Joshua, Nicole, Riley's parents, Tammy, and I sat on the first row of stadium seats and watched as the homecoming court and their escorts made their way out of the tunnel. When I asked Riley to escort Tiffany, he'd told me he thought I'd "officially taken the train to crazy town," so I wasn't sure whether or not I'd see the two of them actually walk out together. I was thrilled when they emerged together, and as soon as people realized who was walking beside Tiffany, the rumbling of hushed voices began. Gasps, chuckles, and questions flowed toward the field in such a downpour that it caused Riley and Tiffany to stop dead in their tracks.

It was obvious by the look on Riley's face as he walked across the field that he still wasn't happy with the request I'd made, but he dutifully accepted it just the same and was managing to be a good sport about it all.

I hoped that he'd thank me for it one day, and I further hoped that Tiffany would prove to have been worth it.

Jesus had been right. Taking the higher road had left me feeling far better than drudging in the mud along with my enemies ever would have.

For the first time in a very long time, I felt free.

chapter 22

The next morning Riley and I sat on the couch across from Joshua and Nicole. Even with her sitting, I could see a small baby bump. Doing the math in my head, it seemed a little early to start showing, but who was I to know? I wasn't a doctor—yet.

"There are two in there," Joshua announced. He must have noticed my stare.

"What?"

"Twins." Nicole laughed. "All that wait and praying for a baby, and God turns around and gives us two at once. Can you believe it?"

"That totally sounds like something God would do." I was in awe of his wonderful blessing. He couldn't have given a more precious gift to a more deserving couple. "Hear that, Riley? We're going to be babysitting twins."

"Twins are special," Riley muttered. "They'll always be close."

The room went silent as we all realized that Riley was thinking about his sister.

I grabbed his hand and gave it a squeeze. "If they're anything like you and Melody, then they better watch out." I turned my attention to Joshua and Nicole. "Riley and Melody were quite a team, and they could do some serious damage if you left them alone too long."

Nicole laughed. "I'll be sure to stay on alert."

Riley cleared his throat and sat forward on the sofa. "We need to get on with our session 'cause Charlie and I have gotta get ready for the dance."

"What dance?" I asked the question even though I knew exactly what dance he was referring to.

"Homecoming, of course."

I looked over at Nicole. "We won."

"We did."

A scowl grew on Joshua's face. "Way to go and blow it for me, Riley."

"Blow what?"

I pulled my hand away and reached over to give Nicole a high five. "I told you it would be today and not a second before. I had a feeling."

"You were right. I'm glad I took your side on the bet instead of Joshua's."

"What's today and not a second before?" Riley asked. "What bet?"

"You just lost me twenty bucks," Joshua announced.

"How did I lose you twenty bucks?"

"I figured you'd clue in long before today, my friend."

I slapped Riley on the leg. "We aren't going to any dance."

"Huh? Why not?"

"You didn't ask me."

"What? Yes, I did."

"No, you didn't."

He turned to face me and crossed his legs in front of him. I did the same.

"Charlie, I asked you to homecoming."

"No, you did not."

His face was full of confusion. "I could have sworn..." He shook his head and looked over at Joshua for help.

"Don't look at me. You made this mess; you dig yourself out."

A glance toward Nicole didn't help him either. She only pursed her lips and slowly shook her head in mock disgust.

"You're my girlfriend," he said, looking back at me. "You're wearing the ring I gave you."

I shrugged.

"We live together, for cryin' out loud. Of course I'd assume we'd go to homecoming together."

"That was your first mistake. You assumed."

Joshua laughed. "You know what they say about assuming."

Riley ignored the teasing and kept his eyes on me. "Are you serious right now? You aren't going to the dance with me?"

"Riley, you didn't ask me."

He stared at me in complete disbelief. "But—"

"I don't care if you're married, old, and crippled; you've still got to ask a girl on a date. Your mom was right. You've gotten lazy."

"Oh dear Lord, you got my mom involved in this?"

"She's the one that warned me that boys get lazy. I didn't think you would, but good grief, was I wrong."

"I didn't get lazy, I just—"

"How could you forget to ask? Do you not think about me?"

"I think about you all the time!" He looked over at Joshua in a panic. "Josh, help me out here."

"He does think about you all the time. I can verify that much."

"And ninety-five percent of the time I'm thinking about you, it's stuff that I'm allowed to think about, so I'm not even screwing that up."

"I guess that's nice to know."

"You're seriously not going to the dance with me?"

"You didn't ask me."

"I'm asking you now."

"I didn't hear an invite. Did you, Nicole? Did you hear an invite?"

"No, I didn't hear an invite. I heard more of a telling than an invite."

He looked at the mother-to-be and rolled his eyes before scooting toward me and picking up my hands. "Charlie, I'm sorry I forgot to ask. And I'm sorry I assumed that we were going together. But will you please, please go to the homecoming dance with me?"

"That's very sweet of you, Riley."

He finally grinned.

"But no." The grin slipped right back off his face. "If you want to go out with me, you have to ask more than a few hours in advance. I've already made plans."

"What?" he shrieked.

"I have. I'm sorry." I pulled my hands away and gave his cheeks a pat. "And as a matter of fact, I've got to get home and change clothes. I'm leaving in less than an hour."

"Where on earth are you going?"

"To Stillwater with Gramps. He's going to show me around the campus, and then we're going to the game. OU's not playing tonight, so I might as well go watch the Cowboys."

"Are you feeling okay?" he asked.

"I'm feeling fine. I mean, if I'm going to go to vet school there, I might as well get used to it a little bit at a time." I got up off the couch, gave Nicole and Joshua a hug, and started toward the door.

"Okay, I get it," Riley announced. "Ha ha. Funny joke. You all taught me a lesson. Charlie, I'll never take you for granted again and assume that you'll go out with me. Are you happy now?"

I threw my hands on my hips and scowled.

"You had me going until you said you were going to a Cowboys' game. That would never happen in a million years. Now, I've got my tux in the car. Let's get you home so you can get in your dress, and let's get to the dance."

"Riley! We aren't going to the dance. I don't have a dress."

He stood in silent shock.

"Your mother and I didn't go dress shopping because you never asked me to the freakin' dance, and even if I wanted to go with you now, she wouldn't let me because you didn't ask until today."

"But my mother loves me."

"She loves me more."

His jaw dropped.

"Well, not really. But asking me the day of the dance is completely disrespectful, and if I wasn't so in love with you, I'd break up with you right this instant. Now you better not say another word or I really will break up with you just because of your stupidity. You went and screwed up. Accept it and let's move on."

"Fine!"

"Fine!" I stomped toward the door, threw it open, and walked out and down the sidewalk. Within seconds, Riley was running up behind me.

"Wait, what time do you think you'll be home?"

"I don't know. Eleven or so. Why?"

He grabbed my hand and stopped me. "I'll wait up for you, okay?"

"You don't have to do that."

"But still, I'll wait up." It was obvious he was worried. He placed his hand on my neck and traced my jawline with his thumb. "Charlie, are we okay?"

"We're okay. This isn't a big deal. It's just a dance."

"I love you. I'm sorry I messed up."

My point had been made, and he'd suffered enough. I couldn't let him worry anymore. Standing on my tippy toes, I grinned before giving him a small kiss. His body relaxed instantly as he wrapped his arms around me.

"I'll make this up to you, I promise."

chapter 23

"Atticus." I felt Gramps lightly tap my cheek. "Atticus, we're almost there. Time to wake up."

I opened my eyes a bit and then closed them right back. "What time is it?"

"Almost midnight."

I felt the truck lurch to a stop, and without even bothering to open my eyes, I felt around for the door handle, gave it a pull, opened the door, grabbed my socks and shoes off the seat, and climbed out of the cab. "Goodnight, Gramps. See you at church in the morning."

"Good night, princess."

Picturing the Bennett house in my mind, I blindly walked toward the porch steps, but even after several steps my feet never found them. I opened my eyes and realized I wasn't even at the Bennetts' house. In a panic, I turned to get back in the truck, but Gramps had already pulled away.

It was extremely dark, and I was all alone.

Squinting into the darkness, I realized I was in the park. I could barely make out the merry-go-round just a few feet away. Not knowing what else to do and too tired to start walking home, I stumbled to the floating metal disc and took a seat.

Naturally, I worried about Gramps. Had he suddenly gone senile? I hadn't seen any other signs, but confusing a house and a park were pretty serious mix-ups. And it had been his suggestion to take me to the OSU game—maybe he had gone senile!

Finally waking up fully, I remembered my cell phone, pulled it out of my sweatshirt pocket, and dialed Riley's number. Hopefully, he was waiting up for me, just like he said he would.

A split second after pushing the send button, I heard a phone ring behind me.

"I wondered how long it would take you to call," a voice said in the darkness.

The merry-go-round turned until I was sitting in front of a smiling Riley.

"What are you doing here?"

"Waiting for you."

His phone was still ringing, so I pushed the cancel button and shoved the phone back into my pocket. "How'd you know I would be here?"

"I arranged it."

"How?"

"I called Gramps as soon as you left Joshua and Nicole's."

"Why on earth would you want to meet me out here in the middle of the night?"

"We've got a homecoming dance to make up for."

"We do?"

"Yep."

"And just how do you think we're going to accomplish that tonight?"

"Hold that thought." He jogged into the darkness and out of sight.

Within moments, small white lights filled the night sky. I closed my eyes and gave them a rub before opening them and refocusing on my surroundings. Christmas lights were wrapped around the swing set and draped over the play fort. The vision was stunning.

"You did this?"

"I did." He walked toward me again; this time he held two items in his hand. He gave the merry-go-round a kick, causing it to start turning, and then jumped on and made his way to the middle. "Join me please."

My heart fluttered as I stood and carefully walked to the middle of the slowly turning sphere.

"I want to ask you a question," he announced.

"You aren't going to ask me to marry you, are you?"

"Not yet."

"All right then. What?"

"I know this is very late notice, but we've got a dance starting in a couple of minutes or so."

"We do?"

"Yep."

"Oh."

"Will you go with me?"

"I don't know if I'm allowed. See, Marme has this rule—"

He held a finger to my lips to silence me and then tucked something shiny up under his arm, grabbed a piece of paper out of his front pocket, and handed it to me. "Here, read this."

I unfolded the paper and held it up so I could read it in the little bit of light that illuminated the playground.

"Read it out loud," he said.

"'I hereby give Atticus Reed permission to go with Riley Bennett to the Second Chance Homecoming Dance. Molly Bennett.'"

"See, you're allowed to go with me."

"How'd you manage to get permission?"

"I blamed it all on my dad."

"You blamed Pops for the fact that you forgot to ask me to the dance?"

"I sure did. Mom and I figured that if he'd raised me right, I woulda known better than to screw up so bad; seeing as how he failed to instruct me properly, I got a pass for just this once."

"Poor Pops."

"He'll get over it. But as his punishment, Mom made him help me hang the lights. So … " He grinned. "Will you go with me?"

I glanced around at the hard work he'd put into decorating. "How could I possibly say no to all this?"

"I was hoping you'd say that." Out of nowhere, he presented a corsage. "First things first. You have to wear this. All girls wear these things to fancy dances."

"We're wearing jeans. What's so fancy about that?"

"Use your imagination please. I know you've got one."

"Oh, sorry. Then I'm wearing an amazing crimson dress."

"I knew you would be, so of course I got the flower to match."

Fearful he might accidently stab me with the needle, I held my breath as he carefully pinned the corsage to my sweatshirt.

"It matches my hat," I announced.

"Funny you should mention that." He reached up, slipped the ball cap off my head, and dropped it onto the ground.

"Wait, I've got hat hair."

"It looks fine." He reached under his arm and pulled out the object he'd placed there. "Don't all princesses need a crown?"

"You got me a crown?"

"Of course. You're the princess of this particular dance."

"Wow. I've never been the princess of a dance before."

"Another first," we said simultaneously, which caused us to laugh.

"Or even been to a dance. So there's another one. And this is my first crown and my first corsage."

"What's a corsage?"

"The flower thing."

"Oh."

As music started playing in the background, Riley stepped back slightly and held his hands out for me.

"I don't know what I'm doing. I've never danced with an actual boy before."

"Actual boy? Have you danced with an imaginary one?"

"Several, of course. All girls have practiced dancing with their Prince Charming. It's what Disney movies train you for."

"Well, I know you've watched enough of those, seeing as how I was forced to sit through hundreds of Disney princess movies with you and Melody growing up. You should be a natural."

"And for the record, it's another first."

"Consider it added to the list." His fingers waved an invite for my hands to join his, and I obliged. "Okay, you put one hand on my shoulder, like this." He lifted my left hand to his shoulder, and once it was in place, his now empty hand lowered and slid around my side until it found its familiar home in the small of my back. Doing so brought me even closer to him. He lightly shook my right hand. "Keep hold of this hand."

"Where did you learn how to do this?"

"My mom taught me way back before my first dance. Well, that and those Disney movies."

I looked down at our bare feet and listened as his instruction continued.

"I know this will be a very hard concept for you to understand, but if we're gonna do this right, you're gonna have to let me lead. That means I'm in charge, at least for the next several minutes, anyway."

"Don't abuse your power."

"I'll try not to."

I watched his feet until he removed his hand from my back, placed it under my chin, and tilted my head up. "Don't look down. Look in my eyes."

"You know what happens when I do that and we're this close."

"It makes you wanna kiss me." His hand went back to its position, and my body immediately felt warmer.

"Right. What if I can't dance and want to kiss you at the same time?"

"I guess we'll have to forgo the dancing at some point, but sadly for you, I'm bound and determined to at least get one dance in, so you're gonna have to control your hormones."

"I can't believe you're telling me to control *my* hormones. That's the first time that's ever happened."

"And it'll probly be the last."

"Then I'll treasure the moment."

"Kinda like how I treasure every moment with you?"

"That's the sappiest thing I've ever heard. You're overdoing it with the sucking up."

"That's not sucking up; it's true. But, if it happens to help get me off the hook, then all the better."

"Uh-huh."

"And have you even noticed we're dancing?"

"We are?"

"Yep."

I looked down at our feet. He was right. We were making our way around the center of the merry-go-round. I was following his lead and hadn't even noticed. It was simple.

I looked into his now smoldering eyes. "You're the first boy I ever dated, the first boy I ever kissed, the first boy I ever danced with, and—"

"And?"

"The first boy I ever loved."

"I hope I'm the last boy you ever love," he whispered.

My heart raced and my legs felt weak. "Is the first dance over yet?"

"Not yet, why?"

"I want you to kiss me."

He shrugged as a crooked smirk perched on his face. "If you insist…"

"I insist."

After bringing his hands to my face, he leaned toward me. I closed my eyes, but just before his lips met mine, I felt him back away. "Quick question."

I opened my eyes in disappointment. "What?"

"Will you go to prom with me?"

"Riley, it's seven months away. Why are you asking me now?"

"I wanna make sure you don't make other plans."

"What if you change your mind between now and then?"

"I won't."

"You could."

"But I won't."

"How are you so sure?"

"I just am. So will you go to prom with me or not?"

"You think you'll still love me seven months from now?"

"Call me crazy, but yeah, I'll still be in love with you in seven months."

"Will you get a crimson tie so it'll match the dress I buy?"

"Consider it done."

"Then it's a date."

"Thank you."

"You're welcome. Will you kiss me now?"

"Love to."

I closed my eyes and puckered up.

"One more thing—"

My eyes flew open again. "Oh good grief, what now?"

"The new song that's about to start . . ."

"Yes?"

"I spent hours searching through my iPod until I found the perfect one. I picked it just for you."

"You did?" My heart was melting to the point that I could practically feel it drip.

"It's a group called Foreigner. They're from the 80s."

"Of course they are."

"Some of the song doesn't fit us, but a lot of it does."

"What's it called?"

He nervously straightened the crown on my head and then let his hands skim the side of my face and body as he lowered them to mine. "'Waiting For a Girl Like You.'"

"'Waiting For a Girl Like You?'" My heart puddled at my feet.

"Uh-huh." He kissed the inside of each of my wrists, and I gulped as his face inched closer to mine.

"Have you been . . . waiting for a girl like me?"

"You could say that." He kissed the small space just above the bridge of my nose and between my eyebrows.

"I could?"

He placed his mouth right next to my ear. "I'll never take you for granted again."

"You won't?"

"No."

His lips grazed the skin just below and behind my earlobe, sending my body into full-blown chills. "If you don't kiss me right now, I'm going to lose it. You're killing me, Riley."

His cheek slightly grazed mine. "It's about time."

chapter 24

Riley, Chase, Tess, and I drove through the streets of Guthrie in complete silence. Due to the boys' moods, it felt just as chilly inside the car as it was outside. Frigid, actually.

It was the night before Thanksgiving, and at the moment the boys didn't feel they had much to be thankful for. As a matter of fact, I was fairly certain they regretted ever going out with us that night at all.

My aggravated boyfriend spoke up, finally breaking the silence. "Every guy in America just lost part of his girlfriend's heart. I know I sure did."

"That's not true," I objected. "Riley, honestly, it was a small sigh and nothing more."

He looked over at me and scowled. "Small sigh? Charlie, you practically hyperventilated."

"Did not."

"Did too."

Tess sat giggling in the seat behind me.

I watched Riley's grip on the steering wheel tighten. "I'm not kidding," he continued. "All the guy did was walk into the cafeteria and the entire theater exploded in ear-splitting screams. It was horrible."

"I didn't scream."

"Not then, you didn't. You waited until he said, 'Hi, I'm Edward.'"

"Technically it was, 'Sorry I didn't get a chance to introduce myself last week. I'm Edward Cullen.'"

He glared over at me again. "Forgive the discrepancy. So I didn't lose your heart in the first five minutes of the movie, it was the first ten."

"You didn't lose my heart."

"Not until the restaurant scene," Tess said. "That was when it was officially gone and the true hyperventilating started."

"Shush, Tess. You aren't helping."

"Hey, you made it longer than me. I lost it before the movie even came out and I found out he was British."

"Edward's not British," I said.

She leaned forward in her seat as Chase sat in a clump against the window behind Riley. "Rob is."

"Who's Rob?" Riley asked.

"The guy who plays Edward in the movie."

"He's British? Oh good grief, I can't even imagine a British accent coming out of that face. Wow." I didn't hide my enthusiasm and regretted it instantly because all it did was add fuel to Riley's anti-Edward fire.

"For cryin' out loud!"

His yell caused the windows to vibrate, but I tuned out his tantrum and spoke directly to Tess. "I didn't notice any sign of an accent. I'll have to listen for it next time I see it."

"Next time?" Riley groaned. "You're gonna see it again?"

"Well, your mom wants to see it, and then I'll have to take Tammy at some point."

He moaned. "Of course you will."

"What about Anne?" Tess asked.

"She isn't allowed to see it."

"Then she'll be the only sane one left in the group of you. Maybe her parents are on to something," Chase said, finally coming out of his disgusted trance.

I gave Riley's shoulder a pat. "I promise I won't see it more than three or four times. Five max."

He didn't speak. His jaw was so rigid I'm not sure he would've been able to even if wanted.

"Honestly," Tess said, "I think it'll take *at least* that many times to see it before we realize there are people in the movie other than Edward. I mean, did you even watch anyone else?"

"I don't think so. Really, why bother? We've only got a set amount of time to watch him on the big screen. We can watch everyone else when it comes out on video."

"Hello? I'm sitting right here," Riley huffed. "Enough already."

I slunk into my seat and looked at the gloomy weather outside my car window until we arrived at our house. Riley sat in the driver's seat and mumbled a good-bye to Chase and Tess as I climbed out and gave her a hug. We made plans to take Tammy to see the movie with us as soon as humanly possible—although it was probably going to be necessary to do it in secret.

I walked over and sat on the patio steps until His Royal Sulkiness finally climbed out of the car after Chase and Tess had driven away.

With his hands shoved in his jeans pockets, he slowly made his way to me.

"I'm sorry. I shouldn't have acted like that over another guy, even if he is just a make-believe character that doesn't have a pulse."

"How would you feel if I did that over some girl while we were watching a movie together?"

"I'd hate it and probably wouldn't talk to you for days."

"At least you admit it." He sat down next to me and leaned back onto his hands. "Really, what's so attractive about him, anyway?"

"You really want me to answer that?"

"No."

"Good."

We sat in an awkward silence for what felt like forever before I finally realized that if the night were going to be salvaged, I was going to have to be the one to make it happen.

"Riley, you may have lost my attention for a few minutes, but you didn't lose even the teensiest part of my heart. To some girls Edward might be the perfect guy, but to me the perfect guy is you."

"Uh-huh." He obviously wasn't convinced.

"I'm being totally honest here. Is he drop-dead gorgeous? Uh, yeah, but there's more to life than looks. And you're right up there with him in the looks department anyway."

"Keep going." His mood was slightly improving.

"He's freezing cold all the time, and who would want to cuddle with that? You're nice and warm, and I love to snuggle with you, even if we are only allowed to do it outside."

"Okay."

"You've got a wicked sense of humor. He had no sense of humor at all."

"And?"

"You look much more athletic when you run."

"Well, thank God for that. Continue."

"He had boundaries with Bella because he was afraid he was going to kill her. You have boundaries because you love me and you want to be respectful. I mean, come on, what's not to love about that?"

"Well, if you would've been awake when I read you the books, you would know that he does respect her. He wants to wait for more reasons that not wanting to kill her. I've at least gotta give him that."

"You aren't helping me make your case."

"Oh, sorry. Keep going."

"You're just as protective as he is. You saved me from some monsters too, and you managed to do it in a lot less violent way."

"True." He sat forward and grinned over at me.

"You're sweet and romantic with just a few years of experience. He's had over eighty years to work on his moves and come up with all those swoon-worthy lines."

"I'm suddenly feeling better."

"You're the perfect boyfriend. No other guy, real or vampire, could ever come close."

He leaned over and kissed my nose. "All's forgiven. Just don't let it happen again—at least not when I'm around, anyway."

"I won't. And did I mention that you're probably a much better kisser than him?"

"You hadn't mentioned that."

"I bet you are, and seeing as how we're just sitting here in the cold, maybe you should let me check."

"And how would you do that?"

"By kissing you, of course."

He shrugged. "I guess I could let you do that."

"I'd just do it to prove a point. It's not like I *want* to kiss you or anything."

"I understand."

"Keep in mind, you're going to have to put on quite a performance to beat what I saw on that movie screen tonight."

"I'll give it all I've got. Or at least all I've got within the confines of what I'm actually allowed to do, which isn't much."

"See, there's that sense of humor I love."

"I wasn't joking."

"Oh."

Grinning, he slid his hand along my cheek and into my hair as he pulled me toward him and kissed me.

Within just a few moments, Riley was well in the lead of whatever his name was and I didn't pay any attention to the sound of the front door opening.

"Attie."

Riley and I stopped midkiss. At first, I was confused. No man in my life called me "Attie" other than Joshua and …

I looked up, and sure enough, there he was. My father was standing in the doorway, and he didn't look happy to see me. Or rather, he didn't like seeing what he'd stumbled upon.

"I … I didn't know you were coming."

"I thought I'd surprise you. Evidently I did."

"Yes, sir."

His angry eyes settled on Riley, who backed away from me and stood. "Mr. Reed. It's good to see you."

"Why don't you go inside and give Attie and me a minute?"

Riley and I exchanged nervous glances before he walked past my father and into the house. He left the door open.

I was left sitting on the top step, looking up at the man who'd shattered my life just a few months before. I hadn't heard from him since August, yet here he was out of nowhere, and he hadn't even given any warning. My thoughts and emotions were suddenly a jumbled mess.

"I'd heard you two were together, but I didn't want to believe it."

"How'd you hear?"

"Cooper told me."

"Cooper Truman?"

"Yes."

I shook my head to try to clear the cloud of confusion hovering in my mind. "What difference does it make if we're together or not?"

"I left you here thinking you were in good hands. I never dreamt Tom would allow this to happen under his roof."

Anger rose inside me. "First of all, you didn't leave me here; you sent me here knowing you wouldn't be coming. And second, Pops has been nothing but wonderful, and you can trust that he's kept his eye on us."

"Pops?"

"That's what I call him."

"It's a little bit disrespectful, don't you think?"

"No. He asked me to stop being so formal, so I gave him a new name."

His body went rigid.

I stood. "Why are you here?"

"I'd heard rumors about what was going on here. I wanted to find out for myself. Evidently they were true."

"Rumors?" My chest physically ached at his response. "So you aren't here because you missed me or because you wanted to see me. You're here because you wanted to check up on me?"

"I'm still your father, and you're still my responsibility. It's my job to protect you."

Pops stepped out onto the patio. "Eddie, don't stand out here and get on to Attiline for something I allowed. If you have an issue, take it up with me. I take full responsibility for what's going on here." He looked over at me. "Attiline, get inside. Let your dad and I deal with this."

"Yes, sir." I ran past them, up the stairs to the landing and into Riley's arms. Marme acted like she didn't see the rule violation.

"What are you thinking?" Dad yelled.

"Would you rather we told them they couldn't date?"

"Yes."

"And what would that have accomplished? You know as well as I do they could've ended up going out behind our backs. Wouldn't you rather they be under our guidance and watchful eye?"

"I'd rather they not be anything."

"That's completely unrealistic. They're in love. Whether you want them to be or not, that's how it is."

"They're too young."

"They're seniors in high school, Eddie. Did you think she wasn't going to date until college?"

Dad didn't answer.

Pops turned back and glanced at Riley and I sitting on the steps, watching the showdown. He turned back to Dad. "They're good kids, Eddie. You don't have anything to worry about."

"Not from what I hear."

"And what exactly is that?" I asked.

Dad walked into the house and stood at the bottom of the stairs. "I heard something troubling."

"What?" I asked.

"I heard you were … I heard you two had a slip-up."

Riley stood. "A slip-up?"

"Cooper's mother mentioned something about …"

"Spit it out already," I shouted.

"Did you have an abortion?"

I felt like I'd been slapped across the face. I wanted to scream at him for being so cruel, but I couldn't. I couldn't even get my mouth to move. It was numb.

I was numb.

"That was a rumor started by a psycho at school." Riley's voice vibrated with anger. "Attie would never, ever do that, and if you spent any time with her, you'd know that." He placed his hand on the back of my head and rubbed it as he stood next to me. I knew he was trying to soothe my anxiety.

Pops spoke up. "You should be more upset by the fact that your daughter had surgery for something that could've been life threatening, but she didn't bother contacting you because she didn't think you'd care. That's what should be troubling you, not pathetic rumors started by people who want nothing more than to destroy her life. What makes it worse? Those very people would be laughing if they could hear this conversation and see how much you're hurting her right now."

"Tom, you and Riley need to stay out of this. This is between Attie and me."

"No, it isn't. Attiline is like a daughter to me—"

"Don't use my daughter to try to fill some sad void left by your daughter's death."

Pops practically fell backward. It was as if my father's words had violently slammed against his body and caused him to lose his balance. He was stunned.

Seeing the pain in Pops's eyes, I jumped to my feet, ran down the stairs, and shoved my father toward the front door. "Get out!"

"No!"

"Get out of this house right now. You aren't welcome here." I shoved him again.

"Attie, I'm taking you home with me."

"No!" I shoved him again. "I am home, and you aren't welcome here. Leave, or I'm calling Gramps."

He grabbed me by the wrists and pulled me to him. There were tears in his eyes. "I've screwed up, Attie. I need you to come home. We can work this out."

"No!" I yanked my hands out of his and shoved him again and again and again, until I realized that I wasn't pushing him, I was hitting him. With closed fists, I was punching him repeatedly in the chest, and he was standing there letting me.

"Attiline..." Pops came up behind me, wrapped his arms around my body, and pulled me away from the man I hated most in the world. The man I wanted to hurt more than I'd been hurt by. Even if I punched him for hours, his pain could've never matched mine. It wouldn't have come close.

I slammed my eyes shut. "I can't even look at you!"

"Attie—"

"Don't say my name!" I covered my ears and shook my head. I wanted his voice to go away. I wanted him to go away and never come back.

Within moments I felt Riley's hands on my cheeks. "Charlie, it's okay. It's okay."

"Go on, Eddie." It was Marme speaking. "You've done enough damage. Go on, get out of here."

"I'm not leaving without my daughter."

I felt my head shake at the sound of hearing him say the words *my daughter.*

My eyes opened to find Riley's green eyes looking right back at me. They were large and full of concern. "Look at me, Charlie. Ignore him. Just ignore him. Pretend he isn't even here."

Pops let go of me and walked toward my dad.

Concentrating on Riley's face and voice, I blocked out the commotion as it erupted in the entryway. I heard their voices, I heard the screams and yelling, but I didn't allow my brain to comprehend the words. I only stood looking into Riley's eyes as he tried to prevent me from hearing their battle.

I'd managed to block it out until my dad said the words that even in my worst nightmares I never thought I'd hear.

Stefne Miller

"I'd asked your mother for a divorce," he announced.

Other than his voice, the house instantly went silent.

"There wasn't anyone else involved. No affair or anything; it just wasn't working." His words were cold and detached. "I couldn't keep it from you anymore. Given the circumstances, I thought you needed to know."

I stood still as the room spun around me and my stomach churned. How could I respond? There was nothing I could say.

"You didn't know it yet, but when you two came back to Oklahoma, you weren't going to be coming back to New York."

Riley pulled me closer. Only his strength kept me standing; my legs felt as if the muscles had turned to ash.

"Life isn't a fairy tale, Attie. I can't leave you here and let you go on living like it is."

I looked around Riley's shoulder. "It shows just how out of touch you are if you think I'm walking around in some fantasy. My life has been hell for the last year and a half. What I've had here is a small amount of happiness, but even *that* you had to destroy." My eyes remained locked on him. "You're dead to me. You died right along with Mom, and as far as I'm concerned, you don't exist. Turn around, walk out the door, and go back to New York."

"Attie, please don't do this," he begged. "I only told you because—"

My hands flew to cover my ears. "Pops, please get him out of here." I buried my face in Riley's chest as he wrapped his arms around me and kissed me on the top of the head.

"Eddie," Pops said quietly, "you need to leave."

"She's my daughter. I'm not going anywhere without her."

"She's asked you to go, and I need you to honor her wishes."

My eyes squeezed tightly closed as Pops's and Dad's voices grew louder again.

Finally, Marme begged Dad to leave.

He did.

• •

206

(Riley)

Attie stood shaking in my arms. Her father had broken her heart. Again.

"Charlie, are you all right?"

She peeled herself out of my arms in a daze. "I think I'll go upstairs."

Her wobbling legs tried to carry her to the stairs, but within just a few steps she fell to the ground and started vomiting.

I dropped to the ground beside her and held her hair out of the way.

"I'll get a towel." Mom ran to the hall closet as Dad ran toward the kitchen.

I could hear cupboard doors slam as Attie's entire body heaved, grief pouring out of her mouth and all over the floor around us. Dad ran up and held a pot under her head as Mom got busy cleaning up the mess.

"It's all right, Attiline." Dad rubbed her shoulder. "Let it all out."

"How—" She tried to speak but only threw up again.

"You're gonna be okay," Dad continued. "We're gonna get you through this. We're right here. Just get it all out."

Powerless to help, all I could do was hold her hair out of the way.

After several minutes, she'd emptied all the contents of her stomach and was left to dry heave into a clean towel. Her face was bright red and wet with tears and sweat, and her eyes darted around the room as if she were searching for something. Maybe she was looking for something to make sense. If so, her search was useless. Nothing made sense at all.

I peeled away the hair that stuck to her face as we all sat on the floor of the entryway. The cold wind blew through the front door that nobody had bothered to close. Attie was in shock. We all were.

All I could think about was how useless I'd become. Her life had just blown up, started to spin wildly out of control, and all I'd done was hold her hair.

chapter 25

(Attie)

I sat on the floor in the corner between the bed and the wall. The night had passed, as well as most of the next day. The Bennetts took turns checking on me throughout the morning, but I finally convinced them to leave me be until I was ready to talk. I knew I wouldn't be ready to talk any time soon, but I didn't bother telling them that. It would only cause them more concern.

"What is it that we're doing locked away in here?" Jesus asked.

"Getting away."

"From what?"

"From everyone and everything. I'm tired of people feeling like they have to help me. And I can't stand to see the way they look at me."

"And how is that?"

"With pity. They feel sorry for me. I've become a huge charity case. I can't even stand to be around myself."

"Were they complaining?"

"Not to my face."

"So you believe you were becoming a burden?"

"Of course I was. What else can they do or say? All of my problems must be wearing them out. I know they are me."

"They love you. They want to help."

"That's the point; they can't help. There's nothing that they can do or say to make me feel better. I just need time, and they don't want to give me that. Riley just wants to rush in and fix everything. This can't be fixed. I'm tired, and I just want to be left alone. That includes you. I want our journey to be over. I want you to go away."

"I won't do that. I won't leave you, even if you want me to."

"I don't want you here anymore!"

"Why?"

"Because."

"Because why?"

"Don't act like you don't know."

"You're angry with me."

"Of course."

"Then come on out with it. Let me have it."

"I don't want to. I may something I might regret later."

"I can take it. No matter what you say to me, it's not going to change my love for you. You need to let it all out. For you, you need to tell me what you're thinking."

"What, like that's even allowable?"

"Allowable?"

"Isn't it like a major sin or something to accuse God of something? To be angry with him?"

"Have you read the Bible?"

"Of course."

"Have you read the book of Psalms? Half of David's prayers were him letting God have it. He was angry with God for all he'd been through. He didn't understand how we could let him experience such pain after all that he'd been promised. He was angry and scared and knew God well enough to know that he could be honest about his feelings.

"Attie, you were created with feelings and emotions. You think I don't know that you're going to feel those emotions toward me at times?"

My tears flowed. "I don't want to be angry with you. I can't lose our relationship."

"Our relationship isn't dependant on you only being happy with me. We survived our disagreement at the river, didn't we? I've been through worse and forgiven much more than your anger, I can assure you of that. Attie, you can't lose me, not ever."

"Once I get started, I could go on for days."

Jesus pulled his sleeves up to his elbows, crossed his arms, and stood tall. "Bring it on. I've been expecting this."

"I'm tired, so if you're expecting a huge production, you're going to be disappointed. I'm too tired. I'm exhausted."

"What are you tired of?"

"Everything."

"Such as?"

"Everything: drama. I'm tired of the fighting and the rumors, and I'm tired of trying to keep it all together. I'm tired of the rejection and insecurity. I'm tired of trying to convince myself that living was worth all this."

I was fatigued. The kind of exhaustion where you can feel it in your chest and it feels like if you don't get some rest your heart will stop beating and your lungs will stop breathing. I pictured it like an octopus resting on my sternum, and the more tired I got, the more he wrapped his tentacles around my organs, squeezing them until they no longer functioned.

Sitting there on the floor, I didn't want to lift my head to look at Jesus. I didn't want to use what little strength I had left to look at another man who was letting me slip away.

Turning toward the open window, I closed my eyes and slept.

"We aren't done," Jesus said, waking me from my slumber. The light outside had changed from bright to a glowing ember.

"What do you want from me?"

"I want you to tell me what you're thinking."

I chuckled. "I'm hardly thinking at all."

"That's not true. Thinking is all you're doing. You're letting your mind go wild."

I finally gave in and said the first thing that came to my mind. "They gave me hope that marriages could work. They were proof that you could love one person forever."

"They shouldn't be your hope, Attie; your hope should be in me. As I've told you before, people will always let you down. If you hold your hope in others, you'll always end up being disappointed."

"Well, you aren't my hope! You aren't anything. I'm sick of this. I've done everything you've asked me to do. I've believed in you, trusted you, followed you, and my life has done nothing but get worse. How much longer am I supposed to tell others how wonderful you are? How do I keep telling people what a loving God you are when all they see is my life in the crapper? I'm tired. I'm tired of following the rules and having nothing to show for it."

"Rules? What rules?"

"What rules? Isn't that what this is all about? Pray enough, trust enough, praise enough, serve enough? When do you uphold your end of this? When does the reward for all of that come?"

"Is that why you've been doing all of those things? For a reward? I never gave you a guarantee, Attie. I never said, 'Follow me and all will go well. Follow me and you'll have everything you ever ask for.'"

"You've taken everything from me."

"I've taken nothing from you. Things have been taken from you, yes, but I didn't take those things from you."

"But you allowed them to be taken, right? You're all powerful. You could have stepped in. You could have changed it. You could have made things better."

"I did make things better. As you told Riley this summer, I brought you to a place where you were loved and where you could love others."

"And that one thing is supposed to sustain me forever? You feel like you can keep letting bad things happen to me because you gave me a boyfriend or new friends? Well, I'm not playing by your rules anymore. I'm done with you. Enough."

We continued, and after what could have been days of arguing with the Lord, all of the energy had drained out of my body and I was weak and exhausted. Feeling completely hopeless and alone, I made the decision to close my eyes and ears to him.

Although the bed looked welcoming, I didn't want to be comfortable. I wanted to feel the cold air on my skin and the tiredness as it overtook me. I wanted to feel something other than the emotional and spiritual pain that I'd been suffering. I wanted to know that I could feel something else. I'd become an expert at not allowing myself to feel pain. Others, Riley especially, tried their best to shelter me from pain of any kind. But here today, all alone, I wanted to feel it—all of it. I wanted to know that my body, mind, and spirit could be overwhelmed with pain, yet I could still survive.

I had to know that I could survive all on my own.

Many more hours passed without me moving from my spot crouched on the floor. My body was numb, my eyes were heavy, and my thoughts a blur.

Finally, I allowed my eyes to close and the pain to go away.

chapter 26

(Riley)

Attie's dad went back to New York the same night he'd arrived. Thanksgiving dinner came and went, and three days passed without seeing or hearing anything from Attie. I left food outside her door at every meal, and within a few minutes she would open the door and take it inside. Other than that, we didn't have any contact.

The Sooners were about to continue their winning streak by beating their rivals, the OSU Cowboys, and I was hoping Attie would be ready to come out of her room and watch the game with the rest of us. Honestly, I didn't have much interest in watching if she wasn't watching with me. Without her antics, it wouldn't be the same.

"Charlie?" I knocked lightly on the door. "The big game's getting ready to start. Do you wanna come down and watch?"

She didn't reply.

"Charlie?" I tried to open the door, but it was locked. "Charlie, you're scaring me. Open the door." I waited a few seconds before pounding on the door and yelling her name more forcefully.

I heard Dad run up behind me. He pushed me out of the way and knocked on her door. "Attiline, can you open the door?"

There was no response.

"Attiline? Baby girl, can you open the door? I just wanna check on you."

Silence.

"Have you talked to her at all?" Dad asked. "Have you seen her come and go?"

"I haven't seen her at all. She's been really quiet."

"We'll give her a minute, and then we'll let ourselves in."

Mom walked up behind us. "Just open the door, Tom."

"Attiline, you've got twenty seconds, and then I'm knocking this door down."

We all stared at the door handle waiting to see it turn, but it didn't.

"That's it." Dad backed away from the door. Lifting his leg, he kicked the door several times until it broke loose from the doorjamb, and he made his way inside.

Instead of Attie's voice, all we heard were screams from my dad. His voice sounded terrified, which caused my heart to stop beating. "Someone call 911. Dear God, someone call 911!"

I ran to Attie. She was pale and lying unconscious on the floor. I looked for blood but didn't see any. There was no sign that she'd done any damage to herself. She was just … gone.

chapter 27

(Riley)

"I'm looking for the guardian of Atticus Reed."

Dad stood. "That would be me."

"Hello." The man reached out and shook Dad's hand. "I'm Eric Dancer, the endocrinologist on Atticus's case. Can you come with me please?" He turned to go, but Dad grabbed his arm.

"I'd prefer for you to talk to me here. Everyone here are her family and friends."

"Okay."

"What's happening with Attie?"

The doctor glanced around the room before looking back at my dad. "She's in renal failure."

"What's that?" I asked.

"Her kidney is failing," he said.

"Kidney?" Tammy asked. "I thought we have two kidneys."

"Most of us do," he answered. "Looking at her chart, I see that Atticus—"

"Her name is Attie," I corrected. "She doesn't like to be called Atticus."

"I apologize. Attie was in a car accident a while back?"

Dad nodded. "Last year."

The doctor continued. "Her right kidney was damaged and removed. So one kidney has been left to do the work of two. Under normal circumstances, people survive with one kidney all the time.

There are usually no complications, and people are free to live their lives as normal."

"So what happened with Char—I mean Attie?"

"We believe she's suffering from acute renal failure, which means that the onset was fast. My guess is that it was caused by dehydration." He glanced around at everyone again. "If she wasn't taking in enough water, her kidney tried to hold on to as much water as it could. Therefore, she wasn't making urine. Her electrolytes got out of balance, and her body wasn't getting rid of waste. Had she been around other people, they would have noticed that she was becoming lethargic and wasn't thinking clearly. But, since she was alone ..."

Guilt. I felt immediate guilt. I should've been checking on her. I shouldn't have allowed her to lock herself away.

"What does all of this mean?" Gramps asked.

"Her BUN and creatinine levels are highly elevated, and her glomerular filtration rate has decreased, causing organ failure. Unfortunately, she's slipped into a coma."

My legs gave out, and I fell into the seat behind me.

"We've placed a catheter into one of the larger arteries in her leg, which will be for hemodialysis."

"What's that?" Anne asked.

"It's a machine that filters her blood for her. The sooner we can remove the toxins from her body and get her rehydrated and her electrolytes balanced, the better her chances of survival."

"Survival?" Dad asked. "Are you saying we could lose her?"

"It depends on the amount of organ damage. Her heart is beating, and she's breathing on her own, but at this point, we just don't know for sure."

Mom sat down next to me and put her arm around my shoulder.

"I suggest you go home and get some rest," Dr. Dancer said. "The dialysis is going to take several hours, and I don't anticipate knowing anything before tomorrow. We have your phone numbers; I'll contact you as soon I know something."

"Can someone sit with her?" I asked.

"She's in ICU, but I'll allow one person back."

I looked over at Gramps. He shook his head as tears filled his eyes. "I can't," he whispered. "I can't see her like that again."

I stood. "I'll go. I wanna be with her."

Dad grabbed me and gave me a hug. "I'll be right out here. I'm not going anywhere."

"Riley?" Mom grabbed my hand. "I'll run home and get some stuff. What do you want me to bring you?"

"Um..." My body shook, and it was hard to think clearly. "My iPod maybe... a book or two... I don't know, Mom. Whatever you think."

"Okay." She kissed me on the cheek before heading toward the exit.

"Oh, and Mom..."

She turned toward me.

"Attie's Bible. It's on her nightstand. She'll want it when she wakes up."

I watched her walk out the door before turning back to the doctor and following him through the hospital corridors. Sadly, they were familiar; I'd seen it all before. The only difference was that rather than spending time sitting with a family friend, I would be standing vigil next to the girl I loved.

"Hello, Margaret." The doctor spoke to a nurse standing outside a patient's room. "This is Riley Bennett." I looked through the glass wall and saw Attie lying in the bed. "He's going to be sitting with Ms. Reed."

"Yes, Doctor," the nurse replied.

"Would you make sure he's comfortable? Answer any questions he may have?"

"Yes, sir."

I was immediately reacquainted with the smell that permeated everything in the intensive care unit. In one way it smelled clean, like bleach or antibacterial soap; but on the other hand, I couldn't deny the odor of sickness. It was a depressing and overpowering smell. I wanted to be sitting in Attie's car, inhaling the scent of her perfume or hand lotion, instead of here.

"Riley?" I took my eyes off of Attie long enough to listen to the doctor speak. "Margaret will take good care of you. I'll be back to check on Attie in a bit."

I tried to speak, but my throat was too dry. No sound would escape.

After giving me a quick pat on the shoulder, he walked off.

"Are you family?" the nurse asked.

I shook my head.

"What is your relation to Ms. Reed?"

"I'm her boyfriend."

Her eyes grew sad. "Oh."

I glanced back at Attie.

"Well, go on in. I've got to go take care of something, and then I'll be right back in to check on you."

I slowly walked along the glass wall until I came to an opening and could make my way into the room. Several machines surrounded her bed, and I heard the familiar sound of their humming. The scene looked eerily familiar to a year and a half before, only this time large tubes filled with blood ran between her leg and a swirling pump of some kind. The sight of the red liquid made me nauseated and woozy.

"You'd better sit down," the nurse warned as she walked back into the room.

I pointed to the tube. "Can she feel that?"

"No. She isn't feeling anything." She handed me a pillow and blanket. The blanket felt hot, as if it had just come out of a dryer. "It tends to get a little chilly in here. If you get cold just let me know and I'll get you a new blanket from the warmer."

"Yes, ma'am."

Another nurse walked in with a pitcher of water and plastic cup.

"Thanks, Penny. Just set it over there on the windowsill," Nurse Margaret said before turning back to me. "Riley, you just push this button right here if you need me, okay?" I glanced at the panel on the side of Attie's bed. Margaret's finger pointed toward a cartoon picture of someone's face. "If you need anything…"

"Or when she wakes up?" I suggested.

Margaret gave a polite smile. "Yes. Definitely if she wakes up."

Closing my eyes, I listened to the machines hum, vibrate, and beep. In an odd way I found the sounds comforting. They were sounds of life—Attie's life. They were keeping her from leaving this earth, and they weren't going to let her give up.

"Heck, if I had a boy as cute as you sitting next to me, I'd surely wake up. She's a lucky girl."

I looked back at Attie as tears filled my eyes. "Actually, I'm the lucky one. She never saw it that way though. You'd probly never be able to convince her of it, either."

"I say you're both lucky then." Margaret continued talking, but I wasn't paying attention, and before long I realized that Attie and I were alone. Ironically, it was practically the first time I'd been in a room alone with her since August. As I reached out and grabbed her hand, I smiled at the realization that if we were home, we'd be breaking rules one, two, and three.

Even if it would have meant I couldn't touch her, I wished we were home.

chapter 28

"Riley?"

A voice woke me. Lifting my head from the bed, I sat up in my chair. The voice hadn't come from Attie; she was still asleep in front of me.

"Riley?"

I looked toward the door and saw Margaret. "Yes, ma'am?"

"I'm sorry to wake you, but I have to ask you to leave the room."

"Excuse me?"

"We've got to get her ready to be moved."

"Moved? Moved where?"

"She's being transferred."

"Transferred where?"

"New York."

I stood and rushed out of the room and into the waiting area. Everyone looked shocked to see me.

"He's taking her," I announced as I ran toward my dad.

"Who?" he asked.

"Her dad. He's moving her to New York."

His face turned red. "The hell he is."

"Dad, they just kicked me out of her room. They're moving her right now."

"Tammy?" Dad turned to face her.

She stood. "Yes, sir?"

"Get your dad on the phone. Tell him what's going on and find out what our legal rights are."

"Yes, sir."

"Molly, run to the nurses' station and demand to see Dr. Dancer right now." His jaw clinched and his back stiffened. "Gramps, get your son on the phone."

Gramps dialed the number and handed the phone to Dad. I sat in the seat farthest from the noise and watched as he paced the waiting room floor.

"Eddie, what are you doing? … I don't care who you are; you aren't taking her away from here." He shook his head violently. "What are you talking about? Your job? Who cares about your job? You'll just have to take some time off and get back down here.…This will not happen; do you understand that? You signed paperwork giving us rights. We have medical rights. I have an attorney on the other line right now, and we'll take legal action if we have to. You will not move her again."

Gramps stood and motioned for Dad to hand him the phone. Dad shoved it into his hand and marched off toward my mother, who was talking to the nurse.

"Son…" I looked back at Gramps, who was now talking on the phone. "You leave her right where she is … We're her family too…" I could hear Eddie's voice but couldn't make out his words. "Enough is enough," Gramps continued. "You're either a parent or you aren't. If you wanna see her, then you come here. She isn't going anywhere." He nodded as he listened to his son speak. "Right then, expect to hear from our attorney." He threw me the phone, and I hung up the call. "Tammy, is that your dad on the phone?"

"Yes, sir."

He grabbed the phone from her hand and put it to his ear. "Greg, what are our options here? They're preparing to move her right now. We don't have much time." He snapped his fingers in Tammy's direction and motioned for her to get my dad. "So we need to file an injunction?"

Dad walked up and stood next to his father.

"Just a second, Greg." Gramps covered the phone with his hand. "Tom, go tell the doctor that our attorney is filing an injunction right now. He's ordering them to stop preparations to move Attie, and they can't move her until this is resolved one way or the other."

"Yes, sir."

"And tell him to be expecting a phone call from Greg Richland, our attorney."

"Yes, sir." Dad ran off toward the nurses' station again.

I closed my eyes and covered my ears as the chaos around me continued. Time seemed to stand still yet run together at the same time.

I don't know how much time passed before I heard Margaret's voice again.

I opened my eyes and looked at her.

"You can go back into her room. She's not going anywhere right now."

Jumping up, I ran toward Attie and left the madness behind.

• •

"Hey, Riley."

I turned toward the door. "Joshua, how'd you get back here?"

"Heck, I'm clergy. I have special powers."

"Glad to know someone does."

He walked into the room and sat on the end of the bed. "Sorry I'm just now getting here. We were visiting family in Texas."

"Aw, it's okay." I turned back to Attie. "Is it still crazy out there?"

"There's a lot of yelling going on. Her dad showed up. Guess he flew in this morning."

"He did?" I must've been losing time. Another day had passed and I didn't even notice. "At least he isn't taking her away."

"I wouldn't say that. I think he just came to fight it out in person."

"Oh."

"Your dad and Gramps aren't going to let it happen though, so don't worry about that."

I nodded.

"How is she?" he asked.

"No change. She hasn't moved at all. The doctor says a lot of stuff, but I don't understand any of it. The longer she's asleep the worse it is, so all I know is that she needs to wake up soon."

"Yeah. How are you?"

"Me?"

"Yeah, you."

I don t even know. This entire thing is like an outta body experience. I m here but I m not kinda thing, or some kinda sick and twisted déjà vu.

"I can imagine. It's some pretty heavy stuff for a seventeen-year-old."

"I would think this would be heavy stuff for a fifty-year-old."

"Yeah, I guess you're right about that."

I looked back at her. It was like she wasn't even in her body. There was almost nothing familiar about her. No warmth, no energy, no color. She was slipping away; deep down inside I knew it was true, but I couldn't let myself believe it.

Tears filled my eyes. They'd been doing that a lot lately.

"Riley, they sent me in here to get you. Her father would like to sit with her a while, and only one person is allowed back at a time."

"Why should he be allowed back? He's the reason she's in here."

"It's easier to woo bears with honey."

"What does that mean?"

"He's her father. Your dad figures that if we give in a little, he'll give in a little too."

My grip tightened on her hand. "Can I have just a few more minutes?"

"Sure." He stood to leave. "I'll let him know that you'll be out in a few."

"Thanks." I watched him leave the room and then sat on the bed. "Charlie, they're making me go outside. I don't wanna go; I hope you know that."

I tried to think of something witty to say. I thought maybe if I were clever enough, she'd wake up just to argue. Nothing witty came to mind.

"I know that things are kinda crazy right now and life hasn't been real fair, but you gotta wake up. If you'll just wake up, we can deal with this stuff." Tears fell from my face and onto the mattress. "Please, Charlie, I know you're in there, and I know you can hear me. You gotta wake up. I love you, and I really, really need you to come back to me."

"Riley?"

I turned and saw Dr. Reed standing in the doorway. My face immediately felt hot. I'd never hated anyone more in my life.

I turned back to Attie and gave her a kiss on the forehead. "I'll be right outside, Charlie. I'm not going anywhere. I'll be right outside."

I climbed off the bed and walked toward the door. Mr. Reed held out a hand for me to shake, but I shoved my hands into my pockets and walked out of the room. As I walked through the waiting room, I refused to make eye contact with any of them. I knew they were looking at me with concern on their faces, but I didn't want to see it. Either that, or they were looking at me in hopes of getting some information, and I didn't have any to give them. Attie wasn't getting any better. What more was there to say?

I sat in the chair farthest away from my friends and family. In a groggy daze, I could hear my parents whispering. They mentioned my name several times as well as Attie's and her dad's. I kept my eyes closed in hopes that I would fall back to sleep.

Growing up, whenever my family took a road trip somewhere, my mother always told Melody and me that if we would go to sleep, we would get there faster. Maybe if I could just stay asleep now, Attie would wake up faster, and the wait wouldn't be as agonizing.

I prayed that God would let me go back to sleep until Attie woke up.

chapter 29

(Attie)

"Atopic dermatitis and flea allergy dermatitis are seasonal in many regions of the world. Malassezia dermatitis may occur more frequently during months of higher humidity. Cyclical pruritus without seasonality can sometimes signify contact dermatitis associated with change of environment. Psychogenic pruritus may begin as a predictable, attention-getting device. Pruritus seen with food allergy should be continuous…"

I woke to the sound of my father's voice. Although I couldn't ask, I knew he was reading from one of his textbooks. Unlike most children who are read fairy tales as a child, I was read veterinary medicine textbooks. Sometimes I wondered if being a veterinarian was actually my goal or if I'd just been brainwashed by an overly enthusiastic father.

My eyes opened, but my vision was blurry. Without turning my head, I glanced over at him. Completely engrossed in his book, he hadn't noticed that I'd woken. I decided not to get his attention and closed my eyes and tried to regain my thoughts.

I was obviously in a hospital bed. What had happened? Had my mother and Melody actually died, or had it all been a dream? Was I dating Riley Bennett and living in his house? If I had been dreaming, the dream felt very real because I wished that he was the person sitting next to me instead of my dad.

"What year is it?" My throat ached as I spoke.

Dad jumped up and screamed for the nurse before kissing my forehead several times. I was shocked at his affection. He hadn't shown me any in...Well, I didn't know. Maybe it was all a dream. My dad never sent me away; he never actually let me go. He never pushed me away.

A nurse ran into the room. "I've paged the doctor. He should be here any minute. Is she talking at all?"

"Just asked what year it was."

"Don't worry," she urged. "You've only been unconscious a few days."

Before I could ask any more questions, a man wearing a white coat entered the room and started talking a language that sounded foreign. Although he spoke English, the medical terminologies only added to my confusion. Some of the words were ones I'd heard my dad use as he read from textbooks, but none of them had actually applied to me before.

I still didn't know where I was and what was real. There were no bracelet or ring on my hand. Had Riley and I actually been together, wouldn't I be wearing the ring he gave me?

Something tickled my foot, and I jerked it back under the covers. Had I ever really kicked Riley in the face?

"Her reflexes are normal," the doctor noted out loud.

I tuned out everyone in the room and tried to force myself to think clearly, but nothing made sense.

Looking around the room as my vision improved, I recognized a face.

"You're here," I whispered.

"I told you I wouldn't go away," Jesus replied.

"Who's here?" Dad asked.

I shook my head and closed my eyes. I didn't know where I was or why, but at the very least I knew that my encounter with Jesus had been real. I would hang on to that knowledge because at the moment, I didn't feel like I had anything else.

• •

A giant snake wrapped itself around my arm and squeezed. I tried to scream, but it sunk its fangs into my throat and silenced me immediately.

"You're all right," a voice soothed. "It's just a dream."

My eyes opened.

"I think you were having a nightmare," the nurse informed me.

"I get them pretty often … I think."

"What was it about?"

"A snake was squeezing my arm."

She laughed and held up a blood pressure cuff. "I was taking your blood pressure. This thing can really be an arm crusher. Especially arms like yours that don't have any meat to them."

I rubbed my arm. She was right; there was nothing but bone.

I glanced over at the seat my dad had been sitting in, but it was empty.

"May I send Riley in now? He's been itching to get in here ever since he heard you were awake."

"Riley?"

"Yes. He's just outside in the waiting room. I don't think he's left the hospital since you were admitted."

"He hasn't?"

"No. What a sweetheart. You're one lucky girl; he's crazy about you."

Finally, confirmation that I hadn't dreamt the entire summer. Riley and I were real. That also meant that my mother and Melody were really gone.

"He talked about you nonstop when I would come in. I feel like I know you and we've only just met."

"He loves me?"

"I'd say."

I ran my hands through my hair. It felt dirty and greasy. There was no telling how long it had been since it had been washed.

"How about this," she said. "We'll get you cleaned up, wash your hair, change your clothes, and then he can come in and see you."

"I'd prefer that. He may be in love with me, but love isn't completely blind."

"Oh, I don't think he'd care a bit, but I bet it would make you feel better. It's amazing what a nice bath can do to a person's disposition."

"It sounds nice."

"We'll make him sweat out there. He's waited this long; what's a few more minutes?"

I spent the next several anxious minutes getting cleaned up, and the nurse was right. I felt much better but still very weak.

"Do you want to put on a sweatshirt? As long as we can get to your IV, you can wear anything up top. You've still got to wear the gown though. You can't wear pants until the catheter's out. Hopefully that won't be too much longer."

"Do I have clothes here?"

"Riley's mom brought you some stuff. I think there was a sweatshirt in the stack." She sorted through the bag and pulled one out. "Voila. Here we are."

I watched as she turned off the IV machine and removed the tube from the needle in my arm. "We'll need to undo this for just a few minutes."

"Blood won't run out?"

"No," she said as she carefully worked away. "It's got a valve that keeps it from coming out. You should have seen the tube that ran to the dialysis machine. Riley almost passed out when he saw it."

"He doesn't like to see me hurt."

"The good ones never do." She unfolded the sweatshirt and held it up in front of me. "Will this one do?"

It was my favorite OU sweatshirt. Marme knew what she was doing when she packed it.

"Moms know everything."

"That one's perfect," a voice added.

"Riley!" I couldn't hide my excitement to see him.

"Give us just one more second, Riley. I've got to get her IV back in. You know how you are when you see her IV. You might want to stay back."

"I'll wait right here." He stood against the doorway and smiled at me as she helped me get my sweatshirt on. He looked tired but as handsome as ever.

I took my eyes off him and watched as she replaced the IV and stuck white tape over it. The top of my hand got cold, proof that the liquid was flowing into my vein.

"There," she said. "That way Riley can't see it." She pulled the blanket up over my hand. "Your hand should warm up in a minute."

"Thank you."

I looked back at Riley. A smile still covered his face.

"And now, the moment he's been waiting for," the nurse teased. "I'll leave the two of you alone."

"Is that even allowed, or are we breaking house rules?" I asked.

Riley laughed. "Who cares?"

The nurse gave him a pat on the shoulder. "Go easy on her. We don't want her blood pressure getting all funky. And remember, I'll be monitoring it on a screen at the nurses' desk."

"I'll be good," he assured.

The nurse pulled the curtain across the window and then closed the door as she walked out of the room.

Riley stood across the room and stared at me.

"Are you going to come say hi?"

• •

(Riley)

"Give me a second. I'm a little overwhelmed by the whole thing. I don't know if my feet will work just yet." They felt like cement blocks, heavy and attached to the floor.

"Take all the time you need. I'm not going anywhere."

"You have no idea what it feels like to see you right now."

"Relieved?"

"Relief doesn't come close to describing it."

Attie's face was sunken in, and her eyes looked hollow, but she was back in my world and that was all that mattered.

"I was worried about you."

"I'm alive," she announced with as much energy as she could muster. "I look like crap, but I'm alive."

"You're beautiful."

"You're a liar."

"And you still have your wit."

"At least I have that." Her voice sounded scratchy, hoarse, and weak, and in that second I wanted nothing more than to touch her and know it wasn't a dream.

My feet finally broke free from their shackles, and I was free to walk to her side. With each step toward her, my heart rate increased.

She sat up and held her arms up toward me, and I leaned over and hugged her. "Gosh, this feels good," I whispered.

"It really does."

Without letting go, I sat on the bed. There was less of her to hold than before.

"When I woke up I didn't know if everything had been real or if I'd dreamt it all."

I kissed her on the neck, then on the jawline, the cheek, and finally the tip of her nose. "If what was real?"

"Us."

"Oh, we're real all right. Very, very real."

"It felt like we were. I was just confused being back in a hospital and waking up to my dad sitting next to me. I guess I assumed that we were back to last year and he never left and I hadn't actually lived here. It was like a *Wizard of Oz* moment or something."

I tucked a piece of hair behind her ear as she continued talking. "Like a 'did that really all just happen' kind of thing."

My fingers stroked her cheek. At that moment I couldn't have forced myself to stop touching her even if I wanted to. The movement of her face as she talked sent energy through my fingers. She was awake and moving, and all I could do was absorb the energy that she'd lacked as she lay unconscious in the hospital bed.

"And now . . ." She ran her hands through my hair and took a deep breath as she gathered her thoughts. "Here you are."

"Here I am. Hair and all." My thumb ran across her dry, cracked lips. "Your lips are really dry. Should I get you some Chap Stick or something?"

"You aren't going anywhere. I'll have the nurse bring me some in a little while." Her forehead scrunched. "Are they too chapped for you to kiss?"

"I don't even think that's possible."

Her face turned into a scowl. "Kissing me?"

I laughed. "No. Your lips being too chapped for me to kiss."

"Oh." The scowl evaporated and a smile returned. "What are you waiting for then?"

I leaned toward her. The hard skin of her lips pressed into mine, but within seconds their texture was the last thing on my mind. Even though she kissed me back, it was lifeless.

I gave her a quick peck and made myself comfortable in the chair next to the bed. "How do you feel?"

"A lot better than I did ten minutes ago. Who knew one kidney could cause so much trouble? Or the lack of one kidney...whichever. I guess I'll know to drink lots of water from now on."

"You don't have to worry about that. We'll be shoving water at you all the time. You'll probly spend the majority of your time running to the bathroom."

"That'll make for an interesting life."

She tried to reposition herself but ended up only causing herself pain.

"What do you need?" I asked as I jumped out of my seat. "What can I do to help?"

"I just need to scoot back a little bit; my rear is getting sore."

I started to pick her up but hesitated.

"What's the matter?" she asked.

"I'm afraid I'm gonna hurt you."

"It's mostly my leg that hurts right now. I'll make sure not to move it."

I slid one arm under the covers and rested it under her knees before placing my other arm around her back. "I'm gonna count to three and then lift you a little and scoot you back."

She nodded and tensed her lips in anticipation of pain.

"One … two … three." I picked her up, moved her, and set her back down. She was light as a feather. Much lighter than when I'd carried her on my back during our walks. "Charlie, you've lost so much weight."

"I'm fine. I've got this stupid IV thing in my arm, and I really don't have an appetite anyway."

"Were you trying to hurt yourself?" The words came out before I could stop them. It was the question that had been burning in my mind since we found her lying on the floor.

"No. You don't need to worry about that. I just wasn't thinking, that's all. As lost as I may feel at times, I'd never get to that point. Really, all I wanted was to be alone for a while. I wanted to get away…"

"From me?"

"From everyone. I needed some time to think. To deal with some stuff."

"I see."

"Do we have to talk about this right now? I'm getting tired and I feel icky."

"No, we don't have to talk about anything if you don't want to."

"Will you just sit here with me?"

"Of course. I'm right here." I grabbed her hand and rubbed it between mine.

Tears filled her eyes. "No, I mean come up here. I need you to come up here and sit with me."

I stood and kissed her on the forehead. "Don't cry, Charlie; I'm right here."

"I just want you next to me for a little while longer."

"Then we'll need to scoot you over and make some room."

After a little bit of careful rearranging, I lay down and wrapped my arms around her so she could rest her head on my chest.

"Is this better?" I asked.

"Yes."

Holding her in my arms didn't seem like enough. It didn't fulfill my need to take her completely in and cover her. Protect her. I took a deep breath, trying to fill my body with her energy, her very essence. "Your hair smells good. It smells like vanilla."

"The nurse washed it for me. Your mom brought my shampoo for me."

"I thought it smelled familiar. It smells like you."

I could feel her bones as her body melted into mine. She'd found her spot and made herself at home.

"I'm tired, Riley." I couldn't see her face, but her voice sounded weak, like a spark was missing in her that had nothing to do with being sick. She was tired, and I understood she wasn't talking about being physically tired. Attie was emotionally and spiritually drained, and my presence alone wasn't going help her.

"Did you dream about Jesus while you were asleep this time?"

"No."

"Did you dream at all?"

"No."

"What about now? Do you see him? Can you talk to him?"

"I see him, but I haven't talked to him."

"Why?"

"I can't. I don't know what else to say."

"Maybe you shouldn't say anything. Maybe you should just let him talk."

"I don't think I'm ready to listen," she admitted.

"That's okay." I kissed the top of her head. "I'm sure he'll wait."

My shirt became wet beneath her face.

"Everything's gonna be okay." I stroked her arm in hopes that it would soothe her to sleep. "Try to get some rest."

"You won't leave while I'm asleep, will you?"

"I'll be right here. I promise you, Charlie, I'm not leaving."

chapter 30

(Attie)

I'd cried myself to sleep, but I was in Riley's arms, and I wanted that to be all that mattered. I hoped that if I held on to him tight enough and long enough, the storm would pass over us, and everything would go back to normal. But I knew it wasn't true. Sadly, there was a large part of me that understood from the moment I saw my dad standing on the Bennetts' porch that my world was changing. Our world, and everything we thought was so certain, was going to change, and there wasn't anything that Riley or I could do to stop it.

Worse, all the changing was taking place inside of me, and all Riley would be able to do was stand at a distance and watch.

"Riley?" My dad's voice brought me out of my sleep, but I left my eyes closed. "Can I spend some time with my daughter please?"

Riley sat up on his elbow but kept his arms wrapped around me. "I don't know if she'd want that," he whispered. They hadn't realized I was awake. "I think you've caused enough damage for a lifetime. What more could you have to say to her?"

"That I love her."

Riley's chest shook as he laughed. It wasn't a funny, ha-ha laugh. It was more of a disgusted, "I can't believe he just said that" kind. I could almost feel hate as it seeped out of his pores and in my father's direction.

He slid his arm out from under me and slowly climbed out of the bed. "Well, if that's what love looks like, then I don't want her to have to deal with any part of it."

"I'm human, Riley. I make mistakes."

"Evidently."

"I came here with the best of intentions. When I finally saw her, I got emotional and didn't think straight."

"And what exactly were your intentions?"

"To fight for my daughter."

"You didn't lose her in a fight; you gave her up. Why would you think you needed to fight for her? I don't think you have any idea what that did to her or anyone else around you."

"Your dad already told me."

"Really? He told you about the days we spent sitting with her in the hospital when you wouldn't come back to Oklahoma to see her? He told you about what it did to Gramps that you didn't even bother to come to your own wife's funeral?"

Dad didn't reply.

"So he told you what it did to Attie when she woke up in the hospital alone? Or that she sat in the rehabilitation center day after day, hoping that it might be the day you would visit, but it never was? And he told you how she felt when your nurse picked her up and brought her home to an empty house? And he told you how she felt when she ate dinner alone every single night or that she ran away to New York City in hopes that you would care enough to go looking for her and bring her home, but of course you didn't?

"Did he tell you she had nightmares every night for a year? Or that, because of what she saw in her dreams, she was afraid to sleep? Or that she was completely sleep deprived? And did he tell you that she cried herself to sleep almost every single night? And did he tell you that she compared herself to trash? She felt like trash that you'd thrown away."

"Riley, I—"

"And did he tell you that they had to sedate her, knock her completely unconscious, for fear she might hurt herself? Or that she's lost all confidence in herself and she can't even see how amazing she is because *you* don't see her that way? Did he tell you that she sees her worth through your eyes, and because of that she feels like she doesn't have any worth at all? Did he tell you there's nothing I can say to her, nothing I can do for her to make her feel better, to fix it? I can't fix what you've destroyed."

I could hear my dad's cries. "That's why I have to try to fix it, Riley. Nobody else can fix what I've done."

Riley ignored him. "Did my dad tell you how he felt when he saw her lying on the floor in her room? Did he tell you how deep the pit in his stomach was when he thought he'd lost another daughter? Do you even think about anyone other than yourself?"

I finally sat up. "Riley, enough."

He looked over at me, face flushed and eyes red and swollen. "I'm sorry," he whispered. "I didn't mean to wake you."

"You didn't. I was already awake."

I looked over at my father. His clothes hung off his slumping body. He looked like Riley had beaten him senseless.

"I'll talk to him," I said. "Just give us a few minutes. I want to hear what he has to say."

"Are you sure, Charlie?"

"No . . . but I feel like I should hear him out."

He walked back to me and kissed me on the forehead as he gripped my hand in his. "I'll be right outside. Just push the button if you need me. The nurse can send me right in."

"Okay."

He placed his face within inches of mine. "I love you," he whispered.

I nodded before he kissed my nose and walked out of the room, leaving my dad in an awkward silence.

He walked over and sat in the chair next to the bed. I watched his eyes scan the room. "You can't look at me?"

He shook his head and looked down at the floor. "I'm ashamed."

"You should be. Unfortunately, nothing Riley said was an exaggeration, and you caused every single bit of it."

"I know." He spoke so softly that I could hardly hear him.

"I don't want to rehash everything that's happened since the accident. You weren't here, you missed it all, and I don't want to bring it all up again. Nothing that we say can change any of it anyway."

He shrugged.

"What I do want to know is why you told me about you and Mom getting divorced. What purpose could that possibly serve?"

"I see you walking down the same road."

"What road?"

"You and Riley. You're too young to be so serious, and when you're young, you're also naive. You think if you love each other now, you always will. Your mom and I thought that when we were together, but things change. How you and Riley feel about each other—it's too much."

"What are you talking about?"

"Attie, there's no doubt this relationship is serious. And Riley, that poor boy is so in love with you he can't think straight. You should see him out there; he's a nervous wreck. He hasn't left the hospital and it's been days."

"You act like Riley and I are talking about getting married or something."

"Are you telling me you haven't?"

"We've joked about it a few times, but neither one of us wants to get married until we're out of college."

"You say that now … and what happens if you get pregnant? What then?"

"Then we've got a massive problem because it'll be another virginal birth. We aren't having sex, and we won't be."

"You may not be now, but another four years is a long time to wait. You think he's going to be willing to do that?"

"I guess if he wants to be with me, he will. I don't know, Dad. I don't have all the answers, but I never thought I needed them right this very moment. It's not like we're making any long-term plans or anything."

"Where are you going to go school next year?"

"UCO."

"Why?"

I didn't answer.

"Because that's where Riley will be, right? You could go to school anywhere. You could come up to Ithaca and be on the fast track like Cooper. Why settle for a small community school?"

"UCO is a good school, Dad. I'm only going there for my undergrad."

"Are you still going to vet school?"

"I think so."

"Where?"

Again, I didn't want to answer.

"This is what I'm talking about. You had a plan for your life until Riley came into the picture."

"I'm not sure how you would know that, seeing as how we've not had a conversation about it since long before Mom died. I was a sophomore last time we even talked about my future. You don't think I have a better idea of what I want now versus what I wanted then?"

"I believe that you made good choices based on good information rather than emotion. Right now every choice you make will be clouded by your emotions. Everything you consider will be viewed through the lens of Riley, and I don't want you making decisions that way. The last thing you want to do is make a decision now that could affect you for the rest of your life."

"Isn't that what college is all about? Finding out who you are? If Riley and I aren't meant to be, don't you think we'll figure that out?"

"I don't know. But if you're meant to be, what harm could a little time away do?"

"What are you saying to me?"

"I want you to come back to New York with me."

"What?"

"You and Riley can get some distance from each other. Both of you can see things a little more clearly, and you and I will have some time to fix our relationship. I've really messed up, Attie; I need you to let me try to fix it."

"And I have to move to New York for that?"

"That's where my job is. What do you expect me to do?"

"All of my friends and family are here. What do you expect *me* to do?"

"I don't expect anything, but I'm asking you to come back to New York with me. Give us some time and give yourself some time to get your head on straight. You've been through a lot. You need some time to think things through."

I shook my head.

"Do it for Riley."

"Riley? Moving to New York is the last thing he would want."

"Did you hear him just now? What kind of life has he had for the last several months?"

Tears immediately sprung to my eyes.

"Attie, what kind of life is that for a seventeen-year-old boy? And if you love him as much as you say you do, then why on earth would you ask him to deal with all that?"

"I didn't ask him to. He made those choices for himself. Plus, I didn't have anyone else, least of all you."

"So you're with him because you need him, not because you want to be with him?"

"I want to be with him. I love him."

"It sounds to me like you needed someone to help you through everything. What is he outside of that? What do you two have in common? Are your lives heading in the same direction? Do you want the same things?"

"We want to be together."

"That's not what I'm asking you."

I turned my head away from him. Truth was, I didn't know what we wanted … or needed. No matter how much I wanted to deny it, the things my dad was saying were true in a lot of ways. I had relied on Riley too much. Not only Riley, but Pops, Marme, Joshua and

Nicole—just about everyone. The only person I hadn't counted on to get me through my messes was myself.

"Are you two what's best for the other, or are you dependant on his help and he gets his self-worth from being the person who gets to be the hero?"

My body was quivering, overtaken with confusion and sadness.

"Are you being fair to him? Should he be put in the position where he thinks he needs to be the person to fix you? You don't want to end up living your life together always wondering if he's with you because he wants to be or because he felt he needed to be."

He reached up and wiped the tears off my cheeks with the back of his fingers.

"I'm a screw-up. I've done nothing right over the last few years. Please, let me try to make this right. Give me the chance to put our relationship back on course."

I finally looked over at him. "I don't know if that's even possible."

"Try with me. Just give me some time—you've got the rest of your life ahead of you. You'll get married and have children. I don't want to miss all of that. I have to make this right. Please, please come home with me. Let's fix what I broke."

Riley knocked on the door but didn't open it.

"Think about it," Dad urged. "Come in, Riley."

He opened the door and walked to the end of the bed. "Is everything all right?"

I shrugged.

"We don't know yet," Dad said. "I guess we're going to find out." Reaching down, he took my hand in his, gave it a small squeeze, and then walked away without saying another word.

"Are you okay?" Riley asked as he sat on the bed next to me.

I shrugged again.

"Talk to me. Tell me you're okay. I need to know that you're all right."

"I need a popsicle." That was a lie. What I needed was a little bit of time to think. "Please go get me a popsicle."

"Now?"

"Riley, please. A popsicle. They've got them at the nurses' station or something."

"Okay." He stood and leaned over to kiss me on the forehead. I closed my eyes as his lips touched my skin.

My mind raced a million miles an hour as he walked out of the room. And though my mind was moving quickly, he seemed to be moving in slow motion.

I thought back over my dad's words. I replayed the words Riley had said to him when they thought I was asleep.

Riley's return snapped me out of my daze. "Are you okay?"

"I don't know, Riley," I snapped. "The real question is, how are you?"

"No need to worry about me." He set the popsicle on the tray in front of me, grabbed my hand, and rubbed it with his.

"Someone needs to." I pulled my hand away and picked up the popsicle. "With all the attention I've been getting for the last six months, I wouldn't blame you if you were getting a bit tired of it all."

"Listen to you talking all crazy; you're back to your normal self. I think we can go home now." He laughed.

"I'm being completely serious."

His smile disappeared.

I looked down at the popsicle and concentrated on peeling the white paper away from the frozen treat. "I feel sorry for you, Riley. Honestly, I do."

"For me? Why do you feel sorry for me?"

"Because you're stuck dealing with all this. There's always something wrong with me, and I've got enough baggage to fill a cargo jet."

"Don't talk like that. I don't feel that way at all."

"Why?" I threw the popsicle back down and looked up at him. His face was pained, but I didn't let it get me off track. "How is that even possible? How can you not feel like all I'm doing is weighing you down?"

"Because I love you, that's why. I wanna help. None of this is your fault."

"But it all becomes my problem, my burden, and my issues. Good grief, my dad issues alone are enough to fill a novel or two."

"Just because some of your circumstances got worse doesn't mean that those of us who love you bail. We're not going anywhere." He pointed toward the door. "You should see the waiting room out there. It's full of people who love you: Mom, Dad, Gramps, Josh and Nicole, Tammy, Anne, Jen, Curt, Matt, Tess, and Chase. Not to mention everyone from school that've stopped by. Even Tiffany spent some time here. And Mitchell King, even—"

"Riley," I interrupted.

"What?"

"I'm talking about you. You and all you're left to deal with."

He waved his hand in the air as if he were pushing the subject aside. "Don't worry about me."

"I *am* worried about you. I'm worried about both of us. I'm really, really confused. Things are really bad right now."

"We'll get through it."

"No, Riley, *I* need to get through it."

"So you'll get through it."

"Riley!" I was losing my patience with him. I wanted him to see what it was I was trying to say so I wouldn't actually have to say it out loud, but he couldn't. Either he couldn't or he just wouldn't. "I need to walk through this alone," I finally said.

His face turned red. "What on earth did your dad say to you in here? I knew I shouldn't have left you two alone."

"This isn't about him. It's about us. It's about me and you and the decision that I have to make in order to do what's best for both of us."

His forehead creased. "What are you saying?"

"I don't know. I think I'm saying we need some time—"

"Don't."

" …apart. I think we need some time apart."

He jumped out of his seat and started pacing. "Seriously, we're back here again? How many times are we gonna have this conversation?"

"This is the last time."

He stopped dead in his tracks. "Watch it, Charlie, you're sounding awfully final."

"I know."

He shook his head. "We're not doing this right now. We're not having this conversation in this room and under these circumstances."

"We need time apart."

"I don't. I don't need time away from you. I don't want that."

"I want that for you."

"No."

"I heard it. I heard everything you said to my dad when you thought I was asleep. You weren't just describing my life over the last year and a half. You were describing your life too. You were describing everything you've had to live through because of me."

He kept shaking his head, as if he was trying to keep the sound of my voice from entering his ears. "No."

"You lost the summer of the accident because you were sitting in my hospital room. Since last summer you've had to take care of me. Whether it was nightmares or bullies at school or my dad, you've been stuck having to pick up all my pieces and try to put me back together again. You've been stuck with all my problems."

"No, I haven't."

"You have."

"It's been my choice. I've not been *stuck* doing anything."

"I want you to have at last part of your senior year to be free."

"No."

"You deserve to have fun."

"We do have fun."

I ignored him. "You deserve to not have to worry about someone else all the time."

He violently shook his head and pressed his lips together.

"And I need to not feel guilty for ruining your life."

"You don't ruin my life. You're tired and sick, and you aren't thinking clearly. We can discuss this later. Right now you just need to rest."

"We don't need to discuss it later, Riley. My mind's made up. I may be confused and I may be sick and tired, but I do know what's best for us right now, and it's not for us to be together."

"Don't. Please don't do this." Tears streamed down his face. "I love you, Charlie. I wanna be with you, baggage and all."

"I need to know that you are enjoying your life, and I need to know that I can carry my baggage all on my own."

He sat back in the chair. "So what are you saying to me?"

"I'm moving back to New York."

"What?" he screamed.

"It's what's best."

"No, it isn't."

"My dad wants me back. I owe it to him to try, and after everything you've done for me and everything you've been through, I owe it to you to let you go."

"No!"

I covered my face with my hands.

"Charlie, look at me."

I shook my head. I couldn't do it. I couldn't look at him. "I'm doing this because I love you. I can't be with you right now. I can't be a burden to you anymore. I can't have you look at me one more time with pain in your eyes. I can't cause you pain anymore."

"*This* is causing me pain. Don't you get that? This pain is worse because not only do I still hurt for you, but now I hurt because I lose you too. You're adding to my pain, not taking it away."

"Eventually it'll be too much for you, Riley. I know it will be. You'll walk…"

"I'm not walking anywhere. I'm not your dad."

"Don't."

"Look at me!" he shouted. I felt him stand, and his face come close to mine.

I slammed my eyes shut.

"If you're gonna do this, then you do it looking at me. You owe me that much."

I lowered my hands and opened my eyes. His face was bright crimson and strained.

"This isn't about what's best for you or me. Don't lie to yourself or to me. You're punishing me for something your dad did. That's not fair."

"I'm not blaming you, Riley. I'm protecting you."

"You aren't protecting me at all. You're pushing me away because of something that *could* happen, not something that has. You're afraid—"

"It will happen. We're young—too young. We fell in love too soon. You had to know this couldn't last forever."

"No, I didn't know that. People last. Relationships last."

"Not very often."

"Often enough. My parents are proof of that."

"And my parents are proof of the opposite. It may have taken twenty years, but my dad—"

His fists slammed into the mattress next to me. "I'm not your dad!"

"Well, I'm my dad's daughter."

He shook his head in disgust. "So what, you're saying you'd eventually walk away because your dad did?"

"Maybe. There's always that chance."

"Shouldn't taking that chance be my choice? It's a chance I'm willing to take."

"I won't let you."

He reached for my hand, but I pulled it away. "And besides, Riley, I have to try to work things out with my dad. No matter how much he's messed up, I have to let him try."

"And you can't do that from here?"

I shook my head.

"So this is it?" he asked. "You're ending us? Everything we've had? After everything we've been through? All over something that may never happen?"

"I guess so." I suppose the words came out more harshly than I intended. I wasn't trying to be cruel. It truly was a guess.

In a daze, he slowly stood from the bed and walked to the door. Without turning to face me, he spoke again. "One of these days you're gonna have to stop running."

He opened the door and walked away.

What else could I have done? If I would have let Riley say any more, he probably would've won me over, and that wouldn't have been what was best for either one of us.

I pushed the nurse's call button and waited in silence until she arrived.

"Yes, Attie?"

"I don't want any more visitors."

"Are you sure? There's a room full of people waiting out here to see you."

"Send them all home. Tell them that I don't want to see anyone and won't for a while. There's no point in everyone waiting around."

"Is there anything I can do?"

"No. Please turn my light off and leave me alone."

"I'll turn the light off, but I'll be in and out to check on you. I won't talk unless you want me to. Just call me if you need me."

"Yes, ma'am."

The room went dim, and I slouched further into my bed as I pretended not to see Jesus sitting on the windowsill.

chapter 31

(Riley)

I walked outside for the first time in days. The bright sunlight practically blinded me as I stumbled out to the cement bench just a few yards away. The cold stone sent a chill through my body, and I realized that I didn't have a coat. We'd left the house so fast that I didn't have time to think about grabbing one, and I'd been inside the hospital for so long that I didn't realize it had turned so cold.

I heard the door open behind me and knew who it was without even looking.

"She's going back," I said.

Mom sat down next to me but didn't speak.

"I shouldn't have left them alone together. It's like one minute all was well, and the next minute everything fell apart."

She looked over at me. "Riley, be honest with yourself. All was not well, and it hasn't been for a long time."

"Maybe things were falling apart around us, but *we* were well. We were happy. We're good together."

"I know you are."

"I can't believe she's doing this to us. The crazy thing is, she thinks that she's helping me. She thinks this is a good thing."

"It might be."

"How can you even say that?"

"I was a lifeguard while I was in high school."

I felt my eyes roll. I wasn't in the mood for one of Mom's strolls through childhood.

"One of the things they taught us in training was how to handle a person that's drowning."

I had to fight the urge to say "duh."

"It's the job of a lifeguard to do everything in their power to save someone if they're struggling—unless by trying to save the victim, you yourself could end up drowning." She picked up my hand and held it in hers. "You see, when someone's drowning, they can lose all common sense. Fear takes over, and they'll lash out at anyone or anything. They think they're saving themselves, but in reality, they're causing both people to sink. The reason it happens is, while they think they're swimming and saving themselves, they're actually working against the efforts of the lifeguard who's trying to save them."

"So what are you supposed to do?"

"You let them go."

I made the connection of what she was saying. It broke my heart. They weren't the words I wanted to hear. What I wanted her to be telling me was that I needed to fight for Attie, find a way to make her stay. The last thing I wanted to hear her say was that I needed to let her go.

"You let go and you wait until they either come to their senses or until they wear out and stop thrashing around. Once all their energy is gone, you can grab them and bring them to safety. But the most important lesson of being a lifeguard is that you don't ever let yourself become a victim when you're busy trying to be the rescuer.

"Riley, Attie's letting you go so she doesn't take you down with her."

I fought the urge to cry, and doing so made my entire body shake.

"She sees what's happening to her, and she doesn't want you to suffer just because she has to."

"Isn't that my choice?"

"It should be. But sometimes we can't make the right decisions for ourselves. She's making the decision that she knows you won't."

"You think she's doing the right thing?"

"I'm not saying that. I'm saying that I believe *she thinks* she's doing the right thing. So, while you have every right to be hurt, I don't think you have the right to be angry. She's trying to protect you. It's like what she did with the cheer squad. She's stepping aside so that life can get back to normal."

"I don't want a normal life if it means she isn't part of it."

"I don't either."

I gave up on trying to keep from crying and let the tears come. Mom held my hand and let me cry. She didn't say another word until my dad joined us on the bench.

"I just talked to Eddie. He told me Attiline was going back to New York."

"We heard," she said.

"I don't know if I can do it," I said through sniffles. "I don't want to let her go."

"When you were six years old, you were bound and determined to get the training wheels off your bike so that you could ride around with the big kids."

I looked over at Dad. What on earth this had to do with Attie was beyond me.

"Your mom thought it was too early, but I thought we should go ahead and let you give it a try. So your mom put on your elbow pads and your kneepads and your football helmet and sent you outside.

"We practiced a few times, had a few falls and knee scrapes, but there wasn't anything I could say or do to make you change your mind. So I put you back on the bike, gave you a push, and ran alongside you for a while as I held on to the back of your seat. Then, when I realized you were peddling hard enough, I let you go. I let you go not because I wanted to and not because I wasn't scared for you—because I was—but I let you go because it's what you wanted.

"That's what we did for Attiline while she was here. We helped get her up on her feet and walked along beside her until she was finally ready to go it alone. Now she wants us to let her go, and it's our job to do it. We have to let her go."

"That's easy for you to say. You're looking at this from the perspective of a parent. You look at it like you've trained her and she's off and flying to a better life. But that's not who I am, it's not who we are. I love her. I wanted her to be a part of my life. I saw her in my future."

"Who's to say that's changing?" Mom asked.

"She broke up with me. She's leaving."

"True. But she's left before and always come back. This is her home."

My mom was wishful thinking. There was no way Attie's dad was going to let her come back. Like he said, he'd come to Oklahoma to fight for her. He wasn't going to let her go without another fight, and I wasn't sure she wanted me to fight back.

"Riley, let her go. If it's meant to be, she'll come back."

"And if she doesn't?"

"Then as painful as it is, we'll find a way to go on without her."

chapter 32

(Attie)

It was ironic. Cheering football fans were celebrating on the television in the family room, and I was standing outside Riley's bedroom door in grief. I could hear my dad and Pops downstairs making polite small talk as they loaded the car with my belongings, but I didn't hear Marme's voice at all.

"Riley?" I stood staring at his door. "Will you please let me say good-bye?"

He didn't respond.

"Riley?" I tried to turn the door handle, but it was locked. I waited a few more minutes before realizing he wasn't going to open the door for me and then finally walked downstairs and out the front door. I didn't step off the porch. I couldn't.

Marme stood completely still. Only her eyes moved as she watched her husband load boxes into my car. If I were touring a museum, she could have easily passed as a marble statue. Her body was lifeless, and her skin was gray. I was fully aware I was breaking her heart—all of their hearts—and I could tell by my dad's demeanor that he too understood the gravity of the moment.

It didn't escape my attention that these moments on the Bennetts' driveway were completely opposite of when I'd arrived in May.

"That's pretty much everything," Pops said as he threw the last one in.

I could only nod. My throat was too dry to speak, and my knees were shaking so violently that any words that did manage to escape would be trembling.

"Is there anything else you need?"

I shook my head before turning and glancing through the open front door. Still no sign of Riley, although I'm not sure why I was surprised. I hadn't laid eyes on him since he walked out of my hospital room just after we broke up.

"I'll let you say good-bye," Dad said as he climbed into the car and pulled the door closed.

Marme ran to me, pulled me to her, and cried into my shoulder; but as quickly as it started and before I could react, she was back inside the house. It was the first time I'd ever been in her presence and didn't hear her speak. I hadn't heard her voice since she'd stood in the entryway the night before Thanksgiving and asked my father to leave. I desperately wanted to hear her voice. I wanted her advice. She was a mom, and she knew everything. I needed her to tell me that everything was going to be okay, but she didn't. She was gone.

My knees finally gave out, and I lowered myself to the porch step. "It's not like I have a choice or anything. I have to try."

Pops sat down beside me and took my left hand in both of his. "I know you do. We understand that, Attiline, but knowing that doesn't make it any easier. We love you and we want you here with us. I guess you can call us selfish like that."

"You're the most unselfish people I know."

"Not when it comes to you."

"Especially when it comes to me." Out of the corner of my eye, I could see tears fall from his face onto the step below us. Seeing his tears caused my own to fall freely. "I don't want to go; I just have to."

He nodded.

"I hope one day you can forgive me."

"There's nothing to forgive. You're doing the right thing. You're taking some time, trying to sort things out, and giving your dad a shot at making things right. Nobody can hold that against you."

"Not even Riley?"

"Especially not Riley."

"But he hates me."

"He loves you. It's the situation he hates."

"What if I'm wrong? What if this ends up being one big mistake?"

"Then you come home. You're always welcome here, no matter what. We'll always want you here."

"Even now that Riley and I are over?"

"Even then."

"Other than Riley, I'm going to miss you the most." I was now sobbing. "I'm going to miss talking to you."

"I want you to promise me that you'll call at least once every few weeks. Call me on my cell phone if you have to. At least let me hear your voice every once in a while, all right?"

"Yes, sir."

"Attiline, my love for you isn't dependent upon your relationship with my son. I've told you before and I'll say it again; I love you like you were my own daughter. Nothing's gonna change that. Not even being a thousand miles apart."

"I love you too. I always will."

I rested my head on his shoulder and looked over at my father in the car. He wasn't watching us.

"Are you ready to get in the car?"

I kept my head on his shoulder. "No."

"All right then."

He squeezed my hand, and the two of us sat on the porch for several more minutes before Dad rolled the window down and told me it was time to hit the road.

"Come on, let's get you in the car before we both completely lose it."

"I already have."

"I have too." He stood, pulled me to my feet, and led me to the car as my dad rolled the window back up.

Finally looking at Pops, I noticed his eyes were bright red and full of tears. He almost said something but stopped himself. Instead, he reached up, gave my cheek a pat, and walked away. As he did, I saw Riley standing in the doorway.

"Ri—"

"Don't. Don't say my name." His dad walked past him, inside the house and out of sight. "If I come down there, you can't talk. I can't hear you say it."

I nodded. It was a silent promise that I wouldn't say the word *good-bye*.

After what felt like an eternity, he bounded down the steps and swept me into his arms. The embrace lasted only a few seconds before he grabbed my face in his hands and kissed me.

I wanted to change my mind. I wanted to tell him that I was wrong and I wanted to stay with him, but I knew I was right. I needed to let him live his life—without me and all my problems. And I needed to deal with my problems so in the future, whether it was with him or someone else, I could have a healthy relationship.

His lips retreated, and within moments he ran right back into the house, slamming the door behind him.

I was left standing alone.

For the first time since before waking up in the hospital and finding Jesus in my room, I felt completely alone.

chapter 33

My eyes scanned the room as the teacher lifelessly read from the Power Point presentation flashing on the Smart Screen in front of the room. His lack of enthusiasm for the subject matter matched my lack of enthusiasm for life in general.

Since returning to New York almost a month before, my life had become nothing more than a series of days that I was left to trudge through until I could manage to make my way back to the sanctity of my bedroom. Back from Christmas break for only a week, as of right now, I had less than ten minutes until the final bell for the day announced that I was free to escape again to the freedom of the weekend.

The noise level increased around me as the students, neatly dressed in their school uniforms, began to get restless. Papers ruffled, chairs slid across the carpeted floor and clanked against the metal desk legs, and pencils pounded rhythmically on desktops as the kids' attention spans reached the nonexistent level.

Even with thirty people surrounding me, I was the loneliest I'd ever been. More lonely because now I knew what I was missing. I'd been given a glimpse into having a full life, and in an effort to repair my relationship with my dad and try to clear my head, I'd given it all up. When I'd lost Mom and Melody, I'd grieved the loss of their lives. Now, I was grieving the loss of my own.

Finally making my way out of the building and toward home, I was surprised at the amount of fog that hung over the college town.

Visibility was less than a few feet, and I was relieved that I'd cho-sen to walk to school that day rather than drive. Traffic was sure to be slow and dangerous, and I for one wasn't interested in risking another car accident.

Staying off the sidewalk, I listened as I sloshed through people's front yards. The ground was practically seeping with water due to the large amount of rain that had poured down on Ithaca over the past several days. Although most everyone was ready for the rain to come to an end, I was hoping it would remain. The sad weather matched my mood and brought me a bit of comfort. Were the sun to start shining, I might feel the need to improve my outlook, and I wasn't quite ready for that to happen.

"Attie, is that you?" Dad yelled from the back of the house as I walked through the back door.

"As if it would be anyone else," I muttered. "Yes," I called back. "The one and only."

He stuck his head out his office door and smiled; I knew the smile wasn't sincere. When his smiles were sincere, they were wide, showed his teeth, and caused lines to form around the edges of his bright eyes. With this smile, the one he'd started giving me once I returned home, his lips were tightly closed and barely curved up in the corners, and his eyes stayed dull. "How was your day?"

"Great." I was trying to act like I was happy to be home. We were living a lie, and I think we both knew it.

"Sicily called and invited you to a party tonight."

"Sicily? A party?"

"Betty's daughter—you remember her, don't you? I think she's only a year older than you."

"Yes," I lied. "I remember her."

A college party sounded like exactly what I needed to pull me out of my funk, if in fact I wanted to be out of my funk, which I didn't.

"Anyway, she'll be here at eight o'clock to pick you up. It'll be good for you to get out of the house for a little while and have some fun."

"Great," I lied. I looked over and noticed Baby lying on the couch. She hadn't been the same since we moved up north. Her excitement for life was completely gone.

"What about dinner?" I asked. "Do you want me to make us something?"

"Can't do dinner, sweetie. I've got to head out. I've got a meeting."

"On a Friday night?"

He gave me a sympathetic smile.

"Okay…well, maybe tomorrow we can go to lunch or something."

"I wish I could, but I've got to work at the clinic tomorrow. Maybe dinner?"

I shrugged. "Sure."

I turned and moped down the stairs, dragging my backpack behind me and letting it fall down each riser as I went. I'd given up everything to come back to New York and repair the relationship with my dad, and so far, he hadn't given up anything. He was gone almost as much as he had been before I moved to Oklahoma. The only difference this time—he was acting like he was happy to have me. And that was the problem. He was acting.

After jumping onto the bed, I fumbled through my backpack, pulled out my cell phone, scrolled through the names, and dialed.

He answered on the second ring. "Attiline! Hey, baby girl, how are you?"

"I'm good."

"I can tell in your voice that isn't true. What's going on?"

"Nothing. Nothing's going on."

"How are you and your dad?"

"We're okay."

"Is he spending time with you?"

"A little bit. Not much since Christmas, or tonight or tomorrow—but eventually I guess."

"I'm sorry. If he doesn't come around soon, I'm coming up there and dragging you home." I could hear frustration in his voice.

He made me smile even though I knew he wasn't telling the truth. It wasn't his place to interfere, and we both knew it. He wouldn't come and get me unless I asked.

"It'll all be all right. I know Eddie; he'll come around."

We were silent for a few moments before I finally spoke again. "I guess we shouldn't go on avoiding the obvious." I took a deep breath. "So do we dare talk about it?"

"I don't know. I'll follow your lead. What do you think? Can you handle it?"

A large, disappointing sigh flew out of my throat. "I'm upset, devastated, heartbroken—I don't know what other words I can use to describe how I'm feeling. It all looked promising for so long, and then it went and ended so badly."

"I know." I could hear his pain. "How do you make it so far and then lose it—again? What on earth is happening?"

"I don't know. They looked horrible. I haven't seen the Sooners look that bad in I don't know how long."

"Since the last bowl game we lost—that's when."

I laughed. "Oh yeah. Since then."

"The entire time we sat watching that game, all we could think about was how on earth you were handling it."

"I wasn't. I wasn't handling it at all. My dad finally had to leave the house. He couldn't listen to me scream anymore."

"Molly and I were afraid you'd end up back in the hospital."

"I almost did. I mean, to end a football season on that note—seriously? It was like they didn't even try, like they'd given up."

"I know." I could picture him shaking his head in disgust.

"Why do I have to care so much? Why can't I be normal and not care? It's just football, for crying out loud. And it's not like I need anything else to be depressed about..."

Pops and I continued talking for over an hour. We managed to talk about everything and everyone—everyone but Riley.

At eight o'clock Sicily rang the doorbell, and by twelve o'clock I was hiding out in the bathroom of some complete stranger's house; I wasn't feeling well and wanted to go home. Problem was, Sicily was nowhere to be found, and I didn't know any of the college students well enough to ask for a ride. From what I could tell, I was the only person in the house that wasn't completely intoxicated, and there wasn't any way I would be getting in the car with anyone there.

I tried my dad's cell phone and our home phone several times, but he never answered. Had it been Pops, he would've had the cell phone attached to his hip until I made it home.

Finally, as a last resort, I called the only other person I had the phone number for, begged for him to come pick me up, and waited a few minutes before I trudged out to the couch to languish until he showed up.

"Hey," a tall boy said with a slur. "Yur new 'round here. I haven't seen you b'fore."

"Yes, I'm the new girl … again. Lucky me."

"You're scrawny."

"You're one to talk."

"Want sum company?"

"Not so much."

He plopped down on the sofa next to me. The smell of alcohol radiating from his body was so overpowering that I almost vomited on the spot. As a matter of fact, the fumes were so heavy, I was beginning to feel a little intoxicated myself.

"Waz yur name?"

"Daphne."

"D—what?"

"D—Daphne."

"Well, that's a purty name."

"Uh-huh." I scooted toward the end of the couch.

He followed. "Where do you live?"

"In a galaxy far, far away."

"Really? Thaz purty cool. So you wanna make out?"

"No."

"You sure?"

"I've never been more sure of anything in my life."

He leaned over a little too much and fell onto me.

"Get away from her!" The boy jumped off the couch as Cooper Truman raced toward him. "You get away from her right now or I swear to God…"

"Stop it, Coop," I screamed.

"Not a word out of you." He held his hand up at me but didn't take his eyes off the boy. "Look, she's messed up right now. Trust me, you don't want to get involved."

"I am not messed up!"

He looked over at me. "Really?"

I shrugged.

He turned back to the boy. "Go on, get of here."

The wimp slinked his way around the room until he could finally slide out the door without Cooper actually reaching him.

"Having fun?" Cooper asked, walking toward me.

"Listen." I tried to climb up out of the couch but couldn't. "He wasn't doing anything you wouldn't have tried if given the opportunity."

"Nice to see you too." He grabbed me by the arm and helped me stand up before shoving his hands in his back pockets.

I started feeling dizzy and latched on to the belt loops of his pants to steady myself. "I'm just saying that you shouldn't go judging others for something you've probably done yourself. What are you so mad about, anyway?"

"This isn't who you are, Attie. The girl I knew last summer wouldn't have had to call me from hiding in a bathroom asking me to pick her up. You don't do this. You don't act like this."

"Maybe I do."

"No, you don't." He glanced around the room as if to make sure the boy hadn't returned.

"Relax, Coop, it's not like I'm drunk or anything. You'll be glad to know that no alcohol passed these lips."

"You're joking, right?"

"No. I didn't touch the stuff."

"I can smell alcohol on your breath."

"I swear." I held up my left hand. "I didn't drink anything."

"Wrong hand, Einstein. If you're going to swear you hold up the right."

"Whatever. I promise I didn't drink anything."

He shook his head in disbelief. "So you haven't had one drink?"

"No. I already told you that." I stumbled a bit. He grabbed me by the arm. "Although I am feeling a little woozy."

"Did you drink anything? A water? Soda?"

"No. I've watched the videos; I know you aren't supposed to trust that stuff at parties like this. I've had a little bit of fruit and that's it."

"Fruit?"

"There was some fruit in the punch."

"You ate the fruit out of the punch?"

"Isn't that what I just said?"

"What were you thinking?

"I got hungry," I whined. "There's no crime against eating fruit."

"Attie, the fruit absorbs the alcohol. You probably got more alcohol in you by eating the fruit than if you'd just drank a few cups."

"Huh?"

"Yeah."

"I wondered why it tasted so weird."

"Girls as innocent as you probably shouldn't be hanging out at parties like this."

"I'm not innocent, you big jerk."

"Spare me."

"Well, how was I supposed to know not to eat the fruit? They don't teach you that in those creepy anti-drug and alcohol movies."

"Trust me, you shouldn't even be allowed to be out after midnight."

"Look, if this is going to turn into a lecture, then I'll find someone else to drive me home. I thought you'd come out of the goodness of your heart and to make amends for your sabotagery. Instead, you came so you could rub it in my face."

"I came because I was worried. And what on earth is sabotagery? Is that even a word?"

"You know exactly what it is."

"No, I don't, but right now I don't care. You were hiding out in a bathroom, for Christ's sake."

"Look at you lecturing me when you just took the Lord's name in vain. You big sinner."

"I think there's plenty of sinning going around."

"Well, you're right about that. I've never seen anything like it. These kids are a bunch of hoodlums."

"I bet they are. Now come on, I'm getting you out of here. Can you walk?"

"We're leaving right now?"

"It's past one thirty in the morning, in case you hadn't noticed."

"It's that late?"

"No. It's that early."

He wrapped his arm around my waist and led me outside to his car.

"Ooh, you brought the Hummer. I've been waiting for months to see this thing."

"Too bad you'll be too hung over to remember it in the morning." He opened the car door and practically flung me inside before fastening my seat belt and slamming the door.

I explored the inside, but the more I moved my head, the more sick to my stomach I felt.

I listened as he climbed into the driver's seat while mumbling. "This isn't quite how I pictured seeing you again."

"How did you imagine it?"

He turned and stared at me for a moment before shaking his head with a laugh. "Not like this."

"Were you hoping I'd run in slow motion across a meadow and into your arms?"

"Something like that."

"Well, I don't do meadows anymore."

"Too bad."

He started the engine and drove away from the party as my head fell back onto the headrest. I closed my eyes, but doing so made my brain feel like it was on a tilt-a-whirl. I tried looking out the window, but after just a few minutes, even that was making me nauseated.

"Coop, stop the car."

"No!"

"Coop … stop the car!"

"I'm getting you home; I'm not stopping this car!"

"Then I hope you don't mind if you have puke all over everything."

His foot found the brake and slammed it to the floor. "Don't you throw up in this car, Attie Reed. My parents paid a lot of money for this car; you better not throw up in it. Do you hear me?"

As we looked at each other, I could feel fear fill my face as my cheeks grew full.

"Don't you dare! Don't you dare!" He threw off his seat belt, climbed across the front seats, and opened my car door before turning and frantically trying to unfasten my seat belt. "Get out before you spew all over me."

In a panic I pushed against him, throwing him back against the windshield as I clumsily climbed out of the car. I hadn't made it twenty feet before throwing up.

"Coop," my voice quivered, "where are you?"

Within a few moments he walked up behind me while I leaned over and spit repeatedly into the overgrown grass below me.

"Here." He held a T-shirt over my shoulder. "Wipe your mouth."

"The shirt stinks."

"Not any worse than you do right now."

I yanked it out of his hand before starting to vomit again. He gathered the hair onto the back of my neck and held it out of the way. "You okay down there?" His voice had suddenly turned soft. "Anything I can do?"

"Don't you be nice to me, Cooper Truman. I don't like you, and I sure don't want you being nice to me."

"I'm not. I just don't want you in the car with the smell of puke in your hair. It'll stink up my car for months."

"Good, because I can't handle you being nice to me right now."

"You don't need to worry about that. The last thing I want to be is nice. I'd rather give you a piece of my mind."

"Spare me the lecture."

"Are you about done?" he asked.

"Done what? Puking or griping?"

"Both."

"I don't know." I was spitting again.

"Well, hang out down there until you're finished."

A couple of minutes passed as I made sure that my stomach had stopped seizing and I wouldn't be throwing up again. "All right, I guess I'm done."

I stood upright, wiped the T-shirt across my mouth several times, and then handed it out to him.

"Uh, no," he said. "You keep it. It can be a piece of memorabilia from your night of sin."

"You think this is funny?" I asked.

"What?"

"You're laughing at me, you big butthead."

"I am not."

I threw my hands onto my hips.

"Okay, well, maybe I'm laughing at you a little."

I felt my face crumble and tears start flowing.

"Oh, come on. It's just funny, seeing you like this. I'm not laughing at you as much as—"

"You're laughing at me!"

"Yes." He threw his arms up in surrender. "I'm most certainly laughing at you. I can't help myself. You look completely pitiful. Your eyes are all red, and you've got snot running down your face. This is priceless."

I sat on the ground, pulled my legs up to my chest, and looked over at him with my head lying on my knees. It was the only way I could keep my head from spinning. "I'm glad you're getting a kick out of all this."

He sat down next to me. "What exactly is 'all this'?"

"I was out partying. Isn't that what people do to have a good time?"

"I wouldn't know."

"Oh yes, I forgot; you don't have a life."

"I have a life; it just isn't anything like this."

"See what you've been missing out on all this time? Doesn't it look like a blast?"

"Can I ask *why* you're doing this?"

"I was going to marry Riley one day, that's why," I admitted.

"Thinking of marrying Riley makes you want to get drunk and vomit?"

"Not exactly." I wiped my face with the T-shirt again.

"What are you, like, sixteen? I can't believe Riley asked you to marry him already."

"I'm seventeen, thank you very much. And he didn't ask me to marry him."

"Then why did you say you were going to marry him?"

"Because I thought I was. He didn't ask me to or anything; I just thought that one day we would be. Like in a lot of years."

"And now? Do you still think you're going to be marrying him?"

"Well, obviously not. We broke up. I moved away. That's it; it's over."

I turned to face him and crossed my legs. I assumed he would do the same, but he didn't. I guess he wasn't aware of the knee-to-knee technique.

"I didn't want to blame him," I sniveled.

"Blame him for what?"

"What if we'd been married for twenty years and I decided I missed out on tons of fun because we'd been together our entire lives. And what if I started to wonder what all I missed out on?"

"You think you'd regret missing out on vomiting on the side of the road at two o'clock on a Saturday morning?"

"Not that part exactly."

"Or having some drunken guy paw all over you?"

"Not that part either."

"Or—"

"Enough already."

"What part then?"

"He's partied and kissed girls, and he had a life before me. My entire teenage existence before him involved a hospital room or my bedroom. I've hardly experienced life apart from him."

"I see."

"It just makes more sense to try it all now. So, when my dad made me go to the stupid party, I figured I might was well let it rip. Although I didn't intend on getting sloshed, I guess it's one new experience out of many that I probably should eventually get around to."

"Well, you better get busy, because if you're going try it all, it could take awhile."

"I know. That's my point."

"So let's see, you've gotten getting drunk accomplished, puking due to an overconsumption of alcohol, attacked by a rabid male...What's left? Drugs, becoming a hippie, maybe a speeding ticket or two? A tattoo? Is that the kind of stuff you had in mind?"

"Not so much."

"So what were you thinking?"

"Well, obviously I wasn't," I cried.

"Obviously."

"This hasn't quite turned out how I'd planned."

"You actually planned this?" He laughed. "Well, that's pitiful. At least when I make horrible decisions it's because I'm an idiot. You actually put thought into this horrible plan."

"It's not like this kind of life comes naturally to me."

"Then why do it?"

I shrugged. "Doing right didn't win me any points. Life was harder when I was doing what I was supposed to. Life just got worse and worse."

"I see. So you figured you'd go out on your own, throw caution to the wind, and see if life got any easier?"

"Maybe."

"That makes absolutely no sense whatsoever."

"Well, now that I say it out loud, it sounds stupid."

"Imagine being the one to hear it. It sounds even worse."

"You're not one to talk, you know. It's not like you're an angel or anything. I know all about you."

His eyebrows raised, and he grinned. "Really? I can't wait to hear this. I'm sure it's priceless."

"I'm not getting into this with you right now. It's one thirty in the morning, remember?"

"I'm not in any hurry."

"My dad's probably freaking out. I need to get home."

"Fine." He stood and held out his hand for me to grab. "Then let's get you home. We'll discuss all of this another day."

"Oh no, we won't." I slapped his hand away and stood on my own, albeit a little wobbly. "I have no intention of ever hanging out with you. I don't like you, remember?"

"Well, you liked me enough to call me and have me come get you."

"No, I called you because you're the only person whose phone number I had."

"So you're using me?"

"Basically. I needed a ride."

"Well, my dear, my rides don't come for free. You owe me."

"Owe you what?

"The very least you can do is tell me why you dislike me so much. It's not as if I've ever done anything to you."

I laughed. "You can't be serious. You sabotaged my life!"

"There's that sabotage word again. What are you talking about? How did I sabotage your life? You lived in Oklahoma, and I lived here. I haven't talked to you in months."

"You didn't want Riley and me together."

He looked shocked. "What?"

"You told my dad on us."

"I told your dad on you? What does that even mean?"

"He came to Oklahoma to bring me home. You told him I was living with Riley and dating him. You told him I'd had an abortion. You're a tattletale and a liar."

"Abortion? I never said such a thing."

"He said your mom told him—"

"Why are you blaming me for something my mom told him? I never even heard that piece of news."

"Then how did she hear it?"

"I don't know. My family lives in Guthrie, remember? Maybe they heard it there. Trust me, it wasn't me. I don't even talk to anyone back there."

"How would your mother get the information to my dad?"

"My parents come to town a lot. They've gone to dinner with your dad a few times to talk about the stables and stuff. I don't know, I don't get involved in their business, but I can guarantee you that I never told your dad you'd had an abortion. Even if I had heard it, I wouldn't be telling anyone about it. It's none of my business."

"Well, I didn't, you know."

"Didn't what?"

"Have an abortion."

"I didn't think you did. Now, I may have mentioned to him that you and Riley were dating, but—"

"See, you did tattle on us."

"You mean he didn't already know?"

"Of course not."

"How was I supposed to know you were hiding it from him? Why would I think you would be?"

"Coop, I hadn't talked to the man in four months."

"And how was I supposed to know that? You can't be serious. You're blaming me for telling your dad something that I assumed he already knew? You're basically accusing me of trying break you and Riley up?"

"Pretty much."

"That's classic." He let out a disgusted laugh before turning and walking toward the Hummer. "I've never been a big Riley Bennett fan, but I certainly never tried to break you two up once you were together."

"Once we were together?" I marched after him. "What does that mean?"

He quickly turned to face me, which caused me to stumble backward. "I asked you out last year; that's no secret. But once I realized you and Riley were together, I backed off. You can't blame me for the two of you breaking up. You did that all on your own." He turned away from me again and opened the car door. "Get in the car."

"No." I turned back around and walked out into the grass.

"Attie?" I heard the car door slam behind me. "What's going on? Am I taking you home or not?"

"Yes. Just not right now."

"Are you feeling sick again?"

"No." I sat on the ground and then lay on my back. "You're right."

"What?" He sat down next to me.

"You're right. I can't blame you. I broke it off with Riley all on my own. I chose to come back here. I made this decision."

"You don't seem happy about being back."

"It's just taking some getting used to, that's all. All of my old friends moved on with their lives. They have new friends. I don't really fit in."

"You don't want to fit in."

"Maybe. I've just got to survive a few more months, and then I'm done and can start concentrating on college."

"Where will you go to school?"

"Here. Dad pulled some strings."

"And Riley?"

"What about him?"

"Where will he be?"

"Somewhere back home—I mean, somewhere in Oklahoma, I'm sure."

"You're not going to try to be closer to each other?"

"He hates me. The last thing he wants is to have me nearby."

"No, he loves you, and you broke up with him. How do you expect him to feel?"

"I didn't break up with him, per se."

He looked at me with eyebrows raised.

"Well, I was moving away. It's what was best."

"Just because it's what's best doesn't mean it doesn't hurt. When he looked into his future, I'd bet he saw you in it. I highly doubt he saw this coming."

"Well, I didn't see it coming either. It's as much a shock to me as him, and I'm just as miserable as he is. What else could I have done?"

"You could have stayed."

"It would have made my dad furious."

"Since when do you owe your dad anything?"

I didn't bother to answer the question.

"Attie, your dad is your past. What if Riley is your future?"

"He's not."

"How do you know that?"

"People don't find the love of their lives when they're sixteen years old. It doesn't work like that."

"Sometimes it does."

"Not this time."

"If you're so miserable, why did you even do it?"

"I had to."

"Why?"

"To prove to myself that I could live without him."

He reached over and peeled a clump of hair off my face. "So when are you going to start?"

"Start what?"

"Living."

chapter 34

I opened the front door and stepped into the silent home and into my room so I could change out of my ridiculous school uniform and into something more comfortable. I dug into the back of my closet and pulled out the first sweatshirt I could grab. Seeing the large OU logo emblazoned on the front, I shoved it back in and reached for another. No need to remind myself of home—or what was once home, anyway.

"Am I going to have to drag you out of this room?"

I looked up and spotted Cooper standing in my doorway as I pulled a blue sweatshirt over my T-shirt. "Hey, Coop."

"Are you ever planning on coming out of the basement?"

"I hadn't thought that far ahead."

His arms folded across his chest as a scowl formed on his face. "Well, that doesn't sound promising."

"I thought you said you'd give me some time."

"That was a while back. We've been cooped up in this house every day after school for almost a month. Don't you think it's time to get out and do something?"

"Do I bore you?"

"Never. I'm just getting worried about you, that's all."

I gave him a quick hug then slid past him and toward the theater room as he followed behind. "Want to watch some *Oprah*?"

"Not really. I'd rather find out what's going on with you."

"Nothing. Nothing's going on with me." I grabbed a blanket and wrapped it around my shoulders as I sat in the chair. "Have a seat."

He sat on the arm of a recliner and gloomily looked down on me. "If this is you better off than before, then I'm actually glad I didn't date you last summer. You would have been a total downer."

"I thought you were here to try to make me feel better."

"I am."

"Well, you're doing a sucky job."

A wide grin covered his face and exposed his bright white teeth. "We've got to get you out of this house."

"I don't want to get out of this house. I like it here."

His smile disappeared and was replaced by a slight frown. "You hate it here."

"Well, I like hating it. It keeps me in my depressed state, which I've come to find very comforting."

"That's never a good sign. Attie, it's not good for anyone to want to stay cooped up in their house all alone. Especially a house that has as many bad memories as this one does."

"It has good memories too."

"Really? Are those the ones that are keeping you depressed?"

"No."

"Are you even thinking about the good memories?"

"No, but don't worry, I'm fine. And I'm not alone. I've had you to keep me company for the last month."

"Not that I haven't enjoyed spending all this time with you, because I have, but your dad's worried, and I'm worried."

"Worried about what?"

"Worried that this depressing routine of yours is going to become your norm." He stood up and motioned for me to follow. "Come on."

"Where are we going?"

"To get you packed."

"Packed?"

"We're going skiing."

"Skiing? I don't know how to ski."

He stopped abruptly, causing me to run into him as he turned to face me. "Attie, you've said it yourself—it's time to try something new." His hands rested on my shoulders as he smiled down at me.

"Has anyone ever told you that you have the whitest teeth they've ever seen?"

He laughed. "No. That's the oddest thing anyone's ever said to me."

"You have a bright smile. It's one of the first things I noticed about you."

His left eyebrow rose. "Oh really?" He playfully pulled me more closely to him. "You noticed me, huh?"

"Yes."

"Like, *noticed* noticed me or just noticed me?"

I shoved him backward. "Quit it. Like you've never had a girl notice you before." I walked past him and into my bedroom.

"So when was it? When did you notice me?"

"Coop," I moaned.

"Seriously, I want to know. When were you checking me out?"

"It was at the pool party, and I wasn't checking you out. It was my job to watch. I was a judge, but you probably don't remember that."

"Oh, I remember. I also remember you only gave me a nine." He sat on the bed and watched as I rummaged through my dresser drawers.

"A nine was all you deserved."

"What else did you notice?"

"Nothing."

"I don't believe you. Come on, make my day. Tell me you noticed something else."

I stopped pulling clothes out of the dresser and turned to face him.

"Please," he asked, grinning.

"I noticed that we have a few things in common."

"Hmm," he said, nodding. "I'll take that. So if Riley hadn't been around..."

"Don't even go there."

"...and I hadn't lived so far away...Maybe, just maybe..."

"No sense in speculating. It is what it is."

"Correction, it was what it was. Circumstances change."

"You better stop talking like that if you want me to go on this trip with you. Wait, what am I saying? I don't want to go on this trip with you."

"You don't have a choice. Consider yourself forced."

"By whom?"

"Me and your dad."

"Is my dad going?"

"No. But he knows you're going, and he's very happy about it."

"He's probably just happy to get me out of his hair."

"I think you need to give him a little more credit than that. He is your dad. He's worried."

"Then it's a change of pace."

"A good change of pace."

I tossed a few more items into my bag and zipped it until it got stuck midway. "Well, if I go, know that I'm going as nothing more than a friend. The last thing I want to do is have to worry about what you're thinking the whole time."

"You don't have to worry about me. I'll be a perfect gentleman. All I want is for you to have a good time. Well, that and for you to return non-injured."

"The non-injured part would be the most important. I've spent enough of my life in a hospital bed."

As he reached over to help me finish zipping the bag, his hands brushed mine, causing me to quickly draw them away.

Once the bag was closed, Cooper threw the bag strap over his shoulder and made his way toward my doorway. "I'll take very good care of you, Attie." He turned to face me. "Nothing bad is going to happen to you while you're on my watch; I can promise you that."

I followed him up the stairs and grabbed my coat from the closet. "And you're sure my dad knows about this?"

"Yes, I suggested it when we talked last time. He thought it sounded like a great idea."

"He must trust you."

"Either that or he really wants you out of the house. Which he does. Here." He tossed me a set of car keys. "You're driving."

"Huh?"

"Last summer I promised you that you could drive the Hummer sometime. Here's your chance."

"Get out! We're driving the Hummer? How obnoxiously wonderful is that?"

He laughed. "Very obnoxious. We'll fit right in with the rest of the show-offs. It'll be great."

I ran past him, out the door and into the driveway.

"Are you going to lock up your house?"

"This is going to be awesome!"

"Attie, are you not going to lock up?"

"You're seriously going to let me drive this behemoth?"

"Why not?" He pulled the front door shut.

"I've had my license for less than a year and Riley usually drove us everywhere we went."

"You're your own woman; I think you can handle driving. Plus, my dad's got great insurance."

I watched Cooper throw my bag into the backseat, and then we both climbed in.

"This is the coolest vehicle ever. You've got to feel like a total stud driving around in this thing."

He grinned and nodded as a blush colored his face.

"You do, don't you?" I teased.

"Maybe a little bit. Wouldn't you?"

"I knew it."

"Can we change the subject please?"

"I don't think I've ever seen you blush."

"Well, the weekend's just starting; depending on how it goes, you may see me blush a few more times."

"Wait, the weekend? We're staying the whole weekend?"

"Why did you think you were packing a bag?"

"I have no idea. You told me to pack a bag, so I did."

"Do you do everything you're asked without questioning why?"

"Tammy was right. You do always answer a question with a question."

"It leads to more stimulating conversation. Wouldn't you agree?"

"No, it leads to a migraine. Where are we staying, anyway?"

"My parents have a cabin. Why?"

"Are they going to be there?"

"No."

"Will there be any adults at all?"

"No."

"Well, who's going to chaperone?"

He broke out in laughter. "We don't need a chaperone. Do we?"

"You're a guy and I'm a girl—"

"Yes."

"We're going to be alone in a cabin."

"We aren't dating, Attie; we're friends."

"I know that."

"And we each have our own separate rooms. There's no need for a chaperone. Unless of course …"

"'Of course' what?"

"Unless you think you can't control yourself around me."

I shot an evil glance his direction before stabbing the key into the ignition and starting the car. "Dream on."

We'd only been in the car for half an hour when I finally couldn't stand the suspense any longer and asked the question that I'd wanted the answer to for months.

"So did you really cheat on Melody with Tiffany?"

I glanced over at him and noticed a shocked expression on his face, which confirmed that I'd caught him completely off guard.

"That came out of nowhere."

"Did you?"

"Why are you asking me?"

"I want to know."

"And you want to discuss it now? Can't we just enjoy the drive?"

"Now's the perfect time because you can't escape."

He leaned forward and rested his head on the dashboard. "All right, where'd you hear it?"

"Some of the girls were talking about it. They said that's why you and Riley hate each other."

He took a deep breath and let it out slowly before leaning back in his seat. "Yes, I cheated on Melody with Tiff."

"Oh."

"I never should have dated Melody in the first place. She was too young…and innocent. And at the time, I didn't want to be so innocent."

My grip on the steering wheel tightened to the point that my fingers throbbed. "So you broke up with her because she wouldn't put out."

"I'm not proud of it, Attie. I know it was wrong. I deserved every consequence I suffered."

"What consequences?"

"Well, I hurt Melody, for one, and she never forgave me—or had the chance to. Riley not only despises me but we got in a fight over it, and from then on all the girls at school saw me as someone who was only after one thing."

"I don't get it. Why do guys have to act like that? It's just sex, for crying out loud. Is it worth all that?"

"Surely you and Riley—"

"Surely me and Riley nothing. Don't loop us into your group."

Out of the corner of my eye, I noticed him twist in his seat until he was facing me. "You're going to sit there and tell me you and Riley never—"

"Is your seat belt on?"

"Yes. So you and Riley never—"

"No. We never did."

"Wow."

"I bet now you're glad you and I never went out. You would've been frustrated and miserable and dumped me in less than a week."

"I wouldn't say that. I'd give it up for the right girl if I had to."

"But you don't give it up for every girl?"

"Not every girl wants me to."

"How are you so sure? For all you know, every girl only does it because she thinks it's the only way she can keep you. I mean, have you ever asked?"

"No, but it's not like its hundreds of girls or anything."

"Well, how many?"

He readjusted again in his seat and turned toward the window. "I'm not answering that."

"I told you I hadn't done it."

"You told me you hadn't done it with Riley. You never said you hadn't done it at all."

"Well, if I didn't do it with Riley, then who on God's green earth would I be doing it with?"

"Nobody, I guess. And for some reason I find the news a huge relief."

"So how many?"

"Attie, stop." He nervously tapped on the window. "Seriously, you need to stop."

"What are you going to do, beat me up?"

"Maybe I should. You're journeying into hostile territory."

"It must be a lot if you don't want to tell me."

"How many do you consider a lot?'

"How old are you?"

He folded his arms across his chest. "I just turned twenty."

"Good grief, Coop, you shouldn't be doing it at all. You're only twenty, you're not married—"

"Obviously."

"You aren't even in a serious relationship."

He spun around and faced me again. "What planet are you living on?"

"It really is a good thing we never went out. We see life very differently."

"I told you I would hold out for the right person."

"No, you wouldn't."

"Yes, I would."

"No, you wouldn't. You'd say you would but then end up cheating or leaving."

"Why would you even say that?"

"You did it to Melody, didn't you?"

"I was a lot younger then, Attie. I was an idiot, and I wouldn't have known a good thing if I saw it."

"And you would know now, at the ripe old age of twenty?"

"Trust me, I know if a good thing is sitting next to me." His voice shuddered, but I couldn't tell if it was because he was angry or amused. "Here's the real question." He leaned forward again. "Would you rule out someone like me?"

"What do you mean?"

"Someone who's made mistakes, maybe has been with more people than they should have, but realizes it and wants to change. Would you give that person a chance?"

"I may not have much of a choice. The older I get, the less chance I have of finding someone who hasn't. It's like I'm some kind of freak or something. No guy wants a virgin, for crying out loud."

"Every guy wants a virgin."

I felt a laugh flow out of my throat.

"They do," he demanded. "They may not think they want to date a virgin, but when it comes time to get serious and find 'the one,' I think every guy wishes they would be someone's 'only one.'"

"Well, I hate to tell you this, but you've got to date people to get to the point of marrying them. So, if guys don't want to date virgins but they want to marry them, then how on earth do they get to that point if they haven't dated them?"

"The guy just knows. When he first gets to know her, he knows."

"He knows what?"

"She's different. She could be the one."

"The one?"

"The one worth waiting for. The one worth … everything."

"You actually believe there's one worth everything?"

"I sure do, and I'd bet she's closer than you think."

"Have you come across anyone you thought might be the one?"

"Once."

"And?"

"She was in love with someone else."

"Well, then she must not have been the one."

"I wouldn't be so sure. Circumstances change. You should know that better than anyone."

"Things have a way of working themselves out, Coop. If two people are meant to be together, they will be."

Resting the side of his head on the dashboard in front of him, he looked over at me with a grin. "I couldn't agree with you more."

"Look at that, we agree on something."

"So is Riley the only guy you've ever kissed?"

"That's none of your business."

"You asked me how many girls I've been with."

"And you never answered me."

"I'll tell you if you tell me."

"Fine."

"Two," he said quickly. "And Tiffany wasn't one of them."

"Only two?"

"Only? Just a second ago you were telling me that I shouldn't be doing it at all."

"I know, but you made it sound like it was a lot more than that."

"I didn't make it sound like anything."

"Two, huh?"

"So how does hearing that make you feel?"

"Disappointed but relieved."

"How's that?"

"I think I'm disappointed that you don't see the importance in waiting, but I'm relieved that it hasn't been more than that."

He gave a solemn nod but quickly perked up. "I answered your question, so you answer mine."

"Riley's the only boy I've kissed. But don't laugh at me or anything. You have to understand, I wasn't allowed to date before my junior year, and then I spent the majority of my junior year either in a hospital or recuperating at home, so it's not like I had many opportunities to go out or anything."

"I wouldn't laugh at you. Why would you think I would?"

"Because I'm seventeen years old and I've only kissed one boy. You're only three years older and you've been with two girls already. I'm sure I look like a complete prude."

"I don't think you're a prude. You know what you want and what you don't. I certainly can't laugh at that. And as a guy who may or may not be interested in you, it's nice to know that I wouldn't have a lot of competition."

"Aw, there it is!"

He laughed. "What?"

"I knew you had ulterior motives."

"Who, me?"

"Yes you. You still sort of have the hots for me, don't you?"

"What?" The smile on his face was so large I thought it would swallow his entire head.

"Don't 'what' me. You just got busted."

"Hey," he squeaked as he squirmed in his seat. "I ... I ..."

"Don't 'I ... I' me. You're done. You're dead to me."

"What?"

"You better not make a move on me this weekend, Cooper Truman. I'll kick your butt if you do."

"I won't be making any moves. I'll be leaving that all up to you."

"Then you'll be waiting forever and ever."

"We'll see about that."

"Your dazzle techniques don't work on me."

"We'll see."

"You're a little overconfident, don't you think?"

"We'll see."

"Uh-huh."

"You think I dazzle?"

"Enough."

He nodded wildly. "You do. You think I dazzle."

"No, I don't."

"I better be careful around you or I'm going to have to peel you off of me."

"No, you aren't."

"I'm going to turn the dazzle factor up so high there's no way you can resist me."

"Trust me, I can and will resist you."

"We'll see."

"If you don't shut up right now, I'm going to turn this car around and take your pompous butt right back home."

"Fine. I'm shutting up."

"Thank you."

"You're welcome."

We sat in silence for several minutes until I noticed him waving his fingers in my direction.

"What are you doing?"

"I'm dazzling you."

"You're such a huge dork that I can't even imagine that any girl would want you."

"They're after my money," he said with a laugh.

"Oh, now that makes perfect sense. Too bad for you I don't care about money."

"I know. Why else do you think I hang out with you?"

"My brilliant and uplifting personality?"

"Okay, I think we can both agree that we're equally delusional. You thinking you've got an uplifting personality and me thinking I could dazzle anyone, least of all you. Truth be told, we're both imbeciles that don't have anyone but each other."

"Very sad, but also very true."

"We might as well make the most of it and just agree to get along."

"Also true."

"So we're all good?"

"Yes."

"Good." He lowered the chair back, lay down, and pulled his ball cap until it almost completely covered his eyes. A few seconds later he lifted the hat rim and smiled over at me.

"So what's with this whole 'crying loud' thing?"

"Crying loud?"

"Yes. You say it a lot."

"Oh, you mean 'for crying out loud'?"

"Yes, that's it."

"It's just a phrase that Riley used to say when he was exasperated with me."

"Then I'm assuming he said it a lot."

"All the time."

"I can see that, you being exasperating and all. You're wearing me slick and we've only been in the car for an hour."

"Get used to it, Coop. If you're going to be hanging out with me, you're going to spend a lot of time on your very last nerve. It's just how I am."

"I'll prepare myself." He lowered the ball cap again. "So you really think I dazzle?"

"Coop!"

chapter 35

I'd never been so out of breath in my life. My chest heaved up and down with every labored breath, and I concentrated on keeping myself from passing out. "I can't believe people think that's fun."

Cooper gave me a sympathetic but glowing smile. "It takes some getting used to." His face was flushed, which caused his white teeth to shine more brightly than normal, and he seemed to have no trouble catching his breath. Just as he'd said, he was much more experienced than I was. Therefore, he was used to the extra exertion on the cardiovascular system.

"I'm going to have sore muscles I never even knew I had. It can't be natural to move your body like that."

"It's natural; you've just never done it before. It'll get easier the more you do it. Trust me, eventually you'll even start to like it. You were getting the hang of it there toward the end. After a few more tries, you'll be incredible."

"I wouldn't count on it. I don't know if we'll be doing it again on this trip. I can barely move."

"I really enjoyed it."

"That's because you've done it a lot. How can it be fun for some-body who knows what he's doing to be doing it with someone who has no clue what they're doing?"

"You aren't going to hear any complaints out of me. I had a great time."

"It's the hardest work I've ever done. Just walking is complete torture. Who the heck designed these stupid boots anyway? I feel like a Transformer dressed up like the Pillsbury Dough Boy. And these skis weigh a ton."

"Give them here," Cooper offered. "I'll carry them."

"No, I can carry them. They're just heavy, that's all … and awkward. I've got to get them balanced on my shoulder just right or something."

I lifted the skis and laid them across my shoulder, but they were off balance and caused me to tip backward and fall.

"You're tired. Let me help you," he offered once he stopped laughing.

"No, I'm not a weakling," I screamed, catching him off guard. "I don't need some guy running in and rescuing me all the time."

"I wasn't trying to rescue you; I was trying to be helpful."

"Well, I don't want your help. I don't want anyone's help."

"Fine." He stomped ahead of me toward the car and left me sitting there with all my equipment scattered around me.

I rolled over onto my knees, gathered my poles in my hands, and pushed myself back to standing before glancing toward the car. Cooper leaned against the car watching me as he hid a smile behind his hand.

"Okay, fine. You can help me."

"I don't want to. Like you said, you aren't a weakling. You can do it yourself."

"Cooper—"

"I'm not helping."

"Fine!"

It took about five minutes, but I finally collected everything and managed to make it to the car. I threw the skis to the ground in disgust, and our once fun day came to a screeching halt as the loading of the equipment and drive back to the cabin were filled with nothing but awkward silence. I didn't feel like talking, and I was certain that Cooper was afraid to say anything for fear I'd bite his head off.

As soon as we pulled into the driveway, he jumped out of the Hummer and quickly made his way into the house, leaving me outside alone.

I stood there for several minutes before the front door flung open.

"For the record, I've never treated you like a weakling, Attie. I was trying to be nice." His blond head tucked back inside, and the door slammed closed, leaving me alone again. Within moments it sprung back open. "And I've heard that you can be overly dramatic, but this is absolutely ridiculous."

"Who told you I was dramatic?"

"Everyone!" The door slammed shut again.

Prepared to defend myself, I stomped up the porch stairs and barged through the door, but Cooper was nowhere to be found.

"Coop?" I frantically searched the house until I finally spotted him through the glass doors in the rear of the house. He was starting a fire in the outdoor fireplace.

I opened the door to give him a piece of my mind, but he spoke before I could get a word out.

"Do you like S'mores?" he asked.

"Yes." I crossed my arms in a tiff. If he thought I could be dramatic, he hadn't seen anything yet.

"Do you want some?"

"Yes." I felt my mood soften a little.

"Are you going to be nice to me?"

"Yes." I was practically whimpering. What in God's name had happened to me giving him a piece of my mind?

"Good, because I'm the only friend you've got. You do realize that, don't you?"

"Yes," I cried. He was right. He was the only person in New York who'd put up with me.

"I've done nothing for the last month but sit by your side while you lay there like a blob on your bed. Most of your homework wouldn't have even gotten done if it weren't for me. I've been a good friend to you, Attie."

"I know. I'm sorry. I don't know what came over me." I slunk to the ground in shame and immediately regretted it. The muscles of my legs shot such an immense pain through my legs that I wanted to rip them off and end the pain as quickly as possible.

His frustration dissipated as he made his way toward me. "You were tired. It was a long day, and skiing isn't easy, especially for a beginner. Don't be too hard on yourself."

I watched as he sat down next to me. "You were just trying to be nice. I shouldn't have yelled at you. I haven't been myself—if I even know who 'myself' is."

"You know who you are. You've just lost track of her, that's all. You'll come around and be back to normal before long."

"You're assuming I was ever normal."

"Of course you're normal."

He had no idea. Other than Riley, Joshua, Nicole, and Tammy, nobody knew about my nightly visits from Jesus, and I sure wasn't about to tell the only friend I had left. He'd think I was crazy for sure. And seeing as how I hadn't seen Jesus since I'd returned to New York, even I was starting to doubt my sanity. Maybe I'd never really seen him after all. Maybe it was just a coping mechanism of some sort. I didn't know.

I didn't know anything.

"…I mean, it's only been a few months or so since you got out of the hospital." Cooper had continued talking, and I hadn't been paying any attention. "Maybe your body wasn't ready for that much strenuous activity. I hadn't really thought about it until now. How about tomorrow we take it easy, hang out at the cabin, maybe take the snowmobiles out for a drive or something?"

"That sounds like fun."

"We'll just play it by ear. Whatever you're up for, we'll do, and whatever you're not, we won't. Sound like a plan?"

"Yes."

"Okay." He slapped his knees with his hands as he stood. "Time for S'mores. Get up and grab a hanger."

"What, you're not making it for me?"

"I hate to tell you this, my dear, but no. I am not making your S'mores for you."

"What?"

"You said it yourself; you aren't a weakling. I figure you can make your own S'mores."

"Whatever happened to chivalry on a date?"

He dropped back onto the step and gave a small laugh before leaning toward me and grinning. "I never said this was a date."

"No," I said, moving toward him, "but you sure hoped it would be."

"Don't flirt with me unless you plan on following through with it."

"Is what I just did considered flirting?"

"Absolutely."

"I wouldn't know."

"For someone who doesn't know, you did it very well. You've definitely gotten my attention."

And he had mine. His piercing blue eyes became a blur as I felt myself lean closer toward him until my lips finally made contact with his. Within seconds he slid his hands through my hair and held my head in place as he leaned over and gently led me to lie down on the porch. His upper body partly covered mine, but the majority of his weight rested on his hip, which was on the ground.

Kissing him was very different than kissing Riley. Cooper's kiss wasn't better or worse, it was just different, and while I was in the middle of trying to compare the two, Cooper pulled away from me.

"Why did you kiss me?" He was slightly short of breath as he looked down on me. "Is this some sick attempt to get over him?"

"I…" Truth was, I didn't know why. I did it without thinking.

He shook his head. "Never mind. I don't have to know. I don't care."

"Are you sure?"

"Completely."

His thumb gently skimmed my bottom lip just before the distance between us evaporated.

chapter 36

Cooper's voice traveled from the hallway and woke me up. "Rise and shine, sleepyhead."

"What time is it?" I asked from under my pillow.

"Almost noon."

I bolted to an upright position, causing the pillow to fly across the room. "Noon? I never sleep till noon."

"We were up a little late last night." Cooper grinned. "How'd you sleep?"

"Sleep?"

Not well. I'd tossed and turned in the huge king-sized bed all night, but it was nothing new. I hadn't been sleeping through the night for a while. No nightmares, thank God, but I was yet again lacking sleep, and it was probably starting to show on my face. Luckily, Cooper didn't know me well enough to notice a difference. Riley, on the other hand...

"Fine. I slept just fine."

He reached down, picked up the pillow, and threw it back on the bed. "Good. Are you hungry?"

"Starving."

"Come on downstairs; I ordered some breakfast." He turned from the doorway and walked away. "And then I threw it in the trash and ordered some lunch."

"Sorry."

His voice got harder to hear as he walked down the long hall-way. "You don't need to apologize."

"Hey, I never got my S'mores," I yelled.

"I didn't hear you complaining about that last night," he yelled back.

I allowed my mind to wander back to the night before. Hours of kissing before I finally came to my senses and escaped to my room for the night. Not that I was trying to get away from Cooper. I wasn't being myself, and I didn't know what I was capable of if I wasn't thinking straight. I completely trusted Cooper. It was myself I wasn't so sure of anymore.

I strolled downstairs and into the dining room. "I was a bit too preoccupied to be thinking about S'mores."

"Are you thinking about them now?" he asked.

"A little bit, yes."

"I could preoccupy you again, if you'd like. I know I'd like to."

"I haven't brushed my teeth."

"You think I care?"

"I care. Plus, I'm hungry. Another round of preoccupation will have to wait until my stomach is full."

"If you insist." He set a plate of food down and then slid into the seat next to me. His blue eyes sparkled against the blue sweatshirt he was wearing, and his blond hair lay neatly on his head—not a strand out of place.

Glancing down at my grungy pajama bottoms and stained T-shirt, I felt uneasy sitting next to his well-manicured perfection. I lowered my gaze in a mix of shame and embarrassment and noticed my toenails. I hadn't painted them since before Thanksgiving, and the crimson nail polish was almost completely chipped away.

He gave my shoulder a light rub. "Is something wrong?"

"No."

"Are you wishing we hadn't kissed?"

"Oh no, it's nothing like that."

"Are you sure? You could tell me if you were."

Rise

"I'm sure. I was just thinking about how horrible I must look while you're all put together."

"You look beautiful, Attie. You always do."

"Flattery will only get you so far, Mr. Truman."

"How far?"

"Ha ha."

"I'm not trying to flatter you. I'm speaking the truth."

"Thank you."

His hand softly slid down my arm to my hand. "I know you said you slept fine, but it sounded to me like you had a rough night."

"Oh really?"

"Yes. From my room I could hear you call out a few times."

"Call out what?"

"I couldn't make out the words, but you sounded a little scared. I thought about going into your room to check on you but decided not to. Should I have?"

"No. Don't worry, Coop. I've got an active imagination that carries over into my dreams sometimes. The best thing to do is just ignore it." I took a bite of the pasta salad and washed it down with soda. "Sonic ice?"

"What?"

"This is Sonic ice. I'd know it anywhere."

"Oh yeah. My parents had their own ice maker installed in the kitchen."

"You have a machine in there that makes Sonic ice?"

"Sure do."

"I've got a crush."

"On me?" he asked with a grin.

"On the ice maker. I'll be spending a lot of time with that thing."

"Even after last night, I've got to play second fiddle to an ice maker? What does a guy have to do to take first?"

"I'll know it when you do it." I reached over gave him a small pat on the cheek. "So what's on the agenda today?"

"Do you want to go on the snowmobiles? There's tons of stuff to do around here."

"Nothing too strenuous. I'm so sore I can barely move."

"We can just hang around here for the day if you'd like."

"Then that's what I'd like."

"As you wish." He hopped out of the chair and made his way toward the kitchen. "I'll call and get some snacks and dinner ordered. I can also have some games sent over if you want."

"There are people that do that?"

"There are people out there that'll do anything if the price is right. You just have to know who to ask." I felt him reach over me as he set another glass of ice down on the table before he leaned over and gave me a kiss.

It felt odd. Riley and I had never been able to touch when we were together in the house, but here Cooper was, holding my hand, kissing me—all in complete freedom.

"You do live a privileged life, don't you?" I asked as he pulled away.

He sat back down next to me. "I do, but I try not to take it for granted or take advantage."

"He says as he phones in his food order for the day," I teased.

"Are you making fun of me?"

"Yes."

"Rude." He reached out, grabbed me by the arms, and playfully pulled me onto his lap before kissing my neck.

"I have an idea."

"What's that?" he asked.

"I'm going to teach you how to rough it."

"Please don't."

"It'll be fun. We'll make our own food, plan our own outings. You can learn what it's like to be one of the little people."

"I'd rather teach you how to be a VIP."

"You can teach me that some other time if you want."

His chin rested on my shoulder. "I want to think I'll have the chance. It's a relief to hear you talk like you're expecting to be spending time with me in the future."

"Why is that a relief?"

"It makes me feel like last night might have actually meant something to you."

"We just kissed; that's nothing compared to what you've done with other girls. Why are you so concerned about it meaning something to me?"

"Because it meant something to me."

"*That* meant something to you?"

"You're going to sit here and act like you don't know how I feel about you?"

"I knew you liked me, but—"

"Since the moment I met you last summer, I've hoped we might get a chance to be sitting here like we are right now."

"Coop, I'm not ready for any kind of relationship or anything."

"I know you're not, but let me remind you—you kissed me. You made the first move."

"I know." And I could have kicked myself for doing it.

"So the way I see it, you may not be ready for a relationship, but you're ready for something. And I'll take something over nothing any day of the week. One day you'll be ready for more, and I'll be here." I started to get out of his lap, but he grabbed a hold of my hips and pulled me back down. "Don't go."

"I don't know how I came off to you last night, but I don't want to mislead you. What happened out there is as far as it's going to go, physically speaking. I mean... I know I probably acted differently than I should have... I was a bit... I don't know, um..."

"You think I don't know that?"

"Do you?"

"Yes. I was a part of the conversation yesterday. I know where you stand."

"And I know what you expect from girls you date."

"Did you not hear what I said?"

"What did you say?"

"I said that for the right girl I would wait."

"I don't think I'm that girl, Cooper."

"I think you might be."

"Okay." I got out of his lap and sat back down in my chair. "I should have given your feelings more thought. I shouldn't have kissed you."

"Yes, you should have."

"No, Coop—"

"I'm a big boy, Attie. I know what I'm getting into. It's my choice, and I'm choosing to spend time with you knowing that my feelings are stronger than yours. But the fact of the matter is that you still kissed me first. You wanted to kiss me, so either you like me a little bit or you just wanted to make out with someone. I don't see you as the kind of girl who kisses just anyone…"

"I don't." At least I didn't think so. I didn't know what kind of girl I was anymore.

"So?"

"I'm attracted to you." And desperately needed to get over Riley. Of course, I didn't say that out loud. "I think that's about all I know for sure."

"It's a start, and it's all I need for right now. I have faith. I'll win you over; you just watch." He slid forward in his chair and grabbed my hands in his. "Can't we just have fun together and let the rest take care of itself?"

"I like that plan. I'd really rather not have to think about it too much."

"I don't want you to have to think about it at all. What happens, happens."

"Okay."

"Good. Now, how does one go about roughing it?"

"About that."

"Uh-oh, I don't like the sound of that."

"It's just…"

"What?"

"The way this is turning." I squirmed in my seat. "Maybe we should head home."

"What? Why? I thought we were having fun."

"We are. It doesn't have anything to do with that."

"Well, what does it have to do with?"

"My age. I'm seventeen."

"I know how old you are."

"And I'm only in high school. And, well…we're whatever we are and doing whatever it is we're doing…"

"I'm still not following you."

"I don't think it's a good idea for me to be alone in a house with a twenty-year-old man that I just spent several hours kissing."

"Attie, I'm not going to try anything. You can trust me."

"It's not that I don't trust you. It's that…I just don't think it's appropriate. And regardless of whether or not you think you'll try anything, I just don't think it's smart to push the limits like that. Last night, we were awfully close to…crossing over."

"I wouldn't have. Even if I wanted to, which of course, I did, I wouldn't. You can trust me."

"Still…it just isn't smart."

His shoulders slumped. He was obviously disappointed.

"See, this is what I was saying. We're on two different planets. We don't see things the same way."

"No, I understand what you're saying. I'm just disappointed, that's all. I'll take you home if that's what will make you feel better."

"And you aren't mad?"

"I'm not mad. As long as we can still spend some time together once we get you home; that's all I care about."

"Of course we can."

"Okay. Well, let's eat lunch, and then we can pack up and head back."

"Thank you for understanding."

"You're welcome. I mean, what can I say? I dazzle. Who can blame you for not being able to trust yourself alone around me?" He laughed.

"You just keep telling yourself that."

"I plan on it." He picked up my plate and carried it toward the kitchen. "You know, I said I'd be willing to hold out for the right girl. I just never dreamt I'd be having to do it the day after I said it."

The right girl. My heart sank when he said it. I was pretty sure I wasn't the right girl for him. Sadly, he didn't see things the same way.

chapter 37

"Green, red, yellow, red."

"I can't do this," he yelled. "This is too hard."

"You're forgetting to strum." I slapped my knee to the beat of the music. "Strum, strum, strum."

"I'm strumming!"

"You're not strumming at the same time you push the button. Hurry, you're losing the audience. They're booing you."

No matter how hard he concentrated, Cooper couldn't seem to get the rhythm, and eventually the song stopped and Guitar Hero had claimed yet another victim.

"That song's hard, Coop. But you still did well on 'I Love Rock and Roll.'"

"I'm playing this one again. I'm not giving up. I'm going to figure this thing out if it's the last thing I do."

"'Iron Man' is kind of hard. We could be here all night."

"What else do we have to do? We're taking it slow, remember?"

"Are you complaining?"

"No way. I love a challenge."

"Are you talking about me or the game?"

"Both. Now push start."

"You're in control of that. You strum when you want it to begin."

Cooper took his rocker stance, placed his fingers on the guitar neck, and prepared for battle.

The song started, and he carefully and methodically moved his fingers to the flowing colored dots. He was doing much better this time around, and his score increased with every successful strum.

For some reason, seeing him so serious about something so trivial was completely adorable.

"Can I be your number one fan?"

"Don't interrupt the master," he warned as he continued to successfully manipulate the buttons.

"A groupie maybe? Follow you around while you're on tour?"

"You're going to make me lose my concentration."

"Would you give me a backstage pass?"

"I'll give you any pass you want."

"And you'll wear those tight rocker pants that show off your butt?"

His hands fell off the guitar as he looked over at me with a grin. "Have you been checking out my butt?"

"Maybe." I pointed at the screen in front of him. "You're losing your audience."

"I'm more concerned with my audience of one and keeping her attention."

"Oh, you've got it."

Removing the guitar strap from his shoulder, he made his way toward me, his grin increasing in size with every step.

I finally reached out, grabbed him by the shirt, and pulled him to me. "You just lost."

"Not the way I see it."

I thought he was about to kiss me, but instead he sat down.

"How did we get here?" he asked.

"You drove over."

"No, how did we get here, to this place?"

"Where?"

"From you wanting nothing to do with me last summer to us not being able to keep our hands off of each other now. That's quite a difference."

"I thought that's what you wanted."

"I did. I do. I'm just surprised, and I'd like to know what changed your mind about me."

"Last summer I thought you liked me a little—"

"A little? Attie, I called you within hours of meeting you the first time. I asked you to lunch and you turned me down. Then I tried to get your attention at the pool party, but you didn't want anything to do with me."

"We talked."

"Yeah, we talked. But then Riley came around, and it was like I never existed."

"Oh."

"Then I orchestrated a deal where I could be near you every week at the clinic—"

"So Riley was right. You didn't do that to get work experience."

"Of course not. I was only doing it to be close to you."

"I see."

"I asked you out to lunch and then out to my house to go horse-back riding—"

"And I brought Chase."

"I finally got the hint. I didn't have a prayer of catching your eye."

"It's not that you didn't catch my eye. I just wasn't sure what to make of you. I think you kind of scared me."

"I scared you?"

"Well, I'd never had anyone like you just walk up and talk to me like that, and then you called right away. I think I thought you were arrogant."

"Do you have any idea how many times I dialed the number and hung up before I finally let the phone call go through? I was a nervous wreck."

"Then why did you do it? I mean, you barely knew me."

"I don't know. There was just something about you. I literally couldn't stop thinking about you. I thought if I didn't get to know you better that I was going to lose my mind. It was ridiculous, but I finally realized that you and Riley were together, and I settled on just being your friend for the time being and hoped that one day you might end up coming up here to school or something. So when the phone rang a few months ago and I saw it was you, my heart just about exploded."

"You mean when I called about needing a ride home from the party?"

"I have to admit I got my hopes up a little."

"And then?"

"I realized that you were in pretty bad shape, both physically and mentally, and just concentrated on being your friend. I didn't give us getting together another thought until—"

"Until what?"

"Until you kissed me. After ten months of waiting, in that spilt second, everything changed. And my question is still…why?"

"Honestly?"

"Of course."

"You're a nice guy and I enjoy spending time with you, but—"

His face wore concern. "But what?"

"I'm just flat out attracted to you, and I think I can be with you and still feel pretty independent."

"And he wouldn't let you be independent?"

"Who? Riley?"

He nodded.

"It's not that he wouldn't *let* me. I think he just worried…a lot. Of course, I can't blame him. There was a lot to be worried about." I shrugged. "Riley was Riley, and there'll never be anyone else like him. He was my first love, so honestly, I don't think anyone will ever compare."

"I don't want to try to compare. I don't want to be in a competition."

"It's not a competition. This is just me trying to go on with life, and I want to be honest with you about it. I can't pretend that Riley and I never existed. All I can do is move on, and spending time with you helps me do that without having to worry about it being something too serious. I think I just want to be a normal seventeen-year-old without having to have everything in my life be so momentous. I want to have some fun and learn to enjoy life as it is now."

"Then nothing else needs to be said." He kissed me on the forehead before wrapping his arms around me and pulling me closer. "This last month since the trip, I've been having the time of my life, and I'm not expecting that to change any time soon."

To Cooper, our time together since the ski weekend signaled the start of something new. For me, it confirmed the end of the life I'd left behind. It was proof that I could navigate life on my own. My outlook on life was a choice, and I'd come to realize that the only option I was interested in pursuing was the one that made me embrace the life that lay ahead and leave the past where it belonged—in the past.

Cooper interrupted my thoughts. "Hey, do you have plans for spring break?"

"Spring break?" I looked back at him. "That's over a month away."

"I know, but I figured if you didn't have plans, we could spend it together."

"Back at the cabin?"

"No. And we wouldn't be alone. My family would be with us."

"Where?"

"So will you go?"

"Where?"

"It's a surprise. You'll find out when we go—if you say yes."

"You've piqued my curiosity."

He grinned. "Really? You've managed to pique far more in me."

"Very funny.

"So are you going with me or not?"

"I'll go."

"Good." He leaned forward to kiss me but stopped himself. "Oh. Do you have a passport?"

"Yes, I've got one, but I've never used it."

"You're about to."

chapter 38

Dad and I sat on opposite sides of the kitchen table eating our blueberry bagels. Other than our chewing and Baby's breathing as she slept on the chair next to me, there was no sound. We weren't speaking.

It wasn't that we were angry with each other; it was just... we didn't have much to say. Well, let me take that back. We had a lot to say to each other, a lot that needed to be said, but neither one of us actually wanted to say it.

"I'm off," he suddenly announced. "I guess I'll see you later on tonight."

He grabbed his computer bag off the table and leaned down to give me a kiss on the forehead. I turned in my seat and watched him walk toward the front door.

"What were you missing?" The words surprised me as they slipped out of my mouth because I hadn't even been thinking them.

He turned to face me. "Pardon?"

"That you had to throw it all away. What were you missing out on, exactly?"

Dad stood motionless as the color drained from his face.

"You and Mom were high school sweethearts. You had a child together. She supported you in everything you did. She loved you. I loved you. So what were you missing?"

"It's not that simple." His voice sounded empty. I heard the words, but there was no life in them. No weight. They came out of his mouth and fell to the ground. They had no meaning to me at all.

"You have an amazing career. You're admired by people that haven't even met you. You travel the globe getting to do exactly what you love. You win awards and impact people's lives. For anyone looking from the outside, you had everything a person could ever ask for: a successful career and a family that loved you. What was so darned important that you had to give us up to get it? What exactly were you missing?"

Again, he didn't answer.

I sat for several moments and forced him to stand in an awkward and painful silence. I wanted the words to settle in his mind. I wanted him to realize what he'd done, and I needed him to realize that nothing could have been worth all the damage he'd caused.

"Well," I said, finally standing, "I hope you found whatever it was you were looking for because I ended up paying the price for you to get it."

"What was the price?" he whispered.

"Everything."

His shoulders slumped.

"And I didn't get the option of giving it away—it was all taken from me. Ripped from me, actually. I was the one left suffering for your actions. They were your choices, not mine. Then I was the one trying to make it all right, as if that were even possible. I gave up everything I'd worked so hard to get back in order to come all this way to try to fix what you chose to break. Finally, what I've discovered is that there are some things that just can't be fixed." I walked to within a foot of him. "You made the choices. You have to suffer the consequences. I'm getting on with my life. I would like for you to be a part of it if you want, but I'm not going to pretend anymore."

"Of course I want to be a part."

"But it's not going to be under your terms. I'm a different person than who you knew two years ago."

"What does this new life look like? Will it be here?"

"I don't know yet. I've got a lot of thinking to do; I need to look at my options."

"I can help you with that."

"No offense, but I'm not so sure you can be impartial."

"I can be." He dropped his computer bag onto the floor and took a few steps in my direction. "I do want what's best for you, Attie. I may not have handled things correctly, but you have to know that I want you to be happy."

"I appreciate that."

"I want to help you. I can't fix what I've done, but at least let me try to improve things going forward."

"Dad, I've been here since December, and you haven't made any effort so far. Why would I think you'd start now?"

"I didn't know what to say."

"All you had to do was say *something*. Anything. Even just an 'I love you' would have been nice."

"I do love you, Attie. I love you more than anything in the world. I don't do a great job of showing it, but it's true. Just give me a chance to prove it to you. What can I do? Just tell me what I need to do and I'll do it."

"No. That's part of what this is all about. You getting to know me and finding out what it is I need. That's your responsibility, so you need to figure it out. I'm here. I go to school, I come home, I hang out with Coop, I make your dinner, and I go to my room for rest of the night. I'm here; I'm easy to find. If you want to fix this, then you're going to have to make some effort."

"I understand."

"If I'm important to you, then you need to figure it out. And you should know—"

"Know what?"

"You're running out of time."

I turned away from him.

"Attie?"

"Yes?" I asked, facing him again.

"And you should know... I didn't find it." Tears streamed down his face. "What I was missing and what you paid the price for. I didn't find it."

"Well, maybe we can find it together."

chapter 39

I sat on the kitchen counter and watched as Cooper washed the dishes in the sink. It was his newest form of entertainment. At my house, he lived like "normal folk," as he called it, and I practically hadn't had to do a single chore since he'd been hanging around. So far, washing the dishes and vacuuming were his two favorite activities. The only thing I wouldn't allow him to do was my laundry. We certainly weren't close enough for that.

"So you don't do the chores around your apartment?"

"No." He threw me a hand towel. "My parents wanted me concentrating on my studies, so I have someone that comes in and does all of that."

"Every day?" I picked up the cookie sheet next to the sink and started to dry it. "Oh wait, you missed a spot. There's some goop right here."

He snatched the pan out of my hand and inspected it. "Where?"

"In that corner over there."

"I thought I got that," he mumbled as he picked at it and then started scrubbing.

"So this person comes every day?"

"Yes. I'm extremely coddled; I admit it. Let's drop it."

"Consider the topic dropped."

"Thank you." He inspected the pan again. "I think I got it ... nope, wait ..." He scrubbed it some more as my phone vibrated on the kitchen table.

I hopped off the counter and gave him a quick pat on the shoulder. "Keep up the good work."

"M-kay," he muttered.

I looked at the caller ID and immediately answered. "Hey, girl."

"Hey, chick," Tammy greeted. "I can't talk long. I was just calling to check on you. What's goin' on?"

"Not much, just hanging out."

"With Truman?" I heard the sound of disgust in her voice.

"Yes."

"Ugh! That's so dang gross. You've seriously gotta cut that out."

I walked into the living room to escape Cooper's earshot. "He's a nice guy, Tammy. Besides, you and I've already talked about this. I thought you weren't going to dog on him anymore."

"I only said that 'cause I thought you would've dumped him a long time ago. How long have you two been going out now, anyway?"

"I don't know. A month and a half or so maybe."

"A month and a half or so too long. It's time for you to come home."

"That's not going to happen, regardless of what happens between Cooper and me."

"So you're gonna keep it up with him then?"

"Tammy, it's nothing serious. We aren't boyfriend-girlfriend; we're just hanging out."

"Well, how long are you gonna be doing that?"

"I don't know. I guess as long as we're having fun and there isn't a bunch of drama."

She sighed heavily. "I do have to admit that you're sounding better and better every time I talk to you. Is he getting you out of the house?"

"Yes, and he's helping me get caught up on school. Really, he's a nice guy."

"Fine then. Put him on the phone."

"What?"

"I said put the boy on the phone."

"Why? What are you going to say?"

"None of your business."

"Don't you embarrass me."

"Put the boy on the phone."

"Good grief." Nervously, I stomped back into the kitchen and held the phone out. "Coop?"

"What?" he asked over his shoulder.

"Someone wants to talk to you."

"Who?"

"You'll see."

He looked down at his wet, soapy hands. "I can't really hold the phone right now."

"Here." I ducked underneath one of his arms and squeezed between him and the sink, jumped on to the edge of the counter, and then held the phone up to his ear. We were practically eye to eye.

"Hello?" His eyebrows raised in surprise. "Tammy?"

His hands played in the water behind me as he got an earful from my best friend. I couldn't hear what she was saying, but by the look on his face, it was nothing less than interesting and comical.

"You don't have to worry about that," he said before going quiet again for several minutes and passing the time by splashing water onto my backside.

"Stop," I quietly scolded.

He shook his head. "That's not what I'm doing, Tammy."

My arm eventually got tired, so I rested my elbow on his shoulder.

"T—... T—... T—..." He couldn't get a word in edgewise and eventually shrugged at me and rolled his eyes.

"Sorry," I whispered.

He laughed quietly and rolled his eyes again. "Yes, I hear you...I will...No, I don't want you to have to do that either."

"Do what?" I whispered.

"Fly up here and kick my butt," he mouthed.

"She said that?"

He nodded with a silent laugh.

" Okay, okay...It was great to talk to you...no, really, it was great. Okay, here she is...here—... here—... here she is. I'll talk to you later, Tammy...uh-huh, bye."

I pulled the phone away from his ear before he got stuck listening to her anymore.

"Tammy?"

"My work here is done," she announced. "He's been warned."

"He's been warned, huh? I appreciate that."

Cooper placed his forehead on my shoulder. His entire body vibrated with laughter, but Tammy was all business. "I gotta go. I'll call ya on Tuesday at the same time."

"All right. Thanks for looking out for me. It looks as if you put the fear of God in the boy, so I should be safe."

Cooper looked up at me and flashed his white smile. "Yes, I treat you so badly as it is," he teased quietly.

"You don't have to thank me; that's what friends are for," Tammy said.

"Love you."

"Love ya too. Bye."

"Bye." I hung up the phone, placed it on the counter, and slid it out of reach. "I'm mortified," I admitted.

"She's very protective of you, that's for sure."

"What did she say?"

"I don't think I can even repeat it."

"That bad?"

"Yes."

"Sorry."

"It's okay." He gently kissed me below my left ear. "I'll get you back."

His breath on my neck caused a shiver up my back, which made him laugh.

"Thanks for putting up with her. You might as well get used to it. I'm sure you'll be hearing from her often."

He leaned back slightly and gazed down at me for several seconds before he leaned toward me again. I prepared for another kiss, but instead he grabbed me underneath the knees and shoved me into the sink, drenching my pants and causing the water in the sink to spill out all over the counter and the floor.

"Cooper Truman!"

In retaliation I turned on the faucet, pulled out the sprayer, and shot water directly into his face. Of course, this caused a tug of war for the spray hose, and the more we wrestled for it, the more water sprayed around the kitchen. Seeing as how I was stuck in the sink, I was at a serious disadvantage. Before I knew it, he had control of the nozzle and was literally showering me with it. I was sopping wet head to toe within a matter of moments, which seemed to only encourage his affections. As he held the spray nozzle over my head, he leaned in to kiss me.

"What on earth?" My father's voice bellowed from the doorway, causing us to instantly stop what we were doing and turn our attention on him. "This place is a mess."

"I'm sorry, sir," Cooper said. "We got a little carried away."

I watched my dad's eyes focus on me, and what he saw caused his face to turn crimson. Although it had happened completely innocently, my legs were straddled around Cooper, and he was practically on top of me.

"Cooper, you better step away from my daughter right now."

"Dad, this looks much worse than it is."

Cooper turned off the water and helped me out of the sink before handing me a towel and walking toward my dad. "Honestly, Dr. Reed, nothing inappropriate is going on."

"Attie, get your butt downstairs and get on some dry clothes."

"Yes, sir." I hopped off the counter and darted out of the room but stood just on the other side of the wall so I could hear their interaction. I could feel water as it ran down my leg and puddled on the floor beneath me.

"Cooper, you clean this mess up and then get out of my house."

"Sir—"

"When you came to me and asked to spend time in our home so you could watch out for her and cheer her up, I never would've dreamt this was what you had in mind. I trusted you! I even let you take her out of town!"

"Sir—"

"You aren't going to come into my house and disrespect me or my daughter like that."

"Yes, sir—I mean, no, sir. I didn't mean to show any disrespect to either one of you."

"Attie's seventeen years old. I'd like to know what about you two hanging all over each other is appropriate behavior?"

"None of it."

"You're older than she is and presumably more responsible. I trusted that when the two of you were here alone, you were making sure you were acting responsibly. Evidently I was wrong. What if I hadn't come home when I did?"

"I promise, Dr. Reed, nothing would have happened. Even if I would have wanted it to, which I didn't. Attie wouldn't have let it. No matter what you may think of me, Attie has her boundaries."

"What about you? What are your boundaries?"

"Whatever hers are."

"Wrong answer. Cooper, you're old enough to know that in the heat of the moment, no matter what boundaries someone thinks they may have, they have a tendency to go right out the window."

"Yes, sir."

"Get this cleaned up and then get out of here."

"Sir—"

"Not another word out of you. And Attie…" Hearing my name startled me. "I know you're eavesdropping. Get your butt to your room immediately or you're grounded for a month."

Without another word, I ran to my room and left Cooper to clean up the mess and deal with my father alone. Poor guy. In one day he'd been read the riot act by both my best friend and my father. I was certain I'd never hear from him again.

I didn't go back upstairs until it was time to make dinner. My hope was that my dad's level of anger would have diminished greatly before he saw me again.

When I walked into the kitchen, he was sitting at the table.

"Sit down," he ordered.

"I was going to make dinner."

"Dinner can wait. Sit down."

I would have argued with him, but he sounded too angry. "Yes, sir." I slid my chair out and took a seat without even looking at him.

"Are you going to sit there and act like you don't have explaining to do?"

"No, sir."

"Then get with it."

I wanted to call him a jerk and tell him he had no right to question me on anything. I wanted to tell him he didn't know me from Adam and therefore shouldn't be accusing me of anything—for the second time, no less. This was the second time he chose not to give me the benefit of the doubt when it came to boys. There were a lot of things I wanted to say, but none of those things would make things better. They'd only cause the gap between us to grow. So I made the decision to let him parent, or at least try. He was making an effort, even if it was pretty harsh.

"Cooper came over and we did our homework. Then he wanted us to go to the stables, but I knew I had to have my chores done first. So he was helping me."

"That was doing chores?"

"Not that exactly. He'd been washing the dishes, and Tammy called to talk to him. So I sat on the counter to hold the phone to his ear—"

"He's in college. Can he not hold his own phone?"

"His hands were wet and soapy."

"And drying them off would have been too difficult for him?"

I shook my head.

"Go on."

"Once he got off the phone, I started teasing him about what Tammy had said, and he pushed me into the sink. I retaliated by spraying him with water, and then we started fighting over the hose. That's when you walked in. Nothing else was going on, I promise."

"Attie, let me ask you a question."

"Okay."

"Would you have been allowed to get away with that behavior in Mr. Bennett's house?"

"No way."

"So why would you think it would be acceptable here? Why would you show Mr. Bennett more respect than you show me?"

"It's not intentional. It's just..."

"Just what?"

I pressed my lips together, not wanting to say what was running through my mind.

"Say what you're thinking."

"I didn't see it as being disrespectful to you. I just—"

"Spit it out."

"You weren't around... by choice. I didn't think you cared one way or the other."

"I do care. And you're right, I wasn't around. I don't know you, or this older you, very well. I don't know how your mind works or what your morals or boundaries are. Or if you even have any."

"When I got here, you never set any boundaries, so I—"

"Really? Are saying that you only follow boundaries that are placed on you? You don't place any on yourself?"

"I do. Dad, you're not being fair here. You're getting on to me for rules and expectations I never even knew you had. Not to mention, it's a little hard to suddenly take correction from someone who just one year ago didn't want anything to do with me. Honestly, I don't know what to think."

"Fair enough, but the fact that I wasn't around last year doesn't mean I don't want to do this the right way now. I'm trying to get to know you, and I'm trying to understand where you're coming from. Can't you meet me halfway?"

I shrugged. "I didn't realize I wasn't, and I wasn't intentionally stepping over your boundaries."

"Okay. Then is what was happening here acceptable under the boundaries that you've placed on yourself?"

"I hadn't thought about it."

"Think about it now. I'll wait for an answer."

I thought back to the conversation about boundaries that Riley and I'd had with each other and the additional discussions with Joshua. "No, sir. None of that would have been allowed under the boundaries that I placed on myself and Ri—" I stopped myself before saying his name.

He sat forward and looked me directly in the eye. "Attie, you're seventeen, and you're telling me that you'd like to start making decisions for yourself. This needs to be one of those decisions. Are you going set standards for yourself and live up to them or aren't you? I made the mistake of ignoring some of the standards I'd given myself, and look where that got me. As you said, I destroyed my family. But just because I made a mistake doesn't mean that I can't instruct you in a way that attempts to keep you from doing the same."

"I see."

"Let me be bluntly honest with you. Guys don't think clearly when it comes to getting physical. You can't trust that they're going to stop themselves. If given the opportunity to go further and do more, the majority of the time they're going to take it."

"But I didn't give the opportunity."

"With what was going on in there, in no time you could have found yourself having to make a split second decision on whether or not you were going to continue. That can be hard to do."

"If he would have tried anything, I would have stopped him. That's been working for us so far."

"Think about what you just said."

"What?"

"Basically what you're saying is that you think it's fair to get him all worked up and then just when you reach your limit suddenly say no. Not only is that not fair, it's also dangerous. Had Cooper been anyone else or less than the gentleman you think he is—"

"You don't have to say it. I get it. You're right."

"And let's just say you went a little further than last time. Where do you start the next time? You think he's going to want to go backward? Go back to doing less?"

"Well, you don't have to worry about that. After today he isn't going to want to do anything with me. I'll be lucky if I ever hear from him again."

"If that's the case, then you've learned a lot about what his true intentions were and what type of person he really is. If Cooper cares about you, he'll try to make things right, no matter how embarrassed he is or how difficult it will be. I guess he and I are alike in that way."

"In what way?"

"I've thought a lot about our last conversation. I get it. I get that I haven't been there for you." He reached across the table and covered my hands with his. "I've got to prove that you're that important to me. I've got to make things right."

"After today, I'll have a lot more free time, so just let me know if you want to work on it." I got out of my chair and went toward the refrigerator to collect the ingredients for dinner.

"No time like the present," he said.

I turned to him. "What do you mean?"

"Will you go to dinner with me? And maybe a movie?"

The feeling of a small smile perching on my face tingled at the corners of my mouth. "Are you asking me on a date?"

"I scared off your only prospect. I figure it's the least I can do."

I looked around the room, almost as if to make sure there wasn't someone else in the room and *that* was who he was asking to go with him. There was no one else. Just me. My heart actually fluttered at the idea that my dad was making some effort to spend time with me. "Okay, I'll go on a date with you. But you better behave."

"I'll be a complete gentleman."

"You'll come to learn that I have very high standards. I hope you can live up to them."

"Me too. Where do you want to go?" he asked.

"A steak joint for dinner and a chick flick."

He rolled his eyes.

"It's the least you can do."

"True." He stood and walked toward his room. "Oh, and don't make any plans for this weekend."

"Why?"

"We're going into the city. I got tickets for a show."

"A Broadway show?" Excitement rose out of my chest and into my throat.

"What other kind of show is there?" He turned to me and grinned. "I even got us a suite at a swanky hotel. I'm going all out."

I smiled back at him. "Thanks, Dad."

"You're welcome. Now go on, get dressed. You've got a hot date picking you up in a little bit."

• •

As Dad climbed out of the car and made his way to my side, I made a mental note to never see a PG-13 movie with him again. Evidently, even movies with that rating had enough stuff in them to make a teenage girl squirm when watching one with her father sitting next to her. And come to think of it, he didn't seem too comfortable with it either. The farther into it we got, the farther away he seemed to lean.

He opened the door and I hopped out. "Sorry about that movie choice," I said. "Only Disney movies from now on, I promise."

He shut the door behind me, and we started walking up the sidewalk. "Why do you think we're seeing *The Lion King* in New York City? Everything else looked a little risqué. You may be seventeen, but I still like to think you re six. I had no idea movies were that bad nowadays.

"That's nothing. The Bennetts and I watched movies almost every night during the summer. Mostly 80s stuff, and you'd be shocked at what they had in PG movies back then. Heck, *Sixteen Candles* even had nudity in it."

"*Sixteen Candles*? I loved that movie when I was younger. I don't remember there being any nudity in it."

"Trust me, there was. I threw my hand over Riley's eyes so fast that I ended up slapping him by accident."

"How'd that go over?"

"Not well. I got a pillow to the face in retaliation."

"Tom and Molly always did love movies."

"While a movie was on, every time Riley and I'd see or hear something we shouldn't have, Pops would yell: 'That didn't just happen. It was a figment of your imagination.' As if that made any difference at all."

Dad laughed, and I could see by the look on his face that he was thinking fondly of his former best friends.

The laugh stopped cold as we turned the corner and saw Cooper sitting on the top step of our patio.

He jumped to his feet when he saw us. "Sir," he said, nodding to my dad.

"Hello, Cooper," Dad said as he stood behind me and placed both of his hands on my shoulders.

"I...I was hoping to talk to both of you," Cooper muttered.

"Go ahead," Dad said. He was playing hardball, not even inviting the poor boy inside.

Cooper rubbed his hands on his jeans before shoving them into his back pockets. It was the first time I'd seen him so full of anxiety.

"First, I'd like to apologize to you, Attie, for crossing into some questionable territory. I wasn't thinking straight. I know where you stand on things, and it was stupid of me to think that I could act however I wanted. I should have put some boundaries in place. I'm sorry I didn't do that."

"Thank you, Coop." My heart wasn't beating at that point, it was trembling. I was so touched to see him standing there under those uncomfortable conditions that I was literally shivering.

"And Dr. Reed, you were right. I'm older than she is, and I've been around long enough to know better than to do what I was doing. It was disrespectful to both of you. But honestly, when I approached you about spending time with Attie, I didn't have any idea we would end up in whatever kind of relationship it is we're in. The ski trip idea was completely innocent. I didn't ask you if I could take her so that I could get her out from under you. I did it because I wanted her to get out the house and have some fun. Honest, I never lied to you or went behind your back in any way."

Dad nodded.

"I understand that Attie's still in high school and she's going to have some rules placed on her. I also understand that if I want to date her, then I have to follow those rules too. I need you to know that I'm willing to do that. Whatever stipulations you lay out, that's what I'll do. Sir, I'd like the opportunity to date your daughter."

"I just sat through a movie with her. It was painful to watch because it was based on how to tell if a man truly likes a woman or not. What was it?" he asked, looking at me. "He just doesn't like you?"

"*He's Just Not That Into You,*" I corrected.

"Yes, that was it. Anyway, to be a dad and to see how horribly my daughter might be treated by the men in her life, including me, made me sick."

I didn't know what to say. I don't think Cooper did either.

"My daughter is priceless, Cooper, and if you or anybody else has any plans of spending time with her, that's how you better treat her."

"Yes, sir."

"And that includes honoring her age and her morals. I don't know anything about you. I know your parents, but I don't know you. I don't know where you stand morally, and I don't know what you expect from the girls you date. But I can tell you this: the first time I catch a whiff that you aren't treating her the way she deserves or that you're putting pressure on her to do something she doesn't want to do or something that I wouldn't approve of, it's over. Do you understand what I'm saying?"

"Yes, sir. One hundred percent."

"Fine then. You can come back tomorrow and the two of you can spend some time together."

Cooper's shoulders finally relaxed slightly.

"I'll head inside and give you two a minute alone. And I mean it when I say 'a minute.'" He walked up to Cooper and held out his hand.

Cooper pulled his hand out of his pocket and shook Dad's hand. "Thank you, sir."

"You're welcome." Dad gave him a firm pat on his shoulder before going inside and shutting the door.

To say the moment standing there staring at Cooper was awkward would be an understatement. I was completely embarrassed.

"I'm so sorry," he whispered.

"No, I'm sorry. He overreacted."

"No, he didn't. He's exactly right. I know better than that. I know how easy it is to cross the line, and let's be honest, if he wouldn't have walked in and you wouldn't have stopped me … well, let's just say we'd be having a whole 'nother discussion right now."

"I know, but it takes two to tango. I hold half of the responsibility."

The front door opened. "Let's go, Attie."

"Yes, sir."

I walked toward the door, but Cooper grabbed my hand and stopped me. "I'll see you tomorrow?" I could tell by the tone in his voice that he wasn't so sure I wanted to see him again.

I stood on my tippy toes and kissed him. As I started pull away, he wrapped his arms around me and pulled me back to him so that the kiss wouldn't end so quickly. After another moment, he let go.

"See you tomorrow," I said.

He kissed me on the forehead before I turned, went inside, and shut the door behind me. Dad was standing in the dining room shuffling through some papers on the table.

"Thanks, Dad."

"You're welcome."

I made it halfway to the stairs before turning around and going back to him. "Dad?"

He turned from his papers and looked at me. "Yes?"

"Not that it matters anymore or anything, but I just wanted to let you know that Riley always treated me with the utmost respect."

"Okay."

"He loved me very much, and he always treated me like I was special."

Dad didn't respond.

"We had boundaries. Boundaries put on us by the Bennetts and our youth pastor and boundaries that we put on ourselves. In all our time together, Riley never crossed them. When I was with him, I never felt pressure; I never worried that he was going to do something that made me feel uncomfortable. He was always a gentleman and always wanted me to be happy. So much so that I think he put my happiness before his.

"I know you didn't get a chance to see that, but I just wanted to make sure you knew it. Cooper's a great guy, but it's only fair that you know Riley was too."

"Thank you for telling me."

I turned, went down the stairs to my room, and before I could stop myself reached into my closet and pulled out the shoebox that I'd shoved underneath my sweatshirts. It was the box that held all the notes that Riley had written me and many of the small pictures he'd sketched.

Just as I went to pull the lid off, my cell phone rang.

I answered and put it to my ear without even checking the caller ID. "Hello?"

"Attie, it's Cooper."

"Hi."

"I forgot to say goodnight to you before you went inside. I didn't want you to go to sleep without hearing it from me."

"Thank you." I picked up the box and shoved it back under my sweatshirts. "I appreciate you calling, especially after the beating you took from both my dad and my BFF. You're quite the trouper, Cooper. Hey, that rhymed."

He laughed. "You're worth it. Although, I can't say I enjoyed it."

I lay down on my bed. "Poor thing. Evidently your dazzling effects don't work on everyone."

"As long as they work on you, that's all that matters."

"Uh-huh."

"So tell me about this movie that has your dad all freaked out…"

chapter 40

Cooper's Hummer was sitting in the driveway as I walked home from school. It was parked directly behind my dad's car, which meant my dad was home to keep his eye on us. Almost a month since he'd caught us in the kitchen, he still wasn't taking his chances. If at home, Cooper and I were delegated to sitting on separate couches and making faces at each other from across the room, and under no circumstances was he allowed in my bedroom or in the basement at all. Not even the theater room.

Although part of me was embarrassed by the way Dad was acting, the other part was happy that he cared. Having him in the middle of my dating business was better than not having him care about any of my business at all.

In an effort to get me out of the house and give us more alone time, Cooper was teaching me how to ride horses equestrian style at a small stable just outside town. Every other day after chores and homework were finished, we'd head out for a lesson. He was a good boy and followed my dad's rules to a tee, but I think it was more out of fear than out of respect. He knew if he crossed the line, he'd lose me. That and that alone kept him from attempting what he'd done with so many other girls in his past, and I couldn't help but worry that as time went on, his patience and understanding would start to fade.

I walked into the house to find Dad, Cooper, and another man standing in the living room.

Cooper gave me a hug before turning toward the man. "Attie, this is my dad, Alex Truman."

Mr. Truman and I shook hands. "It's a pleasure to meet you, Mr. Truman."

"You too. I've heard all about you."

Mr. Truman turned his attention back to my dad as Cooper pulled me away from them and into dining room.

"Why is your dad here?" I whispered.

"There's no way your dad's going to let you go on the spring break trip unless my dad can talk him into it."

"He came all this way to talk to my dad about that?"

"Of course. He knows it's important to me that you go."

"Why is it that big of a deal?"

"Attie," he said, grabbing my hands in his, "you've never left the country. I want to be there with you the first time you do."

"First time?" My heart plummeted. This would be a first that I wouldn't be experiencing with Riley, and even though we'd broken up months ago, the realization was painful.

"What's wrong?"

"What?"

"You look upset. Is something wrong?"

"No, I just—"

"Attie," my dad called, "can you two come in here please?"

Cooper led me back to our fathers.

"I was just telling your dad here that my son would like to take his girlfriend on our family spring break trip."

Girlfriend? I'd never thought of myself as Cooper's girlfriend, and we'd certainly never discussed him wanting to appoint me the title or me wanting to accept it. Hearing the word made me very uncomfortable, and for some reason I glanced down at the ring finger that had been empty since waking up in the hospital back in Oklahoma.

"I told him that our entire family is going," Mr. Truman continued. "And that you'd be in good hands, so to speak." He'd made himself laugh.

I tried to smile, but I suddenly wasn't feeling well. By the look on my dad's face, he'd caught on to my distress.

"Attie and I will discuss it. How's that sound?" he asked.

Mr. Truman shrugged. "Fair enough."

I felt Cooper come up behind me and slide his hands around my waist before he kissed me on top of the head. It was something Riley never would have done in front of his parents. "It's going to be a great trip. I'd really appreciate it if you'd let her go."

"We'll talk about it," Dad repeated.

"All right." Cooper kissed me on the head again. "Well, Dad and I've got to head out." He let go of my waist and turned me to face him. "Sorry I can't stay. We'll go to the stables tomorrow, okay?"

I nodded.

"It was great to meet you, Attie." Mr. Truman pulled me to him and gave me a hug. "I look forward to spending more time together."

"Thank you," I squeaked as he squeezed me to him. His hug reminded me of the hug Cooper gave me at the pool party that slightly freaked me out. It felt overly friendly.

Mr. Truman let go of me, and the two of them made their way to the door.

"I'll call you tonight," Cooper said.

Within seconds they were gone, and Dad and I were left standing in the entryway.

"What was that about?" Dad asked. "Do you not want to go?"

"Yes, I do. I think."

"You think?"

I didn't respond. All I could do was stare at the door.

"Attie?" My dad touched my arm. "What's going on?"

"Cooper's dad called me Coop's girlfriend."

"And?"

"I'm not. I'm not his girlfriend."

"You aren't? You've been together for more than a few months—"

"Just hanging out. Nothing serious."

"What I saw...what you've been doing with him is nothing serious? Does he know that?"

"I'm not his girlfriend." I turned and walked toward the kitchen. My dad was only a few steps behind. "I'm not ready for that. Riley's the only one . . ."

"This is about Riley?"

"Yes . . . No." I shook my head in an effort to clear my confusion. "It's not about Riley; it's just that he was my boyfriend. I loved him. I don't love Cooper like that. I don't feel that way about him."

"You don't?"

"I don't think so." I sat down and laid my head on the table. "No. I know so. I don't feel for Cooper what I do—did for Riley."

Dad sat down across from me. "But you like him, right?"

I sat up. "Yes."

"You enjoy spending time with him?"

"Yes."

"You don't have to love someone to do that."

"But—"

"Don't 'but.' You need to go on the trip. You'll have fun and get to go somewhere you've never gone before."

"Do you hear yourself right now? You're actually trying to talk me into going on a trip with a boy that you'll hardly leave me alone with."

"His dad promised he'd hardly leave you alone either."

"Oh, I see."

I got up and walked to the pantry. "You do realize that one of these days you're going to have to stop trying to protect my virtue and trust me enough to protect it on my own."

He laughed. "Hopefully not for another ten years or so."

"Ha ha." I grabbed some cream of chicken soup and then put it back down.

"You miss Riley," he said out of nowhere.

"Yes." I hid my tears by pretending to be looking for something. "I miss all of them."

"I'm sorry that I doubted you, and I'm sorry that I pulled you away from them. Riley especially."

"What's done is done. It's been four months and everyone's moved on. No sense in crying about it now."

"She says as she stands in the pantry crying," he teased.

I trudged back to the table and plopped back down in my seat. "Cooper's a great guy, he is. I really like him a lot. I'm very attracted to him, and we have a lot in common."

"But?"

"But I just don't know if I'll ever get the fireworks I got with Riley."

"You can't ever match the feelings of first love, Attie, no matter who it's with."

"Maybe that's true. Maybe that's all it is. I actually told Cooper something similar."

"Look, I'm not going to make you go on the trip. Go if you want, don't go if you don't, but be fair to Cooper. The boy is obviously crazy about you, so if you don't think you can ever feel the same, then—"

"I didn't say I couldn't ever feel the same. I said *wasn't sure* if I could feel the same."

"Then there's only one way to find out."

"How's that?"

"Go on the trip, have some fun, and see where that leaves you."

I sighed and looked over at my dad. "You're the doctor. I'll follow your orders."

"Good. Now go on and watch some television or something. I'll make dinner."

"Really?"

"Sure. I'm practically forcing you to go on some exotic vacation on a private jet with an extremely good-looking guy. I have to make it up to you somehow."

I stood. "That's true. How dare you try to make me enjoy my life?"

"How dare I."

"I'm going to go to my room and pout about it for a while."

"You do that."

I kissed him on the cheek as I walked past him. "Thank you, Daddy."

"You're welcome."

chapter 41

I stood on the airport tarmac and ogled at the small private planes that surrounded us. Not only had I not been on a private plane before, I don't think I'd ever even seen one in person. I'd been told that while I was unconscious I flew from Oklahoma to New York on a small plane, but I doubt it had anything in common with the plane that I was about to get on.

Cooper's family lived a completely different life than what I was used to. When Cooper and I were alone together, we lived a normal life; we did normal things and spent normal amounts of money. When his parents came to town, we only ate at the nicest restaurants and attended the swankiest of events. It was a life that didn't really fit me, and to be totally honest, it didn't fit Cooper either. I was beginning to comprehend what Cooper had explained when we talked at the pool party and at lunches together during the summer before. He was putting on a show for his parents. He was living out their expectations, and he was lying to himself any time he said he enjoyed it.

The only thing that Cooper and his parents did agree on was me. Cooper's parents saw me as the daughter of the wonderful Dr. Reed, not just another girl from Guthrie. I was going to be attending the right school, and eventually I'd have the title of "Dr." before my name. They also knew that I loved Oklahoma and that if by chance Cooper and I ended up together, I would have a much better chance at getting him to return to Oklahoma than they ever could. In their eyes and his, I was perfect for him.

I also realized that part of his attraction to me was that I didn't have any expectations on him, and with me, he could be himself. Funny thing was, I also realized that when I was with him, I wasn't myself at all. He knew nothing about the real me: Nothing about the nightmares or the pain caused by my father. Nothing about the Lord that I'd loved and left. He didn't want to know those things about me. Not because he didn't care, but because talking about them would also involve talking about Riley. It had been Riley who'd walked through it all with me, and Cooper could never compete with those memories. And like he'd said, he didn't want to have to compete.

"Are you excited, Attie?" Mr. Truman asked.

"Yes, sir. But I'd be more excited if you guys would just tell me where we're going. Can't you give me a hint?"

"Cooper would kill me if I spoiled his surprise. We'll be there soon enough, and you'll be out of your misery."

"Thank you for letting me join you on your family vacation. I really appreciate it."

"We're glad to have you. You're welcome any time."

I felt Cooper's hand slide into mine as he came up from behind me. "Plane's ready, Dad. They just need you to go sign off on the flight log."

"You five get on the plane. I'll be right there."

I followed behind Mrs. Truman, Cooper's sister, and her boyfriend, Trevor, but Cooper held me back. "Let's wait for a minute. We'll have plenty of time with them around. I want a few more minutes alone with you."

"I think you've had plenty of time alone with me over the last few months."

"I can never get enough."

He kissed me lightly under my ear and then glanced around to make sure nobody was looking before moving his lips to mine for a brief moment.

We heard the phone signal from my purse, which caused him to groan. "Tell whoever it is that we're busy."

"It's just a text; I can tell by the signal." I pulled the phone out, and as soon as I pushed the button, my heart froze.

"What's the matter?"

I shook my head and tried to push the button again to open the message, but my hands trembled so badly that I could barely manage.

He gently grabbed my elbow. "Attie, what's wrong?"

"It's from Riley."

Cooper's face turned rigid. "What does he want?"

"Um." I looked back down at the phone and read the message out loud. "Just curious whether or not you were coming home for spring break. I'd love to see you."

I couldn't stop the tears as they filled my eyes.

"It's been four months," Cooper yelled. "Why is he contacting you now?"

"I don't know." I tried to keep my body from trembling but couldn't. Just seeing his name and reading the words was mental torture. He'd been thinking of me and had taken the huge step of reaching out, but I was going out of the country with Cooper.

"Have you two been in contact?"

"No. I'm as shocked as you are."

"Well, text him back and tell him that you're spending spring break with me."

"I don't want to be mean, Coop."

"That's not being mean; it's telling him the truth."

I stared down at his words and tried to think of what to say back. I knew he was sitting a thousand miles away anxiously waiting for me to respond.

"We've got to get on the plane, so say what you're going to say so we can get out of here." The hostility in his voice was undeniable.

"Don't be angry with me, Cooper. I didn't ask him to contact me."

"I'm not mad, Attie; I'm upset."

"About what?"

"Look at the effect he's having on you. Two minutes ago we were kissing; now all of a sudden your head is right back in Oklahoma."

"I'm sorry."

"Where's your heart?" His face turned crimson. "Is it here or there?"

I involuntarily turned and looked behind me as if I could actually see my past, and when I did, I saw him.

"Jesus," I whispered.

"Where is it, Attie? Where is your heart?" Cooper was saying behind me.

I walked toward the Lord. I was desperate to talk to him. With him was where my heart was, and I was trying to make my way toward it.

"Where are you going?" Cooper yelled. "We've got to go."

As quickly as the vision appeared, it was gone.

I startled at Cooper's sudden touch. "Are you still coming?" His voice had slightly softened.

"Yes," I whispered. "Just let me handle this. I'll be right there."

He grabbed my hand and gave it a squeeze before dropping it and running toward the plane.

My fingers quickly worked their way across the phone keyboard.

"Not this time. It would've been great to c u though."

Within seconds, I received Riley's reply.

"Bummer. I hope u r doing great. Every1 here misses u."

I cried as I typed my response.

"I miss every1 there 2."

Again, he replied within seconds.

"Don't b a stranger. I'd love for u 2 keep in touch."

My fingers flew across the buttons.

"I will."

My heart beat through my chest as I waited for his response. I could tell by the delay that he was contemplating what to say. Finally, the phone signaled again.

"Take care of yourself. Gbye."

My fingers typed more slowly this time.

"U 2. Gbye."

Cooper was right. A part of my heart was right back in Oklahoma. I couldn't help myself. Another part of my heart was still hiding from the Lord, and it wanted to come out. Every feeling I'd suppressed when I left home was knocking, wanting to be freed.

I turned back to see the Lord again. He appeared and smiled at me.

"Attie?" Cooper called.

I turned to him.

"We need to go. Everyone's waiting."

I walked toward the plane but looked back momentarily. The Lord was gone.

After regaining my composure, I walked up the stairs and down the aisle to Cooper. His body was tense as he sat looking out the window. He didn't make eye contact with me.

I leaned over and gave him a small kiss on the forehead before sitting down next to him and grabbing one of his hands in mine.

"So you're still not going to tell me where we're going?"

His body seemed to relax as he finally looked over at me. "Aruba," he whispered.

"Really?" I squealed. "Wow."

His face wore a full grin again as he soaked in my excitement, and although my mind was somewhere else, I was determined not to let it show. I'd made the choice to go on the trip with Cooper. I now had to make the choice to give him my undivided attention.

chapter 42

The turquoise-blue water radiated in the orange light cast by the setting sun. Other than my first glimpse at the inside of the University of Oklahoma football stadium, nothing had taken my breath away quite like the view I was taking in while standing in the sand next to Cooper. It was stunning. We'd landed just a few hours before, dropped off our bags at the condo, and he and I immediately took off on our own.

A wonderful dinner at a local Italian restaurant that overlooked the ocean followed by a walk on the beach at sunset should have been the perfect evening, but ever since receiving the text from Riley, I wanted to be nowhere but home.

"Where are you?" Cooper asked.

"Aruba, and it's amazing. Thank you."

"That's where your body is." His voice sounded deflated. "Where's your mind? Your heart?"

I squeezed his hand and gave him a large smile. "It's right here. Why do you ask?"

"You seem far away, distant. Back in Oklahoma, maybe?"

"No," I lied. "I think I'm just overwhelmed. It's the most beautiful place I've ever seen. I think I'm in shock that I'm here."

"Are you sure?"

I nodded before I forced myself to rise up to my tippy toes and give him a kiss. As I did, he wrapped his arms around me and pulled me to him so tightly that I almost lost my breath. It was as if he was trying to hold on to me, trying to keep me from leaving—either physically or emotionally.

I rested my cheek on his shoulder, and we stood in silence. His arms wrapped around me as we watched the sun slip away behind the ocean's edge. I could feel bursts of warm air on the top of my head, and with each exhale it was as if I felt his hope escape a little more.

"Do you happen to have any plans for April twenty-fifth?" I asked.

He pulled away and looked down on me with a quizzical stare. "Um, I don't know."

"How do you feel about going back to high school?"

"It doesn't sound very appealing. I didn't even like it the first time around. Why do ask?"

"That's the night of the prom. I just thought—"

"Are you asking me to your prom?" Life filled his voice again.

"I know it's totally stupid, but I was hoping you might want to go with me."

"I'd love to go with you."

"You would?"

His beautiful white smile reappeared. "Absolutely."

"Proms really aren't my kind of thing, but I didn't get to go last year and ... and well, I only have one more shot at it, and I wouldn't want to look back and regret not going."

"And you want to take me?"

It was a loaded question and I knew it. "Of course. Who else?"

"A cousin maybe?"

"I don't have any cousins, so you'll have to do. And besides, I think we'd look pretty great all dressed up."

"I'm sure you'll be gorgeous. You always are."

"So you'll put me on your calendar for April twenty-fifth?"

"You're on my calendar for any day you want to be."

"I guess I've got to get a dress and you'll have to rent a tux."

"I own a tux."

I laughed. "Of course you do. What was I thinking? A Truman in a rented tux? Perish the thought."

"We wouldn't be caught dead in one of those things," he admitted.

I dropped onto the sand below me and lay back so I could watch the stars as they appeared in the night sky. Cooper did the same.

"It's a date then," I whispered. "It gives us something to look forward to."

"I look forward to every day with you."

I turned my face toward him. "That's sweet, Coop."

"It's true. It doesn't have to be a special occasion for me to look forward to spending time with you. Every second with you is special."

I wished I loved him, that I felt what he did. I wanted to be happy that I was in the most beautiful place I'd ever been and with a boy who was absolutely crazy about me. The truth was that I was in pain because I was in the most beautiful place I'd ever been and I wasn't there with Riley.

Unsure of what to say, I changed the subject. "Oceans have the most distinct smell, don't they?" I asked. "Sort of that combination of salt and seaweed. There's something comforting about—"

Cooper shut me up by covering my lips with his.

chapter 43

The month between Aruba and prom passed quickly. Cooper and I spent practically every waking, nonschool moment together. Problem was, my past kept presenting itself.

Although I hadn't told Cooper, Pops and I had texted each other a few times a week. Nothing more than small talk, but enough to keep my mind from concentrating solely on my life in New York. Pops never asked if I was seeing anyone, and he never offered information as to Riley's dating status, but I was left to assume that he'd moved on with his life just as I had. Our "conversations" were never anything more than him checking in on me and giving me updates on the goings-on in Oklahoma. Pops missed me and I missed him.

I still talked to the girls back home regularly. They were all getting ready for prom just like I was, and I was sad to know that they would be experiencing the night without me. Although part of me couldn't wait for them to post the pictures on Facebook, I knew that seeing them would be painful.

I shopped alone for my prom dress, orchestrated my hairdo, and made sure to buy the perfect shoes to match the dress. With every shopping spree, I wished that Marme had been there to help me or at least make it more enjoyable.

"So you're ready for Saturday night?" Cooper asked from the recliner next to mine as we watched *Dr. Phil* on the small upstairs television in the living room.

"Ready as I'll ever be. Are you?"

"I've got everything all planned out."

"How much was there to plan?"

"You'd be surprised."

"And you've got your tie and that cumber thing?"

He laughed. "Cummerbund? I've got it covered. I got red, just like you told me to."

"Crimson."

"What?" He looked confused.

"I told you my dress was crimson."

"That's what I just said."

"No, you said 'red.'"

"Red is crimson."

"No. Red can be Husker-red or Bama-red or Razorback-red, but those are all different than Sooner crimson."

He scowled. "That's the most ridiculous thing I've ever heard."

I was angry, and there was no way to hide it. Him saying that the way I associated my colors was ridiculous was basically the same as saying that *I* was ridiculous. "Are you saying that I'm ridiculous because I know my colors?"

"No. I'm saying that it's ridiculous to categorize them by team. Don't you think you're getting a little carried away? There's more to life than football, Attie."

"You think I don't know that?"

"I don't know. You just chastised me because I didn't know the difference between Husker-red and Sooner-crimson."

"I didn't chastise you. I was making a point. I just want us to match, that's all."

He reached out for me to take his hand. "Look, I don't want to fight with you."

"This is who I am, Riley. I'm—"

His hand dropped back to his side. "My name is Cooper."

"What?"

"You just called me Riley. My name is Cooper."

Realizing what I'd done, I felt the blood drain from my face. "I'm sorry. It slipped out."

He nodded grimly.

"We were talking football." I was making up the excuse as it flew out of my mouth. "Riley and I talked football all the time, that's all. It's just habit. Nothing more."

"I watch football too, Attie. I'm not obsessed, but I watch it. Riley isn't the only person in the world you can talk football with."

"I know that."

"But I guess he knew the difference between crimson and red. Right?"

I stayed silent.

Cooper shook his head slightly. "I'll take that as a yes."

I looked back at the television and watched as Dr. Phil lectured a woman sitting in the chair next to him. She looked about as uncomfortable as I felt.

"Are you ever going to give me a chance, or am I wasting my time?"

"You're not wasting your time."

I climbed out of my chair, crawled into his lap, and took his face in my hands. "It was a slip of the tongue, that's all. This fall we'll make our own football memories, Coop. I promise."

"This fall?"

I smiled and gave him a small kiss.

"I hope we'll be together this fall," he whispered.

"We will be."

He pushed the footrest back into place, slid out from under me, and stood up. "I guess I better be going."

"But it's early. You never leave this early."

"I've got a lot to do before Saturday."

"Cooper." I stood and wrapped my arms around his waist. "Please don't go away angry. It was an accident. It doesn't mean anything."

"I'm fine. I just have a lot on my mind about Saturday and everything."

"It's just a prom; it's not a big deal. You don't need to get all stressed out about it."

"I know, I just … it's going to be a big night for you, and I'm hoping it's everything you want it to be."

"It's only a dance."

"I know." He took a deep, seemingly nervous breath. "I'll be fine." He turned and started making his way toward the front of the house. I followed closely behind and finally grabbed a hold of his hand just as he opened the front door.

"You're not going to say good-bye?"

His face changed from showing nervousness to admiration as he placed his hands on either side of my face. "Attie, I …" He stopped midsentence and nervously bit his bottom lip. "You know how I feel about you, right?"

"I think so."

"My guess would be that you're totally underestimating my feelings."

"Oh?"

"I … I …" I waited as he fumbled around for words. "I better go," he finally said. "We can talk about all that stuff later."

"Are you sure?"

"Yes. It's not the right time."

"Tomorrow then?" I urged.

"I'll be busy tomorrow. But Saturday night, the car will be in your driveway at five thirty."

"I can't wait."

He quickly pulled me to him and gave me one last kiss before heading out the door.

"See you Saturday," I yelled.

He turned and smiled at me. "See you soon."

chapter 44

I took one last look in the mirror and let out a disappointed sigh. I looked nothing like I'd hoped I would. My hair wouldn't pouf the way I'd wanted, and the bust of the dress wasn't filled quite the way I'd imagined. It looked a little deflated, and my mood was starting to match.

Dad threw open the door. "You ready to go, Attie? He's waiting on you downstairs. You need to hurry."

"I guess so. Not much else I can do to fix myself now."

"You look beautiful. Just try to have a good time."

"Yes, sir."

"Now put him out of his misery and get on downstairs."

As I walked toward the door, he called after me. "Attie?"

I turned and noticed tears in his eyes. "Yes?"

"You're stunning."

I walked to him and kissed his cheek before turning and leaving him in the room alone. He never followed me down the stairs.

A corsage sat on the stair banister. Cooper was nowhere to be seen, but Baby barked loudly in the living room. "I can't believe you didn't let me make a grand entrance or anything. I should go back upstairs and make you watch me as I walk gracefully down the staircase. I was gliding, you know? I was literally gliding down the stairs and you missed it. I got ready upstairs for the sheer reason I could glide." I picked up the corsage and began to put it on.

"I believe that's my job."

His voice startled me and caused me to drop the corsage onto the floor.

I looked up in utter shock.

"Hey, Charlie," Riley said, followed by a crooked grin.

My heart raced out of control, and my hands began to shake. "Riley? What...?"

"I couldn't miss your prom. We had a date, remember?"

"But I thought Cooper was taking me."

A beautiful laugh floated out of his mouth. It was one of the most wonderful sounds I'd ever heard. I'd desperately missed his laugh. "Well, plans changed."

"They did?"

"Yeah."

"He's okay with you taking me instead of him?"

"Yeah. Why? Would you rather go with him?" He pulled his cell phone from his pocket and prepared to dial. "I'm sure if we called him up he'd be here in a matter of minutes."

"Don't you dare call him. I'm so happy you're here."

Looking down, I watched as Baby yapped at Riley's feet. She was happy to see him, but he didn't pick her up.

He walked toward me and knelt down to pick the corsage up off the floor. "Do you wanna wear this thing?"

"Did you pick it out?"

"Yeah."

"Then yes, I want to wear it."

I held my arm up for him to slide the flower onto my wrist, but he hesitated before doing it. I wondered if he'd realized I wasn't wearing the ring he'd given me.

He regained himself and slid the corsage on before jamming his hands into his tuxedo pockets.

"You look very handsome, Riley."

"Thanks. I feel kinda weird all dressed up in this thing. It isn't very comfortable."

"Well, you look great."

"Thanks."

"Do I look all right?"

"Oh yeah, sorry. You look amazing. Beautiful. Not that I'm surprised or anything."

"Thank you."

"Your hair's gotten longer."

"It has?"

He nodded as he shuffled his feet on the hardwood floor. "In case you can't tell, I'm a nervous wreck right now. I had everything all planned out, but as soon as I saw you, I forgot everything I was gonna say."

"Are you happy to see me?"

"Of course."

"That's all I need to know."

"Should we go?"

"Yes."

He opened the front door, and I immediately noticed Cooper's car sitting in the driveway.

Apparently Cooper had lied. He wasn't okay when he left me standing at the door two days before. I couldn't even wrap my brain around what was happening, and I couldn't help but worry that I'd broken his heart. "Riley, I don't understand what's going on."

"I know. I'll explain it over dinner."

· · · · · · · · · · · · · · · · · · · ·

As the waiter took our order, Riley nervously messed with his hair and then finally gave me a smile when the man left us alone.

"I hate fancy restaurants," he announced.

"I know you do."

I placed my elbows on the table and looked over at him.

"So I guess you wanna hear why I'm the one sitting across from you instead of Cooper?"

"Yes."

"Well, when I came home from school yesterday, he was sitting in my living room. He looked like he'd lost his puppy or something.

Rive

"My first thought was that something happened to you, which of course threw me into a complete panic. But he finally told me you were fine, and he just came out and asked me if I wanted to take you to prom."

"Why?"

"He said that he thought you might want me to take you."

"He said that?"

"The way he tells it, the two of you have been hanging out, and the closer it came to prom, the more he thought you might want me here."

I thought back to the conversation in the living room when I accidently called him Riley. "That's it? That's all he said?"

"Basically. He said if I wanted to go, I needed to pack my bags and come back with him. He let me borrow his dad's tux and everything. Oh, and he told me that you were wearing crimson."

"Did he say 'crimson'?"

"No, he said 'red.' But I knew you wouldn't be caught dead in Husker-red and he must have meant crimson."

"Cooper doesn't really get the difference."

"Then he doesn't know you very well."

I didn't reply. Riley and I both understood that nobody knew me like he did.

"How's school?" he asked before dipping into his salad.

"You know school, it's … well, school."

"Yeah."

"How is school back home?"

"Close to done, thank God. I can't believe I'm going to be out of there before long. Then off to UCO."

"So you decided to stay close to home?"

"I got a scholarship, so I couldn't pass it up. My parents were completely freaking out. I mean, it's not a full ride or anything, but it's enough that my parents can afford the rest."

"Good grief, Riley Bennett! I'm so proud of you I think I might explode."

"Thanks."

343

"Are you proud of yourself? Excited?"

"Both."

"Have you decided what you're going to major in?"

"Not for sure, but I'm thinking criminal justice."

"Good for you."

"Hey," he said, jabbing his fork in his salad again, "I know this is random, but the gang and I went to Johnnie's a couple of weeks ago, and you know what I found out?"

"What?"

"Their pie is amazing."

"It is?"

"Yeah. All these years I've gorged myself on frieds and coneys, and I've been missing out on the pie."

"Well, I'm glad you finally figured it out."

"Me too. I can't wait for you to taste it. You're gonna love—" He stopped himself and shook his head. "Sorry, I forgot we aren't back home."

"It's okay. Who knows, maybe I'll come visit soon."

"That would be great. You can meet Anne's new boyfriend. Oh, and Jen's finally dating the guy from the golf team. They seem to really like each other."

"She told me, and wouldn't you know it? As soon as she stopped chasing after him, he went after her."

"You've kept in contact with them all this time?"

"I talk to them every week on Skype, and we're on Facebook almost every day."

"Uh yeah, Facebook. I haven't really gotten into that."

"You should. It's a great way to keep in touch." I looked down at my plate and sighed. "I can't believe that much has happened since I've been gone."

"You look disappointed," he whispered.

"I'm not. It's just—"

"What?"

"It's not like I expected time to stand still or anything, but it's just weird to know that life just kept right on going—like I was never there."

"That's not the case at all. We just didn't have much of a choice."

"Look, Riley, about the way I left—"

"Let's not," he said. "I don't want to ruin the night. There's no need to go back and rehash all that. It is what it is."

"It is what it is." I spoke in a quiet whisper that even he couldn't hear.

"Let's talk about something happier."

"Like what?" I asked.

His face went blank, which caused me to bust out in giggles.

He sat back in his chair and threw his hands into his moppy hair with a laugh. "Seriously, are we so far gone that we can't come up with something to talk about?"

"We're pitiful," I announced. "We really are."

"I sure hope we dance better than we talk, or this is gonna be a long freakin' night."

"No doubt."

"Oh, I guess you heard that Nicole had the babies."

"Pops told me. I've been meaning to call her."

"They're the cutest babies I've ever seen. Joshua can't stop talking about them. He's crazy in love."

"What did they name them?"

"Libby Grace and Sophie Rae."

"How cute is that?"

"I know."

"I'm sad I wasn't there to see it all."

"It's been fun. It's kinda neat to see new life come into the world like that. It makes you realize that there's still some good going on around us. Lord knows we could all use more good."

"Tell me about it."

The mood was instantly lifted, and Riley and I were able to spend the rest of our dinner enjoying each other's company over very interesting conversation, none of which included Cooper or any girls back home.

Unfortunately, our dancing wasn't nearly as effortless as our talking, and within less than an hour we were more than ready to leave the lamest prom that had ever existed. It didn't come close to comparing to the Second Chance Homecoming Dance that Riley had thrown for me.

"We needed some eighties music or something. How can you dance to that hip-hop crap?" he asked as we made our way toward the car.

"We can't, obviously."

"I think I looked like I was having convulsions or something."

"Well, I didn't look much better."

"Yeah, you did. You've at least got that booty-shake thing down."

"How could you even tell with me wearing this dress?"

"Oh, I could tell."

"You aren't supposed to be looking at my booty, Riley Bennett."

"Hey, you were shaking it in my direction; how was I supposed to ignore it?"

"I wasn't shaking it in your direction."

He rolled his eyes at me.

"At least I wasn't meaning to."

"Well, you were."

"No matter how bad the dancing was, I still had fun. Thanks for coming, Riley."

Without thinking, I leaned in and kissed him. He didn't respond. I pulled away, but he grabbed me by the waist and brought me to him as I ran my fingers through his hair.

I'd been wrong about kissing Cooper. Kissing him didn't come close to kissing Riley. The touch of Cooper's lips on mine had never caused my knees to buckle, my hands to tingle, or my mind to blur. Kissing Riley was, in my opinion, what a true kiss should be.

Riley's hands slid around my back. Keeping his left hand stationary, he slid the right up my back before cupping it gently around my neck. The way he held me was familiar and wonderful. For a split second it was as if nothing had ever changed. We were right back in Oklahoma standing on the side of the house, hiding from the view of his parents.

Out of nowhere, his body went stiff, and his arms fell lifelessly at his sides before he slowly pulled away and cleared his throat.

I stepped closer to him. I wanted him to kiss me again.

"Charlie, we can't." His left shoulder shrugged up to his ear as he looked down at the ground.

"Why?"

"Because I can't kiss you knowing that I have to turn around and leave tomorrow. I can't let those feelings happen. It'll kill me to feel that way again and then turn around and have to let you go."

"But Riley—"

"Maybe I shouldn't have come. I just . . ."

"You just what?"

"I wanted to take you to prom. That's all."

"I see." As if a bandage was ripped off my heart, it shattered into pieces.

His hand touched my face, and he softly stroked my cheek with his thumb. No matter how much I may have wanted to, I couldn't hide the pain, the pain caused by his rejection. My shoulders trembled, and tears spilled down my face.

"Charlie . . ." His hand moved from my cheek to the back of my neck, and he pulled me to him. His right arm wrapped around me, and I was in his arms again. "This is so much more painful than I imagined it would be. I just don't feel like we should start something, especially with me going right back home."

"When are you leaving?"

"Early tomorrow morning."

"So soon?"

"Yeah. Maybe I shouldn't have come at all."

Anger rose in my chest. "You're right." I shoved myself away from him and walked toward the car. "Why did you come, Riley? Why now, after all this time?"

"I wanted to see you."

I turned to face him but quickly turned back around. It was too painful to look at him.

"I'm sorry, Charlie; I was being selfish. I missed you and wanted to see you. This hasn't been easy on me."

I turned back to him. "And you think it's been easy on me? I tried calling you when I first got here. You wouldn't even talk to me."

"You broke up with me and moved away. What did you expect me to do?"

"I expected you to understand."

"So help me understand." He took a step toward me. "You left me and everything else good about your life behind. Why?"

"My dad finally wanted me."

"I wanted you too."

"I needed to repair my relationship with him before it was too late."

"By ending ours?"

"Ours was going to end anyway."

He looked as if I'd slapped him. "I see."

"It was inevitable that we'd end up apart, whether it was then or later; we wouldn't have lasted."

"You really believe that?"

"We've survived this long without each other. I think that proves we weren't meant to be."

"I guess I didn't realize it was all so final."

"I've been gone for six months, Riley."

"You don't have to tell me that. Trust me, I know how long it's been." He shoved his hands in his pockets and shrugged his shoulders to his ears. "Are you and Cooper dating? Have you kissed him?"

"Yes."

His shoulders sagged and his head dropped. "Anything more? No, never mind, I don't want to know."

"Of course not."

"Are you in love with him?"

"I like spending time with him. We have fun, and we have a lot in common—"

"That's not what I asked."

"What difference does it make?"

"Do you love him, Charlie?" he screamed. He shook his head as a tortured grimace filled his face, and lowering his voice, he continued. "Do you hate waking up in the morning knowing you won't get to see him until later in the day? And when you've been away from him and you finally hear his voice, does your heart race? How about when he grabs your hand? Do you wish he wouldn't let go?"

I recognized the words. They were the words I'd spoken when we sat together by the river and I told Riley how I felt about him the first time.

"No," I whispered.

"Then what on earth are you doing with him? Why settle for that when I'm here? I'm standing right here."

"And you're leaving tomorrow."

"Come home."

"This is my home, at least until I get some stuff figured out, maybe even longer." The hurt on his face was undeniable and painful to look at. "Look, let's not talk about this anymore. You're only here for a night. Let's just go try to have some fun."

"I traveled a long way to get here, and I'm tired. I'm really not in the mood to go to an after party with a bunch of people I don't know. Can't we just hang out and talk like we used to?"

"I want to go to the party."

He shrugged. "Fine. We'll go."

"No, I don't want you to go because I made you. You don't owe me anything."

He started pacing. "I can't even believe what a mistake this trip was. I should've just stayed at home."

"It probably would have been easier if you had."

He spun around to face me. "I had to know."

"Know what?"

"Where we were." His hands covered his face. "I guess I needed closure."

"You came all this way for closure?"

His hands dropped to his side, and his shoulders slumped again. "Apparently."

I yanked off my corsage and threw it at him. "You could have just sent me an e-mail. It would have hurt a lot less."

He watched it land on the ground before bending down and picking it up. His jaw grew tight and his eyes narrowed. "I'm sorry for bothering you. I shouldn't have come."

"At least we know where we stand," I said sternly.

His eyes closed as he shook his head. "I guess we do." We stood in silence until he finally walked to the car. "My plane leaves in the morning. I'll be out of your life, and we can both move on." He opened the car door and then turned to face me. "Are you going to be able to get a ride home after the party?"

"Yes."

He sat in the driver's seat. "I guess if I see you in the morning I see you."

"Maybe it's best if we don't," I suggested.

An angry laugh escaped his lips. "Unbelievable," he whispered. "Riley, you've got to know I never dreamt we would end like this."

He swung his legs into the car and grabbed the door handle. "Funny, I never thought we'd end at all."

The door slammed, and within seconds he was gone.

chapter 45

It was a cool early morning. I'd been walking the streets of Ithaca for hours. I wished I'd brought a rain jacket. A light mist had begun to fall, and my hair and dress were getting damp.

My chest ached knowing that when I returned home, I would be forced to say good-bye to Riley. What made it ache even more was the understanding that this time, more than likely after everything I'd said and done to hurt him, I would be seeing him for the last time.

Looking around, I realized that I didn't have a clue where I was. I wasn't sure how to make my way home.

The raindrops grew larger as they fell quickly from the sky. Frustrated and now sopping wet, I looked around for the nearest building that offered shelter. A small building across the road had a large eave where I could seek shelter, so I hurried across the street and ducked behind a pillar.

"Now look what I've done. I'm stranded."

"Nobody's ever truly stranded."

Looking around, I spotted a man standing a few feet away.

"I'm just opening up the church. Would you like to come in out of the rain?" the man offered.

"I don't know if I should—"

"You'll be safe inside. I promise."

I gave the man a small smile and once the door was open followed him inside. The small church had several rows of old wooden pews lined up on either side of a small aisle that led to the front of the sanctuary.

"Thank you very much," I said. "Maybe the rain will slow down soon."

"In the meantime, go ahead and make yourself comfortable."

"Thank you." I took a seat in a pew on the last row.

"You seem lost," the man said as he sat in the pew across from me. "Do you know where you are?"

For some reason, his question brought tears to my eyes. "You have no idea how lost I truly am," I said as I tried to control my emotions.

"Can I help?"

Looking around, I noticed the beautiful artwork and the statue of the Virgin Mary at the front of the left side aisle. "I'm a Christian, but I'm not Catholic, so—"

"Well, luckily we serve the same Lord. Why don't you tell me why you're crying?"

My eyes now rested on the large crucifix at the front of the sanctuary. I pointed at it. "I pushed him away," I cried.

"Oh?"

"I got angry and asked him to leave me alone."

"Why were you angry with him?"

"Many reasons. A lot of really bad stuff happened, and just when I thought the worst was over, something else happened. It's like he never—" I stopped and shook my head.

"He never what?"

"He never put up a fight."

"He never put up a fight with whom?"

"With Satan or who or whatever causes all the bad stuff to happen. He sat back and let it keep happening. He never stepped in and said 'Enough is enough; it's time to leave her alone.'"

"You've lived a life with no happiness," the man observed. "I'm sure that's a hard thing to accept."

"No, it wasn't like that."

"So you did have happiness?"

"Yes."

"Was it before or during the pain?"

My crying became heavier. "Almost the whole time."

The man was silent for several seconds before speaking. "Maybe in reality, the Lord did step in. He gave you moments to refresh and regain your strength. To enjoy life."

I wiped my eyes and nose with my arm and looked back over at him.

"Human nature causes that sometimes," he continued. "We tend to blame God for the bad things but not give him credit for the good."

I could only nod.

"Take rain, for example. It can rain for days on end. Days and days of cold, wet, windy weather. But even during those times, every once in a while the rain will let up to a more manageable mist or sprinkle. Sometimes we may even get a little bit of sunshine that will peek out from behind the clouds. It doesn't last long, but it's just enough to show, if we'll just pay attention, that this too shall pass. It's just a question of which you're going to focus on, the rain and all the problems it causes or the rain and all the good it does because it came.

"In the book of James it says: 'Consider it pure joy, my brothers, whenever you face trials of many kinds, because you know that the testing of your faith develops perseverance.' It goes on to say: 'Perseverance must finish its work so that you may be mature and complete, not lacking anything.'

"The Bible also tells us that God doesn't ever allow us to come up against something we can't handle."

"I *haven't* been handling it, and he *did* allow too much."

"Well, here's my take on that. Alone, we can't handle it. But if he's at our side, or even carrying us if necessary, that's what makes us able to handle it. That's what makes us survivors. And call me crazy, but I'd bet you're a survivor."

"But like I said, I gave up on him. I ran away. That's probably why all this has been so much more difficult."

"Do you still believe in him?" he asked.

"Yes."

"And you still love him?"

Fresh tears started falling down my face. "Yes."

"I'd be willing to bet he never went anywhere. If you look hard enough you'll see him, just like you used to."

He let his words sink in before continuing.

"Our life is about choices, Attie. We can either choose to fight for what we know is good and right no matter what our circumstances, or we can chose to give in and let the enemy win."

I sat silent and still.

"Here's my question for you," he said, standing and beginning to walk down the aisle. "Are you going to stop running and fight, or are you going to give in and let the chips fall where they may?"

I didn't respond.

"And one more thing," he said, turning to face me. "There are many things in this life that are worth fighting for, and I have a sneaking suspicion that God isn't the only one you've run away from." The man gave a small bow. "I'd better be going. I've got the Lord's work to do."

"Thank you," I mumbled.

"It was my pleasure." He turned and walked away, but I heard his voice carry from the doorway he'd exited. "Feel free to stay until you can remember your way back home."

"Wait, how'd you know my name?" I yelled.

There was no response.

I sat in the silent room and stared at the statue of Jesus in front of me. "Where are you?" I whispered. "I don't see you anymore. I don't know where you are."

The Lord didn't answer.

"I'm drowning." I stood and looked around the small chapel. "Do you hear me?" I screamed. "I'm drowning."

The room remained silent.

Defeated and lost, I walked toward the crucifix. "You reached in once," I whispered. "Reached in and pulled me out of the pit. I was restored; you'd salvaged me. I need you to reach in and pull me out again."

I fell to my knees.

"You don't even have to change my circumstances. I just need you here with me. I don't want to do this without you anymore. I want to go back to our journey, no matter what. I want to go back." Tears streamed off my face and onto the floor in front of me. "Please, let's go back to our journey. There's no place else I'd rather be than with you on our walk."

"Rise."

His voice shocked me. I turned on my knees until I saw Jesus standing next to the pew I'd just left.

"You're here." Focusing on his bare feet, I frantically started crawling toward him.

"Rise," he repeated.

Ignoring him, I continued crawling until I was right next to his feet.

Bending down, he looked me in the eyes, a large smile on his face. "Attie, it's time for you to rise."

As he'd requested, I slowly stood to my feet.

"I'm right here," he whispered.

"You never left?"

"No."

"I expected you to reach down and save me, but you didn't. You sat there and watched me struggle, watched me start to drown. You saw where I was. Why didn't you pull me out?"

"You hadn't reached out. I can't make you call out for me. You had it in you the whole time. All you had to do was call my name. I would have reached down and pulled you out. I was there, waiting for you to call out."

"But I pushed you away instead," I muttered.

"You tried. I didn't really go anywhere, but you shut your heart to me. You didn't want to hear me...or see me."

"I know."

"You wanted me around under the condition that I kept your life the way you wanted it. As soon as I didn't meet that condition, you chose to stop walking with me."

"It sounds so horrible to hear it said like that. True, but horrible."

"But I wasn't and I'm not giving up. Not until I have your whole heart—even if it takes forever. Your whole heart, even when it doesn't feel good and even when circumstances make it nearly impossible. I don't want you to try to act a certain way or do specific tasks; I just want your heart. I want you to love me because of who I am and not for what I do for you. No different than what you would want from someone."

"I know that now, and you do have my whole heart. I understand now that by loving you I get a peace that stays around even when the world around me seems to be falling apart. As soon as I walked away, that peace left. I've felt so lost."

"You've felt lost because you walked away. Home didn't leave where it was. I didn't leave; you left. You ran."

"I was scared."

"Yes, but you were also mad. You wanted to believe that since you'd survived so much hardship, you wouldn't have to suffer anymore. But unfortunately I can't make that promise to you. Everyone will suffer, some much more than others. All I can do is promise that I'll walk through it with you."

"That's enough for me. I know that now."

"If it's just you and me, that's enough for you?"

"Yes. Without you, none of that other stuff even matters. I want to walk with you again, no matter what."

"Then you're going to have to stop running from me."

"I will."

"Then let's go," he said, turning and waving over his shoulder.

"Go where?"

"Back to our journey. We've got work to do."

chapter 46

By the time I made my way back to the house, Riley was gone and Cooper was sitting on the porch steps. He was slouched over, and his face was emotionless. It was one of the rare times he didn't flash his white smile as soon as he laid eyes on me. Riley must not have told him how our night ended. If he had, Cooper would have been on cloud nine.

Afraid of what lay ahead, I slowly walked to him as a small part of my heart broke to pieces.

"So you arranged everything?" I asked.

He only shrugged.

"Why? You must have known what might have happened if Riley and I saw each other again. And what that would mean for you and me."

"I didn't know for sure, but I knew it was a possibility."

I sat down next to him.

He took my hand in his, and I immediately started crying.

"Attie, I'm in love with you. But I can't make you love me back. And I couldn't be in a relationship with you all the while knowing that I was your second choice. In the back of my mind, I would have always worried that given the opportunity to go back, you would. Riley's trip here confirmed all that. It was never really over between you two."

"It is over between us."

He looked at me with wide eyes, full of surprise.

"And as much as I hate to say it, it has to be over between you and me too."

Squeezing his eyes shut, he shook his head and then looked back at me. "But if you two aren't together, then why can't we be?"

"I'm not where I need to be, emotionally and spiritually speaking. It isn't good for me to be with anyone right now. I was crazy to think we could spend so much time together and act how we were acting without it getting too serious. I should've stopped and thought it all through before I drug you into my messy life."

"I don't blame you. I only have myself to blame. I walked in with my eyes wide open. I knew it was too soon, but I couldn't help myself. When we went on that ski trip, I honestly had no intention of it being more than just helping out a friend. I never expected to feel the way I felt, and I certainly didn't expect you to respond the way you did."

"I know. I didn't expect any of it either."

"You and I have a lot in common. We want the same things out of life, and we could be an amazing team together. I want you. I can give you all the love you could ever need."

"Just because something looks like it should be perfect doesn't mean it feels right," I whispered.

"It does feel right—to me."

"I'm sorry; that was insensitive of me. I really shouldn't say anything, because no matter what I say, it'll be wrong."

"Was any of it real, Attie? Or was it just an effort to try something new?"

"It was real, Coop. I love spending time with you; we have a great time together. And we have a lot in common. I do have feelings for you, just not as strong as what you have for me. And I can't sit here and promise you that I ever will."

"Like you said, you've got a lot to sort out. If you want to come back, I'll be here."

"As flattered as I am, I don't want that for you. I want you to go out and find the perfect girl. The girl who's going to choose you first and have no doubt, no confusion. You deserve that."

"I deserve you, and if it didn't work out with you and Riley, and once you've come to a better place in your life, then there would be no doubt or confusion left. We'd be free to go on with our lives together."

"Coop—"

"Don't think I'm noble, Attie. I didn't bring him back here for you; I brought him back for me. I believed all you needed was some closure and you'd be right back here. I still believe that. I'm living out that old saying 'If you let something go and it comes back, it was yours, and if it doesn't, it never was.' I have to let you go to find out if you'll come back."

"Coop—"

"We may not have the history that you and Riley have, but we have something. I'm not giving up."

I laid my head on his shoulder.

"All you have to do is pick up the phone. I can be here in a matter of minutes."

"I'll probably never make that phone call."

He dropped my hand and stood. "I'm choosing to believe you will."

I tried to stand, but he gently pushed me back down. "No, you stay right there. I can't say good-bye to you, so I'm just going to walk away."

"Coop, please."

"I can't," he said behind tears. "I hope to see you soon, but if I don't, I hope you have a wonderful life. You deserve it."

I watched Cooper climb into his car and drive away. In less than twelve hours, I'd said good-bye to the only two boys I'd ever cared about. I'd broken three hearts—theirs and mine.

Jesus caught my eye as he walked around the corner. Looking down, I noticed he was standing on one of the stepping-stones that led to our backyard. His feet were bare.

I looked at my own feet. My toenails had no crimson left.

"It's just you and me," he said.

I looked back up at the Lord. "Yes."

"Welcome back."

I felt a sincere smile form on my face.

He grinned back at me. "What are you smiling about?"

"It feels good to see you again."

He sat next to me on the porch. "Trust me when I say it's good to be seen by you again."

A large yawn escaped my throat.

"You're tired," he said. "Go on, go get some sleep."

"I've missed you. I don't want to take my eyes off of you yet."

"I'm not going anywhere, Attie. I'll be right there when you wake up."

"And then what?"

"And then we'll get to work on sorting things out."

"All right." Placing my hands on my knees, I pushed myself up and walked to the door.

"Attie," he called.

I turned and looked down at him.

"You've done well."

I rolled my eyes. "I ignored you for months. I don't know if you can call that 'well.'"

"But you rose above your circumstances and what your heart wanted and you let me back in. That's the very definition of a job well done."

I started to go back inside but stopped myself.

"Lord?"

"Yes?"

"Thank you for being so easy to find."

"You didn't have to find me, Attie. I was never hiding, and I never left."

Giving him one last smile, I turned and went inside. My dad was sitting at the dining room table.

"Riley told me what happened," he said.

"And what was that?"

"That you broke it off for good. He's devastated."

"I thought I'd already broken it off for good. I just don't think he was willing to accept it, and honestly, I don't think a large part of me was either."

"I think he hoped that he'd come up here, talk some sense into you, and you'd go back."

"He thought wrong."

"So then you chose Cooper?"

"No. I broke it off with him too."

Dad's eyebrows arched high. "Really?"

"I've got issues, Dad. I need to fix them. I shouldn't be with anyone right now. And besides, I don't want to make the same mistake you did."

"What mistake?"

"Falling in love too young. Getting serious and missing out on everything else life has to offer."

He sighed as he rubbed his face. "Please don't tell me you're making decisions based on what I said in the hospital."

"Of course I am. You were right. And isn't that why you told me all of that? So I would make the decision I did?"

He groaned. "Attie, I've got issues too, and a lot of what I said in that hospital room came out of a completely unhealthy frame of mind."

"What?"

"Marrying your mother was not a mistake. What you said a couple of months ago was spot on. I had everything a person could ever ask for. I was the problem. I got lazy."

"Lazy?" My conversation with Marme came to mind.

"And selfish. Relationships are work, and I stopped putting in any effort. All my time and attention went to the clinic and the school. You and your mom were left to live a life almost completely separate from me, and I didn't put forth any effort in trying to be a part of it."

"But you said you went looking for something."

"I did, and I still am. But I also said a lot of other things. A lot of things to make myself feel better about the choices I was making.

Things that kept me from accepting the fact that had I not made some of the choices I made, your mom would still be alive. You never would've had to suffer the way you have over the last two years." Tears filled his eyes as he spoke. "You were right. The people I love most in the world ended up paying the price for my immaturity, and I've got to find a way to live with knowing that.

"Attie, I sent you to Oklahoma because I couldn't bear to see you suffering due to something I caused. So rather than cause myself pain, I turned around and caused you more pain than I can even imagine.

"Horrible choices," he whispered. "I've made one horrible decision after another."

I remained quiet and still as he spoke. I was afraid that if I said anything, he wouldn't be able to get it all out in the open, and it was obvious that getting it all out was exactly what he needed to do. He was being eaten alive from the inside out.

"I never should have believed the lie that the Trumans told me; I never should have come to Oklahoma the way I did, and I never, ever should have brought you back here."

"I don't agree."

"What?"

"The way you did it wasn't the best, but I did need to come back here. We did need to work on things, and I needed some time to heal on my own. We've both got a lot of work to do, and I don't think either one of us would have done it where we were. We've got to get busy."

"Doing what?"

"Finding what you were searching for." I got up from the table and walked toward the kitchen. "I'll get the coffee started."

"Are you serious?"

"If you don't figure it out, you'll just end up searching for it again some other time."

"You just broke it off with two boys in one day. Don't you think we should be working on you?"

"That *was* working on me."

"How's that?"

"I say that part of the reason I came back was to heal and learn how to depend on myself, but I haven't actually done it. I basically went straight from Riley to Cooper. I never took the time to be alone and deal with stuff without a guy trying to help fix me. I can't be half of a couple if I'm half of a person, and for the last year and a half, I've been half a person. I'm ready to be whole, and no guy is going to be able to help me get there."

"Then how do you plan on doing it?"

"The same way you are."

He shook his head and shrugged in silent questioning.

"It starts today with church."

"Church?" His face flushed as he picked up a spoon and started stirring his coffee. "I don't know about that, Attie. I haven't been to church for a couple of years or more."

"Gee, I wonder if that's when your life started losing direction. What do you think?"

"Don't back-talk me. You're still my daughter, and I'm still the adult."

"I wasn't back-talking. It was an honest question; I just said it with a bit too much sarcasm."

He looked up at me and scowled.

"Really, Dad. We're both pretty messed up right now. Even if I'm wrong and we don't find what we need there, what can it hurt to give it a try?"

"Why would you think that would work?"

"Because it's the only thing that worked for me before."

His head cocked to the side. "Before?"

I sat in my seat again. "We haven't talked at all about what my life has been like since the accident. And honestly, I don't think you need to know every detail. But what I do want you to know is that the Lord met me right where I was and he stayed with me. It was through him and the people he put in my life that I made a lot of progress. Even after I found out you weren't coming to Oklahoma, he walked me through it, and I was able to walk out the other side. It sucked, I'm not going to lie, but I survived it.

"When you came back and told me about you and Mom, I lost it. I pulled away from the Lord completely. I didn't want to see him, and I didn't want to hear him. He wasn't doing exactly what I wanted him to do, and because I didn't get my way, I walked away."

"Like father, like daughter," he muttered. "In more ways than one."

"Do you want to know where walking away got me?"

"Of course."

"Nowhere. It got me nowhere. I was more confused, more lonely, and more messed up than ever. No matter what it's looked like on the outside, since I got back here I've been miserable, and not just because I miss my family and friends but miserable because I missed the Lord. Miserable because even though I needed to go back to him, I wouldn't."

He didn't respond.

"Look, even if you don't agree with me, will you go just because I'm asking you to? Because it's important to me?"

"I'll make a deal with you."

"Okay."

"I'll go to church with you every Sunday—"

"And Wednesday."

He rolled his eyes but smiled. "And Wednesday if you'll go with me to counseling. I think we both need it."

"All right."

"You don't even need to think about it?"

"Why should I? I was going to counseling in Guthrie."

"You were?"

"It was Pops's idea. It helped their family a lot, and he asked me if I'd give it a go, so I did. And I think it ended up saving my life. Not to mention, it helped me get my driver's license, and Joshua and Nicole are two of my favorite people in the world."

"Your time spent there was good for you."

"And we'll make my time spent here good for me too."

"Yes, we will."

"Now get up and get dressed; we've got work to do."

I started to get up from the table, but he reached out and stopped me. "First things first," he said.

"What first thing?"

"Stay right here." Dad left me sitting at the table for several minutes as he disappeared up the stairs, and when he finally reappeared, he was holding a book. More specifically, a Bible. He held it out for me to take. "Here. I thought you might want to have this."

I took it from his hand and sat it on the table in front of me.

"It was your mom's. I found it when I went through her stuff. I set it aside for you. Well, that and a lot of other stuff you might want to go through at some point since you never did it last year." My finger traced her name, which was engraved in gold on the lower right hand corner of the front cover, as he continued to talk. "She must have spent a lot more time reading it than I thought. She's got a lot of notes in there. A lot of highlights."

My heart beat wildly as I ran my finger along the gold-lined paper edges. I was about to see my mother's handwriting again, and oddly, I was nervous about it.

"I'll go get dressed," Dad said quietly.

Once he left me alone in the room, I slid my finger into the middle of the book and opened it. The pages fell to Psalm 23, and I recognized the chapter. "The Lord is my shepherd, I shall not want…" I read quietly. While I loved the chapter, it was a small note my mother had written in the margin that caught my eye. "Take your attention off the problem and focus on the one who can fix the problem. Look up, and cry out to the shepherd."

I could almost hear her voice in my head, the sweetest sound I'd heard in almost two years.

chapter 47

Graduation came and went the second week of May without any pomp and circumstance. I opted out of taking part in the graduation ceremony, and instead, Dad and I went into the city and saw *Wicked* at the Gershwin Theater. I loved it; he didn't. But he still bought me the soundtrack and let me listen to it all the way home and then tried to convince me that I should try to make it as a singer on Broadway. I informed him that he was delusional.

We spent the remainder of May and all of June and July in family counseling together. I also spent that time in my room soaking in time with the Lord. College was fast approaching, and my time and attention were soon going to be monopolized by studies, friends, a career, and possibly, one day, a family. I knew that although the Lord would always play a vital part in my life, I wouldn't again have the ability to spend this much time getting to know him and getting to know who I was in him. I had a lot to learn, and not just learn so that it was in my mind. It wasn't memorization; it was learning it in my spirit. It was believing it and living it out. It was allowing his words to transform me and create a whole new person—one who knew who she was and who she wasn't.

In the process of learning about who I truly was, I discovered something that I never would have expected. I discovered that while I loved animals, I didn't want to be a veterinarian. I realized that God didn't allow me to experience all that I had so that I could care for animals. He allowed all of those things so that I could turn around and help other people in the same situation. I decided I was going to become a therapist like Joshua. I was going to use all that I'd suffered and learned through the process to help others salvage their lives.

Since we were in counseling, I took advantage and told Dad my decision about a change of career in front of our counselor. Much to my surprise, he ended up taking it much better than I'd expected; and as soon as we got in the car, he started calling his contacts at Cornell to find out how I could get on the fast track.

I, on the other hand, had other plans.

· ·

I sat on the front step waiting for my dad to get home from work. He always got home between four and four thirty, and I only had a few minutes left to get the speech together in my mind.

I'd done what I thought was best. I'd come back to New York to repair my relationship with my dad, and I'd succeeded. Although it wasn't the perfect father-and-daughter relationship, it was *a* relationship, and it was more than either of us expected to ever have again. I'd also spent some much needed time learning about myself and what it was I needed and what I could realistically expect from another person.

The car pulled into the driveway, and through the windshield I could see him turn the key in the ignition to turn the car off, but he didn't get out.

Somehow he knew.

After several minutes, when he still hadn't exited the car, I walked to the driveway, opened the car door, and climbed in the passenger seat.

"You're going back," he whispered.

"How did you know?"

"I've known all along. As school got closer I expected it to happen any day, and when I pulled up and saw you sitting there, I knew this was it."

"You're my dad and I love you. But my life is in Oklahoma. My heart is there. Mom's there. It's where I belong."

"I know. As much as I wish it wasn't true, I realize you don't belong here. Who knows, there's a chance I don't either. Maybe one day I'll end up going back to Oklahoma too."

"That would be nice."

"So what's the plan?"

"I was hoping you could take a few days off and drive me back. If not, I can call Pops. I'm sure he'd fly up and drive back with me."

"No, I want to. When are you wanting to leave?"

"Tomorrow?"

He gave a deep, sad sigh. "That's fast."

"School starts soon, and I want time to get settled. I've already talked to Joshua and Nicole, and they said that I could stay with them for a little while until I find an apartment or something. So you might want to get the checkbook ready."

He laughed. "I'll do that."

"Thank you."

"Not that I want you to, but why aren't you staying with the Bennetts?"

"They would let me if I asked; they'd probably prefer it, but that's Riley's home. I don't want to make things too awkward."

"So you aren't planning on getting back together with him?"

"That isn't really up to me. As much as I'd love to be with Riley again, it's been a long time, and I hurt him. I can't see a situation where he'd take me back."

"And I didn't see a situation where you'd take me back, but you did."

"It's different. You're my dad. I couldn't have lived with myself if I hadn't given us a chance."

"And will you be able to live with yourself if you don't try to get Riley back?"

"You didn't see his face the last time I saw him. I'd be lucky if he even looks at me again, let alone speaks to me. Besides, I'm not going back for him. I'm going back because I feel like it's where I belong. It's where I feel most comfortable, and it's where I'm most myself."

He finally pulled the key out of the ignition and opened his car door. I climbed out of the car and waited for him to join me before walking back toward the house.

"Then I guess we need to get you packed up."

"I may have a lot of boxes to pack up, but at least this time when I head home, I'll be taking a lot less baggage."

chapter 48

The water was cool on my bare feet, and I watched it squirt between my toes as I walked along the sidewalk. A rare August rainstorm had stalled over Guthrie, and the hard, dry ground was getting a much-needed soaking.

My welcome home had been an emotional one. Almost everyone I loved stayed up late to be at Joshua and Nicole's when Dad and I finally pulled into town. Riley was the only person who wasn't there, and after a few hours of catching up with everyone, Pops suggested I get it over with and go see Riley. As it turned out, Riley didn't want the first time we saw each other to be in a room full of people. I couldn't blame him.

The Oklahoma wind whipped around me as I walked toward the Bennetts' home, and I hoped the storm wasn't an ominous sign of how my reunion with Riley was going to go.

I quietly opened the front door and stepped into the entryway. He was lying on the couch in the family room. After tiptoeing to him, I knelt on the floor and watched as he slept. He was beautiful, just as he'd always been.

He repositioned himself on the sofa, causing the sleeve of his left arm to bunch up on his forearm. My heart leapt when I saw that he was wearing two bracelets. One was the *Salvaged* cuff I'd given him, and the other was mine—the one I'd left behind.

Reaching over and lightly tracing the letters with my finger, I thought back to the day I'd made the bracelets and how I'd realized that God had salvaged my life. He'd rescued me from the depths and dropped me into a place of joy. He'd given me a place of refuge. A home.

"What'cha looking at?" Riley moaned.

I pulled my hand away.

"You." A giggle escaped my throat. "And as someone once said to me, it's the most beautiful scenery I've seen all day."

"Ah, nice one." He smiled and gave a small nod, though his head was still on the pillow and his eyes remained closed.

"'Perfection personified.' Isn't that how you put it?" I asked.

"Yeah, and you accused me of stealing the line from a movie."

"It still sounded good."

He didn't respond, which caused my anxiety to escalate.

"Are you going to look at me, Riley?"

"Eventually."

"Okay."

I looked around the room at the familiar and wonderful sur-roundings. Nothing had changed, and I was relieved.

When I finally looked back at him, our eyes met.

"Well, good grief, it's Riley Bennett," I teased in a whisper.

"Hey, Charlie." A familiar crooked grin appeared just before he rubbed his eyes with his fingers.

"Are you happy to see me?"

"I guess so," he teased back. "Do you realize you're sopping wet?"

"Yes."

He sat up, grabbed a blanket off the arm of the couch, and wrapped it around me before sitting back down. "You're gonna catch a cold if you don't watch it."

"I'll be fine."

Holding his hands in his lap, he leaned toward me. "What were you doing out in the rain?"

"You're wearing our bracelets."

He glanced at them and then back at me as a heavy crease emerged between his eyebrows. "Yeah."

"Do you still love me, Riley?"

He leaned away from me and back into the couch. "Why are you asking me that?"

"I need to know."

"Why?"

I took a deep breath and let it out. "I'm hoping you do because I'm willing to do whatever it takes to get you back. I'll fight for you if I have to."

"What?" His hands immediately gravitated to his head. His fingers ran through his brown hair over and over again as he processed what I'd said.

"I realize I gave up on us without even giving it a fight, but I've learned that some things are worth fighting for. You're one of those things."

His breath sucked into his chest and his eyes were wide yet blank. I could read nothing from his response.

"I love you, Riley." I lifted up onto my knees. "If I asked you, would you give me another chance?"

There was no response, which caused my heart to stop midbeat. "Look, I realize I screwed up. I said things I shouldn't have; I ran away. I made very, very bad choices. But I was confused and scared, and I wasn't thinking clearly." I glanced at the bracelets. "You're wearing our bracelets; surely that means something."

He stood up and walked into the entryway before turning and looking back at me with a cloud of confusion hovering on his face. "You were gone for nine months."

"I know."

"At prom, you said we were over."

"Yes."

He shook his head, walked up the stairs, and disappeared into his room. After a few minutes, his head peeked out the door. He stared at me for a moment and then ducked back into the room.

Several minutes passed without him returning. With my heart shattered, I walked out the front door and back into the storm.

. . . .

(Riley)

After managing to get my heart rate back to normal and grabbing a wad of tissue off my dresser, I went back down the stairs to Attie, but she was gone.

Rushing out the door, I looked toward the sky and watched as the rain poured down in sheets.

"Charlie?"

She turned to face me as I stood on the patio. Her body trembled under her cold, wet clothes. She was drenched from her blonde head to her shining, crimson toes.

"Come in out of the rain; you're gonna get sick."

She shook her head in defiance.

"Quit being ridiculous. Come on inside."

"No!" Her foot stomped, causing rain to fly through the air. "Are we going to discuss this or not?"

I walked to the bottom step. "Charlie…"

"Don't 'Charlie' me!"

I shrugged. "Okay."

"I have something I want to say, and I need you to listen."

I watched her through the water that dripped off my eyelashes. A shiver visibly ran through her body just as her face crumbled and tears mixed with rain drenched her face.

"I left because I needed to work things out with my dad. I didn't lie about that. At the time, I honestly thought that was why I was going. But now I realize that I was also running away. I ran because I was scared… of us. I knew that with as many issues as I had and as confused as I was, you and I could never last. I truly believed that by leaving, I was doing what was best for both of us."

She closed her eyes and shook her head. I could tell she was trying to get her thoughts together. They were probably running through her mind faster than she could say them. While she tried to collect her thoughts, I kept any thoughts from running through my mind at all. I wanted to hear and understand every word she was saying. But mostly, I wanted to hear her voice again.

She opened her eyes and looked at me again. "I had to know that, I could be with someone because I wanted to be, not because I *needed* to be. I want to trust that I can love someone because of who they are, not because of the things they do for me or the security they give me. I realized in my time away that I had to heal so that if and when I was in a relationship, I could do it without all the baggage and without the insecurity. I want to be a whole, complete, healthy person. I believe that's what I'm becoming."

She shivered again but kept her eyes locked on mine.

"And after all that, what I've come to realize is my heart's yours, Riley. It always has been, and it probably always will be. All I want to know is if you'll come back to me."

I wiped the rain out of my eyes. "You don't get it, do you?"

"Get what?"

"I don't need to come back to you; I never left. I never let you go."

Her eyes widened in shock.

"I knew that you needed time, you needed to think things through, try it on your own. But I also knew that you weren't gone forever. I trusted that you'd be back. Granted, after the whole prom debacle it seemed pretty hopeless, but part of me still believed you'd come back."

"You never gave up?"

"I always told you I wouldn't."

She made an ill attempt at wiping the rain off her face.

Reaching into my jeans pocket, I pulled out the wad of tissue.

"I'm drenched, Riley. A tissue isn't going to help."

"Shush."

"Okay," she whimpered.

I slowly uncrumpled the paper until it revealed her ring. Seeing it, she gasped.

"You left this behind. I was hoping that you would want it back. I hoped you'd want me back—eventually."

"I wanted you back the entire time. I was just being stubborn."

I couldn't help but laugh. "You, stubborn? I can't imagine."

"I'll work on it—the whole being stubborn thing."

I rolled my eyes at her.

"Or I'll try to, anyway," she corrected.

"I'm not gonna hold my breath waiting for that to change."

"That's probably smart."

"Probly." As I walked up to her, she finally flashed a full-faced, nose-scrunching smile. "There's the smile I fell in love with. It's good to see it again."

"It's good to have a reason to do it."

I turned away from her.

"Riley?"

"Shh." Reaching behind me, I grabbed her by the hand and led her toward the side of the house. She didn't resist. She knew exactly where we were going.

When we'd finally made it to our spot, I turned to her and grabbed both of her hands in mine as the rain washed over us. "I have a question for you."

"You're not going to ask me to marry you, are you?"

"Not yet. You'll have to wait about four years for that."

"Okay. Then what's the question?"

"Will you be my girlfriend—again?"

She nodded.

"That's a yes?"

She nodded again, causing tears to overflow her eyes and fall freely. "Yes," she whispered. "And this time, I'm not gonna run."

"Did you just say 'gonna'? You finally getting a little Okie in ya?"

"I *am* an Okie. I might as well start sounding like one."

For the second and hopefully the last time, I slipped the ring on her finger. Then, bringing my wrist up to my mouth, I used my teeth and free hand to untie her bracelet from my arm.

"I've had the ring and this cuff since you were put into the hospital." I wrapped it around her wrist. "I put it on so that it wouldn't get lost and then never took it off." The loops pulled tight, and the bracelet was secure. "There, both back where they belong."

Attie looked up at me with so much admiration that I couldn't resist grabbing her and pulling her into my arms. Her breath warmed my entire body as she whispered in my ear. "I love you, Riley. No matter how lost I was, that never changed."

I was so overwhelmed by relief that I started crying too. She stood back and looked at me. "So off we go, on an all new adventure."

I wiped the wet hair off her face "I love you, Charlie. Welcome home."

A single raindrop ran down her face and rested on her bottom lip, and without even thinking, I leaned over and drew it into my mouth. She responded by pressing her body into mine.

Attie was mine again and in my arms where she belonged.

Epilogue

(Riley)

I heard screaming.

I jumped out of bed and sprinted out of my room. Throwing on the bedroom light, I found her sitting up in bed, hands covering her eyes and her mouth wide open as wails poured out of her throat.

I ran up beside her, and she removed her hands from her face, revealing large eyes filled with tears. Her arms flew into the air, and her hands clasped open and closed in a fit of wanting to be comforted.

"You're okay," I whispered. "I'm here." Reaching over, I took her into my arms.

"Riley?" Attie's voice was groggy.

"It's okay; I'm here. Go back to sleep."

"No," she said softly as she walked my direction. "You've got to go to work in the morning. Give her to me; I'll take her. You go back to bed."

"Silly girl." I kissed Attie on the tip of the nose. "I'm wide awake." I slightly bounced the baby in hopes that she would fall back to sleep, but it was no use. She was wide awake.

"Poor Melody," Attie soothed. "Are you sick? I wish you could tell me what's wrong."

I placed my cheek against our daughter's forehead but kept my eyes on Attie. "You can probly tell better than me, but she doesn't feel warm or anything. I think she just had a bad dream."

Attie rubbed Melody's bald head as I continued to bounce. "Why don't you just bring her to bed with us?"

"I thought we weren't gonna start the whole 'baby sleeping in our bed' thing."

"Good grief, she's ten months old. One night isn't going to hurt her."

I shrugged. "Hey, you don't have to convince me. If I had my way she'd be in our bed almost every night. I mean look at her; she's irresistible—just like her mother."

Somehow I managed to bounce and walk simultaneously as we made our way back to the bedroom. Attie looked over at me and giggled, causing her nose to scrunch up ever so slightly.

"What?" I asked.

"Nothing. You're just cute."

"I'm glad that after ten years you still think so."

"Ten?" She climbed back into the bed and under the covers. "Try twenty-seven. We've known each other our entire lives, remember?"

"Well then, ten since you finally came to your senses and agreed to go out with me. Or wait, make that nine, seeing as how you dumped me and it took you almost a year to take me back. Or seven years since the last time you broke up with me—"

"That time lasted less than a month."

"Still."

"Well, if you hadn't gone and acted like such a guy, I wouldn't have had to put the fear of God in you like that."

"Now why ya gotta go and bring that up?"

"I gotta bring it up because I know it drives you crazy, and you know how much I like to drive you crazy."

"You're so good at it."

"It's a gift."

"Uh-huh." I handed her the baby before climbing into bed.

"Still, here we are after all these years," she said with a tired smile.

"Here we are." There was no place I'd rather be.

Attie laid Melody onto her back in the space between us on the mattress, and after several minutes both Attie's and her daughter's eyes were growing heavy.

"Go to sleep, Charlie. I'm wide awake; I'll keep an eye on her."

"Are you sure?" she mumbled.

"Positive."

She gave me a small smile before closing her eyes and allowing herself to drift off. Melody's hand was clasped around Attie's pointer finger.

"You too," I whispered to Melody as I rubbed her fat little belly. "I'm right here. You can go back to sleep now."

Finally, after several minutes, the baby's eyes closed, and I listened as her breathing became soft and rhythmic. Propping myself up on a few pillows, I watched them as they slept.

I was near, and no more monsters would come for them tonight.